OWEN MARSHALL is an award-winning novelist, short-story writer, poet and anthologist, who has written or edited 35 books, including the bestselling novel *The Larnachs*. Numerous awards for his fiction include the New Zealand Literary Fund Scholarship in Letters, fellowships at Otago and Canterbury universities, and the Katherine Mansfield Memorial Fellowship in Menton, France. In 2000 he became an Officer of the New Zealand Order of Merit (ONZM) for services to literature; in 2012 was made a Companion of the New Zealand Order of Merit (CNZM); and in 2013 he received the Prime Minister's Award for Literary Achievement in Fiction. In 2000 his novel *Harlequin Rex* won the Montana New Zealand Book Awards Deutz Medal for Fiction. Many of his other books have been shortlisted for major awards, and his work has been extensively anthologised. His short story 'Coming Home in the Dark' was made into a feature film that premiered at the 2021 Sundance Film Festival.

In addition, in 2003 he was the inaugural recipient of the Creative New Zealand Writers' Fellowship, and was the 2009/10 Antarctica New Zealand Arts Fellow. In 2006 he was invited by the French Centre National du Livre to participate in their Les Belles Étrangères festival and subsequent tour, anthology and documentary. He was the President of Honour of the New Zealand Society of Authors 2007–08, and delivered the 2010 Frank Sargeson Memorial Lecture.

He was a school teacher for many years, having graduated with an MA (Hons) from the University of Canterbury, which in 2002 awarded him the honorary degree of Doctor of Letters, and in 2005 appointed him an adjunct professor.

Return to Harikoa Bay

New work from
the master
of short stories

Owen Marshall

VINTAGE

VINTAGE

UK I USA I Canada I Ireland I Australia
India I New Zealand I South Africa I China

Vintage is an imprint of the Penguin Random House
group of companies, whose addresses can be found at
global.penguinrandomhouse.com.

Penguin
Random House
New Zealand

First published by Penguin Random House New Zealand, 2022

10 9 8 7 6 5 4 3 2 1

Text © Owen Marshall, 2022

Design by Carla Sy © Penguin Random House New Zealand
Cover art: Grahame Sydney, *Night House II*, 1995, oil on linen,
760 x 1215mm.
Author photograph by Jackie Jones
Prepress by Soar Communications Group
Printed and bound in Australia by Griffin Press, an Accredited ISO
AS/NZS 14001 Environmental Management Systems Printer

A catalogue record for this book is available from the National
Library of New Zealand.

ISBN 978-0-14-377653-6

eISBN 978-0-14-377654-3

The assistance of Creative New Zealand towards the production of
this book is gratefully acknowledged by the publisher and author.

ARTS COUNCIL OF NEW ZEALAND TOI AOTEAROA

penguin.co.nz

MIX
Paper from
responsible sources
FSC
www.fsc.org   FSC® C009448

For Jackie

Contents

1.

Resurrection of the Dolls

'Fuck, and fuck again,' said Emma with vehemence. She was alone and so could say it loudly without fear of reproof, yet she wished Mr Torres were there to hear her, or Hilary or Eddie. Impropriety in the presence of others would have given greater emotional release. The photocopier was in revolt again and she could hear the A4 sheets scrunching up within its innards, but nothing was coming out. It did this from time to time and always to her and not the others. The photocopier surely had a reptilian animosity at its core. Eventually it became so constipated that there was just a grating sound and the flickering of red, baleful eyes.

Emma was in the photocopying room of Hoffman, Utterlay and Smith. A room the size of a modern laundry, and although its purpose and location were quite obvious, there was formal designation on a green plastic tag above the entrance. Emma knew she should go and tell someone the copier had seized up again, but she went instead to the small window and watched the new person moving into the adjoining commercial space. A modest showroom, a poky back office and even smaller area for toilet and basin. Mr Torres, who was HUS office manager, called it the swamp of dreams. Eleven different enterprises had foundered there in his time, he said, and he took a bitter satisfaction in that. Transfixed in such a barren life himself, he had no pleasure in the success of other people.

Even within the four years of Emma's time at HUS, three enterprises had begun with hope and trumpets and left in tears and disarray. The premises were occupied by Pooch Pamper when she first joined the firm: two middle-aged women who offered to wash and sanitise dogs, and exercise them safely in the municipal park. There was occasional barking to be heard for a few months and a variety of breeds to be observed, but after a malign mastiff killed a black swan in the reserve while nominally supervised by the taller of the Pooch Pamper owners, it was all over. The less tall woman, diminished even more by tragedy, moved to Australia to re-establish the business in a country unaware of the disaster.

After a two-month vacancy Pandora's Box moved in, a speciality chocolate concept created by Vanessa Prendergast — handmade chocs in white, red and blue as well as the traditional colour. They were packaged in cellophane tied with striped ribbon, or in small cardboard boxes in pastel shades. The window display attracted the attention and admiration of many, but the prices were such that sales were insufficient to maintain a business. Mass-produced chocolate won, as mass-produced goods usually do. Emma had bought Vanessa's chocolates and talked sometimes with her in the small shop, but that, of course, was not enough. Vanessa had resorted to offering individual elocution lessons among the chocolates, but nothing could prevent failure. Mr Torres sneered and said she hadn't even understood what Pandora's box really contained — afflictions from the ancient gods. Didn't she know that? So Vanessa had finally surrendered and taken a job at the auction house in Glutt Street.

The Reverend Ewan Mosley was the next tenant, but even a divine connection was insufficient to ensure success. He set up the Modern Christian Bookshop, which he stocked not just with Bibles, New Testaments, Billy Graham speeches in three volumes, religious novels and biographies, but also with up-to-the-minute gospel music discs and even paintings with inspirational themes — robed figures caught in shafts of heavenly light and clustered children with beatific expressions. How few the customers — the only regular a homeless and toothless man seeking warmth in winter — and the Reverend Mosley reluctantly decided that philanthropic provision was not sufficient to justify the stock held and the rental for the premises.

And so Emma watched from the window the arrival of the latest lessee. An attractive young woman with short hair dyed red, who carried in sewing machines and other such apparatus, then cartons of material, and also boxes of dolls, some pinkly and smoothly naked, some elegantly clothed. When Emma went back into the offices she told her colleagues of the new neighbour and the nature of her enterprise. Most wished her better fortune than her predecessors, but when Mr Torres heard later, he assumed a hangman's smile and said he gave her six months. Six months max and he'd bet on it. The HUS partners were not interested in such gossip. They passed through the open office and its undistinguished denizens as if it were a supermarket.

The next day, during her lunch break, Emma went next door to meet the red-haired woman and welcome her. She was good looking, as already said, and blithely untroubled by existential anxiety, as is conventional in such a story as this. The shop was not yet officially open, the door was locked, but Emma could see the woman working inside amid the cartons and new shelving. She came to the door in answer to Emma's knock. 'We're not open yet,' she said cheerfully. 'I'm still setting up. Sorry.'

'I've just come to wish you well. Success and all that. I work next door at HUS.'

'HUS?' the woman said.

'Hoffman, Utterlay and Smith.' Emma had forgotten that not all the world was aware of the acronym so customary for her. 'I'm Emma.'

'Just like in Jane Austen.'

'In name only,' said Emma. 'I lack gentility.' She was impressed a little, however, by the woman's knowledge of the literary connection.

'I'm Paddy.'

'I won't interrupt. I just wanted to say hi.'

'You're not. Come in,' said Paddy, stepping back, so Emma went in and they chatted.

The shop had no name displayed, but Paddy said it was to be called Paddy's Dolls. 'I know,' she said. 'It's not that great, but the good ones were taken — Dolled Up, Doll World, Dolls' House. I couldn't believe how many names turned up on Google.' Paddy said she wouldn't just sell dolls, but clothe them, to the owners' specifications even, if so requested, and she was considering having a section for second-hand dolls that she'd buy in, refresh and hopefully make a useful profit from on resale. Infused with her enthusiasm, the project sounded like a winner, as had many of those in the same premises before her. But Emma said nothing of those, instead asking what Paddy had done before. 'Oh, I had this job at the hospital laundry and hated it. I've always wanted to have a business of my own. I've actually got a polytech qualification in media and entertainment studies, but it didn't lead to anything. I had heaps of dolls as a kid and I've always been keen on sewing and dressmaking. I knit too. Most people aren't interested now, are they?'

'I suppose not.' Emma wasn't interested herself. They seemed skills like blacksmithing, or candle-making.

'At last I'm my own boss,' and Paddy stood among the boxes of fabrics and dolls, the partly assembled shelving, the brooms and mop, and she smiled, gave a shiver of delight at her own accomplishment.

'Good on you, and good luck,' said Emma, and she meant it, yet even then, even before Paddy's Dolls had been christened, there seemed miasmic and incongruous apparitions lurking in the corners of the small shop: faint shapes and smells of laundered canines, multi-coloured chocolates in their transparent wrapping and levitating bearded Hebrew prophets with warnings of retribution.

Emma and Paddy became friends. Emma would wave as she passed the shop, go in often at lunchtimes and after work. In the first few months, when Paddy was still optimistic of sufficient patronage, Emma even went in to help on the odd Saturday morning. Customers were scarce, but she could fit the garments on the dolls, covering their asexual pink bodies with beautiful clothes that bestowed femininity. They became confidantes, Emma and Paddy, sharing expectations and grievances and their views on all the world. Paddy had hoped her qualification would lead to a career as wardrobe mistress in the film or television industry, but instead ended up in the hospital laundry. Emma had gone teaching after gaining her degree, but had been so buffeted by indifference and insolence that she'd accepted the hierarchy and boredom of HUS clerical work, where she found herself in a so-called open office, but cubicled, with partitions chest high around her. Mainly women fellow workers, their heads questing from cells like despairing battery hens.

Both Emma and Paddy had lives beyond their work. Unlike Georgian heroines they were not past their use-by date at twenty-eight and thirty. Both had a boyfriend whom they dominated, and could easily have had others. Relationships were conducted on their terms, and their satisfaction in independence was far greater than any wish to live with a man. What they sought in addition, however, was achievement and pleasure within a career.

Emma envied Paddy. She envied her despite the private conviction that Paddy's Dolls would fail as its predecessors had failed. Paddy would surely go down with the ship, but at least she was its captain. When she was photocopying at work, Emma would go to the window and look out to see the frontage of the adjoining shop, with 'Paddy's Dolls' painted there in bold gold letters and she would wish herself there, rather than in the useless bustle of HUS. In truth, she felt herself demeaned in her job, surrounded by petty and materialistic concerns, subject to people of inferior nature and talent — Mr Torres especially.

Mr Torres knew of her friendship with Paddy and took pleasure in snide references to the inevitable fate of the shop. Open derision too. 'Dolls. Jesus Christ,' he said. 'What sort of person thinks you can make a living selling and dressing dolls. Some folk just have no understanding of the realities of business. I'd put a burger joint in there, or a betting shop. People have to eat and they're suckers for a chance to win big.'

Mr Torres was an embittered man, as I've mentioned: the necessary counterweight to the more sympathetic characters in a story of this sort. He envied the partners above him and chafed at being no more than office manager when his ego demanded more. His wife had grown cold and his children had dispensed with him. His bitterness was such that it couldn't be contained internally and manifested itself in his appearance. Sardonic lines were as sabre cuts on his cheddar cheeks, his upper lip curled from the teeth and his eyes had a restless dissatisfaction. 'Oh yes, the signs are there, I'm afraid,' he said. 'The writing's on the wall. It's just a matter of time for your friend. The novelty wears off, you see, Emma. We've seen it all before.'

And yes, the signs were there. Emma had to admit that. Paddy's dolls' clothes were attractive and individual, but time-consuming to produce. Even at a modest mark-up, the prices were significantly higher than for the cursorily dressed dolls in the chain shops. 'I'm working for peanuts,' Paddy admitted. 'In fact peanut singular. I don't know what to do.' She no longer opened the shop on Saturdays, or weekday mornings, and instead went to the homes of successful people to clean their showers and toilets. 'It's worse than the bloody laundry,' she said, 'and some stuck-up bitch accused me of stealing her Coco perfume.'

'It's not fair. Your dolls are fantastic: better than anything else I've seen.'

'Yeah, people say they're fantastic, come into the shop and drool over them, ask me about the fabrics and how I come up with the ideas. But do they buy them? Not bloody often. I always thought if you made something really nice, the best you could and better than other stuff, then you couldn't miss. But people won't pay.'

'It's just not fair,' said Emma again. 'Your dolls are the best.'

'And I really love doing it. It's the greatest feeling ever.'

They were sitting together in the small shop, close to Paddy's embroidery machine, which she had still not fully paid off. Her natural mood was one of cheerful optimism, but she knew the place was failing. Even cleaning bathrooms and kitchens couldn't save it. Emma hated to see her sitting there, sad faced, and crowded around her the multitude of dolls, all sizes, all ethnicities, all beautifully dressed, wide eyed and with fixed smiles that admitted of no misfortune in life.

There had to be an answer, and it came fortuitously after Emma had twice had sex with Reyansh in his apartment in a new block close to the university. Reyansh hasn't been mentioned before because he isn't as integral to the story as Emma, or Paddy, or even Mr Torres. Sex was very important to Reyansh, but less so to Emma, and that's another reason why his role is secondary. A pleasant enough guy, ethnically distinctive and well toned, but inessential here except for his knowledge of marketing on the net. Selling online was his business, and when his lust had been sated for at least a few hours, he talked of his job. At the moment his work was preparing a programme for top-end running shoes. 'There's a vanity market for almost anything,' he said. 'People who want the most expensive product just because it's the most expensive and exotic. Not many people, okay, but they're there and with online selling you can cream them off from anywhere in the world.' He was watching Emma preparing to leave and already aware of stirrings that made him reluctant to see her go. 'Limitless possibilities if you pitch it right,' he said. 'Perception is everything.'

That's what gave Emma the idea for the salvation of Paddy's Dolls. 'There's something I want you to do for me and Paddy,' she told him.

'We need to go top end.' Was Reyansh going to say no? And you need a happy ending in a story of this nature.

The three of them had meetings at Paddy's small shop to discuss a new modus operandi. Even more design time and expensive costuming were to be lavished on the dolls, Indian silks and real jewels, complimentary perfumes in tiny crystal bottles, birth certificates with wax seals. The price was more than quadrupled and Reyansh devised his most scintillating online advertising in order to retain Emma's favours. The enterprise was rechristened Petite Perfection as Paddy's Dolls was too plebeian. How those dolls sparkled and smiled, some no taller than a pencil, some larger than human babies. They were an ageless perfection unattainable by anything organic, undemanding in upkeep and with no capability for disobedience, all of which made them the more desirable.

What a gamble it was, but Reyansh was right, for orders began to trickle in, and a trickle was more than enough to provide a generous profit. Paddy worked happily in the shop, troubled no longer that people came to stare and wonder at her skill and inspiration, yet almost all unable to make a purchase. Mr Torres couldn't understand how the business survived. It hurt him to see apparent guilelessness win out. 'I don't see hardly anyone buying any friggin' dolls at all,' he said in exasperation. 'It should have gone under by now.'

Nothing succeeds like success, as the adage tells us. *Seven Sharp* even came calling, and Paddy and her dolls were on early evening television. Emma was able to add to Mr Torres's chagrin by informing him she was resigning from HUS to join Paddy in Petite Perfection. Even the HUS partners deigned to notice Emma's resignation and presided in the firm's tearoom over a modest cheese and chardonnay farewell. They had a nose for money. Emma's last action was to secretly force-feed the photocopier with a wet serviette.

'Your business is saved by the world's preening vanity,' Emma told Paddy the next day as they sat together in the shop admiring newly arrived Florentine leather, velvet from La Rochelle, tourmaline and topaz from Madagascar.

'Just in time,' said Paddy. 'I thought I was going to have to resort to giving blow jobs in the office.' It wasn't quite as Jane A would have expressed relief, perhaps, but sincere in its own way, and sufficient closure to a gentle satire.

2.

Rue de Paradis

osalind Sandringham was almost in tears. She was newly arrived at Charles de Gaulle Airport and unable to find the baggage claim area. She had followed her fellow passengers, but they had hastened into the general throng and she'd lost any sense of direction. And she needed the toilet. She should have gone on the plane when she knew they would be landing within half an hour, but by the time she thought of it there were queues, and besides, the cramped facilities had become unsavoury during the long flight from Singapore. She disliked, too, the awkwardness of coming out to the close confrontation with those waiting. People didn't care, did they. Unsightly scraps on the floor even. She should have gone, though. She always told her primary school pupils to go before setting out anywhere. She was tired, bewildered, she didn't speak the language and she needed the toilet. People around her seemed brisk, purposeful, and carapaced with a disinclination to relate to others.

There was, however, a tall, elderly man with polished, quality shoes standing to one side of the escalator, talking on his cell phone. Rosalind came close enough to hear that he was speaking in English, and so she stood at his side waiting for him to finish. Because of her proximity the man glanced at her and smiled, but continued his conversation — something about a rental car and a trip to Fontainebleau — but the bustle around them prevented any sense of eavesdropping. He turned to her and smiled again when his call was over, raised his eyebrows in enquiry.

'Excuse me,' she said. 'Could you please tell me where the baggage claim is? I'm a bit at a loss.'

'It's a jungle, isn't it, like all big airports. No problem — I'm heading there myself.' His speech was deliberate and unhurried, that of a man accustomed to being listened to. 'First time here in Paris?' he said.

'Yes.'

'And you're from?' he asked, almost as if they were in interview as they walked among the crowd.

'New Zealand,' said Rosalind.

'Antipodean,' he said. Despite his age the man had a long stride and Rosalind felt a little pressured to keep up. To the side she saw the illuminated sign for toilets and stopped, thankful, but also slightly embarrassed. He came back towards her, again raised his eyebrows in interrogation. 'All right?'

'I think I'll go in there,' and she made a small gesture towards the sign.

'Oh, very well. Afterwards just keep going this way. Go down, not up. You'll find yourself at the baggage claim.'

'Thank you.'

'Enjoy your stay in Paris, Antipodean. Goodbye then.' He stood for a moment with a smile, then went off briskly through the crowd, trailing his small, wheeled cabin case expertly behind him so as not to obstruct anyone else. When Rosalind came out she looked for him, despite knowing he'd gone. She was unable to resist the fanciful image of his waiting — stooping slightly, his eyebrows raised. As she followed his directions she wondered what his profession might have been — a banker, perhaps, or a senior civil servant.

She found the carousel, and her case with the blue ribbon as additional identification circulating there. She experienced a familiar relief: always when she travelled she had a fear her luggage would be mislaid. Her suitcase wasn't just a container for possessions, but her companion, and a familiar friend in places where she had no other. She knew she had to catch a train into central Paris, but sat a while with her case to settle herself and to watch the people around her. She would write about them later in her journal, about them and so much more, but not the interior of the Charles de Gaulle Airport, which was grimy, worn and lacking any French chic. Singapore had been more impressive, more negotiable and cleaner too. Travel, for Rosalind Sandringham, required the strategies of a military campaign. She began to plan her sortie to the train station and the subsequent discovery of her hotel in the tenth arrondissement, made more hazardous by her lack of accomplishment in French, despite the instructional CDs and Alliance Française meetings before the trip.

She found the station in terminal two, but was bewildered by the ticket vending machines with their different colours and purposes. She sought assistance at one of the manned ticket offices and was treated with cursory indifference, the sallow man's voice unchanged, but his expression one of increasing insolence and superiority until she finally understood that a small British flag on the corner of a ticket window indicated that the staff member spoke English.

Her hotel was three stars, and chosen from the internet not because of enthusiastic reviews, or special deals, not even so much for the reassuring name, Endroit Sûr, meaning safe place. Its location was what appealed most to Rosalind. Hôtel Endroit Sûr, in Rue de Paradis. How often she had murmured that to herself, or in a voice only slightly louder in conversation with others regarding her trip. Rue de Paradis. How could charm and wondrous experience not be waiting for her there?

On her map of Paris the Hôtel Endroit Sûr seemed not far from the Gare du Nord, but on the ground the distance seemed to stretch, more noticeable because she had to walk with her case through a fine drizzle that darkened everything, although morning wasn't over. People move more rapidly in the rain, and withdraw into themselves, so that there is little sense of the camaraderie often felt by strangers strolling the same city streets. The outside café tables were empty and Rosalind wasn't tempted to stand long and observe the life going on within. And she was feeling chastened somewhat because on the train two women had disparaged her trousers. Yes, they were unflattering and unfashionable in cut and cloth, but more practical when travelling than a dress. She hadn't understood all of the brief exchange, but caught the reference to 'pantalon démodé' made by the taller woman, whose svelte attractiveness was marred only by the large nose common among French women.

'Surely comfort and modesty in clothing when you travel,' murmured Rosalind to herself in self-justification as she hurried through the fine, drifting rain that lacked the force of impact to saturate and instead gathered on her coat as a glistening congregation. Yet she recalled the young women's derisive, complicit glance and felt diminished.

Rue de Paradis is renowned for its boutiques selling china, glassware and porcelain, and as she passed by, Rosalind resolved to come again to the shops after lunch when she was without the encumbrance of her case. She would buy something petite and beautiful — small so that it was easily and safely carried, beautiful so that it would always be a reminder of Rue de Paradis and her time in Paris. The anticipation of finding such a piece, and the glimpses she had of the window displays, were enough for her to forget the comments on the train, to ignore the drizzle and the dog droppings on the pavement. To smile to herself in that inward, closeted way that lonely people do when self-absorbed, despite being among others.

Hôtel Endroit Sûr may well have been the safe haven its name proclaimed, but the number who could find refuge there was limited. It was a cramped place, like so many of the old hotels in central Paris. Everything was confined and there was a sense that the buildings on either side were squeezing it further, but not in any expression of tenderness. The main foyer was little more than an alcove with a bench of faded blue leather around it and two small glass-topped tables. The reception desk was only a couple of paces away, and all that was done and said by those waiting could be both overseen and overheard by staff.

Rosalind didn't immediately approach the desk, for the male employee there was in animated conversation with a colleague who seemed on the point of leaving, but continually paced back with a laugh to resume talking. She couldn't understand their quick-fire conversation, but was struck by the disparity in their builds and clothing. The receptionist was small, thin, nimbly active as if about to spin top-like on the spot. His wrists protruded from his jacket, bony and hairy as those of a chimpanzee. His companion was large, almost hidden in a full-length black coat and he held in one hand an umbrella that he would begin to unfurl when stepping towards the door, and close again on returning. Each seemed determined to have the last word, but in a way that confirmed their friendship and reluctance to part.

Eventually they separated, both talking and laughing simultaneously, so the competition was unresolved.

The immediate aftermath of such explosive, rapid conversation was a noticeable silence, during which the receptionist assumed a professional presence and concentrated briefly on the desk computer. He then looked up, smiled at Rosalind and raised a hand palm uppermost to suggest his availability. She rose from the worn, smooth, blue leather of the bench, left her case and approached the desk. 'J'ai une réservation,' she said. 'Rosalind Sandringham.' She had prepared the phrase carefully.

'Quand avez-vous fait la réservation?' Rosalind understood the question, knew the answer, but struggled to express it in French. The receptionist allowed her to embarrass herself for a time then interrupted with, 'Better we speak English I think, yes?'

And so they did. His English was impressive, and although brisk in manner he wasn't unfriendly. The cage lift was barely big enough for two, although neither of them were large people, and Rosalind was aware of his simian arms brushing her sleeves, and the tobacco smell on his breath. Her room seemed not much larger than the lift. He opened the window, which looked down on a cobbled delivery bay, told her the hot water in the shower would take some time to come through, but 'would arrive'. He gave Rosalind the door key, then went back down to get her case. Although not large, it couldn't be brought up with them. At no time had he given his name, and when she answered his tap on the door, intending to ask, the case was there, but he was already on his way to resume duty at the desk.

Rosalind partly unpacked, but to give herself maximum floor space she left her case on the bed. There was no carpet on the floor, just scarred and faded cork tiles that were especially stained in the cramped bathroom. She hung her damp coat on the shower nozzle and went to the single window for a wider view. It was just a courtyard with bins at one side and scaffolding opposite, but it was old, it was cobbled and it was in Paris. 'Cobbles,' murmured Rosalind. Even in the reduced light because of the surrounding walls they winked and glittered in the drizzle. It was as Victor Hugo might have described it, or a scene in which Chief Inspector Maigret appeared in unhurried walk, cradling his pipe in thought. Just a grimy, cobbled service courtyard, but a stage set for Rosalind Sandringham as she stood in her 'pantalon démodé' at a third-storey window of the three-star Hôtel Endroit Sûr.

She would, she decided, have lunch at a café and then buy her keepsake. At night she would eat in her room. She could afford to eat out only once each day, and it was less safe in the streets after dark. More important than either of those considerations, however, was the knowledge that she would be less aware of being alone. At night the cafés and restaurants of Paris were the domain of groups and especially of couples. People whose talk and laughter, whose glances and smiles, had the assurance that they mattered to their companions, that they had a place in the lives of others. To someone of Rosalind's sensibility it was no pleasure to have a solitary twilight meal, even in Paris, with lovers at a nearby table, or boisterous students in the flush of youth.

Though many of her friends and colleagues would have been surprised to know it, Rosalind, although unmarried, was not unacquainted with love. An affair, though not of the tempestuous and scandalous nature the word suggests to most. She'd never been a beauty, and was forty-three before she met Philip, who had moved into a flat in the same building. He was an architect and had owned a rather fine home of his own design, but his wife suffered from clinical depression and had become incapable of housekeeping. A tall, lean, balding man, socially awkward despite his professional accomplishments: considerate, well intentioned and with the same pressing needs as most men. Rosalind was supportive of both husband and wife, even when after many months she and Philip began to have occasional sex. He would confide in her, and sometimes afterwards lie with her on the narrow bed with the yellow duvet and make love in a brief, urgent way before resuming gentleness and talk, sometimes weeping at his wife's condition and his guilt, his confused life. Rosalind didn't dislike the unaccustomed physicality. His pleasure in her body exalted her, but the intimacy of the friendship was even more important, and when he no longer made love to her, she'd remained a friend to them both until they moved to another city. At no time had she expected Philip to abandon his wife to be with her, and he never mentioned the possibility, but she allowed herself, only briefly, to imagine being in Paris with him now.

In Paris, in the Hôtel Endroit Sûr, in the confined room with scuffed cork floor, in the bed where she sat with only her case beside her. He'd liked to finger her as they lay together, and their breathing would intensify though they were silent otherwise. She taught herself not to look away at such times, but to meet the gaze of his faded, blue eyes.

Before leaving the hotel room, Rosalind cleaned her teeth and did her hair in front of the wall mirror, the backing of which showed through in faint whorls like a dimly glimpsed oyster shell. She took her coat from the shower and checked the purse in her handbag. She looked out from the small window, but nothing had changed on the dark yet gleaming cobbles below. Maybe when she came back from lunch she would take a photograph with her phone.

The desk was unattended and the foyer empty when she left the small cage lift. Rosalind was a little disappointed, for she'd intended to ask the hairy man for his recommendation as to a café. Not everyone spoke English as well.

The soft, fine rain was still falling and there were more people on the street than earlier. There was better light, though, once she was out of the hotel, and some of the building frontages had protective awnings. Had the day been fine she would have walked farther on Rue de Paradis and taken longer in choosing somewhere to eat. The selection of a café was often for her a greater source of pleasure than the meal itself. She liked to sense the ambience of a place before making her choice. 'Ambience,' murmured Rosalind to herself as she walked. Now, however, she came to a decision quite quickly: a corner place, Orléans, which was both well lit and well patronised. Her guidebook gave the advice to choose cafés frequented by locals, and away from sites of tourist interest. The crowd in Orléans seemed Parisian by dress and the loud spill of their own language. Although Rosalind's nature inclined her to quieter places, she was dutifully impressed by informed advice.

She regretted the choice. Not because of the food, but because the small table finally vacated for her was dirty and the waiter impatient. A tall man with a yellow waistcoat who cut through her halting French by indicating she should use her finger to point out her menu choice, and who assumed a slight smirk of disdain when she chose banana Nutella crêpes and frites. He took no notice when she also pointed to the food scraps on the table, but openly regarded more interesting and sophisticated customers. A further disadvantage became apparent at the next table where two elderly women ate and talked with equal enthusiasm. Rosalind had to admire their clothing: whatever their age, French women are not afraid of colour. The woman nearest to her, however, had a very small dog in a bag at her feet, and its head was out, quivering inquisitively at Rosalind, who very much disliked the continental laxity towards pets in restaurants. Once she became aware of the dog she was convinced she could smell it as well.

But if she looked away, concentrated on the street beyond the large window, she could see a small, flowering tree. The leaves were sleek with moisture and reflected the light from within Orléans in jewelled sparkles. It had flowers too, large, pyramid-like, made up of tiny blossoms in two tones of purple, lighter where fully out, darker at the tips where the petals remained enfolded. A lilac, that's what it was. How beautiful and still amid the busy street. Rosalind was pleased to be able to recognise it. When she came out of the restaurant, free of the yellow waistcoat's disregard and the bag dog's whining for scraps, she stood by the lilac for a time before going on down Rue de Paradis in search of her keepsake. The small tree was undamaged, its flowers complete despite the many passers-by.

The rain had stopped while Rosalind had been having lunch and there were brief bursts of sunlight as low clouds moved overhead. She was able to linger before the shop windows, enter some premises and admire the fine pieces on display, although she knew those most desirable were far more expensive than she could afford. One small place, however, offered second-hand goods, and she entered eagerly, gave her 'Bonjour, madame' to a dark-haired woman intent on a computer screen, went carefully among the shelves and trays of bric-a-brac. She began with porcelain in mind, but even in a second-hand shop those pieces she most admired were too expensive. Close to the window, though, was a locked cabinet containing glass ornaments, assorted in size and origin. Rosalind recognised the delicate, highly coloured Venetian glass, but what took her attention immediately was a very different piece with no exterior decoration, but two glass arum lilies within its rotund solidity. How was it possible to accomplish such a thing?

She made her way back towards the shopkeeper, but the woman saw her coming, left her desk and without speaking walked to the cabinet and unlocked it. Rosalind pointed to the lilies. The woman reached in with accustomed dexterity, took it out and held it up between them.

'Spéciale,' she said. 'Très spéciale.'

'Oui.' Now that they were close together, Rosalind could see that the woman was older than she had first seemed. Her upper lip was finely wrinkled, and the veins and tendons of her small hand plain beneath the thin, sliding skin.

'Allemand,' she said. She turned her hand to show more of the internal glass lilies: each orange stamen a vivid lance within the perfect whiteness of the flowers. 'Très spéciale,' she said.

'Oui.'

'Bouteille de parfum,' the shopkeeper said. The woman took Rosalind's right hand and put the bottle in it, continuing for a moment to give support, for it was surprisingly heavy, although no more than nine or ten centimetres high. The glass stopper was rather like an eye dropper — a ball grip and then a tapering stalk. The bottle had almost no capacity, which accounted for its weight, and Rosalind wondered if it was a scent container at all, but didn't dispute with her. It was special, that was the thing. It was beautiful. The white lap of flowers and orange stamen, green tendrils around them, set eternally within the glass.

'Combien est-ce que ça coûte?' Rosalind asked.

'Nous n'avons que celle-ci,' the woman said, which Rosalind couldn't understand.

'Combien ça coûte?'

'Cent soixante euros,' the woman said. Rosalind handed the bottle back reluctantly. Far too much for her travel budget, especially as the exchange rate for the Kiwi dollar was so poor. If her French had been better, Rosalind might have attempted to haggle, but she just thanked the woman and went resolutely towards the door. The shopkeeper made no attempt to detain her.

The rain had returned, people had their heads down again, there were no lilac trees on that part of Rue de Paradis, the shape even of familiar things seemed gratingly awry. A listless futility was heavy in the air. Rosalind told herself there were other shops and better pieces, but couldn't convince herself. When she paused in front of windows, nothing she saw could put the perfume bottle from her mind. Having admitted that to herself, she turned round, went back to the second-hand shop and smiled in surrender at the dark-haired woman, who showed no surprise, who went to the cabinet without a word.

When she paid, Rosalind expected the shopkeeper to congratulate her on having made such a purchase, for becoming mistress of something très spéciale, but the affirmation wasn't given. Possession was a fierce joy, however, and as Rosalind went back towards the Hôtel Endroit Sûr she was aware of the weight of the scent jar, and in her mind saw the arum lilies, immobile and lovely within the glass. What expense, though! There was guilt as well as exhilaration in the shiver at her own audacity. She bought just a baguette, cheese and two apples on her way back to the hotel. How costly fruit was in the city.

A different man was at reception: bull necked and wearing a light, grey jacket. He barely glanced at her as she went through to the cage lift, and so Rosalind suppressed her intended bonjour. Her room appeared to have shrunk in her absence, but it was warm, private. She unwrapped the bottle and placed it on the bed by her pillow where there was no chance of a fall. How beautiful it was even there, lying on its side on the plain, thin cover. It made her happy, and she sat there smiling because of its perfection, and the conviction that she'd been right in her decision to purchase. She put her hand on it again to experience the smooth coolness. She brought to mind the neat living room of her flat in Ilam and imagined where the bottle could be most advantageously displayed. A place where the sun could make gleam flowers that would never wilt, never lose their lustre.

When she was rested, Rosalind had her meal — bread, Cantal cheese, the smaller apple, which she cut with the Swiss Army pocket knife Philip had given her before he and his wife moved away. 'The traveller's friend,' he'd said, 'and from your friends.' The knife had been given when the three were together for the last time, but Philip had earlier brought a gift when alone with Rosalind. A flat, silver bookmark shaped like a quill. As she used the knife, she thought of that greater gift, not because of its silver sheen, but for the difficult love of which it was a token.

Rosalind was accustomed to being by herself, but was most aware of it when she ate alone. Perhaps for that reason she didn't linger, but briskly put what remained back into the paper bag and brushed crumbs from her lap and the bed. The scent bottle still lay alongside her pillow, the arum lilies eternally fresh within the solid glass, safe from decay, safe even from time itself. Already it had become a companion. There was no electric jug in her room. At first she thought she would just drink water, and calculated the saving to be made if she did, but then she rebuked herself for both timidity and stinginess. Being a tight arse, as she had heard guys express it. What point in being a tight arse on the one occasion she would ever be in France? Coffee in the hotel dining room perhaps, even a venture to the streets before it became late.

So she went down in the clattering confinement of the cage lift, and along the corridor to the entrance of the dining room, which was no bigger than the lobby, and more shabby. Five small tables and a potted fern in its never-ending death throes as sentinel inside the door. Two tables were occupied by couples with their backs to Rosalind and there was no conversation. She turned, walked past the grey jacket man at the desk who remained as if an effigy, and into the Rue de Paradis.

Natural light was fading and the streetlamps gaining. The slightest drift of rain still, through which people went undeterred. Oh, it was so much an impressionistic painting, so much Paris, and she was glad she'd come out. Mindful of her disappointment with the Orléans, she kept walking until she found a small place, half shuttered behind an iron railing. There was a table close to the window, its surface clean. Other people were there and she watched them as she nursed her café crème. Quite close was a man by himself, slanted well back in his chair and with his legs stretched far under the table. He was English, as his conversation with the waiter showed, but what attracted Rosalind was his resemblance to Philip. The same lanky, slightly clumsy frame, same loss of hair on his crown, even the tendency to tilt his head far back as if his neck had a crick. But he was younger than Philip and better looking, though wearing jeans and worn, pale sneakers. She wondered what would have happened if she'd met Philip when he was this man's age and maybe unmarried. She imagined herself coming afresh into the café, and him drawing up his lanky legs, turning with a smile as welcome and rising to greet her.

The man did draw up his long legs and rise. He came and stood at Rosalind's table. So close she saw his face was quite unlike Philip's in all but shape, lacking any suggestion of inner reflection.

'You're too old,' he said. 'If you'd been giving me the eye twenty-five years ago I'd have fucked you for sure, but you're too old now. No offence.' He left her sitting there with a small muscle twitching in her cheek and her hand clenched on the coffee cup. The noise of other people went on just the same around her. She looked out into the Rue de Paradis and concentrated on the flux of light and movement. She told herself that cruelty was itself often a consequence of suffering, or of self-loathing.

On her way back to the hotel, Rosalind thought of the perfume bottle waiting for her there and she rejoiced with herself at its perfection, and at her courage in the purchase. She determined to be happy in a city with such depth of history. The present was vivid and active, but it seemed to her that just beneath it flickered layered scenes of people equally intent on life in their time, equally justifiable, and eager still to supplant the living and renew possession. The rain was so light, almost mist, and tickled on her face so that she rubbed her nose and chin. The soft wind, made visible by the mist and street lights, seemed to unravel against the starless sky.

At reception in the Hôtel Endroit Sûr was the English-speaking hairy man, and he smiled a welcome and told her that it was supposed to rain again the next day.

'I don't mind,' Rosalind said. 'I'm going to the Musée d'Orsay.'

'Aha. Of course.'

In her room she hung her coat on the shower nozzle and took off her wet shoes, lifted the scent bottle to the light. Then she looked down again into the cobbled courtyard with its bins and scaffolding. It was enclosed and the light was almost gone, but the cobbles still had a wet gleam, and there was life down there, though no movement. A cat was sitting at the entrance, well out from the wall. Its colour was difficult to distinguish, but it was very upright, not crouched at all, front legs straight beneath its head as in the feline statues of ancient Egypt. Rosalind stood watching for some time, but there was no movement. 'A cat,' she said quietly to herself in affirmation.

Soon she would write in her journal, always an important time and task. The capture of experience. Before that, however, she needed the lavatory and went into the adjoining bathroom. She was a small woman, but felt unpleasantly enclosed in such a tight space. She made a good deposit; always a satisfaction when travelling. Number twos, her kindergarten teacher had always called a movement of the bowel. So antiquated was the plumbing, however, that the cistern flow wasn't sufficient to flush it away, and Rosalind was left bewildered and embarrassed. She knew she should be candid and practical; go down to the desk and make a firm complaint, but she just couldn't. Instead she closed the door on the problem and closed her mind to it as well. Maybe later the cistern would function as it should.

Rosalind had a last look from the window. No cat, just the dark, jewelled cobbles and the soft, drifting rain briefly golden, circling before the single bulb at the street entrance. She made herself comfortable on the bed, with her journal and the scent bottle.

'I write this in my third-storey room in the Hôtel Endroit Sûr on the Rue de Paradis, Paris. My first day in the city of light and love.' And so Rosalind Sandringham began to shape and burnish the nature of her experience. The bright bird doesn't always have the sweetest song. There was no conscious deceit, just the bringing forward of things of fitness and grace, and the exclusion of the mundane, the squalid, the ungenerous. Nothing of the defective lavatory, nothing of the slights inflicted by the women on the train and the airport ticket man, or the discomforts, delays and apprehension of solitary travel, nothing of the dismissive lunchtime waiter with the yellow waistcoat, or the quivering, mucus-covered snout of the dog in the restaurant. Nothing even of the Philip lookalike who didn't wish to fuck her. Nothing of loneliness, regret and unrequited ambitions, or apprehension concerning the future.

She wrote of the English gentleman at the airport and his kindness, his addressing her as Antipodean. In retrospect he became more distinguished, more concerned for her. She expressed her intuition that if they had talked longer an affinity would have been evident between them and he might have invited her to accompany him to Fontainebleau. She wrote of Rue de Paradis's history, which she'd discovered on Google, including the information that its original name was The Meadows of the Daughters of God and that in 1710 it was still the site of a kitchen garden belonging to the nuns of that community. She wrote of the obliging hairy man at reception and his comment that although slow, the shower's hot water 'would arrive'. She wrote of the purple flowers on the lilac tree set in the pavement outside the Orléans café, of the Egyptian cat on the cobbles and the lightest rain lit like a swirling lace dress by the single courtyard bulb. She wrote the names of those places she was still to visit and spoke them aloud to savour the cadence of the syllables — Moulins, St-Étienne, Montpellier, Carcassonne and Perpignan. She wrote of the costly and lovely scent bottle, and held it up to see again the lily flowers that could never fade. She wrote of the things that mattered, that transformed experience, and what she wrote would become her authentic recollection, would be the truth. Rosalind wrote her own life and in doing so became content with it.

3.

The Drummer and the Stoat Killer

Sometimes your relationship with a friend, or colleague, undergoes a significant change even after years of the same accustomed degree of familiarity: moving to the next level, as people glibly say. Something happens in the small cosmos of your lives and other aspects are revealed.

Nothing dramatic necessarily. Not a road to Damascus moment. It certainly wasn't with Malcolm Enderby and me. We've worked together for years in sales at Metropolis Autos in Auckland, which is a big outfit. It doesn't have Toyota , but Volkswagen, Ford, Hyundai and Nissan are just some of its franchises. Malcolm and I head up the teams in good-natured rivalry. Each of us has quite a few guys answering to us, even women more recently. Metropolis is progressive in that respect, even in the service and parts departments. Lots of women in the office and accounts, of course.

All successful salesmen have their own style. I tend to get in there pronto, without being too pushy. I like to encourage people into a test drive. Let the vehicle sell itself, I tell my guys. Let them smell the new upholstery and hear the sexy turbo-charged engine. Talk to them when they're *in* the vehicle. Malcolm, he's got a laid-back air, waits to be approached, and seems happy at first to talk about anything but cars. He gets people to open up about themselves and eventually they find they are also open to his advice about which vehicle to buy. He gets more repeat sales than any of us: folk coming back and asking for him. Efficiency and enthusiasm, that's what I'm known for, but I'm not as memorable as Malcolm. I guess he's likeable, that's what it is.

Out of work time we didn't see a lot of each other. A couple of barbecues, work dos, and once a group of us went to the races. I think that was jacked up because someone was leaving. Charlotte and I have our own friends, but at work I got on okay with Malcolm. We usually sat together and supported each other in the meetings of department heads. Ours was the only group that had co-leaders and I think that was because management thought there were too many franchises for one person to cope with. Liaison with the various suppliers is just about a job on its own, let me tell you. Apart from work, though, Malcolm and I didn't have much in common. He was Catholic, for one thing, though that's no big deal these days. It was more that we had no shared experience apart from work, and that just circled around on itself and became a pattern of behaviour — amiable enough, but also containing in a way. An easy and shallow predictability in how we got on together.

Anyway, things changed between us a couple of years ago. Malcolm's wife, Trish, rang me up at work on a Tuesday and said he wasn't well and wouldn't be coming in. There were occasional days when he didn't show, and he did tell us once he was susceptible to respiratory infections. Now, of course, I can guess at the real reason. Trish said he'd left his phone in his office the day before, and would I mind having it dropped off at the bank where she worked. She knew there was always someone from the sales team out and about in the city.

As it happened, I was taking a top of the range X-Trail to Avondale to show to a client, and could drop off the phone on the way back — at Malcolm's home, which was pretty much on my way. The Enderbys had a nice place in Orchard Street, roughcast and with a recent wooden deck. Just a little hemmed in perhaps. Nobody answered the front door, or the back, and I would've left the phone in the letterbox and gone, except that there was drum music coming from the basement, and so I walked down to that narrow door and small window. It was a sort of rumpus room and Malcolm was in the centre of it, surrounded by fancy drums and cymbals and going at it like a madman. He wasn't normally an animated guy and it was odd to see him so hyped up, so self-absorbed. There was a vulnerability about it that made me feel embarrassed, and I stood aside from the window when I knocked — loud, and then louder again. The drums stopped, but it seemed a long time before he opened the door.

Nothing about him suggested sickness. He was wearing jeans and a blue jersey without a shirt underneath. He was just as embarrassed as me. 'You got me,' he said.

'I just came around with your phone, that's all,' I said.

'Come in,' he said, and turned back to an old sofa that was hard against one of the walls. 'I just traded up to this new drum kit yesterday and couldn't resist spending time with it.' I told him I thought it looked pretty flash, but that I didn't know anything about drums. 'Tama Superstar Hyperdrive six piece,' Malcolm said. 'Bass, tom toms, snare drum, cymbals and all the gear that goes with them. All top spec.'

'I thought tom toms were Tarzan of the jungle stuff.'

'I love the tom toms,' he said and laughed. 'No, tom toms are a fixture.' Everything in the drum kit except the cymbals were a matching glossy dark red. When something of quality is new, you have an urge to touch it, don't you, to feel the finish and freshness of it. Every day I see people reach out to touch the panels of a new car without conscious decision, let their hand slip over the deep, waxed paint, rest it on the silver glitter of chrome. I felt like doing that with Malcolm's drums, and I knew nothing about music, couldn't play a note on anything. No wonder he'd taken a day from work. 'Don't tell anybody, will you,' he said. 'The guys would give me heaps about playing bloody drums at my age.'

It was a different Malcolm there in his basement with the newly purchased drums and cymbals, and in temporary escape from his sales responsibility. He seemed younger, and not just because he was wearing jeans, a jersey with the sleeves pulled up and no shirt. I asked him if he'd always been into drums. 'Ever since a kid,' he said. 'It's been a thing with me all my life just about. It's why I didn't make it at varsity, because I got into the pub band scene. At one stage I thought I could make a go of it full time. Ever heard of Catch Cry Brotherhood?'

'No.'

'I played drums with them. All over Auckland and holiday gigs in places like Tauranga and Nelson. Even went to Aussie and almost starved to death despite playing most nights in grotty pubs. So much depends on getting the right management, and we never had any luck there. We had some great times together, although it couldn't last. We were mad bastards then. Real mad bastards.' He shook his head in wonderment at the life he'd had, and come through. He told me about those Kiwi drummers he admired. The only name I recognised at all was Geoff Chunn, because he'd been in Split Enz. Even I knew Split Enz.

'Why don't you play me something then,' I said, 'before I take the X-Trail back to work. I reckon I've as good as sold it.' And he did. I've no idea if it was a proper arrangement, or if he was just making it up as he went along, but it sure impressed me. He was into it. He looked and sounded as good as the guys I saw on TV. He loved doing it too: it released something in him that I'd never seen before.

When he finished, Malcolm started fiddling with one of the tom toms. 'I haven't got them tuned properly yet,' he said, 'but I'm really chuffed with the lot. Bloody expensive, but why work if you can't have what makes you happy?'

Malcolm said he'd come in after lunch. 'Nothing to anybody about the drums, remember,' he said. 'Just say it was a twenty-four-hour bug.' That was okay by me. People don't need to know everything about you. Most people don't deserve to. Malcolm came in later, as he said he would, and got on with the job just as he always did. He was good at it. Well, you don't get to head up a double figure sales team at a place like Metropolis Autos without talent and application, and I should know.

It was different with us after that, though, as if some barrier between outer and inner dimensions of personality had fallen after I found him in the basement at Orchard Street with his new drums. To my surprise he asked Charlotte and me round not long after just to listen to him playing. It became a thing and we'd have a few drinks and talk as well. Trish said he never played for anybody else, and he said not to go on about it to other people. The four of us clicked, and Charlotte and Trish started doing things together too.

Malcolm reckoned I, too, must have some hidden talent. 'What about you?' he asked me one rainy day when we stood together in his living room with the dahlia flowers in their garden distorted by the flux of water on the window. 'You didn't grow up dreaming of selling cars, did you?' He was right. I told him that when I left school what interested me most was conservation stuff, visions of tuatara, yellow-eyed penguins, spending time monitoring native birds in the bush and exterminating introduced predators.

'I had an uncle who'd worked for the New Zealand Wildlife Service, as they called it then,' I said, 'and he got me enthusiastic. I imagined myself rediscovering an extinct species just as Geoffrey Orbell did with the takahē. The huia maybe. That would be something. All I actually did was track maintenance work at Kahurangi National Park for a few months after leaving school. I applied for a job with DOC, but they're pretty selective and I didn't get it.'

'But you're still into it?'

'I'm still a Forest & Bird member and enjoy the mag, but I'm way too busy to get involved.'

'Make time,' said Malcolm. 'We all need something else, not just the day job. It's exercise for a different part of the brain.' I thought that quite perceptive, and remember standing there with him by the large window with the heavy rain slanting in on the glass and the crimson, white and yellow flowers writhing in a sort of migraine dance outside. 'So make time,' he said again.

I did make time. I joined up with a local volunteer group planting native vegetation, monitoring bird life, trapping predators, escorting school groups, all sorts of stuff. Charlotte came along sometimes. She wasn't much interested in cars and said it was something we could do together. I don't want to give the impression that either Malcolm or I dislike our jobs at Metropolis. You meet a lot of people in sales and see all sorts of personality traits, and the vehicles themselves are constantly improving. You wonder what they're going to come up with next. They're even talking about self-drive cars now, for God's sake. And it's a damn good living if you're good at it: the more you sell the more you make. The drumming and conservation are an enlargement and relaxation, though, for both of us. Very different things, but serving the same purpose. I was perfectly okay with people knowing my interests, but Malcolm remained secretive about the drums and preferred others not to know.

That seemed to me a pity when surely music is something you share, especially if you're good at it. If you'd played so often in front of pub crowds here and in Aussie, why would you worry about people knowing? Trish said he didn't want to be some pathetic has been.

In March DOC was having this big push against predators. Even the government's more onside these days, and my volunteer group was raising money for new self-resetting traps. Some of the latest are even Bluetooth enabled. Modern traps are expensive, though, and you need plenty of them to make a difference. We wanted to use them in the new Northland enclosures where bush is regenerating splendidly. The usual fund-raising activities were suggested — stalls, raffles, a ball. Charlotte said we needed something unusual to get people's attention. 'Drums,' she said. 'We need Malcolm on drums as well as wine and nibbles.' It was brilliant really, but how to get Malcolm to agree? We talked to Trish first, and she thought it a great idea.

'I'll work on him,' she said resolutely. But after a few days she came round and said he didn't want to do it. 'I think there's only one thing left that'll work,' she said. 'You have to ask him as a friend, ask him as a favour.'

So I did that when we were driving back together from the opening of the new branch in Devonport. 'It would be something different,' I told him. 'And what other way could our interests come together? A fun thing in a really good cause.'

'I haven't played in public for friggin' years. Who wants to see an old prick who imagines he's still got the moves? I'm happy just rattling away in the basement.'

'But you've still got it. You know you have.'

'Who would come, for Christ's sake, and where would you hold it? A venue would cost most of your takings.'

But I'd thought about that and come up with an answer. The Metropolis showroom would be ideal, and we could tap into the firm's client list as well as greenies. I kept on at Malcolm and he agreed finally. I knew, as Trish had said, that in the end he was doing it for me: doing it as a sign of friendship. I think he rather hoped there was still an out, that the general manager would put the kibosh on the idea. The boss was a bit taken aback at first, and wanted to hear Malcolm play before agreeing, but of course after coming round to Orchard Street one evening and hearing for himself, he was all for it. 'Jesus, Malcolm, that's great,' he said. 'I had no idea. Bloody marvellous.'

The boss is pretty shrewd, though. Sure, he's willing to support a worthy cause and environmental issues are good for the firm's image, but he always has an eye for profit. He had the showroom cleared for the event, and spruced up, but he also had extra lighting installed in the yard and had the latest SUVs, utes and hatchbacks artfully arranged there with their doors open, a couple of the junior salespeople drifting about in case there were queries.

Everyone said it was a great night. People even danced with the kākā and kiwi cardboard cutouts we had there for publicity. We charged $50 a pop, over 350 people came and we ended up with a donation of over $12,000 for the traps once expenses were stripped out. We hired a DJ, and Charlotte and Trish chose the music, but it was Malcolm's drum sessions that were the star turns, just as we knew they'd be. He was transformed in front of the crowd, even more than he had been in the basement. He wore black jeans and T-shirt and a leather jacket and really played up to the image of a band drummer. Everybody loved it. People danced, or stood and clapped. A certain city councillor collided with the office door and had to be taken to hospital, and Martin Binns, senior partner of Gimlet and Freyer, our auditors, sang 'The Winner Takes It All' from start to finish.

Even the weather co-operated — such a warm evening, and through the glass of the showroom you could see folk mooching among the well-lit vehicles outside when there wasn't any music. Yeah, there was sure a spike in sales that month.

But it was the drummer's night. The sweat ran down Malcolm's face and into his smile while he played, and the rich plum-red of the Tama Superstar drum kit had a brilliance that seemed more than mere reflection. It was bloody marvellous, just as the boss said.

Naturally, after that lots of people wanted him to do gigs at weddings, office parties, send-offs, launch events, you name it, but he wasn't keen. He said you can't go back, and that a drummer is part of a team, not a one-man show-off. He still plays in his basement and doesn't mind if close friends drop by. Mostly, though, he plays by and for himself. He's become quite interested in the conservation stuff Charlotte and I are into, comes with us often when we're planting natives, or bird spotting. He can get quite vehement about possums now.

Sometimes when I'm in the showroom and see him soberly dressed, in conversation with a client among the cars, or relaxed in his office before the computer, I think of his alter ego as a helter-skelter drummer before the wild crowd. I'm glad I went down to his basement that day and found him there. We're much closer friends because of it — the drummer and the stoat killer of Metropolis Autos.

4.

Dancing on Another Planet

I don't get back here much. Partly that's because I live in Darwin now, but also there's no one here any more to whom I'm close. All of the family have shifted away to one place or another. Even my parents, after living here for more than thirty years, moved to Nelson to be close to my sister and her family. Maybe there's people I once knew well, but have now lost touch with, but Boof Sandri's the only one I know for sure still lives here. I don't think I'll call on him again, however, even though he was just about my best mate in my last high school years. He visited me in Aussie a couple of times and I saw him here eleven years ago, but we've taken different paths for too long now and haven't much in common except a receding past. He's become mad keen on horse racing and yachting, and I don't think his wife likes me much. I don't recognise in him anything of the Boof from the old days, even when we talk about them. His wife said he should have done a lot better for himself at school and university. They snipe at each other a lot and that's not a pleasant atmosphere for a visitor.

Places bring back people, people bring back places, and both conjure the cinema of your past. I'm not a great one for nostalgia, but being here for a couple of days, mooching around by myself, has evoked memories both good and bad. Our family home's gone: a rambling, two-storeyed wooden building with apricot and apple trees behind, and in its place two crouching townhouses in Oamaru stone with Decramastic roofs. There's still the dentist's house next door, but its garden is neglected now. The town itself hasn't changed that much, and although the high school has a new gym and a couple of prefabs behind the hall, I found my way around the grounds quite easily, and saw a retrospective shimmer of myself and others in familiar places. I stood in the concrete fives courts where I lost to Trevor Parkin in the final.

I drove out to Kimbers Crossing too. The old weir and the pool beneath the willows where we hung out a lot in summer. The track through the gorse and broom seemed shorter, but just as overgrown, the yellows of the small flowers glowing in the sun. Steers used to roam there and they could get quite stroppy. Warren Pugh was charged by one and ended up with two broken ribs. I didn't see any stock today, but Kimbers Crossing brought back to me a happening of greater significance than Warren's encounter, and one for which I share a lingering sadness, even guilt. Yes, Esme Porrit. All those years ago.

Esme wasn't really part of our gang. She was Derek's younger sister and just tagged along when she could. Belinda and Anne were two years older than her and bona fide members. They went to the same school as Esme and didn't mind her as long as she knew her place — which was to maintain subservience to them and, by the contrast of her asexual figure, emphasise the nubile attraction of their own. Odd how important a year or two is at school in terms of seniority, yet means nothing when you've grown up. It wasn't really a gang: people came and went on the fringes of it, as with all adolescent groups. Derek, Maaka, Kevin, Stuart and I regularly hung out, though, and sometimes Marty and Carol, though she often had music practice and couldn't come when we decided to do things. Stuart was always called Boof for no reason that anyone remembered. There were others too, some just faces now rather than names.

Esme didn't seem to have many friends of her own. She was a bright kid and won prizes, but was different, as the brightest kids often are. She liked being with us, even though she wasn't fully accepted. She would cycle at the back of the group, or wait as we got into a car to see if there was room for her. Esme was very thin and blonde. She laughed a lot and showed her teeth and her skinny legs kicked out to the side when she ran. When she went up to get the fourth form award for general excellence, the principal said she was a student of special ability, but that didn't count for much with us. If she hadn't been Derek's sister, we'd have told her to bugger off, and often we did anyway. She seemed happy to flit around the edge of things: a sort of lesser citizen of the group. She knew to wander off if any of us were pashing in the cars, or if any argument blew up.

Dancing by herself was how she passed the time when she knew she wasn't wanted. Quite unabashed she would dance on the tennis courts, the patio of Belinda's parents' place, even among the gorse and broom, the lupins and drooping willows of Kimbers Crossing. We got used to the oddity of it and took no notice. While we were involved with undertones of competition and sex, with our poses of careless rivalry and display, she would dance alone and disregarded, except for our occasional flippant dismissal. Twirling and sinking, arching and reaching, her hands out, bent at the wrists as if she held pails, or lifted high with the fingers spread. It was as if she heard a music denied the rest of us, or maybe it was her way of showing she didn't need our acceptance.

Once she danced in the carpark of the Palace Theatre when we were walking through after seeing *Spartacus*.

'Why always the dancing?' I asked her.

'It takes me to a different planet,' she said and gave her high-pitched laugh.

'A bloody odd one,' said Boof.

'I'm going to learn dancing,' she said. 'Mum said next year I can have lessons,' and she twirled away between a blue Corolla and a Volkswagen Combi.

'I learnt dancing for years,' said Anne, and she gave a sort of sliding skip that took both Boof's attention and mine. She had all the curves in the right places, did Anne. Sometimes she would just look at you without saying anything and then smile. There was a lot in that smile.

I suppose if what happened to Esme hadn't happened, Anne would be the one I'd remember best, for Esme wasn't important in the hierarchy of the gang. No one was jostling for her favour, or attention: she was just Derek's younger sister who tagged along.

I remember it had been hot that day at Kimbers Crossing, just as it was today, but it was evening then. Nine of us in two cars and room

Return to Harikoa Bay

for Esme to tag along. The river wasn't all that far from town, and we often biked, but it was more cool, more American, to use the family car. The girls changed in the Ford Falcon and the guys in the Triumph, or blatantly beneath the trees. It was always a time of towel swishing, dashing between the vehicles, laughter and false modesty. Niles was with us that evening. He'd only come to the school that year, but thought himself a bit of a hotshot because he was first fifteen and his mother was a paediatrician. Not all of us in the gang took to him, but Kevin had become a close mate and so he started coming along. We swam and mucked about with a blow-up ball, playing a sort of water polo without rules. A lot of ducking and grappling went on. On land Maaka led us in a haka he'd made up himself. Afterwards we lay on our towels on the bank, dappled through the swaying willows by a sun still strong, and we drank beer and vied with each other to be cool, to be smart, to swear a lot and be offhand. How urgent, how devastating, is sexual longing in young guys. Carol was there that day too. I remember because she said coconut oil was giving me a good tan.

Niles had taken a fancy to Anne, join the club, but at that time she was favouring Derek in a rather noncommittal way. She didn't laugh when Niles told a joke about cow girls and told him to cut it out when he flicked his towel at her legs. Esme didn't take part in any of this. She changed back into her clothes straight after swimming and after wandering upstream for a while, came back and began dancing close by. A customary thing for all of us except Niles, who watched her gyrating stick figure in a simple pink dress, her happy preoccupation, her difference, and still found it derisory.

'What's Cinderella up to?' he said. 'She's weird.'

'She just likes to dance,' said Belinda.

'Hey, weirdo,' shouted Niles, 'What the hell is that?'

'I'm dancing,' said Esme and she came closer, danced around us in the dappled evening light. 'Just dancing 'cause it makes me feel good.'

'Doesn't make me feel good. Why don't you piss off, you titless wonder, and find your own friends,' Niles said.

'Leave her alone,' said Anne. 'She's okay.'

'Yeah, lay off,' said Derek. He never fussed over his sister, but was a good brother in his own way. He was a big, quiet guy, but you didn't want to stir him up. He'd front up to Niles, first fifteen or not.

'A titless wonder and a crappy dancer too,' said Niles, but quieter and directed towards Esme, who stopped dancing and came and stood near him.

'You won't make me cry,' she said, although she seemed close to it.

'Find some friends of your own,' he said.

'Knock it off,' said Derek and he sat up to look directly at him.

'You won't make me cry,' said Esme again.

'Take no notice, Esme,' Anne said.

Esme turned back and began to dance again, but you could tell she was hurt. She didn't dance for long. She picked up her towel and togs and said she was going home. 'Don't be silly,' said her brother. 'Take no notice of him: he's a nong. It's getting late to be walking all that way by yourself. We'll all be going soon.'

'I'll be okay,' she said and started down the track dangling the blue towel and her black togs. Soon she was lost in the shadows of the gorse and broom. She didn't look back and her jaunty steps were an obvious defiance.

She wasn't okay, though. We weren't to know that, of course. How could we, sitting there in the quiet warmth of a summer evening and none of us having experienced anything really awful. We continued to laugh and talk and posture in that summer extravagance of youth: the low, deeply coloured sun reflecting from the quiet river, and the drooping willow foliage soft and still.

Esme never did reach home, and no sign of her was ever seen again, despite a mammoth search and long-term police investigation. None of us wanted to speculate. I guess her disappearance is one reason that not many in the old gang kept in touch once we left school. Whenever I met Derek afterwards, she was the sad, unspoken barrier between us.

'You won't make me cry,' she told Niles. I never did see her cry, but I remember her dancing, and that's a whole lot better. I don't think of Esme in a culvert somewhere, or hustled away, but dancing on another planet, one more hospitable than our own. Dancing, dancing even now.

5.

Night Nurse

Was she ever there, the night nurse?

Brief companion within the cavernous expanse of unending shadow beneath the raven's wing. The reluctant clock faint on the wall, the saline drip stand and the entry needle taped to the back of your hand. The flush tubes lower down that glow and pulse with more blood, it seems, than piss. The automatic pressure pads on the ankles, the firm, but friendless, clasp of the blood pressure band on your upper arm, the switch close by that permits the bed head to be raised, or lowered — ah, such limited excursion as you lie tethered there. Despite the generous warmth of the private room come sudden shivering fits and twitches that are the body's response to physical shock and the mind's misgivings. And you are conscious that outside in the undergrowth are silent creatures, snouts raised, scenting in the dark.

The raven night crouches over everything: spreads its wings of apprehension. No more is there laughter and chatter drifting from the nurses' room, no more cheerful women passing doors with trolleys of fancy food that can only be a mocking irrelevancy to so many grey and reduced people peering tortoise-like from their beds.

Doubts and fears flock in with night. Regrets and threats that flourish in the heavy soil of darkness and solitude. How isolating illness is, how intractable, how insistent and embracing in unwelcome ways. But — she comes in that silence despite the menace, the night nurse, to bring her comfort even as she employs the customary checks of finger clip, blood-pressure wrap and thermometer within your ear. She is older than the day nurses, more senior perhaps. She uses your Christian name in a way that is not at all false and lifts up the bag of ruby urine as if it were a wine to prize. Her pleasure is a reassurance and she holds your hand as she explains the removal of the catheter. Breathe fully in and out three times, then hold your breath, she tells you. The clock follows the same instruction. Your reluctant and abused cock shrivels back like a snail's antennae, but you and she are both beyond embarrassment. She talks and holds your hand. Gives you a plastic container. Tells you what you must expect and what to do. The clock still holds its breath at four and thirty-two.

You drowse and challenge the clock to move whenever you awake. Indeed the raven gradually lifts, dissolves and day comes. Light and growing cheer. A sense of an active world, and healthy, well-intentioned people. You wish to thank the night nurse for her nurture, but she is gone and bright, fresh people are her replacement.

The night nurse will come again, however, will hold someone else's hand in the small room with its paraphernalia of recovery, will use their name with a comforting familiarity and move surely in the dimness to fulfil their needs.

So to the night nurse, already dreamlike in your consciousness — thank you and farewell.

6.

Family Ties

Whenever I think of coming to punish my father, it's always in a strong wind, and that's blowing now as I drive up the long, unsealed track to the house and sheds. A southerly, noisy as it shoulders through the windbreak pines and harries the distressed clouds across a platinum sky. (How often I biked, or walked, into it as a boy.) Always it seemed a head wind rather than giving assistance, no matter what my own direction. But in those days everything in nature seemed predisposed to opposition. It was how my father viewed the world and so the world obliged him.

It's a banal truth that all in childhood is bigger and diminishes as you yourself grow up. It used to be a journey to the road gate and back, and one that held possibilities for both gain and loss. In the first term of my third-form year I hid for two mornings in a row in the gorse hedge until the school bus had gone on without me and spent the warm days in the creekbed reading Tolkien, ate my lunch enclosed in the stink of fennel, and the sound of the snapping seed pods of broom, dreamed of faraway places. The school rang home, of course, on the second day, and my father gave me a hiding with his trouser belt, so it was back to the tedium of the classroom and accomplishment without pleasure. It's possible to do well without having any respect for the institution that rewards you.

My father has a fundamentalist view of life without any formal commitment to religion, or even a Bible in the house. He's an Old Testament sort of man and would suit a fringing beard and an Appalachian collarless shirt, but he's clean shaven, seated in the living room without a smile as he watches through the window my arrival. I drive the Jaguar as I come to punish my father. I park it now side on to his view to emphasise its opulence. See how I have done well, my father, despite your predictions and desire for failure. See how Mammon has favoured me, despite my contamination in your eyes. A Jaguar XF in Odyssey Red Metallic looks good outside the wooden farmhouse, even if dusted from the gravel road.

I don't knock, or call out, at the door, but step over his boots and go on through. 'Hello, Dad,' I say.

'How are you?'

'As you see.'

'The jug's hot, if you want a coffee,' he says. He gets up, not as a greeting, but to follow me into the kitchen where he takes Gingernuts from the packet, places them on a white saucer, stands as I make an instant coffee, then follows me back to the living room. For a moment I think to seat myself in his brown vinyl armchair by the window, but it would be too obvious a challenge. He has weathered well, my father: tall and spare, his skull increasingly apparent as the soft tissue of his face has worn away. High cheek bones and the bridge of his prominent nose taut against the skin, though there are folds and creases elsewhere. Only the slight forward stoop seems accentuated. He never shirked the physical work the farm required. He looks a lot like the guy in *American Gothic* except he has more hair. He was handy enough with a pitchfork. 'We're hellish dry here again,' he says, dunking a Gingernut. He has those narrow frame glasses too, like the Gothic man. 'If it wasn't for irrigating the river flat we'd have hardly any winter feed at all.' The 'we' doesn't include my mother, who's been dead for years, but refers to my brother, Peter, who runs the farm now from the adjoining property.

'I'm calling in on Peter and Lorraine for lunch before heading back, so I can't stay long,' I say, 'but I wanted to pop in and see how you are.

You could've come over too. Lorraine said she invited you.'

'Yeah, but I've got a bit to do at the sheds,' he says. 'There's something not working properly with the bale feeder. Damn thing was a pain last winter and I want it up to scratch before the next. There's always something.'

My father's good with machines as well as stock; not many cockies have both strengths. It's just the recent computer genetic programs that are beyond him and he leaves that stuff to others. Peter's good with machines too. He's only a little more than two years older than me and when we were kids couldn't understand why building and dismantling things had little fascination for me. He was into team sports too, while I preferred the solitary test of the runner. There's no one else to blame when you're a track athlete: just you, your opposition and the tape to break at the end. Even the training regime is a self-imposed test. I succeeded at running as I succeeded at most things, though not all. That's why I was seldom hassled at Boys' High, I think. A couple of provincial junior titles put me up there with the first fifteen boys. A lot of stuff is sublimated for teenagers.

'So you're off again overseas?' my father says. He's looking out of the window, past the Jaguar to the old macrocarpas by the tractor shed. Macrocarpas are resistant to wind sway, not like poplars, or silver birches, but the strong southerly forces even them into a clumsy dance. He scratches beneath his chin: a dry rasp.

'Just Sydney. A conference there for three days. The usual — tax stuff.'

'Why go to Sydney to talk about Kiwi taxes?'

'Well, it's about tax everywhere. How global corporates can be made to pay their fair share in each country they operate in.'

'So it's another worldwide swizz?'

'Pretty much at the moment, yes,' I tell him. What's the use of boring him with the intricacies of concerted government attempts to make digitally based multinationals like Google and Facebook pay a fair tax in the countries in which they do business? It's all a long way from a downland farm in drought and a tricky hay feeder.

'It's odd you've ended up in tax, isn't it,' he says.

'Someone's got to do it.'

'You're right there, I suppose.' He gives a slow grin as if he's caught me out, as if there's some admission in what I said, then looks back to the landscape. Even when indoors, he's really living outside. 'Maybe this'll bring rain,' he says, 'but it'll just blow through at this rate. We need a long, steady fall.' His hands are large and worn, the backs finely wrinkled and with the dark, shallow bruises that old hands suffer easily.

I certainly didn't set out to become a tax specialist. When I left school I thought I might become an architect — the opportunity for creativity, the constant progression of material and design — but I chose law. There are so many ways to go in law. The senior partner at Penrose, Wills and Unthank encouraged me to specialise in corporate law, and that narrowed down to the multinationals because of increasing political awareness of their tax evasion. Governments follow the scent of money. A new, complex area of law and I was right there to take advantage of it. Not many people would think of international tax law as exciting, but chasing the big, fire-breathing dragons of commerce can be quite engrossing. I chair a panel appointed by the PM and I'm the Kiwi representative on an international committee trying for a common approach. There's cowboys everywhere these days, even in skyscrapers.

I ask my father about his health, for he won't volunteer such information. He's got no time for people who bleat on about their troubles. He tells me he's no better and no worse. 'They're keeping an eye on it after the treatment. That way they can send a regular bill. Monitoring it, they say. God knows what the difference is between an ultra sound, an MRI and a CT scan. All black magic to me.'

'But it hasn't got worse, I hope?'

'Monitoring, like I say.' He doesn't want to talk more about it. My father lives a life unto himself. My mother never gave up on attempts to draw him out, but he submitted only what he had to. What manner of courtship they had, who knows: perhaps she found his secrecy a challenge and he her persistence equally so. How well I recall the years of her endeavour to find his essential, inner self, and his equally powerful need to hold that inviolate.

I loved my mother. I love her still, though we can no longer touch. I talk to her sometimes in my head as that helps me to see her. Farm work was never able to coarsen her and she was tall, slim, white haired and gracious even at the end. She turned more and more to classical music, and when my brother found her dead by the hen house, with the eggs unbroken in the plastic bucket, Vivaldi was still playing on her headphones. Music is the one truly international language she used to say. I like Vivaldi, partly because he reminds me of her. She told me once she used to play the cello, but I don't recall any musical instruments in the house.

As an adult I understand my mother better than I did as a child, although my love was no less. Peter and I had been entirely focused on the present and the future — nostalgia comes later in life — while she'd liked to talk of things and places important to us when we were small. The red trike with the big front wheel, the Noddy books, the trough by the tractor shed we persistently climbed into, the hot water cupboard where I would hide when disgruntled with the world, the highchair with a tray that caught our fingers. (A mother never forgets that time when her children are fully dependent on her, when she is the absolute centre of their lives and guardian as well.) 'Remember the pet lamb we called Dozy,' she'd say, 'that chased the cat. Remember when you decided to run away and got as far as the shearing shed before it started to rain, and the time you got your hand stuck in the vacuum cleaner.' As well as photographs, she had a folder with my first crayon drawings, and she wouldn't throw away the diminutive, blue gumboots that Peter and I wore in turn, but kept them in the laundry corner by a soft broom and her father's walking stick. She let me wear her hats and just smiled when I used to hold to my face the red velvet jacket she'd worn as a young woman.

'Eli might be able to find time away from his practice to come to Sydney too,' I tell my father, who replies with a small, indifferent grunt. He never uses my partner's name. 'And he's keen for us to go to Vietnam sometime soon. People say it's a fascinating place. Both of us feel we need a break. Maybe we'll work in another few weeks in Italy. We love the Umbrian and Tuscan hill towns.'

'Your mother was always keen to travel to Europe.'

'But you never went, did you?'

'The time never seemed to be right somehow. Farming's an up and down sort of thing. Mostly there was some call for the money here, and anyway Peter was busy enough on the new place without looking after here.' My father always talks about the 'new' place, but it was bought years ago now and is pretty much integrated with the original property. My father would be at home in one of those societies that reckons individual worth in terms of how many goats are owned or hectares commanded. Land is what matters to him and the right to decide who walks over it. He's uncertain, suspicious even, of any possession you can't hold, or stand on. He's slogged, though, you have to give him that. He's come from nothing, to use a phrase he's fond of employing himself. Recreation for my father is an occasional visit to the races, or a Christmas dinner at the home of a wider family member. I don't think I've ever seen him with a hardback book in his hand. For him, reading is a form of idleness and he rebuked me for it when I was growing up. 'Get off your butt and do something useful, for Christ's sake, boy,' he'd say.

'Anyway, how's wool doing these days?' I ask him, and he looks to the sway of the reaching poplars along the drive as if the answer can be found there. 'And Peter tells me the stud's doing okay.'

'It's all fine wool that buyers want these days. The merino guys are happy enough. The rest of us have to get by.'

'The stud rams, though. That's going okay?'

'Not so bad,' he says, 'but it's an intensive sort of thing with a lot of handling and record keeping. Finicky stuff.'

My father is fearless in regard to animals. It's not valour so much as a calm assumption that fellow creatures lack the presumption to challenge him, even if they wish to do so. I find this characteristic of his nature somewhat at variance with other aspects of his personality, but true nevertheless. He will walk up on a bull, or steer, or stag, and win the confrontation. And he shows no awareness of such casual mastery.

'You should get out more,' I tell him. 'You don't have to do every-thing here now. When's the last time you visited your sister, or had anyone round? And Auckland's not the other side of the world, but you've never come to stay.'

'There always seems to be something needs doing here,' he says, 'and my gut plays up when I travel these days.' He inclines his head back in that characteristic way and strokes beneath his chin, still looking to the window and not at me.

'Have you been to Mum's grave much lately? When I went this morning there weren't any flowers.'

'Don't tell me when to visit your mother's grave,' he says, his voice oddly reproving rather than angry. And he's right, of course. What can I be sure of about their marriage, even if to me they seemed poorly matched. I recall no displays of affection, but no serious disputes either. Best I keep judgement to those things of which I'm sure.

'No, it's just that it seemed a bit neglected, that's all.'

'I go,' he says. 'I go.'

'The rain's coming now,' he says after a pause, and so it is: sudden, wind driven from the south so that it strikes the glass with striations and everything outside seems quivering and indistinct.

'What about the rabbits these days?' I ask. When I was growing up we waged war on them: Peter and I out with the .22. We had a lot of rabbit casseroles. Sometimes old man McKinney would bring ferrets over.

'They haven't been too bad, but of course they're becoming immune to the virus now.'

I think I've always admired the masculine figure, even long before I was aware of sexual attraction. The stretch and draw of muscle, breadth of shoulder and narrow hips, the ease of stride, the carriage of a young man who is fit and strong, the conscious resilience of one who is older. It was one reason I took up athletics, though prompted as well by the determination to excel at something esteemed by regular guys. To run with grace and purpose among others stripped to numbered singlets and shorts and be equally fit and balanced; the flex of arms and thighs in accustomed and purposeful movement, the steady depth of breathing, the competitive awareness of other bodies — and then, hopefully, to put the pressure on and glide away with no one able to match you. (Winning is a way of forcing people to recognise your worth.)

Alan Johnson was a year ahead of me at secondary school and I fell in love with him. The first person for whom I felt a focused and physical desire. He must have had some Māori blood, because his skin wasn't pasty at all: so even, with no freckles or blemishes. Naturally I never said or did anything, and he had no idea of my crush. It didn't make me unhappy. I think I always knew that in time I would be able to express myself quite naturally. I even had girlfriends, and that's exactly what they were. I enjoyed their company, went to dances, hung out with a mixed group. I think only Abby realised the truth. 'I can tell girls don't turn you on,' she said one night after we'd been to see *One Flew Over the Cuckoo's Nest* at the Odeon. We were parked by the reservoir and could see the headlight beams like fireflies in the lit city streets below. I had an arm around her shoulders, but we'd been talking of the film, not kissing.

It was different at uni. A gay world existed there and in the city. You could be in, or out, or halfway between. I never made any declaration to my family, but it gradually came to be recognised — unreservedly understood by my mother, accepted by my brother, incomprehensively resented by my father. 'How come he's grown up a homo?' I once heard him ask my mother, as if my orientation was a deliberate slur on his own lifestyle. He was always uncomfortable if I came to visit with a male companion, always found some reason to go away, as if there were disease in the air. What point could there be in telling him of the Ancient Greeks, who exalted equally the beauty of both the male and female body. The famous warriors of Sparta and Thebes fought most valiantly when shoulder to shoulder with their lovers. Since my mother's death I've always come alone, and seldom, to visit my father.

For the time at least the rain is gone, but the wind is still insistent. My father and I are accustomed to being together without much communication. It's easier that way, but I've made a considerable journey, in more ways than one, and wish to be acknowledged as a son and as a man. 'I'm glad of the chance to see Peter and Lorraine,' I tell him. 'I enjoy time with their kids. Smart boys, and affectionate.'

'They come over here sometimes when their mum and dad are away. Squabble over stuff sometimes, but mostly they get on well.'

'Just like Peter and me then.'

'In some ways, I suppose,' he says, without conviction or interest.

'I know you think I'm different, but I'm much the same as everybody else. Just because I sleep with a guy doesn't change everything. Have you ever thought about that? It's not a big deal for most people these days.'

'No big deal for me either, but I don't want to hear about it. Nothing to do with me. I hardly see you, do I.'

'It's not a choice I made just to piss other people off, you know.' I hope a bit of offhand humour might make it easier for him. 'It's a natural thing.'

'Whatever,' he says, and tips his head back. 'I never think about it,' he says, and then gets up from the armchair and takes both our cups to the kitchen bench.

His brief absence establishes a sufficient break in our conversation for him to feel comfortable about beginning a new subject on his return. 'Do you still run?' he asks. 'Not competitively of course, but do you still run to keep fit? You used to be a tiger for training.' Sport is a manly thing and one subject my father has always found easier to talk about, although in my case I'm sure he sees it as an anomaly. In his own upbringing there was no time for games.

'I still run when I can, though these days jogging's a more accurate term. It's not easy to find the time, or a place, either, if you're travelling. I try to keep off pavements. I like running in parks. Grass is so much easier on the joints. I have an exercycle too.'

'On a farm you don't need any gadgets to exercise.'

What is it I expect from my father as we sit here, together and apart? There will be no apology for the repugnance made obvious over many years. He is what he is, but if I'm honest with myself then I admit I would rather my mother had been granted the longer life. It's not that I wish him dead, but that I love her more. My father didn't come to either of my graduations and felt no need to give a reason. 'You know what he's like,' my mother said. 'I did my best.' Surely I would have looked no different to others in gown and hood, would have caused no embarrassment for him, but it was his signal, and mine in reply was never to refer to it. To show no pain is a means of diminishing the satisfaction of those who inflict it.

He always thought 'something could be done about it', as if it were an abnormal growth to be surgically removed. My mother said his generation was like that, but I haven't found that universally true. He finds in me some criticism of himself, some failing of his own masculinity.

My father has begun complaining about his neighbour — the overstocking, neglected fences, a reliance on my father's machinery without offering any form of return. 'Drives a flash car and heads up the local Rotary, but can't keep his stock off our property. Always asking for favours.' My father has an entrenched aversion to being taken advantage of in any way.

'But he's been the same for years, hasn't he?'

'His father was a first-rate chap. Colin's not half the man his old man was. It's not the same now.'

'It's a pity then,' I say. 'Neighbours are important in the country.'

I hardly remember Colin. A couple of years behind me at school and with neither talent nor peculiarity to make him stand out.

As we talk I'm aware of the smell of the house: a smell of perfunctory upkeep, slightly sour and musty, woollen socks and pan-cooked bacon, unwashed towels. The odour of a widower's domain, and a further alienation from the home I knew. The house seems leached of colour too — all a common indistinctness as if even the curtains, furniture, crockery and covers realise they are no longer valued.

'Well, I'd better get going now,' I tell my father.

'Okay then,' he responds. 'I've got eggs somewhere for Lorraine,' and he pushes himself up from the chair, goes through to the kitchen again and returns with a clear plastic bag of large, brown eggs. But he doesn't come farther than the door. 'Look after yourself then,' he says in farewell.

He's watching from the window as I reach the car, but neither of us waves. The wind tugs unkindly at the open car door and I take firm care to close it when I'm seated. While driving out today I wondered if I should tell him that Eli and I are planning to get married, but it would be a gratuitous challenge and serve no purpose. My mother would have come to the wedding: would have come with love and understanding just because it was me and needing to know no more than that. Just being who I am, and happy enough with it, is sufficient punishment for my father.

I don't hate my father. I never did, but he isn't willing, or maybe able, to accept me. Forgiveness is possible as a conscious moral act, but none of us can make ourselves forget.

7.

The Penguin Cap

I became involved in the death of Simon Furness purely by proximity. I'm a bookseller and have no expertise concerning medical agencies, or the law. On 22 July 2020, that cold, sullen day, I was setting up a small display of Scandinavian noir fiction by the main door when two men came quickly in, and I still recall the chill air that accompanied them despite the speed of their entry, before the doors swung back. And a momentary surge of cold drizzle. They were both better dressed than most of my customers, with long, dark overcoats, and one at least had a leather cap, also sombre and with a penguin motif above the brim. I can be sure of that detail because not long after I had ample time to look at the cap as it lay beside a body close to the fiction and biography shelves.

Yes, Simon Furness was the one who died, although I had no knowledge of his identity at the time. They were, I presumed, just two well-dressed customers who went quickly into the aisles. In a bookshop you give people time, rather than approaching immediately to offer assistance: time to find an author, or a title, a genre, time to be drawn in by the attraction of a cover, or the unreserved endorsement by a celebrity on the back. Books are like eggs and thrive in a broody silence. They hatch in a quiet intimacy.

Now, however, I realise that a regard for reading was not perhaps the only reason these men came into my shop. Kate, one of the assistants working that day, said she could hear them from her counter, talking urgently, but in undertones. She told the police the one phrase she could recall with certainty was 'moral recidivist'. It stuck in her mind she said because of its singularity. Kate is keenly aware of language and has a diploma in journalism, although poetry is her ambition. Who was the recidivist, I wonder — Simon Furness, or his companion?

Three of us were serving in the shop, yet even Kate, who was closest to the men, heard nothing to suggest that help was needed. Just briefly the urgent, but lowered voices, then the resumption of the pensive peace that is a bookshop's atmosphere. The high shelves and packed books were barriers to both sound and sight, but there were no indications of tragedy. I don't remember the other man leaving the shop, but when I was making my way back to the office I came across dead Simon sitting on the floor with his back supported by the shelves and the penguin cap by his side. It didn't look like a body and there was no dishevelment. For a moment I thought he'd just made the unusual decision to sit down and read. It made me smile, but when I stopped beside him I saw that there was no book, no recognition of my approach, and his face had an empty slackness: a downwards expression as if in disapproval of what had happened.

I called to Kate and Toby, but the first person who appeared was a girl in a yellow puffer jacket who stood about, got in the way and said nothing. Kate took control, beginning resuscitation with Toby's assistance. I rang for the ambulance, ushered the puffer jacket girl from the shop and stood at the door to meet the medics and dissuade other people from entering. Damn cold, and the icy drizzle blew into my face. It seemed a long time before the ambulance came, but at least it was able to park close to the shop, for traffic was light. It was a relief to have professionals take over, and the police too came soon after. I'm not sure who contacted them. A corpse and a visit by police aren't the ideal forms of publicity for a retail business, and though there was a minor and temporary influx of nosey parkers in the next few days, there was no increase in sales.

To be honest, I don't remember feeling any immediate sorrow for Simon Furness. He was unknown to me, and uninvited. I recall a selfish relief that he'd died without leaving blood on the floor, or damage to any of the fittings. Almost a considerate death, you could say. Kate and Toby found a welcome distraction in the happening, and Kate especially achieved a passing fame because of her closeness to the event and her assured attempts at resuscitation — a public response that I endorsed wholeheartedly. All three of us were questioned quite closely, although there was little we could contribute, by a detective sergeant called Craig O'Connor, who assumed a grave manner, but whose natural buoyancy and good humour constantly broke through. He was able on a subsequent visit to tell us a good deal more than we were able to tell him, and I came to a greater understanding of Simon — who he'd been, and what form of loss resulted from his death.

Simon had been a lawyer of some note in the city. Not a barrister, but a man skilled in the intricacies of corporate law. The sort of man who sits down at his desk for an hour and rises several hundred dollars the richer. Also someone who had given service pro bono to various social organisations. He left not just that reputation, but a wife and three boys who had to go on without him. The more I knew of him, the more I regretted his death, and wondered if I could have done something to forestall it.

There had never been a death in the shop before, and Kate and Toby were quite exhilarated by it, while sympathetic at the same time. Toby was convinced it was murder, Simon Furness eliminated by dark forces: an ice dart with instant poison, or a sudden needle, as used by Russian assassins. The morning following the death, Toby noticed the blue spine of just one book protruding slightly from the alignment of its fellows close to where the body was found. It's a joke among my staff that all my books must be on parade, and I have a habit of brushing my hands along the shelves as I pass to ensure conformity. The book was at shoulder height and Toby was convinced that Simon was responsible for drawing attention to it in a last gasp effort to identify his assailant. *Maurice* was the title: a novel by E. M. Forster, and not his strongest in my opinion. Toby was convinced the name was a clue that would lead to the murderer and imagined himself solving the mystery — being an amateur detective, like Father Brown, or Miss Marple. Toby is a bookish young man who thinks crime is like a board game.

There was no murder, no nefarious, shadowy Maurice to be tracked down, no international web of corruption to be exposed. A heart attack, the autopsy confirmed, after a history of medical treatment to guard against it, and the dark-coated companion came sorrowfully and voluntarily forward once he learnt of the death. Not a Maurice, but Barry Lockyear of Lockyear and Furness, a senior partner and a former swimmer of some note, who came to see me at the shop the following week wearing again his full-length dark overcoat, for it was cold that day also, but without wind, or rain. He thanked us for our efforts, ineffectual though they'd been, told us of the impressive turnout at the funeral and the generous provision that was being made for the family despite its own very considerable resources. 'I just wish I'd waited with him a few minutes longer,' he said, 'but of course it would've made no difference at all. The worst of it is, we had a bit of a disagreement before I left. Nothing too bad, but not the ideal final note, is it? No way of knowing, naturally. We've been friends and colleagues for years.'

I was tempted to ask him who was the moral recidivist referred to in the conversation Kate overheard, but it was no business of mine and just intrusive curiosity. We went to the place where Simon had died, stood by the fiction shelves with the blue spine of Forster's *Maurice* close to our faces. 'Was he a reader?' I asked.

'Very much so. It was a relaxation from the rigorous and involved scrutiny of his legal work. Yes, a great reader.'

'The enduring names — Kipling, Dickens, Austen, James, Brontë, Forster?'

'Not so much,' said Barry. 'Simon liked Stephen King, Le Carré, Grisham. Stuff to take his mind off work.'

'I don't remember him coming into the shop often,' I said, but without any tone of censure.

'He read mostly online, often when he was travelling. He did come in here sometimes, though. Simon was comfortable around books. I wished we hadn't disagreed that day, though. How trivial it seems now.'

'I heard he had a history of heart trouble.'

'Yes, he did. He was only sixty-six, you know. Nothing these days. I'll have a browse around while I'm here,' Barry said, and that's what he did. Afterwards he bought a book on exercise and health, and a biography of Spike Milligan. I haven't seen him since.

I did have a brief phone conversation with Simon's wife. It came about because I found that although Toby had reluctantly given up his theory of murder, he had retained Simon's black cap, had it hidden in the tearoom cupboard behind the ice-cream container holding Handy Andy, Ajax and scourer pads. I discovered it while looking for the screwdriver. Toby said he'd put the cap there because it was surely too sad to return it to the family, but I told him the decision wasn't ours to make.

Explaining to Mrs Furness why I was offering the cap so long after her husband's death was awkward, and I made up a story about it getting hidden under a ledge, but she wasn't interested in the apology, or in having the cap returned. 'I don't want any reminder of what happened,' she said, 'but thank you and your staff for trying to help him. The police told me all about it. Actually that cap was one I disliked anyway. Our son found it wedged in the netting of the chimpanzee enclosure when he was on a school zoo trip there. Who knows where it had been. Simon only wore it if he was walking on rainy days. I'd forgotten all about it.' I've never met Mrs Furness, but an image of her formed in my mind from her voice and her opinions. A tall brunette of considerable assurance concerning her place in society. A forthright woman who would persevere in the world despite her loss.

So the penguin cap wasn't returned, but I didn't tell Toby that. I kept it for myself at home and wear it sometimes when I walk in the evenings. I have a dark, full-length coat too, rather like those worn by Barry and Simon on the day of the latter's death. I think of him sometimes when I'm walking alone: how he turned into my shop that day to escape the weather without any realisation that he would die there after a minor disagreement with a colleague and friend. I'm on the outside of Simon's life, a bit player at the end of it purely by chance. How often experiences seem to have no greater connection than a dismissive randomness. So I walk in the evenings sometimes wearing Simon's cap — a man I never knew who died close to me, a cap of uncertain provenance apart from once perhaps having graced the head of a chimpanzee.

8.

Hīkoi

My brother's dead now, but I walk and talk with him often in memory and find him quite cheerful, as was always his nature, no matter what befell him. He once told me that life is largely a matter of attitude, and although he provided no philosophical basis for his belief, he acted on it. My brother's name is Laurie.

I thought of him this morning when I read of the severe and uncharacteristic drought in Northland. Neither of us ever lived there. We are South Islanders, but our father came from Te Tarehi in the wop-wops, kauri country, and often talked to us of a childhood there: bush clearing, horse riding, kiwis and the ghosts from ancient Māori battles. All a long way in time and space from the Canterbury Plains.

I've been there only once: years ago, with Laurie. He rang me at the Christchurch City Council offices where I worked. He often did. It never seemed to occur to him that I might not have time for a chat. 'Te Tarehi,' he said firmly.

'Yes?'

'You remember?"

'Of course I do. Where Dad grew up. He told those stories about it.'

'It's time for a hīkoi to the valley,' Laurie said. I think he was a little pleased with himself for such display of te reo. I wasn't all that sure of the meaning, but I didn't admit that. A march, isn't it? A trek?

'But we wouldn't be walking, would we?' I told him.

'A driving hīkoi,' he said cheerfully.

'Why now?' I asked.

''Cause we've talked about it for years and never done it. Any longer and we'll never find the place. It'll be fun and Dad would've liked us to go. Karen and Bev will get a kick out of it too.'

Our wives, however, decided it was a kick they could do without. There are no shops in the valley and they had no genealogical reason to prowl the partly tamed hill farms and wetlands of that part of the tropical north. In fact, there is no gathered settlement in Te Tarehi, just the occasional farmhouse and cannabis bach. There's one store cum post office where the valley's dirt road meets the sealed one close to the coast, miles from where we were headed.

All that knowledge was still to come when Laurie and I flew to Auckland and after some initial jostle at the airport picked up a Corolla rental.

'You can drive. I'll navigate,' he said, in a bestowing tone and settled in the passenger seat. Laurie's form of navigation was to recognise every necessary lane indication and turn-off ramp after we'd passed it, and we spent an hour and a half getting out of Auckland. He enjoyed seeing the city, he said, some parts of it more than once, and was sorry not to go over the bridge. He was impressed with the motorway. 'No head-ons here,' he told me as I tried in vain to get out of the slow lane. 'Chips?' he said, offering me the packet, onion and vinegar flavour, as I clenched both hands on the wheel.

We had lunch at Wellsford: burgers and ginger beer in a corner café with murals of indigenous sea fish on the wall. Moki, lemon sole, groper, John Dory, kahawai, orange roughy, snapper, trevally, even a stargazer. I hadn't realised we had such diversity. When I returned from a visit to the loo, Laurie was explaining to the owner, who looked about twenty, the pros and cons of solar panels. Laurie was an electrician by trade and quite happy to share his professional knowledge. I gathered that panels were the thing for the future, but that they were becoming progressively cheaper and more efficient, and a waiting game might well be the way to go. The café guy was reluctant to see someone of Laurie's expertise leave, but I said we had to be on our way.

'It's no wonder many ancient peoples were sun worshippers,' said Laurie when we were driving again. 'So much depends on it. If I were starting off again, I think I'd concentrate on the natural sources of power: tides, winds and the sun, and all free. How lucky can we be.'

'They have to be harnessed though, don't they.'

'True,' he said. 'Maybe better that they're free in that sense too. Did you know that there's a fish called stargazer?'

'Not until today,' I said.

'Already we're learning things on this trip and we're not even there yet.' Laurie settled in his seat and gazed contentedly over paddocks that seemed to smile back at him. Terrible things were happening all over the world, but there were goodness and peace to be found also and Laurie understood that. 'Stargazer,' he mused, 'I like that.'

Both of us were keen to visit the Kauri Museum in Dargaville and both of us were impressed with its size and diversity. I spent most time in the amber room; Laurie was interested in the antiquated and ponderous logging machinery. I found him deep in conversation with Gavin Glumm, who was a volunteer worker there. When Gavin found that Laurie was an electrician, he asked him for advice concerning the museum's switchboard. There were problems with overload cut-offs. Laurie's knowledge was often called on and not just because it was practical, but because his engaging personality encouraged the approach. I know as much about urban zoning regulations as anyone in the country, but it's rare for that to spark rapport with folk met casually. Zoning has a distancing effect.

Laurie said he'd have a quick look and spent almost an hour with his head in one or other of the large fuse boxes. He fixed it, naturally, and as proof all the lights were put on briefly, the whole place, and nothing failed. The museum director thanked him personally and gave him a wad of tickets, gratis.

'Where are you staying tonight?' Gavin asked when we were walking back from the director's office.

'We thought either here, or in Aranga,' Laurie said.

'No, no, Ethel and I would like you to stay the night with us. I sent her a text. We'd like that,' Gavin said. 'You too, of course,' he added as an afterthought, turning to me.

'That's kind,' my brother said. 'What do you think, Carl?'

'Very kind,' I said. I knew Laurie had asked my opinion as a sign of my entitlement to inclusion in decision making.

The Glumms had a home at Baylys Beach, on the coast close to Dargaville. A single-storeyed wooden home that Gavin said had been transported there in two parts from somewhere else. That remained apparent because of a strange single step halfway up the hall. Ethel was an exceedingly tall woman, taller than any of us: six two, or six three at least, I'd say. I'm not accustomed to looking up to a woman in any sense other than admiration. She was thin, too, with her skeleton apparent beneath pale skin. Her hair was noticeably glossy, worn very plainly, perhaps so that there was no emphasis of her height. I had time to observe her as we stood in the hallway and for some time Gavin told her of Laurie's electrical feats before getting round to introducing me — as Carlos.

We had potato, corn and salmon fritters for tea. Dad used to talk of fritters, and I experienced a brief memory frisson as Ethel spoke of them. The taste was welcome too.

The dessert didn't disappoint: a similarly retro treacle pudding with ice cream. Laurie said he'd decided never to leave, and Ethel seemed to grow another inch. Laurie himself wasn't a small man, but with horizontal rather than vertical dimension.

Ethel had recently retired as a dental nurse, but her interest and enthusiasm were for family history. Not the Glumms, who were German in extraction, she said, but Maslins and Coopers, who were her own people. She'd done a lot of online research, and DNA testing. She was interested in our surname — Lecompte.

'Not a common name at all,' she said. 'Quite la-de-da. What do you know about it?'

'Not a hell of a lot. French, of course,' said Laurie.

'First found in Languedoc,' I told her. Our family background was sketchy but it was one of the things about which I was better informed than Laurie. 'There was a coat of arms with three trumpets on it. We haven't made a direct connection, though.'

'What else?' she asked.

'We don't know much more. Our Lecomptes have been here since the 1860s and were ordinary people from East Anglia: labourers and servants. Such people don't leave much of a record.'

'You must dig, dig,' enthused Ethel. 'So much can be done now through the net without much expense.'

It was odd to be sitting with the Glumms, unknown to us until a few hours ago, and be quizzed on our family history. After dinner Laurie and Gavin sat comfortably in the small living room and talked about the present world, but Ethel kept me at the table, spread out a mass of documents and photographs, and for two hours educated me in the history of Maslins and Coopers. Bearded and mustachioed men in waistcoats and boots, serious, and dimly seen in front of small, primitive businesses, or tramcars: overclothed women standing amid children, or straight backed in their wedding dresses. The one thing I have retained from immersion in Ethel's family history is that a Maslin, or a Cooper, named Shadrach, died after being keelhauled for insubordination while serving in a British naval vessel. Who could forget such a terrible demise?

The bedroom Laurie and I were later shown to was large, with a high, coffin-like free-standing wardrobe and window drapes with blue tasselled cords, but it had only one bed, though it was a double, with four patterned pillows artfully arranged at the head. 'I hope you don't mind,' said Ethel. 'Just for one night and you're brothers, after all.'

'Absolutely fine, thank you,' said Laurie, and I murmured agreement. It was a comfortable bed and after a cheerful and fulsome recitation of the day's delights, Laurie fell asleep, snoring loudly and creating other noises, not all from his mouth. I slept myself eventually, woke abruptly at the climax of a dream of Shadrach Maslin/Cooper being dragged beneath the hull of a man o' war — the plunging timbered hull, dark snouts of the cannon, tossing green waves and the seamen lined on deck as sullen witnesses of punishment.

I needed to pee. Although I located the bedroom light switch, I couldn't find the hall one, and while groping my way down the passage I tripped on the unusual and forgotten junction step and smacked my face into the sharp-edged, wooden body of a grandfather clock, as it was later revealed to be. I was struck once and the clock struck four chimes. In the bathroom I plugged my nose with toilet paper to stop the bleeding and perused a split left eyebrow. Aroused by the noise, Gavin appeared, put a plaster above my eye, apologised for no fault of his own and pointed out the hall light switches. The step seemed to smirk at me as I returned to the bedroom. I lay the rest of the night, swallowing a little blood, breathing through my mouth, with Laurie snoring peacefully beside me.

He was, however, genuinely solicitous at breakfast, as were the Glumms. Gavin said they'd discussed the hall step several times with tradespeople and considered a gradient section, but the quotes were rather steep. Ethel said the clock did take up too much room, but that there was nowhere else in the house for it, and it had belonged to a Maslin forebear who had captained a coastal trading vessel. Rivers were the roads in those days, she told me, and went to the trouble to find a photograph of him and several others — all wearing waistcoats. At least the bleeding had stopped and my nose was unplugged, though I was still unable to breathe through it. And admittedly the breakfast was another of Ethel's triumphs. Pancakes with banana, bacon and maple syrup.

The Glumms came out to the car to see us leave, Gavin again thanking Laurie for his electrical wizardry at the Kauri Museum, and then turning to me to say, 'And nice to meet you too, Mal.'

'Carl,' I said.

'Of course,' Gavin said.

'Laurie and Carl Lecompte. I'd rather like to be a Lecompte: better than Glumm, better than Maslin, or Cooper. Make sure you do more research and get right back to Languedoc and the three trumpets. There's a story there, for sure.' Ethel was so enthusiastic I wondered if she would do the digging herself, despite having no bloodline connection. Personally, I've always found the name a bit of a drag. People keep asking how to spell it.

'What great people and so friendly,' said Laurie as we drove away and their waving figures diminished behind us. 'This trip's an absolute boomer, isn't it. And that Ethel sure can cook. A considerable saving too, rather than a motel and meals out. We got lucky there.'

'Nice couple, true enough, but I did do a header into the grandfather clock, remember. Not a hell of a lot of fun.'

'Yeah, that was a bit of a bummer. How do you feel now?'

'Still can't breathe through my nose,' I said, 'otherwise okay.'

'It's a bit swollen.'

'My nose is?'

'More round your eye where the plaster is.'

'Who would have a damn step halfway down a hallway, eh?'

'Remember Gavin said the house was moved in two halves and so—'

'Yeah, yeah,' I said. 'But I mean who would have a step halfway down their hallway and a bloody great clock in ambush next to it?'

It started to rain after we passed Aranga, quite heavily and with a closing drapery of cloud, but we stopped at the Waipoua forest and walked in to see the giant kauri. We took photographs of each other, and I still have one showing me with patched and swollen face standing before a vast tree trunk. 'Marvellous,' enthused Laurie. 'What a privilege to be with such grand, ancient living things. Venerable, that's what they are — venerable.' I still remember the moisture creeping through my shoes and large drops from the venerable foliage anointing my head. And a cloud of very small midges dancing close to my mouth.

We had coffee at Ōmāpere, and on the way back to the car stopped at a small wooden general store, purpose built and very old. 'Dad would have known this place,' Laurie said, and so we went in to its heterogeneous collection of stock: everything from fishing tackle and seed potatoes to Gingernuts and candles. Its aura was not unlike that of the Kauri Museum. Laurie found a packet of Van Hartog cigarillos and bought them for old times' sake, although he'd given up smoking years before. 'We used to smoke them at city hall dances,' he said, his voice rich with sultry reminiscence, and we each enjoyed one, sitting in the car with the doors ajar and the misty rain insistent on the glass. It was a long time since I'd smoked a cigarillo, and with a sense of defiance I drew the strong flavour deep, and with it came, yes, memories.

Laurie studied the map before we set off again. 'We turn off before Rawene,' he said. 'Go inland into the valley.'

'But how far before the old family place?'

'From what Dad said, it's a fair way, but we'll have to ask. Some local cockies will know. Lecompte isn't a common name. Someone will remember, for sure. Country people have long memories.'

'Ewart and Eliza, that's who our grandparents were.'

'Yeah, that's right. Someone will remember the place.'

We found the turn-off without trouble and drove up the narrow valley: lots of dark, native bush on the hills and occasional clearings on the flanks, more open ground on the flats along the small river. After driving for fifteen minutes or so, I suggested we stop at the next farmhouse we came to. We'd passed few buildings and the distance between them was increasing. So we pulled into the gateway of a small, wooden place close to the road. The rain had almost ceased, but a misty drizzle rolled down from the bush and flattened over the riverbed. Laurie and I walked the short, unsealed path, stood on the sack at the front door and knocked. A scampering sound from within, then almost immediately the door opened and two small boys looked up at us with their mouths open. Not twins, but surely less than two years between them. The smaller boy held a green plastic water pistol at the ready and his T-shirt was wet. Before anything could be said their mother appeared and stood uncertainly behind them, a hand on the shoulder of each as if to restrain, or protect. A small woman in jeans and pink socks, but no footwear. A woman whose anxiety was plain. I suppose unexpected visitors were unusual in such an isolated place.

I told her we were sorry to bother her and just wondered if she could give us directions to the old Lecompte property. Our father had lived there as a boy, we explained. 'No,' she said immediately. 'We haven't been here very long. I've never heard of any Lecomptes. My husband will be home soon.' The last information was obviously meant as an indication she would soon have reinforcements, rather than a suggestion her partner could be more helpful.

'That's fine. Thanks. We'll be on our way,' said Laurie. As we moved off she felt relieved enough to say more.

'The Shallish family have the next farm a few k's further up,' she said. 'The place with a new milking shed close to the road. Old Tāmati's lived here almost for ever.' We thanked her again and she watched us until we drove away, the intent faces of the two small boys lower in the doorway, also watching.

'I think we made her nervous,' I said.

'Well, with your face the way it is, you could be a murderer on the run,' said Laurie.

'Thanks for that.'

'The bruise is coming out and it's more swollen. That clock must have given you a real wallop, but never mind, the rain's over, I reckon, and the sun's starting to burn off the mist. Fantastic scenery here. No wonder Dad often talked about it. It's wonderful to be here.'

The new milking shed was easy to spot: set in the largest grassed flat we'd seen so far. The house, also quite new, was on a slight rise farther back from the road. We had seen few new buildings in the valley. 'This place must be doing okay,' Laurie said. A man was walking down the track as we drove up. A thin Māori guy with red-topped gumboots, a green singlet visible beneath his unbuttoned shirt, a stick and two dogs at his heels. A thin, elderly man, but upright and with a good head of hair. We stopped beside him and introduced ourselves as the dogs sniffed at the car wheels. It was Tāmati Shallish and he *had* lived there almost for ever and he did remember the Lecomptes. He had known our father as a boy.

'David was a few years older, but I remember him all right. I knew Mary better who was my age. David was a bit of a dreamer and not cut out for farming: neither was his father, for that matter. What did your dad end up doing?'

'He was a real estate agent. Mainly lived in Christchurch,' I told him.

'That figures, eh. He had a way with people, David did.' Something that Laurie had inherited and he soon had old Tāmati sharing his memories of the Lecomptes. It was a bit disappointing to find that our grandfather hadn't made a success of the property, that it had finally been incorporated into the reserve, the house taken away and just a shed left in which predator baits and traps were stored by the reserve guardians.

'The place was too steep anyway,' Tāmati told us. 'Probably no one could have made a go of it. By the time old man Lecompte came out, the best land in the valley had been taken up. He wasn't the only one. It's not easy country. We get one of the highest rainfalls of anywhere, eh.'

'Well, you seem to have done okay,' said Laurie admiringly.

'We've got the flats, and better roads and transport have made all the difference. Things have got easier over the years. Your father rode a horse to primary school and so did I.'

'Was it always cows here?' asked Laurie.

'Pretty much. The logging went on closer to the coast.'

Tāmati seemed to know everything about the valley and its history. He was interested in our hīkoi and the reasons for it. Interested, too, in finding out what had happened to the Lecomptes once they'd left. He wanted to be remembered to Aunt Mary and said she'd been one of only three girls at the school. When Laurie asked for directions to the old farm, Tāmati said we'd never find it by ourselves because it had largely gone back to bush and even the shed remaining wasn't visible from the road. 'I'll come with you,' he said generously. 'Just hang on a minute while I get the dogs chained and tell my son.' He walked back up to the house and we saw him talk to someone at the door, wave a hand and then start down the track again.

'What luck to come across him,' said Laurie. 'A nice old guy. We wouldn't have had a clue, would we? Dad never said anything about the house going, did he?'

'Maybe he didn't know. Nothing about the farm failing either.'

'He'd have shot through by then.'

Tāmati showed his age for the first time as he climbed into the back seat of the Corolla. His knee got stuck against the front seat and the seat belt twice escaped his grasp and retracted with a clatter. He still had his stick; not a city walking stick but a long, rough-cut farmer's stick that struck the side of my face as he struggled in the back.

'Oh, sorry about that,' he said. 'And you've had a knock already by the look of you. Sorry.'

'It's okay,' I said.

'What happened?' he asked. The stick striking me gave the question a natural lead in, rather than being an intrusion.

'I slipped going to the toilet last night. In the place where we were staying.'

'He fell onto a grandfather clock,' added Laurie helpfully.

'Jesus,' said Tāmati. 'Not so good.'

'Really nice people, though,' said Laurie. 'The guy worked at the Kauri Museum and his wife's a great cook.' Laurie extolled at length Ethel's fritters and pancakes as we drove.

Tāmati was right. There was no way we would have found the Lecompte place without him. No house and the shed hidden from the road. Just a netting gate in the sagging fence and an overgrown slope stretching back to original bush higher up. As we walked in, Tāmati pointed out a large indentation, grass and fern covered. 'That was a saw-pit,' he said. 'A man at the top and some poor bugger underneath who copped all the sawdust and crap. Really tough yakka, pit sawing.'

The old shed was made of pit-sawn timber. It had originally been part of the milking shed and held material needed by the guardians of the reserve. Tāmati was a guardian and had a key to the padlock that fastened a heavily rusted chain. He had come often here as a boy, he said, remembered the house, the horse paddock, our father and Aunt Mary. Just the shed remained, and it was special to stand in its dimness alongside the deeper shadows of past and lingering Lecomptes.

'Wow,' said Laurie. 'This is what we came for, though it's not quite what I imagined. I expected a house and yards: people still living on the place maybe.'

'A few more years and there'll be no sign at all,' said Tāmati. 'The bush regenerates so quickly in this climate. This block was never really farming country. Bush is better here, and we're maintaining tracks through the whole reserve for people to enjoy.' Outside the sun was strong and there was just an evaporation mist rising from the bush, but in the old shed Tāmati's dark face was barely visible.

Laurie wanted to look at a stack of traps, and as I stepped back to give him room I shouldered a shelf, and a large cardboard packet there fell on its side with a slap, puffed a little powder over my head.

'What have you done now,' exclaimed Laurie, and laughed, but Tāmati was more serious.

'That stuff's poisonous,' he said calmly. 'We use it to put at the entrance to wasp nests. You'd better come and wash it out.'

'The river's just over the road,' said Laurie.

'Nah. We'll go back home where you can have a shower. It'll be okay, but better not to take any bloody chances.'

So the visit to the old place was brief and came to an ignominious end. Tāmati told me not to pat my hair, or clothing, and when we had driven back to his home I went through to the bathroom with just a quick introduction to his surprised son and daughter-in-law in passing — Taika and Erena. It's embarrassing to be naked and uninvited in someone else's bathroom, even though unobserved. I didn't get the shower door closed properly and so a good deal of water ended up on the floor, and because the plaster came off during my wash, traces of blood were left on the towel. When dressed again, I went out and apologised for the imposition, but the family was relaxed and hospitable. Erena gave me a new plaster for my eye and invited us to have lunch with them. 'If things had worked out differently you could easily have been our neighbours,' said Taika, a man of presence like his father and close to our own age. He and Erena had two children away at boarding school and a share in a fishing venture at Rawene. Obviously not all the inhabitants of the valley were lifestyle hippies.

Tāmati talked most during the meal, because he knew most about the Lecomptes, had lived with them as rural neighbours when a boy. It was interesting to get a view of our grandparents from a perspective other than that of our father. I hardly knew my grandparents, but from Dad's account had imagined them as resourceful and accomplished. From Tāmati's more objective, yet sympathetic, recollection I realised that certainly Grandad had struggled as a farmer and relied much on his neighbours, including the Shallish family.

Tāmati, Taika and Erena all came out to farewell us. Laurie gave them the Kauri Museum tickets as a thank you for their hospitality. Old Tāmati had put on his red-topped gumboots again. 'Haere ra,' he said and raised his stick as we left. At the road gate we admired the new milking shed before beginning the return journey.

'How lucky was that,' said Laurie, 'to come across him. Otherwise we'd never have found the place. There's nothing there now really, is there, except the shed in the trees. Lucky we came when we did.'

'And we wouldn't have gone to the Shallish place if it hadn't been for the nervous woman,' I said.

'It all worked out,' he said. As it usually did for Laurie.

The sun shone as we returned down the valley. A white ute was the only vehicle we met, and the driver raised his hand. The bush on the close hills was dark and glossy; puddles gleamed on the unsealed road. I thought of our father, and his father, being here all those years ago, our grandmother, too, and Aunt Mary.

'Couldn't be better, could it,' Laurie assured me. 'Absolutely great. Marvellous. The Glumms, the museum, old Tāmati, finding the Lecompte place. A hīkoi to remember, don't you reckon? Loved it. Loved it. Way to go.'

I'd been savaged by a grandfather clock, dusted with poisonous wasp powder and hit in the face with a farmer's staff. Sometimes on the trip I thought the Lecomptes would have been better to have stayed in Languedoc with their trumpets. But it had been a trip with Laurie, in the glow of his enthusiastic brotherhood, and that was its true and lasting significance.

9.

The English Visitor

On Thursday morning he walked again from his apartment in Palais Lutetia to the Villa Isola Bella. The quickest way was the low road through the tunnel and past the marina, but he preferred the climb up to the old cemetery where William Webb Ellis was buried, and then the stroll along the Garavan boulevard, past the Parc du Pian olive grove with hunched, ancient trees set against the blue sea, on to the ornate villas of Garavan, some lacking love, but all with wonderful faded colours of green, yellow and rose. He walked slowly because of the heat, and carried the small backpack from his hand, rather than having it in contact with his shirt. On his way home he would buy the few supermarket items that are all a guy living on his own needs.

He was glad to be above the clatter of the seafront, to pass the pepper and carob trees and hear the doves. The distinctive calls reminded him of his time in England. There were plenty of pigeons in New Zealand, but there he never heard the very different voices of doves. The sky was criss-crossed with vapour trails like chalk streaks on the clear arch of blue, another reminder that he was a long way from his isolated homeland.

Through the narrow streets of Garavan he descended to the Villa Isola Bella, opened the gate to the enclosed garden of the writing room and entered quietly, hoping to see lizards on the wall, or the door frame, sunning themselves. Sometimes, when returning to his apartment at night, he would find one or two close to the external light, seeking warmth he supposed. It intrigued him that they could hold so easily to perpendicular walls, like suction toys.

There were no lizards at the room that morning, no letters, no notes slipped under the door of the single room. He went inside, opened the window and sat down with his journal. Mansfield had been a journal writer, hadn't she: all writers were, surely. Writing in the journal lessened anxiety and guilt concerning lack of progress on his novel. Journal entries would be the basis for fiction in due course, he reassured himself: a restocking of the creative larder.

What the hell was he doing in Menton, on the Côte d'Azur, trying to write a novel set during the New Zealand Land Wars? The dislocation was surely too great. He didn't want to confront those doubts again and so he wrote of his visit to Ventimiglia only days before. The market by the seafront with its stalls of local produce, the cobbled and sloping alleys of the old town, the cemetery with its fresh flowers, oddly tiered repositories and occasional crypts. Many of the graves had photographs embalmed in glass, people looking out as in life to greet their families. People in their best clothes and standing, or sitting, erect in awareness of formality. In contrast to the ruinous neglect of so many cemeteries in his own country, those in France and Italy were embraced by their community, cared for and visited. In Ventimiglia there had been two women singing at a graveside. They looked like mother and daughter, but neither was young, and as he'd passed they had smiled and held up their hands without ceasing the song.

He wrote about the women singing, their dark clothes and the way they held up their hands as he passed. The heavily lined face of the older woman, almost masculine with its bold features and black eyebrows. He wrote about the wonderful paella he had later in a family café next to a dental surgery, and of the Algerian hawker's attempts to sell him a belt when he left. They were no good, those belts. They looked shiny and had smart buckles, but they weren't leather and the holes soon stretched and tore.

Menton, so close to the border, had much of Italy in its complexion:

the names in its own graveyard were proof of that. He was thinking of writing something of this in his journal, when through the window he saw the street gate open and a woman enter. She came to the window, not the door, and stood with confidence to look in. Smiled. A tall woman, elderly, with a long, pleasing face and a lot of grey hair piled in a rather haphazard bun. Previous fellows had told him about visitors who came to the room, some as unwelcome distraction, but he'd been bothered little, and he got up and opened the door. He was transient himself with no right to deny access to others, but was wary nevertheless.

'I'm here at last,' the woman said cheerfully, as if she had been long implored to come. She put out her hand in greeting, already looking past him into the interior. She wore a loose, blue dress that came well down her legs, and new sandals like those he had seen at the Ventimiglia market. 'Brenda Beauchamp,' she said, switching her gaze to him to gauge reaction. The accent was English, but not pronounced.

'Ah, a relative,' he said.

'Who knows? At one stage I did a bit of digging. Nothing came of it and now I prefer to leave the possibility open, rather than continue research and be disappointed. I love her stories; I love her life, I've always wanted to come to Isola Bella. I couldn't find the place she lived in at Ospedaletti, but then she was unhappy there anyway, not like here in Menton.'

He introduced himself rather than responding to mention of Ospedaletti. He knew nothing of it. Because he was on the fellowship people assumed that he was familiar with everything concerning Katherine Mansfield and strongly influenced by her work. He knew and valued the stories, of course, was aware in outline of her brief and rather tragic arc of life, but he wasn't a devotee, claimed no special insight. If pushed he would probably say he was a Sargeson man. 'Would you like to have a quick look at the room?' he said with conscious generosity, yet containment.

'How kind of you,' said Brenda, and matched his backward steps with forward ones of her own. The room was not large, and she was the sort of woman who seems to fill a greater space than that occupied by just her body. Large feet and lifting hands, a swaying torso as she moved, and the loose, long, blue dress. 'How marvellous,' she said, and, taking glasses from her bag, she bent to examine the bookcase, while he closed his journal on the desk. 'You don't live here, even though there's a bed. Is that right?'

'Some of the early writers who came did, but it's not allowed now. The rest of the villa is privately owned. This used to be the gardener's room, or the wine cellar, so I've been told.'

'K.M. spent a lot of the time on the terrace just above us. Right above our heads. There's photographs showing her sitting there. She loved this place even though she was so sick and couldn't get around much. She said she became conscious of it as she used to be conscious of New Zealand.'

He had remained standing, but when Brenda rested on the edge of the bed he knew she wasn't ready to leave, so he sat down at the desk. He was aware of her enthusiasm and the long way she had come, and wished to make no rebuff. She asked if he'd mind if she took some photos, and drew a small camera from her bag. She wanted to take one of him at the desk, and afterwards he encouraged her to sit there herself while he took a photograph. 'I can't get you into the villa. You can't even see the terrace properly from down here, but you'll have this one of you sitting at the desk in the Mansfield room.'

'Am I being a nuisance?' she asked after the camera was put away.

'Not at all, but I am meeting someone later in the old town for lunch. How long are you here in Menton?'

'Just today. I fly out of Nice tomorrow morning to London.' She was back at the bookcase again, her head angled awkwardly to read the titles, the grey bun of heavy hair catching the light. Most of the previous fellows had left a copy of at least one of their books behind as evidence of passing presence, some with a brief rhapsody within as well as a signature. He wondered what Katherine would have made of them all, this string of different personalities with only their nationality and a devotion to words in common.

'She wrote some of her best stories here,' said Brenda. Her large feet in open sandals were pale, small blurred veins crossed the rise of an ankle bone. '"Miss Brill", "Life of Ma Parker", "The Daughters of the Late Colonel", all written at Isola Bella,' she said. Finished with the books, she took off her glasses, stood looking out of the window to the courtyard garden, her gaze drawing his own. 'She will have looked down on this from the terrace,' she said.

'When I first came the garden was neglected,' he said. 'There was mould in here too and the room had a musty smell. The place must have been shut up for months. I had my formal meeting with the mayor and afterwards gardeners turned up. I haven't much French, and the kind wife of an acquaintance came along as a translator. The mayor called the English les boeufs, I remember, but seemed better disposed to Kiwis.' The enclosed garden had pale gravel, seats, a palm tree. Brenda gazed at it almost fiercely.

'What's your favourite?' she asked.

'Out there?'

'I mean your favourite story.' It could have been annoying, interpreted as a test, or display of superiority, but her tone and expression held only a disarming conviction of shared enthusiasm. He did know many of the stories. He had studied some at university and sought out others for himself. He mightn't know a lot about Mansfield's life, but he knew her work.

'A Dill Pickle,' he said. 'I know others get the limelight, but I guess I like it best.'

'Oh, what a good choice,' said Brenda in a sudden softening, and she smiled, lowered her eyes a moment, as if he had paid her a compliment. 'Tell me why,' she said. They remained looking into the garden, she still nodding her head in affirmation of his choice, so that the long wisps of hair free of her bun wafted in the light.

'It starts just when it has to,' he said. 'The guy's trick of interruption, the scenes within scenes like Russian dolls, their differing memories of the same moments. Most of all though, for me, is the evening picnic by the Black Sea and the coachman offering the dill pickle. Just a paragraph, but what colour and emotional power. The yearning dream, and the stripping of the dream away.'

'She sees the red chilli like a parrot's beak through the green glass of the jar. She loved Russia, of course. Well, she loved a Russia that she created for herself.' Brenda held both hands before her, palms uppermost, as if presenting proof of what she said. A train went past on the line just below the villa, just as trains must have passed when Katherine lived there, and they waited as the noise faded.

'Once when I'd been here late and was going back to the apartment, I saw three African men walking along the railway line from Italy. They come in illegally that way, I'm told. They went past silently in the dusk with their heads turned away as if that made them invisible.'

'I'm going on too much, aren't I,' said Brenda. 'It's being here in her place, and you knowing the stories. But you're meeting someone for lunch, so I'll be off.'

'I lied,' he said. 'Just to give me an out. I don't have to be anywhere. I've just got sensitive about privacy and writing time. The more solitary I've become, the more accustomed I am to it. It's a form of selfishness.'

'Necessary, though, if you want to get work done.'

'Pretty much.'

'Well, you'll be relieved to hear that I'm being picked up on the seafront road at one. Friends are taking me on to Nice where I'll stay with them. I'll be out of your hair.'

He suggested they go out to the garden seats. There was more space for her to occupy there. He brought out tumblers and a bottle of lukewarm cheap wine. When he apologised for it, she smiled, but offered no rebuttal and drank little. She had no hat, and he gave her his own, and sat with a hand towel on his head. 'Enough of K.M. for now,' she said. 'Tell me about your own work.' Her interest was genuine and he gave a dutiful account of himself. Brenda had never been to New Zealand, but she knew something of the literature. Then he asked about her own life. Brenda was a doctor. Well, she had been — a specialist in Bristol and now retired. A widow of two husbands and a grandmother of seven children. He was surprised, but kept that to himself. He thought a retired English oncologist would be more contained, more groomed, rather than a woman in a loose cotton dress, with roughly bundled grey hair and large feet in Ventimiglian sandals. There seemed no shortage of money, however, and she spoke of a holiday home in the Lake Country. Both her husbands had died of cancer. 'My life has been spent in the company of illness,' she said, 'but I've been blessed with robust health myself.'

But they were in Katherine's place, weren't they, who knew all about illness. Katherine was the reason they were there together, sitting in the walled garden of Isola Bella. As if to signal the irrelevance of their own stories, a small lizard scampered up the wall and posed on the top. 'I see them here sometimes,' he said, 'and at my apartment. For some reason I get a bit of a lift when I see lizards. They remind me of my Marlborough boyhood. Skinks especially.'

'K.M. loved them. She wrote about them, and the grasshoppers and the tiny frogs on the path. She described one lizard as a miniature crocodile and said it winked at her.'

'How is it that you're so drawn to her, that you know so much about her, when you must have been extremely busy in a professional career that had nothing to do with writing? The Beauchamp name?' The lizard had posed for a brief time with its head raised and then in a flicker was gone. They were left looking at a point of emptiness.

'The Beauchamps originated in Aquitaine and had an aristocratic history in the Middle Ages. They're all over the place now in all manner of spellings. I don't imagine I'm any traceable relation, but it's just that possible point of connection. If she were alive I could use it as a way of introducing myself perhaps. No, I came to her work through a book group. Very suburban, but a necessary distraction for me. K.M. would be scathing, wouldn't she. I thought of her this morning when my friends and I had an early espresso by the seafront. There was a man close by with a broad hat and white trousers, and as he smoked he cut the hair on his knuckles with a small pair of black-handled scissors. She would have noticed that.'

'She died so young. That's what I always remember about her. Just thirty-four, wasn't she? Imagine what she could have written if she'd been given more time.'

'That's why she never missed anything,' said Brenda. 'At Ospedaletti she had a dream of death. There was shock and noise of breaking glass, bodily disintegration amid green, flashing light. She died in that dream, she said, and was never the same afterwards. There's something about the colour green and K.M., isn't there? So often it's in the journals and the stories.'

In the face of Brenda's enthusiastic familiarity with Mansfield's life he felt at a disadvantage, almost embarrassed at his own ignorance, but he knew she didn't intend, or wish, either response. He'd been invited to give a talk about Mansfield at the university in Nice, but had delayed giving an answer partly because he felt his knowledge of her was insufficient. He told Brenda about the lecture and encouraged her to talk. The books about Mansfield were on the shelf in the room only a few steps away, as they both knew, but he wanted to hear the things that were dear to his visitor.

So she talked of the early love of Shakespeare and Oscar Wilde, the maid Katherine hired in Menton, Madame Reveilly, a police inspector's sister. She talked of the lovers and the haters, the selfishness and the compassion. She talked of atheism, black depression and laughter. She talked of raindrops as big as marguerite daisies and the fur coat of Fontainebleau. As Brenda spoke, a single filament fell across her face from the empty sky with a tiny spider clinging to the end, and she instinctively brushed it aside and continued talking. The spider glided to the knee of her blue dress as she sat, then like an agitated full stop scuttled out of sight.

She would be in her late sixties, maybe more. She had an attractive face still, no set lines of dissatisfaction, though his hat was oddly perched above it on the stack of hair. There was confidence without assertion in her manner, and he could imagine her in comforting discussion with her patients. She broke off her animated talk suddenly when she realised it was almost one o'clock. 'My God, the time. I almost forgot. So now I'll go, and you will have K.M.'s place to yourself again. Lucky you. Thank you for letting me come in and stay a while. It means a lot to me. I couldn't pass Menton by without coming here.'

'I'll walk down with you,' he said, and he took the towel and glasses into the room, before returning to go with her across the railway line and towards the sea road. They stopped on the way so that she could buy a bunch of clementines for her friends, still attached to the leafy sprig as was the way in Menton.

The waspish crescendos of passing scooters forced pauses in their easy conversation, and after one brief silence she said, 'You won't make her ethereal, will you? In your talk, I mean. You won't be fooled by surface girlishness as some readers are. She was a great mimic, a complete player of parts to chosen audiences, but my God she was tough beneath it all. Remember the Graham Greene comment about the splinter of ice in the heart of a writer? That's K.M. all right.'

Had he ever thought of Mansfield as ethereal? Perhaps he had. There was no time to discuss her any more, however, for Brenda's friends were waiting at the corner in a large, red Audi, and they showed good manners by getting out to meet him. A couple well dressed and affable, who had been to the Basilica of St Michel and the beach while Brenda was at Isola Bella, and who were eager to be off for lunch at the Hotel Riva. The woman had the tanned desiccation common on the Côte d'Azur, and the man wore pale shoes and no socks. 'Come with us,' said Brenda. In the company of her friends she seemed older, larger, more English.

It was no longer polite to talk of Katherine Mansfield, and the general conversation had no real significance, just guff about Queen Victoria loving Menton and Churchill coming to paint there. At the end he leant down at Brenda's open window and they shook hands, which was at once a conscious formality yet perfectly natural. 'Good luck,' she said.

'Yes, good luck,' he replied. They knew they would never see each other again, and they knew that each held that thought in the same moment, though neither spoke of it. In the front seat her friends started to talk of the Hotel Riva, and Brenda smiled and held her large hands palm uppermost as she had in the room at the Villa Isola Bella, and then she was driven away.

He walked on to his accustomed café where he would have the cheap rosé and frites before returning to the writing room. In the late afternoon he would take the Mansfield books and walk back to his apartment, sit on the small half balcony, endure the brief rain of dust from the mats being beaten on the balcony above him and prepare a lecture for the university in Nice. A talk on K.M., as Brenda liked to call her, and there would be no emphasis on the ethereal.

10.

Living in the Moment

To be honest, my move to that private boys' school in Sydney was a calculated one. I figured it would be worth something on a curriculum vitae if I made a success of my time there. That's the reason also that I accepted the additional role of hostel manager after only a year. Appointment committees like to see a spread of expertise, especially for senior administrative positions. There were over two hundred boys in the hostel, ranging from year seven to year twelve — their schooling level, of course, not their age. The hostel responsibility was just about a full-time task on its own, with a good deal of direct contact with parents as well as boys, and I had a teaching load as well, but the combination of comparative youth and ambition is a high-octane fuel.

You may well have had a similar experience in your own career and understand the crucial significance of building a good team around you. You burn out quickly if you try to do everything yourself. I got rid of a couple of slackers among the housemasters, appointed in their place part-time younger guys who weren't teachers, but had sporting abilities that were useful. Adolescent boys bond well through sport. The domestic side of the hostel I was less familiar with: laundry, budgeting, resident nurse, catering. For a few weeks I just watched how things worked, or didn't work, and soon realised the kitchen was the only serious problem. The chef was hopeless. A middle-aged woman with bursitis who had abandoned committed enthusiasm, if she'd ever possessed it, had abandoned even stoical professionalism, and churned out a repetitious menu, the main consideration being ease of preparation. Sausages in gravy every Tuesday, scrambled egg on Thursdays, lettuce, beetroot and cold meat on Sunday. For dessert a quivering, yellow custard, or a motionless cordial she termed jelly. The boys gave a chorus of assumed surprise as each arrived and had their own terminology as well. The sausages with sauce au jus de viande they called rhino turds.

So Mrs Ainsley was let go, as the euphemism is, and I advertised the job. The headmaster was quite happy to leave the appointment to me, but I asked for a board representative and someone from the parents' association to join me in interviewing applicants. I knew better than to be solely responsible for the selection if it proved a disappointment. Graham Sidrose came for the parents, and rather predictably, Jocelyn Plannett from governance. She was the only woman on the board, and although she was a lawyer specialising in tax and insolvency, no doubt it was assumed she would have expertise in domestic matters because of her gender. Her son, Sean, whom I taught for two years, inherited little of her intellectual ability, but was a pleasant boy and more than useful as a halfback.

Catering manager was how the job was described in the advertisement. Cook was too plebeian for a private school, and the position did entail supervision of other kitchen staff. There was no deluge of applications. Twelve in fact, and five of those could be discarded immediately because they showed no evidence of useful qualification, or experience, in cooking for large numbers. One candidate stood out clearly from the others — Sefton McGill. We called four people for an interview, but really it was no competition. We included Mrs Rubenstein only because she was the sister of the science HOD. Sefton was even more impressive in person than on paper. He'd been a warrant officer in the army, responsible for catering for considerable numbers of men in a variety of situations, ranging from active duty in Afghanistan to formal dinners in the officers' mess. The military testimonial he provided was fulsome. He was fifty-seven years old and looked younger: tall, slim, with a calm manner and voice that had nothing of the parade-ground bark. He was at ease before us, but with no presumption in that ease. His hair was dark and neat, although such a cut was no longer enforced by regimental custom.

It was Jocelyn who came to the point quite early in the interview, after some conversation about the school's expectations. A good lawyer soon recognises the nub of any matter. 'I looked on the net,' she said. 'Warrant officers are paid a good deal more than we can offer you as catering manager here. Without meaning to pry, I wonder if you might tell us why you would consider such a move.'

'Military life's for younger people,' Sefton said. 'Also my wife and I divorced eighteen months ago and I needed to make changes in how I lived. You'll see I've since done some hotel work.'

'We're looking for someone who's committed,' I said. 'Someone who's not just passing through.'

'I'm looking for a permanent job. If it worked out for both the school and myself then I'd be expecting to settle in for some years at least. I'm accustomed to young men, a lot of them not much older than your seniors. I'm used to being with them as well as feeding them.'

Graham Sidrose asked some questions about menus and nutrition that he'd obviously mugged up beforehand, I talked a bit concerning hostel routines and expectations, Jocelyn had some direct questions concerning alcohol, drugs, guests, and hostel adults as role models. Sefton answered everything with openness and assurance, and had queries of his own. As we wound up, I told him we would be in touch with a decision within three days, and was there anything further he wished to raise. 'Thanks,' he said. 'There are three things that I'd need agreement on if offered the job. First, that I have the responsibility of hiring my own staff. Second, that the kitchen oven is replaced. What's there at present is far too small and just isn't up to producing good meals for that many.' Graham asked for the approximate cost of a new commercial oven and was taken aback when Sefton gave a ballpark figure of $25,000.

'And the third thing?' promoted Jocelyn.

'My daughter, Anna, still lives with me and would come into the flat.'

We had no problem with the first request, and the inadequacy of the existing oven had been the subject of complaints by Mrs Ainsley.

Although $25,000 is a good deal of money, private schools have reputations to maintain and are usually well resourced. Sefton's third stipulation required more consideration. There were women who worked in the hostel, and two housemasters were married, both with daughters, as it happened, but it was an issue that needed care.

'How old is your daughter?' Jocelyn asked.

'Twenty-five,' Sefton said.

'What does she do?' I said.

'She's a tour guide. Mainly wine tours, but also river cruises and historic sites. She'd be away sometimes, but mostly she'd stay here. Her mother's married again, and Anna doesn't get on all that well with the new guy, who's got children of his own.'

'Would she be happy, do you think, living in a boys' hostel?' asked Jocelyn. 'There are restrictions. Noise, number of visitors, things like that. Nothing too limiting, but she couldn't have loud parties with lots of her friends, for instance, and obviously drinking can be problematic. We have a lot of responsibility in regard to our hostel boys.'

'Anna's got past that. She'd want to be able to have friends, of course, and so do I, but she'd understand the protocols of the hostel. She's lived in an institutional environment almost all her life.'

'Nothing else you want to ask?' I said, and Sefton said that if he was appointed, and if there was time, he'd like to have some interaction with the boys apart from just the catering — in sports coaching and maybe orienteering. I saw no problems at all with that being given a trial. Most staff sought less contact with the boys rather than more. At the time, of course, I thought it might just have been a comment to increase his chances of selection.

The three of us on the committee talked when the interviews were over. Sefton McGill was the only candidate who figured much in our discussion, and we agreed on him as our choice. Jocelyn said she'd check with the finance committee regarding the oven and a couple of lesser items Sefton wanted, I was to inform the headmaster and Graham was to canvas parental opinion regarding the improvement of meals.

There were no hitches and Sefton started in term two. He was the best appointment I was ever part of at that school. The food underwent a marked improvement with little increase in costs. Being unmarried, I took most of my meals in the dining room and appreciated the positive changes in variety, nutrition and presentation. Even the married hostel staff were noticeably more regular in taking advantage of their entitlement to eat in. And Sefton proved his offer of involvement with students in other ways wasn't just talk. He coached tennis and badminton, even sometimes helped out with slower kids during prep, and there was no extra money for him in that. Most of the boys liked him and he liked most of them.

I think I can say that we became friends and I hope he'd agree. It didn't happen all at once, but the longer he was there the more I saw in his personality and outlook that I valued. He could be pretty direct and forceful, but he was prepared to listen, and although he was more able than most in positions of greater status and authority, he understood the reality of hierarchy. I liked his daughter too. Anna was bright and capable: a good conversationalist and with a shrewd understanding of how the world worked. She was there at the flat often when I went round and was good company. She loved music and had impressive qualifications in it, and after a term we offered her some evening hours with Mrs Deighton, giving tuition to boarders. She proved quite a success.

Sefton and I liked to watch the same TV programmes, especially nature and travel docos. Sometimes he came to my place, sometimes I went to his. We also talked about all sorts of things, not just the boys and hostel stuff. His background was very different to mine, and I enjoyed hearing about experiences that had nothing to do with teaching and students. His father had also been in the military, which meant they'd had postings all over the place. Sefton had seen a good deal more of life than I had, and not merely because he was older.

Every institution has its individual milieu, no matter how many others have the same function. It has to do with the people within it and sometimes with its history too. That first year as hostel manager I was conscious of a wariness, almost tension, among the seniors in Rosella House. Something not quite right. Richie, the housemaster, was aware of it too but couldn't account for it. When he and I had a talk with his prefects, they said everything was okay, but we weren't convinced. Both of us had experience enough to pick up the vibes.

It was Sefton, though, who cracked it. A wet, cold Wednesday night and I came back from a check of the dorms to find him standing under the overhang. 'Have you time for a chat about Bevan Prue?' he said. Bevan was one of the Rosella seniors. A large boy of uncertain temper and with the soft beginnings of a moustache. A boy, I think, who was given considerable latitude at home and chafed under the restrictions imposed on him as a boarder.

'Come into the warm,' I said, and we went into my flat, which was the smallest in the hostel, though with a pleasant view. As hostel head I could have chosen otherwise, but I had no wife to please then, no children to accommodate. We left our dripping coats on the lino of the kitchenette and went through to the sitting room. 'What's he been up to now?' I said.

'His mates have started calling him bin boy. I've heard them in the dining room and when I was on the courts too. It started me thinking, and I checked the council bins, kept a bit of an eye out, but there wasn't anything unusual. Then I thought, what about the pig bin?'

There's always waste food in a hostel, no matter how careful the husbandry: leftovers, stuff gone off, or half eaten, slops. A pig farmer had the contract to come and take it away from a bin behind the kitchen. He came early on Tuesday, Thursday and Saturday mornings, in a surprisingly flash truck with a hoist and tank. Sefton said he'd waited by the slatted stores window on Thursday and after watching the pig man make the collection without incident he'd been on the point of going back into the kitchen when he saw Bevan Prue come and reach into the empty bin. 'Something's going on,' Sefton told me. 'You don't go rummaging in a stinky bin for nothing. Anyway, there it is and I thought you should know.'

'Just Bevan? No one with him?'

'Not that I saw, but others know something's going on. There's this bin boy nickname that's suddenly caught on, and he's an odd kid.'

That's how I came to be waiting at the stores window myself early on Saturday morning, when usually I had a lie-in. I watched the white Hino come in, and the pig man in blue overalls dump the bin with the hoist, replace the heavy rectangular lid and then drive away, all without furtiveness, or hesitation. And, sure enough, within a few minutes Bevan came and with no less assurance lifted the lid and took something, not large, from the bin and wandered off.

I caught him just before he reached his dorm. 'I want a word, Bevan,' I said, and he stood there obediently. 'What did you get from the pig bin?'

'What pig bin?'

'There's only one, and just now you took something out of it, didn't you?'

'I haven't got anything. I just looked in,' said Bevan. 'I've got nothing.'

He didn't have anything, not with him, but he would've seen me coming and so I told him to wait where he was and walked back the way he'd come. Sure enough, there was a plastic bag lying behind the low wall that ran from the laundry to the caretaker's shed. A double-wrapped plastic bag that stank. Bevan was waiting obediently. 'What's this, then?' I asked.

'Never seen it before. No idea,' he said. 'I was just having a wander around.' He looked at me without evasion, but his face was flushed, the incipient, downy moustache more noticeable. It was a fair cop, and he knew it.

Weed was what it was, and a fair bit of it. I hadn't found it on him, of course, but I had his mates in one by one for a talk and eventually the whole thing came out. There's always someone who cracks in such circumstances, and some of those seniors in the know had been unhappy anyway. There was no fuss about Bevan's departure from the school. Neither his parents, nor the board, wished to draw attention to the circumstances. Best dealt with internally was the headmaster's summation. He gave a talk in assembly about the dangers of drug-taking, but without any specific reference to Bevan, or the hostel. And the pig man's contract was cancelled with immediate effect without riposte from him. Maybe I should have insisted on more being done about him, but then the whole thing could have blown up.

Bin boy Bevan was only one example of the help Sefton gave me. He wasn't a snoop and took no pleasure in uncovering the misdemeanours of others, but he was observant, shrewd and confided in by the boys. There was the pilfering from the tuck shop, the bullying of young Fraser and the Labrador pup kept secretly in Kookaburra House. There was also the positive advice that I was happy to encourage concerning the large number of likeable and deserving boys in our charge. I hoped Sefton would be at the school at least as long as I was, but the longer we live the more we realise life is neither predictable, nor concerned with our advantage.

A few weeks into the first term of the following year I found out something about Sefton that brought change and difficulty for us both: disappointment too. I'd been to a dinner party at the Harrisons', who had boys at the school. Eddie Harrison owned three home-appliance shops and was an old boy supportive of his alma mater. Dinner party always sounds rather collar and tie, and the Harrisons certainly lived well, but it was a relaxed and enjoyable evening. When I got back to the hostel it was long after lights out, but I took a stroll around the darkened buildings as I often did. Coming towards the rear of the block that Sefton's flat was in, I saw a shadowy figure drop from the fire escape and vanish soundlessly into the shrubbery by the garages. Boys are always up to something, often just for the fun of it, or a dare. I was in good clothes and almost decided not to bother, but finally I did haul myself up and climb to the second-storey window. The Venetian blinds inside were closed, but hung in a way that left a gap at the sides, and I could see quite clearly into the bedroom. Anna was crouched on the bed with her blonde head well down, and Sefton, in just a white singlet, was fucking her energetically from behind and slapping the side of her pale thigh.

I didn't want to be there, didn't want to acknowledge it, and got down as quickly as I could and went back to my own place. I'd seen it, though, and nothing would change that. I couldn't ignore incest, no matter who it was, or how consensual. It really rocked me, and throughout the next day I agonised over what to do. Maybe I should have gone straight to the headmaster, or the police, but Sefton was a friend. I thought of just saying nothing, as if I hadn't seen, but I knew at least one boy was aware, and I had responsibilities to them all. I thought of firing him with immediate effect and without reason given, but he wouldn't have stood for that. I thought of Anna, too, and what it must have done to her life.

How do you start a conversation with a friend about such a thing? I rang him, asked him to come around after he'd finished in the kitchen the next evening. It doesn't make sense, I know, but from the time I knew about him and Anna I somehow expected him to be different, but he looked and acted just the same. There was no easy way to start the necessary exchange, and so I got straight to it once he was in the flat. 'I know what you're doing with Anna,' I said. He looked away and then back at me again. He didn't seem surprised.

'I'm not doing anything with Anna against her will,' he said.

'Jesus, she's your daughter. Your own daughter. What sort of father does that?'

'But she's not my daughter,' Sefton said. 'She's my wife.'

'What are you telling me? That you married your own daughter?'

'I'm telling you that she's not my daughter. She's a woman I met when I was married, and when I was divorced I married her. There's no law against that.'

I remember that we'd been standing close to the window and it was still fully light outside, the sky was blue, and boys were wandering past on their way to prep, and some waved, and both Sefton and I waved back as if nothing had changed. He sat down and waited for me to say something. I did. I asked him if he was bullshitting me, and he said that Anna was home and, if I didn't believe him, I could ring her, even ask her to come over.

'Why lie about it then?' I asked him. 'Why tell us she's your daughter when she's not?'

'You know why. People don't like it when much older guys marry much younger women. It's seen as creepy, predatory, isn't it, and there's often a discarded wife, as there is for me. No one cares that they might be in love. No one thinks of the companionship, the friendship, the shared laughter and interests. All they see is the age gap and them in bed together. There's no law against it, but people don't like it, especially women. It's a threat, maybe, to something people can't quite pin down: to what's normal, if anyone knows what the hell's normal. What about love conquers all? Nah, not then.'

Sefton didn't ask me how I knew about it, and I didn't tell him. We sat in the warm room with the last of the day's summer sun slanting in, with the large eucalyptus trees at rest around the sports fields, and he told me about Anna joining his team in the catering corps, about her ability and affability, her intelligence and a friendship long before they ever had sex. He told me how they fell in love despite thirty-two years between them, and that because of love they gave up a lot of things, hurt and lost other people, came down in the world, but were happier than ever before nevertheless. 'It's not easy,' he said, 'especially for her. If we tell people it changes the way they see us. If we don't, it makes it bloody hard to be together out of the house in the way we want. I've told her she can call it quits any time, but she doesn't want to. She says she loves me, and I love her, love her so much.'

Why shouldn't love conquer all, as the movies show us. If Anna wasn't his daughter then I was fine with it. I knew them both and liked them: I knew there was no exploitation, or intimidation, going on. But it wasn't that simple of course. Whatever my personal attitude there was also my responsibility as hostel manager. At least one boy was aware that they were lovers, and thought them father and daughter. Maybe others as well. What I was okay with personally wasn't necessarily something I could accept within the hostel. I told Sefton that and he said he wanted to stay, but that he'd accept whatever decision I made. There was no pleading. He was quite realistic about it, as he was about everything, except perhaps his love for Anna. And he'd told that one lie, hadn't he, at the interview about her being his daughter. I knew how the headmaster would view that. 'You do what you feel you have to do,' he said as he left, walking into the warm, quiet evening just as calmly as he'd come.

Anna came to see me during lunchtime next day. I was leaving the dining room and on my way back to the main school. She must have taken the day off work after hearing what had happened. 'Sefton's told me,' she said. 'Can we talk about it?' So we went to the wooden seating along the side of the music suite, with blue and white agapanthus flowers nodding close and the sound of traffic far off by the main gates. 'I can show you a birth certificate,' she said with a smile.

'I should have twigged, with you being so blonde and Sefton dark, but that often happens anyway.'

'We should've told you, but we've been through all this sort of thing before and it seemed better at the time.' She did seem older than her years: not physically, because she was attractive enough, though not beautiful. She seemed older because of that calm self-possession that she shared with Sefton. 'You can't choose who you fall in love with,' she said. 'Not if it's real love, and if it is you don't care about an age gap.'

'Thirty-two years, though, must have made you both blink. You know, how will things be when he's seventy-five? And what about children?'

'If you're in love you live in the present,' Anna said. 'With love the present's everything, and the present goes on, doesn't it.'

'I'm okay with it myself,' I said, 'but it's not that easy here in the school.' Williamson, a day boy from my year twelve history class, was walking past and he grinned to see me sitting there with a young woman. Maybe he thought she was my girlfriend.

'Did you have a good meal?' Anna asked.

'We did. No complaints there,' I said. I knew why she said that, despite the apparent switch of subject.

'Well, all that might be lost if Sefton goes. We don't want to go and don't see any reason to, but I know it's not easy for you with the boys and everything. Sefton won't say much, but he's keen to stay, and so am I. We like it here. I just wanted you to know that, and also that he's enjoyed working with you. You're a friend.'

'I feel the same,' I said. 'It's a bugger of a situation really. The worst of it perhaps is that everybody thinks you're father and daughter.'

'Yeah, we made a mistake there, I think, but when we tell the truth we so often get knocked back for jobs and everything. People sniggering, or being stand-offish.'

'I'll come around,' I said. 'I'll come around when I've had a chance to think.'

'I just wanted to tell you how I feel. Sefton too.'

'I'll come around quite soon,' I said.

I thought a lot about it. I couldn't think about much else, although I took my classes as usual that afternoon and did the hostel stuff afterwards. If there had been just myself to consider it would have been fine, but it was more complicated than that — the peeping Tom and maybe more boys who knew and thought they were father and daughter, my obligations to the hostel, the school and the board, the one lie that Sefton had told. I sat up until late that night, thinking, veering from one possibility to another and none without cost.

Sefton would have to go, I decided finally, but go as painlessly as possible. I wouldn't tell the headmaster, or anybody else, how things were, and Sefton could leave with the school's blessing and my positive testimonial. The least hurt to the greatest number. You might think I'd have a poor sleep after such pressure — I expected so myself — but the unconscious mind has its own priorities, and I had a dream of being with my Uncle Alan on his sheep farm in the Maniototo. Dry, golden country with tors rising high above the tussock and grasses, and he and I out with the dogs. A clean wind from the south and not a road in sight.

Sefton and Anna accepted the decision. Without giving detail, I told them that their relationship was known among the boys and they realised the significance of that. They were grateful, too, that I would say nothing to the headmaster, or anybody else. Sefton gave notice that he was leaving at the end of term, and before that came around had no difficulty in getting a senior position at the Belham Hotel close to the airport. There was a job for Anna there as well, which would enable her to use her training and increase the time they spent together. It was all accomplished without embarrassment to anyone. And why not? No criminality was involved, no immorality, just a social convention broken and a harmless lie exposed that might have led to awkwardness and unwelcome public interest. The headmaster himself came to the hostel two days before they left and wished Sefton well.

Our friendship survived the pressures of the change. Sefton and Anna got a small, modern flat close to Angland Park and not far from the hotel, and I visited them when I could. It gave me pleasure to see them relaxed and natural as man and wife: pleasure too in getting to know Anna better and doing things with them both. There seemed a special and positive intensity in their relationship, as if they were aware it had no far horizons. Living in the moment, as the saying goes. The three of us went sometimes to the theatre, and to musical events which, with Anna's instruction, were an education for me. I know the difference now between an oboe and a clarinet. Sefton bore no grudge against me, or the school, and liked to hear how the hostel boys were getting on. When I did once ask him how things were at the hotel, he said at first there were raised eyebrows and occasional insinuation, but people seemed to get used to them being a couple. Normality increases with familiarity.

After I came back to New Zealand, we kept in touch for some years, but gradually communication became both more perfunctory and less regular. Finally it lapsed, as happens with friendships not refreshed by opportunities to be together. I think of them, though. I think of them with interest and affection as two people who put love first. The present is all that matters if you're in love, Anna told me, and I find no argument with that.

11.

Giving the Finger

Yes, quite a lot of people do ask me how I lost the little finger of my left hand. It's not a large appendage, or a crucial one; people have prostates and kidneys out, wombs, whole lengths of bowel, and aren't asked for explanation by casual companions at a café table. But a finger's absence is markedly obvious and enquiry as to the cause seems less a personal intrusion. The outcome of momentary carelessness perhaps, rather than concession to some grim disease.

My own case is, I suppose, more unusual than most, for I lost my finger as the consequence of a dream. I'm a practical sort of person and not especially imaginative. Like so many people in the modern world, I put my faith in science, not religion. I'm an architect and deal in precise, physical things. The calculation of failure risk and stress bearing as well as an appreciation of aesthetic elements. I've never been a great dreamer, either in the sense of envisaging extravagant success in life or the involuntary paradoxes of the night. The usual dreams from time to time — those arising from anxiety, or the re-emergence of minor boyhood trauma. We all have the running late dream, the desperate need to pee dream, the nasty surprise dream, and all are explicable in origin, no matter how bizarre in their internal sequence.

The dream that led to the loss of my finger was different. It first came to me four months ago. Summer, and I'd been to a meeting of my share club group. No anxiety there. Our power company holdings were doing especially well. I hadn't drunk much, just a glass of Central pinot noir. Natalie was asleep when I got home, and I was too, quite soon afterwards. In the dream I saw Gemma, our granddaughter, riding with other children on what looked like one of those flat freight wagons, just the deck and iron wheels, but it seemed to be on a road, not a track, and swooped around bends with city buildings and parks flowing by and a high, white concrete overpass ahead. Gemma was smiling. She has a beautiful smile. All the children were happy. The images were bright and quick. I didn't realise there was no sound until there was a clear, male voice that said quietly, 'Gemma's turning nine on the twenty-fifth of June, isn't she? I have to tell you that she'll die on her birthday unless you cut off a finger before then. I'm pleased that I'm able to give you this warning. Glad for you both.' I woke up then.

In the morning I told Natalie about it. The oddity of it, as often with dreams, but it didn't bother me that first time. All sorts of stuff turns up in dreams. I read somewhere that scientists are realising the brain's like a computer and spends the night sorting and reorganising material. Masses of sensory data. Neurologist Oliver Sacks said everything we've experienced is in there somewhere, even though we can't consciously access it.

The dream recurred, though. Not every night, but often several times a week. I've never had recurring dreams before, although I know they're not uncommon. The details varied: different children around Gemma, different buildings — once I saw a flash of my old primary school — and sometimes the vehicle seemed more a bus, sometimes more train, but always it was silent, and the dream too, except for the pleasant, confiding voice that told me the same thing in slightly different form. 'She'll die on her birthday unless you cut a finger off before then. You know that now. I'm glad I've been able to warn you.' And always ahead of Gemma and her friends was the clear outline of the high bulk of the overpass.

Natalie got upset about it. She told me not to mention the dream to the family ever, and that I should see someone: a counsellor, doctor, psychologist. There must be something that's triggering such an awful dream, she said. I came around to that view myself and asked Wynton Green, who's our doctor, and also a friend, to recommend someone to talk to. That was Gwyn McNally, who had an office above Rebel Sport in Flyte Street. I didn't especially take to Gwyn: he seemed a bit too conscious of his own urbanity and professional poise. When you faced him his expression was as if he were looking into a mirror — all self-awareness. A psychiatrist has medical qualifications and I respect that; I'm hazy on what gives psychologists their standing.

I had only a couple of sessions with Gwyn. He said I shouldn't be troubled by the dreams. That as Gemma was our only grandchild we had a powerful emotional focus on her and that could manifest itself in indulgence, overprotectiveness, unreasonable expectation and anxiety, of which dreams were an expression. He said nature directs our love down the generations and that's both necessary and just: we love our children and their children more than we love our parents. All of that was probably true enough, but I didn't find it much help.

As Gemma's birthday came closer, my concern shifted increasingly from my own welfare to hers. What if something did happen and I had done nothing despite the opportunity? She and her parents were unaware of the dream, but as they planned her party, as she danced and laughed in anticipation, I found it increasingly difficult to share their pleasure.

Three nights before the birthday party the dream came again. The flat deck held more children than before, all elated, and Gemma most excited and happy of all. It passed an expansive, empty park with swings, a dinosaur slide and a duck pond. It passed a merry-go-round on top of a supermarket with the empty chairs flared out because of a menacingly accelerated rotation. It passed a polar bear sitting at a window seat in McDonald's. All of this without sound. 'We are drawing close now,' the voice said. 'I'm glad I have given you a warning. It's up to you now.'

Gemma was to have her party at The Mystery House in Sanderton, out past the zoo, and before the main highway overpass. During the afternoon two days before the birthday, Natalie went to her book group and I made a decision. A rational choice after the consideration of probability elements and fail-safe precautions. I put on old but clean clothes. I rang the ambulance service then went to the shed, where there was a small chopping block, and had an accident there. The paramedic was disappointed the severed digit couldn't be found in time for later reattachment. I paid the minimum permissible price — the smallest finger on the less used hand — but would have given more. Most of our significant decisions in life are calculations of risk.

The birthday party was a great success. I was even able to be there and share the happiness, despite some discomfort. Gwyn McNally was concerned when he heard, and later told Natalie to keep an eye on me, but there's no longer danger for any of us. I have only ordinary dreams now. So that's it really. The answer to your query about no little finger.

I have a question for you, though. What would you have done?

12.

Cecily

My sisters, who are younger than me, thought Aunt Cecily was weird and didn't like staying with her. 'She's kooky,' said Lisa.

'Bonkers, eh,' said Mia. 'Lala land.' But then there weren't many adults they wished to be seen with anyway, especially not relatives. They hooked up with others indistinguishable from themselves, just like those little flocks of goldfinches, or yellow hammers, that swoop down and then away together. In different groups, though, my sisters, because there's three years between them. Three years is almost a generation when you're a teenager.

Art history was my thing at uni, despite my parents' warning that it was a dispensable qualification and an unreliable career. That choice in itself gave me an affinity with Aunt Cecily, who was then deputy director of the Auckland Art Gallery. She liked me to call her Cecily and so I will henceforth here too. What's a generation between friends, she said, if you share a similar outlook on life. What does it matter if you're man or woman, black or white, religious or otherwise, goatherd or philosopher, if you laugh at the same things and scorn the same things.

My mother says that's all very well, but that Cecily had escaped the usual impositions that engender caution. She was unmarried, unharried by children, or financial worry, healthy and a citizen of a free country. She was successful, admired within her circle, displayed an unwitting and uncensored flamboyance that in someone less aware of others would be seen as egotism. I was Cecily's favourite, not because she discriminated against my sisters, but because of their wariness concerning her. They'd had their chances to commit when we were all much younger.

I remember Cecily taking me to the zoo when I was at primary school. Not just once, but several times, although the recollections coalesce. The tigers she loved. 'Oh, what glorious, fierce colours,' she said, and quoted Blake's poem about the forest of the night. I recall her once singing to a tiger, which came close to the fence and regarded her quizzically as she did so. Delacroix liked tigers, she later told me, and so he did, but my choice now would be John Collier's *Circe*, even though he is mainly remembered as a portrait painter. The juxtaposition of a naked woman and a tiger creates a powerful image.

Cecily admired the lordly giraffes also, despite their disproportionate appearance, but never lingered before the chimpanzees, or the gorillas. 'Too much like ourselves to be in captivity,' she said. 'They have awareness of being on show, and of our condescension.' And she understood childhood well enough to ensure we always ended a visit with an ice cream, or a chocolate milkshake. By the time I was seventeen our sightseeing had moved on to art exhibitions and collections, where more rigorous instruction was offered, but we still ended in the cafeteria.

Once she asked for my trousers. She'd been to our house for a meal during my second university year. I had on a new pair of light-blue, stone-washed jeans: narrow legs and double stitching. Cecily took a fancy to them, asked me where I'd bought them. When she later found that no more were available, she asked me for mine — and paid generously, of course. She had slim hips and the jeans quite suited her. She wore trousers often, but had some expensive dresses too — bold without being fussy. French women understand simplicity as a frame, she said. Cecily had worked at the Petit Palais Gallery, even done a course at the Sorbonne. My mother told me that a titled Frenchman had proposed to her, but been refused. An aristocrat, my mother said, and with money too. But when I questioned Cecily she said he was merely the brother of a baron, and quite obtuse despite having artistic pretensions. 'As to money,' she said, 'who knows. He was generous in restaurants, but often that's just show.' A baron's brother, though, it has a ring to it.

A very articulate woman who could open an exhibition, or give a floor talk, with accomplishment that was achieved both by her sense of presence and the perspicacity of what she said. Cecily's voice had a slight metallic ring to it that was unusual, but not unattractive, and everything she said was imbued with the enthusiasm she had for art, for enterprise, for life. The dullness that is an inevitable part of existence for most of us seemed to have no place in hers, but then my observation was incomplete and from the distance of a nephew. Whatever disappointment she experienced was kept to herself. My mother said Cecily always wanted to dance through life rather than walk.

Cecily wrote a book on the work of surrealist trailblazer Dorothea Tanning. It received critical commendation and sold quite well in the United States. She gave us all a signed copy, and in mine wrote. 'To my best man.' She also had enthusiasms that were quite outside her intellectual focus. Skiing was one of them. She said that on the slopes she felt most free, could leave even herself behind. And she collected antique gold and silver thimbles on her travels, although she never sewed. Beautiful, elaborate little objects: some with intricate scrolling, some with rainbow ceramic inserts, or jewels, some with all three. They clustered around the glass-domed clock on her mantelpiece like chickens about a hen.

Despite her wide interests and adventurous joie de vivre, Cecily maintained an academic rigour in regard to her profession and could display a fierce concentration, often working late into the night, or even through it. When I was at the university I found her extempore oral examinations more searching than any official written tests I faced. 'Enter the work,' she would exclaim. 'Enter the work without presumption and so be receptive to the intention of the practitioner.' She knew many of our artists: some were her friends. She valued them according to their talent, but also for the degree of empathy they displayed towards others. She gave respect and praise where she thought it due, not just where she knew such responses would be endorsed, and could be scathing in both private and public concerning work she considered inferior. She loved art, but wasn't in awe of it.

Most Kiwis aren't greatly into the visual arts, and Cecily had no wide renown, although there was considerable publicity when she exposed the guy from Hastings who was selling work he claimed was by Tony Fomison. Her analysis of brushwork, colour matching and materials was irrefutable. I've always been pleased to acknowledge kinship, although one of my lecturers insinuated she had undue influence on my thesis. I went to the department head over that and eventually received an insincere and cursory apology.

At my graduation dinner she clapped her hands with pleasure and assured me I would be happy. How could it be otherwise, she said, when one worked surrounded by the very best visual expressions of life from the most talented people. A gallery is like a garden, she said, and just as therapeutic. She danced with all the family in turn, including my sisters, and intrigued the wine waiter by speaking French. She bought a bottle of Château Haut-Bailly and told a story of my mother's first romance that was tender, humorous and revealing.

For a couple of years Cecily had a red Mazda MX-5. Not new, but pretty exciting for me at the time when my own transport was a 90cc step-through. She let me drive when we went out together and took pleasure in my excitement. She sold it, though, because she got sick of coming back to it and finding the seats wet after rain. Auckland's not a place for convertibles, she decided reluctantly, and the hood was a hassle. 'Italy, or the south of France, Tony,' she said, 'that's where we should take it. I could wear a pink scarf, you could drive wearing just a shirt — and pants of course.' We never got there, but after the Mazda she bought an Audi saloon that was a special ride too in its own way. I wish we'd done the Cote d'Azur thing, though. Cecily would have been right at home in a sports car and with a pink scarf — maybe dark sunglasses too.

I remember a trip to Melbourne, where Cecily curated a retrospective of Ralph Hotere's work at the National Gallery of Victoria. I'd had a small part in the preparation of the exhibition and she invited me to come and see it in place, paid for my airfare with typical generosity. I had the pleasure of sitting with many others and listening to her talk, surrounded on the walls by her selection from the artist's oeuvre. She made us think and also made us laugh, and the latter is not an immediate association with Hotere's work. Afterwards, quite late, seven of us went to the renowned Flower Drum Chinese restaurant, and to my relief, and Cecily's easy acceptance, a short man with a bow tie, whose name I can't remember, paid for her meal and mine. Perhaps, like the baron's brother, his generosity was not indicative of wealth, but welcome nevertheless. It was a group happily united by the love of creativity. There were two other women there, one markedly attractive, both intelligent, but Cecily was the centre without any thought, or need, to inhibit others. She drew them out, bolstered them, even as she blossomed herself.

Later, at our hotel, she and I had a coffee in her room, which overlooked a broad, main thoroughfare on which car lights still swarmed like fireflies, although it was well after one. We talked of the exhibition, of the meal and our companions there. We talked of the future more than the past. 'Go to Europe, Tony,' she said to me.

'We have our own art, though,' I said. 'We're doing some good stuff. I reckon we've come of age.'

'Go to Europe and then come home again. Go to America too. You won't really understand what's important and different for us until you understand the journey that's been made. Go to China and Japan as well.' She tossed me a packet of nuts from the mini bar as if it were both passport and ticket to the world.

'Bring it on,' I said, 'but I need some decent opening: a job where there's useful and exciting work going on. I'm past just bumming around visiting galleries. It's not that easy, especially from here, to get something challenging and to get paid for it. Bugger those internships.'

'I'll help,' Cecily said. 'American institutions are the best resourced, and you could bounce on from there: get a variety of experience under your belt before you commit to any one field. I know people of influence at San Francisco and the Boston Museum of Fine Art. Blair Kelman was in Paris when I was there. I'm damned if I know how he's done so well, but some just find a niche, a passion, and blast off.'

'I'd like to blast off.'

'You just need to find the fuse. Overseas is good for that.'

'I'd be up for it,' I told her. Sitting with Cecily, several storeys high, with the firefly lights below in shades of red and white and yellow, I felt it was as good as done. It was that sort of night, that sort of conversation, when achievement and choices seemed assured.

Cecily did reach out, just as she said she would. I didn't get to San

Francisco, or Boston, but I had some happy years at the Seattle Art Museum — SAM to everybody there. I was an archivist, although I didn't end up as one. It's good to have a wide gallery experience. Corinne, my then girlfriend, was a conservator. Seattle's a lot bigger than I'd realised, and funky with it. A swinging place, with close links to Ray Charles and Quincy Jones, Jimi Hendrix and Nirvana. I'm not that musical, but I like those associations. The city's cultural without being stuffy. I've been back twice and still enjoy the place. Barbara Earl Thomas, John Grade and Amanda Kirkhuff are all Seattle artists. Kirkhuff's just fantastic.

They say the good die young, but Cecily reached seventy-nine without any suffering of which I'm aware. A fierce intelligence and a firm grip on life. I visited her a year or so before she died and we talked until almost midnight, and argued with enjoyment too. She showed me again the small Hammond that she'd decided to leave to me. What taste she had, and generosity.

I was in France when she died — suddenly and painlessly, my mother said, just as she wished. Lucky, splendid Cecily. No wretched decline, or prolonged death throes, just a sudden clash of cymbals and the curtain drop before the applause could turn to tears. I was in Arles when I received the news, and two days later returned from the small Van Gogh gallery there to find a card from her with a reproduction of Pissarro's *Peasant Women Planting Stakes*. She had a soft spot for old Pissarro. Everything is beautiful if you are able to interpret it, he once said. As ever, Cecily's message was full of her activities, and enquiry about mine. I stood with the peasant women and thought how fitting that my last news of her was not of her death, but a message of her life. I saw us together in the red Mazda on the high Riviera motorway, driving fast. Cecily with a pink scarf tied around her hair, and laughing.

13.

Taking the Fall

There are lots of fulfilling jobs in the world, but Wesley Brown didn't have one of them. Often he woke up thinking he was still a success — you can't easily cast off twenty-one years of upward mobility in professional life — but then he'd remember that the Lawyers and Conveyancers Disciplinary Tribunal had disbarred him. He would confront that reality for a moment, then begin another day with resolve that he had a new life to build, even if it was bound to be a diminished one. Official punishment had been home detention, not prison, and a financial penalty, but the greater consequence was Debbie's decision to leave the marriage, but not the house, and fourteen-year-old Patrick's decision to remain with her.

Wesley's place was now a small flat in a different part of the city, number nine in a concrete block high-rise containing fourteen just the same. Reasonably modern, however, and he did own it. He'd lived in a lot of worse places as a student. The divorce had been a greater financial disaster than the court's imposition. He'd felt unable to deny Debbie anything she demanded after he'd destroyed their former life.

He could have applied for low-level administrative positions with the hope of gradually rehabilitating himself, but even that would have meant being open about his past. He wanted to start without the hindrance of his history: to be just the new guy people would come to know and judge purely on their own experience of him. He could do that as an unskilled worker surely, and so he looked in the paper, rang places, walked into factory buildings to make enquiry.

The Hadley Group were hiring. Hadley were big players in the manufacture of pharmaceutical and hospital dressings. Wesley rang the office. He gave his real name, but didn't mention his professional qualifications, so no lies were told. Any sort of work, he said, he was interested in any sort of work. He'd done time in wool stores and warehouses he said, and it was true. Unlike the upper echelon at Hodgkiss, Wilkin and Finn, he'd made his own way to a career and was familiar with casual workplaces from his own experience and that of his family. No silver spoon boy, our Wesley, adept at fitting unobtrusively into whatever social milieu he found himself in.

Packer. That's what he was offered. Well, the job wasn't confirmed, but he was told if he was interested to come to the factory the next morning and ask for Ruben Best. The factory wasn't as the name might suggest — no furious machines, belching furnaces, hooters, escaping gases, shouts and jangling overhead tracks. An airy place with subdued, highly technical manufacture of quality goods in hygienic surroundings, but also with a sense of urgency and delicate balance among the components responsible for integrated creation of the product run.

'I'm here to see Mr Ruben Best,' Wesley said to a young woman with green hair who was hitting an upturned photocopier with a transparent ruler.

'It's not what it looks like,' she said cheerfully. 'Something fell into it.'

'There's always something. And Mr Best?'

'See that door by the hand-sanitiser dispenser. The one with the glass panel. That's Ruben,' she said. Wesley thanked her and went on. He could see Ruben even before he got there. He sat in suit trousers and shirt sleeves at a desk that took up almost all of the very small office. Just room enough behind it for one person and in front of it for a chrome chair, its red vinyl seat patched with Hadley medical tape. Ruben was tapping his keyboard with clumsy rapidity, but looked up and motioned Wesley in.

'Wesley, right?' he said. 'Sit down and I'll be with you right away,' and he renewed his concentration on the keyboard.

In such a confined space it wasn't easy to reach the chair when the door was open, but Wesley managed it and once seated closed the door with just a sweep of his arm. He sat quietly while Ruben completed his task. Wesley was aware of novelty in the situation, but interested rather than affronted. Wesley's hourly billing rate and professional status had been such that he was almost never kept waiting, and certainly not in such circumstances, but here in the small office of a minor administrator he was not a highly qualified legal consultant, but Wesley Whatever, applying for the job of packer. Life has many perspectives.

Ruben finished quite soon, leant back in his chair for relief, put his hands behind his head briefly so that faint yellow stains showed in the armpits of his white shirt. 'So, Wesley,' he said, 'the packer's job, right?'

'Yes.'

'You've done this sort of stuff?'

'I've been storeman, wharf work, that sort of thing.'

Ruben could have asked for a CV, for testimonials, but he was hiring a packer and despatch, someone of whom not a lot was required, and he preferred to use his own experience and intuition in selection. He hired a good many people for such positions and they came and went. He had a nose for those who were lazy, disruptive, dishonest or invisibly disabled by some circumstance of life. He noticed that Wesley's clothes were casual, but clean, that he could look him in the face, that he spoke well, that he didn't smell of booze, that the pupils of his eyes weren't enlarged. What he couldn't know was that Wesley was just as aware of what was really going on during their relaxed conversation, that he, too, was making a personal assessment. Wesley experienced Ruben in his natural habitat and true form, and found him pleasant enough even though his name seemed incongruous.

Wesley was hired and asked if he could start the next day. Things move rapidly in the world of an unskilled workforce. 'Check in with me before 8.15 tomorrow and I'll introduce you to the floor,' said Ruben. 'Bring in your driver's licence for me to have a gander at. Just routine, and we'll need to talk about KiwiSaver and other stuff. And there's a staff canteen that most of us use, but that's up to you. Okay then. No questions? I hope you'll like it here.' He didn't stand up, but smiled as a sign the interview was over, and was already occupied with his keyboard as Wesley squeezed out.

Quite a lot of women worked at Hadley Group; it was the sort of business in which muscle had little advantage. Ruben took Wesley into the factory the next morning and passed him over to Mrs Herangi, who was a supervisor. 'Somebody at last,' she said. 'We've been short here, Ruben, for days now.'

'Had to get the right person,' said Ruben placidly and as a passing compliment to Wesley.

'Things go wrong here if we don't have the staff.' She nodded to Wesley, but her focus was her immediate superior. 'We're under pressure at the best of times. Maybe you could get the upstairs chardonnay drinkers to understand that.'

'For the moment,' said Ruben, 'let's concentrate on getting Wesley here sorted, shall we. You and I can chat about staff levels later.'

Mrs Herangi's Christian name was Pauline, but she discouraged that informality. On the factory floor it was customary usage, but not to her face. All women of lesser status were known by their first names, whether married or not. Executive women were different, of course, but Wesley was yet to know that.

'Germs,' said Mrs Herangi when Ruben had gone. 'Hygiene is important here. A lot of our products have to be sterile. Good to remember that, even though what you'll be doing is well down the line and generally involves material already safely packaged. Use one of the dispensers for your hands every time you come in, and you don't eat in here. Not even a cough lozenge. Not even your own fingernails.'

'Of course,' agreed Wesley. Mrs Herangi's instruction and explanations continued as they moved around the factory, becoming more specific as they came to the plebeian functions of packing and despatch, where he was assigned. 'That's it then,' she said finally, standing by the belt, the trolleys, the stacks, with the doorway of the loading bay behind lit golden by the morning sun. 'I've got to get on. Rhonda here will settle you in, and Malohi's around somewhere.'

Rhonda, who was packing small cartons of hypoallergenic adhesive dressings, looked up with a smile as Mrs Herangi went back to her post in the more sensitive areas of production. There was no formal introduction and simply by continuing with her work Rhonda showed Wesley what was required of him. She was young, pleasant and at least six feet tall — a netballer surely. Her face was free of make-up, attractive in its naturalness. 'The only thing really,' she said, 'is to make extra sure every container or package has its line sticker and that you've recorded that with the computer stick. They go ape if stuff leaves without being zapped.' With a phallic-shaped remote she showed him how that was done and said he'd better put on his smock.

Everyone on the factory floor wore a smock, even Mrs Herangi. Dark blue garments with the Hadley Group logo over the heart. Wesley remembered his mother saying that the provision of an overgarment was worth hundreds of dollars a year. She'd worked for a cleaning firm, away most nights of the week in empty offices in the city. The Hadley smock was of good-quality cotton and with full-length Velcro. Wesley thought of taking a selfie and sending it to Serge, the only one of his former legal colleagues he was still in regular touch with.

'Who's this then, Rhonda?' This uttered by a Polynesian guy not only taller than both of them, but broader as well, who had come in from the loading bay.

'This is Wesley,' Rhonda said, barely pausing in her work.

'Malohi,' he said and put out his hand. 'About time we got someone. About bloody time. You from round here?'

'Most of my life,' Wesley said.

'Move over and I'll show you how me and my girlfriend here get things done at *pack-ing* and *des-patch*.' His voice attained a TV commercial falsity.

'You wish,' said Rhonda.

'She's not all that bad looking,' continued Malohi, 'but talks sex all the time. Like *all* the time. It's rude really.'

'Shut up,' said Rhonda cheerfully.

'A–ll–ll the time,' said Malohi, drawing it out, almost as if musing, and then to Wesley, 'See these forty-gram ones fit better if you always have the date stamp uppermost. There's a slight curve caused by the seal. Don't let them get stuck together.' His large hands moved with quick precision and the tightly sealed oblongs seemed to dance into the container.

'Thanks. I guess it'll take me a bit to get the knack,' said Wesley.

'It's not rocket science,' Rhonda said. 'Just practice.'

'What job you had before, man?' asked Malohi.

'I worked at a legal firm,' said Wesley. 'Routine office stuff. I've been a fruit picker, done shop front, store work and so on.'

And so the mild interrogation went on, with questions from Rhonda too, but it didn't last long. It was more sharing than probing, and all the while they worked, and Wesley was shown how things were done, what was expected of him. As Rhonda said, it wasn't rocket science, but every job has its skills; the accomplishment of task with least effort. Wesley had always been a quick learner.

Work breaks were usually taken in rotation so that the flow of production wasn't interrupted. Wesley's first lunchtime in the cafeteria was spent without the company of his fellow packers, but Ruben Best was there, sitting at a corner table before a plate of bean and green-leaf salad that Wesley wouldn't have picked as a likely choice. Wesley understood hierarchy. He didn't go over to where Ruben sat and wasn't invited there, but the floor manager got up and accompanied him to a table where there were five smocked workers. 'This is Wesley,' he said. 'He's just joined us this morning in packing. I'll let you all get acquainted.' Maybe he couldn't remember all their names, more likely he thought it better they introduce themselves. He went back to his corner table and his own concerns.

Wesley was met with noncommittal acceptance by his fellow workers during his first few days. Some people were less friendly than others, but as an expression of their natures rather than any particular reaction to him. People came and went in the cafeteria, as their breaks ordained, so he found himself giving his name and sometimes his hand quite often. Some faces and identities became familiar with no introduction at all. For Wesley that first day, gender and age were the superficial markers of his blue-smocked companions, but he knew full and individual personalities would become apparent.

One of those was Bruce Norris, a technical guy responsible for keeping the machines up to scratch, and who had also been chosen by his fellow employees as their official representative with management, and endorsed by the CEO and board, who had no wish to have a union presence within the workforce. Bruce was an honest and affable bore, respected by his fellows, but not someone they wished to be stuck beside in the cafeteria for long, or anywhere else. He took a liking to Wesley, perhaps as a newbie to impress, and often came to sit with him whenever their breaks coincided.

'Jeez, man,' said Malohi, 'you don't want to get landed with old Brucie that much. What a bloody yawn. He collects stamps, for Christ's sake. Who collects stamps these days?'

'Maybe he just feels he's bringing me up to speed,' said Wesley.

'Some speed,' said Rhonda. 'The way this place is going we'll all be looking for new jobs next year.'

'Why's that?'

'Hadley's going down, you betcha, down, down, down.' Malohi's voice became deeper with each repetition, and he slapped his hand on the boxes he'd piled on the trolley. He seemed happy at the prospect, as if proletarian satisfaction at the prospect of capitalist enterprise failure was greater than the fear of losing his job. 'Sinking ship, man.'

'Really?'

'Share price down. Understaffed. Underpaid. Management crap fights,' said Rhonda. 'The signs are there, aren't they. It's not rocket science.' Wesley was becoming accustomed to this mantra. 'Susan went to Medaid a couple of weeks ago. She saw the writing on the wall.'

'Our best admin person by a friggin' mile,' Malohi said.

'There's been deliberate spoilage, here in the factory, but no one knows who.' Rhonda looked at the busy people not far away, as if a guilty aura would form about the head of one of them.

'*Sab-o-tage.* I tell ya, there's people here hacked off for sure.' Malohi leant in confidently. 'Liam told me they've put in secret cameras. Scratch your bum and they're watching upstairs.'

'Liam's a stirrer,' said Rhonda.

'Wouldn't surprise me, though,' the big man said.

Wesley got to know Liam in a superficial way. A shark-faced man who worked a machine that made wad pouches for hydrogel dressings, gave Bruce a hard time for not getting everyone better conditions and had a braying laugh to draw attention to himself. Wesley didn't take to Liam, and preferred Averil, who tended a similar machine. An older woman who had taken the trouble to explain the intricacies of the Hadley payslip to him. She had been with the firm for a long time and had the in-house knowledge helpful for a newcomer.

The most disconcerting and difficult times for Wesley during those first weeks had nothing to do with his job at Hadley, but came when he visited his former home to see his son. Sometimes as he drove up that familiar drive and stopped before the house, Patrick was standing behind the French doors to the patio, unsmiling, but more often he would be in his room having screen time. Debbie would give her brisk hello, there would be a civilised, short conversation for Patrick's benefit and then she would busy herself not far away to allow Wesley time with their son. Wesley liked to encourage Patrick out of the bedroom — onto the patio if it was sunny, a walk with him onto the golf course, a drive to the city waterfront. Patrick wasn't antagonistic, just somehow removed. Wesley told himself it was accountable teenage withdrawal, but missed the closeness they'd once had. He found himself the one starting conversations and with a false enthusiasm for topics he thought might engage his son. Patrick accepted his arrival calmly, and his departure with equal composure, never once showed any interest in coming to the flat. While they were together, Wesley kept up the cheerful pretence that it was okay to be this sort of family, when he knew it wasn't. Not for him anyway. And he knew whose fault it was.

He kept in touch with Serge too. The only colleague from his professional life he felt inclined to see, although there were others who hadn't distanced themselves. Twice he went to Serge's for a meal. His wife was a good cook and could talk intelligently on a range of subjects, but there was no discussion of the hubris involved in the temporary use of a client's trust fund for financial advantage that didn't eventuate. No talk of promotions within Hodgkiss, Wilkin and Finn, the importance of family, or the emotional readjustment required when one is a criminal. Once, when his wife was away at a conference, Serge came to Wesley's place, but found it difficult to suppress his uneasiness at having his new Volvo parked at night in such a neighbourhood. They talked of mutual colleagues, of sport, the pantomime of politics, and Wesley mocked himself and Hadley by exaggerating his insignificance there and the company's in-house peculiarities.

Wesley hadn't done any research on the place of his employment. For him Hadley was just a temporary source of a bare living wage, but after hearing of the firm's problems he was interested enough to use Google and a couple of trade magazines to learn more. Sure enough, things weren't great. Underlying profit down twenty-two per cent in three years and reports of a dysfunctional relationship between the CEO and the lab director. The former was Cathleen Hadley, granddaughter of the founder. The director was Dr Renee Beardsley, who had moved from England two years before. The increase of female executive power generally was something Wesley was well aware of and of which he approved. That it existed within the Hadley Group gave the situation added nuance. There was Keith McEwan, sales and product growth, but he was only third in line.

Wesley had been several weeks at Hadley before he saw either of these significant women, who had little cause to be hanging around packing and despatch. They did occasionally, however, visit the cafeteria, though not together. Ms Hadley he saw first. She came in on a Friday afternoon with Ruben and a handsome though completely bald man whom Wesley never saw again. Ruben accompanied them, fetched coffee and muffins, then left. Wesley was half listening to Bruce talking about Second World War stamps, but was more interested in the CEO. Hadley Group was a public company, but the family were major shareholders and Cathleen was at its head. She must have had a privileged upbringing surely, private schooling, ski trips from a Queenstown holiday home, and now dinner parties, board meetings, the patron of various philanthropic organisations. When Wesley had been a partner in his firm, he'd met such people on equal terms despite a very different background, but now he sat in a blue work smock at a far table with no reason to be included.

Ms Hadley was small, neat and upright, relaxed among people who owed their employment to her family. Before leaving, she came to Wesley's table, nodded to him and others, and talked briefly to Bruce about an arranged meeting that involved him as staff rep. 'Thank you, Bruce,' she concluded without hauteur and then left with her companion.

'You're well in there,' said Janie, but without malice, and Bruce tried not to show his pride at preferment.

'It's just being liaison for you lot,' he said.

'Well, get a pay rise for us at this bloody meeting then,' said Sayed.

'Yeah, well, but things aren't going that well these days. Not well at all,' said Bruce.

Dr Beardsley was a different sort of woman, though equally small, neat and upright. She was younger, and more combative, less assured of a place in the world, but determined to claim it. She bristled easily. Bruce told Wesley she came from Manchester, had beavered her way to a good degree in science technology and had experience in major firms. She spent a lot of her time in the product development lab on the second floor and Wesley first saw her when she came down to address the only full meeting of the workforce that occurred during his time there. A Friday, and the floor was shut down an hour early so everyone there could crowd into the cafeteria and be warned of dissent among them. No board members, no Ms Hadley, no Keith McEwan, but Ruben and his equals with the supervisors at the corner table.

Tampering. That's what Renee was there to talk about. There had been a spike in contaminated products and also in the failure rate of the more sophisticated machinery. She gripped the chrome support at the end of the cafeteria food cabinet and leant forward urgently. 'There's no margin for error in the health market,' she said. 'We lose our product reputation then ultimately jobs will go too. You can bet on that. I can't believe there's more than one very stupid person doing this, but we'll all suffer. We're the company, we're Hadley, you need to remember that. Whoever it is, they've got to be stopped and you people are most likely to find who it is, because that person's almost certainly sitting here with us now. Think about it.' Renee paused for effect. Her delivery was forceful, but the *Coronation Street* accent was still evident enough to be distracting in a Kiwi work cafeteria, and often mocked in her absence. She was about to sit down, but was seized with the need to be blunt. 'Not just tampering,' she said. 'Outright sabotage, that's what we're talking about. Absolutely.'

Ruben was more temperate when he spoke. 'No one's being accused here,' he said. 'Maybe some nutter's coming in somehow from outside. We're looking into that possibility, but there's definitely some dodgy stuff going on that we need to get to the bottom of and we have to work together to do that.'

Neither speaker gave any examples of tampering and Wesley asked Bruce about that when the meeting was over. 'They reckon giving specific examples could encourage copy-cat crimes,' he said. 'Like those needles that started popping up in strawberries everywhere. I haven't been told a lot, but at one meeting Keith McEwan said several packets in a run of OPX surgical mesh had been contaminated with fly spray.'

'Why would people do it?'

'God knows. Well, there's been no decent increases for years, pay or conditions, but then look at the problems Hadley's got anyway.

Putting the boot in now doesn't make much sense, does it. I dunno . . .'
It's not rocket science, Rhonda would have said.

The whole business interested Wesley, rather than alarming him. He felt no particular allegiance to Hadley and if he lost his job there he would find an equally unskilled one somewhere else. He had some understanding, though, of the pressure that management would be feeling — Ms Hadley, Dr Beardsley, Keith McEwan and others. As a partner he had shared responsibility for the success and reputation of a firm, understood the alignment of personal mana with the status accorded the organisation one represented.

Renee Beardsley's address had an unsettling and somewhat divisive effect on staff. Some resented her assumption that the saboteur was one of them. Some were adamant they wouldn't snoop on their fellow workers. Some were fervent in their wish to find the culprit. Some didn't give a bugger and just went on as before. Malohi entertained himself during the monotony of packing by naming likely suspects: Estelle because she'd been passed over for a supervisor's job; Ricky because his wife had gone off with a diesel mechanic; Sayed who was a communist; Liam the loudmouth; even Dr Beardsley herself, because of her feud with the Hadley dynasty.

He hadn't thought of Averil Knowles, but eleven days after the cafeteria meeting she was placed on compulsory leave and a week later dismissed. There was no official announcement, but such news always gets about within an organisation. Averil was the saboteur, and through Bruce's privileged information Wesley got to know that contaminated individual packs had been tracked to her station and bore her fingerprints.

Your profession has an important influence on how life is viewed. A psychologist automatically seeks sincerity in a smile; a farmer checks the sky for weather. Although Wesley was in the present merely an unskilled manual worker, his natural perspective remained that of a lawyer, experienced in both assessment of human nature and the pedantry of the law. The dismissal didn't seem right to him.

Averil still had a landline, unlike many of the younger folk at Hadleys. Wesley found her address from the phone book and rang on the following Saturday morning. She was a long time answering and as he waited he noticed several dead flies on the windowsill of his small living room: a rebuke to his cursory housekeeping. The curtains too, baggy in places because a plastic hook or two had come off the runners. He thought of Debbie and of Patrick, the house above the golf course, the outward gloss his life once possessed. He vaguely recalled a woman who had come in twice a week to clean, and whose existence he'd otherwise never bothered to show an interest in.

'Hello?' said Averil uncertainly, bringing Wesley back to his concrete block flat and his disgrace.

'It's Wesley,' he said. There was no immediate reply. 'From Hadley.'

'Oh, yes, Wesley,' she said, making the connection, but obviously surprised to hear from him.

'It's just that I heard you've been laid off. I'm sorry about that.'

'Sacked,' she said. 'I've been sacked after seventeen years. They say I tampered with a batch of OPX. As if I would after seventeen years.' She sounded sad rather than angry.

'I know. The thing is, I used to work in the office of a legal outfit and I think you've been treated badly. I'd like to come around and talk to you about it. I could help, I think.'

'Come around here?'

'If that's okay.'

'What, you think you know who did it?'

'No,' said Wesley, 'but I think you've been treated unfairly, according to the law. There are procedures laid down for dismissal, you see. I don't know that they were followed in your case, Averil. That's what I'd talk to you about. Just to make sure.'

He went to her place the next morning. Ten-thirty as arranged. Wesley assumed she chose that time because it would be morning tea, the proper time women like Averil considered to have a talk. The house was small and wooden, with the front door central like a mouth. In the garden plot by the door was a plaster gnome holding a fishing rod and smiling despite the absence of a pond. Wesley had almost forgotten how such houses were, though he'd been brought up in one. Tight, separate rooms instead of the open-plan design of modern homes. Reduced, heavily framed windows. Averil took him down the narrow passage and into the kitchen that had a table with a shiny top and chrome legs. 'I've got the jug on,' she said. Through the window above the sink he could see an aged apple tree, the branches dark and arthritic, the fruit large, fully formed, but green. Cookers, his mother would have called them.

Yes, he'd have coffee rather than tea, Wesley said in response to

Averil's offer, and he took a buttered half of date scone. He knew that, despite her courtesy, she found it odd that he should want to come and talk. They both worked at Hadley, sure, but they weren't friends and he was a newcomer. 'I hope you don't mind me coming, but I think you've had a raw deal. Have you talked to anyone?'

'I've talked to people. People at work and my family.'

'I mean professional advice.'

'Well, the job's already gone, isn't it.'

'But there are laws that protect employees against unfair treatment because there's a natural imbalance of power in employment relationships.'

Averil didn't say anything.

'What I mean is that Hadley has to act fairly and reasonably. Even if there's good cause for dismissal there are rules to follow. Bruce said you just got a letter of dismissal, no earlier one raising issues and giving you an opportunity to put your side of things.'

'I was just hauled into the office with McEwan and Renee Beardsley, informed my fingerprints were on the packets and told to go home. Then a letter that sacked me, after seventeen years. After that long, why would I start mucking around with stuff?'

'It's not fair and not legal, not even if you did it.'

'I didn't do it.'

'All the more reason to do something now,' said Wesley. He knew how it must seem to Averil. A guy she hardly knew, a guy with one of the lowliest jobs at her workplace, telling her the bosses at Hadley were wrong. What would Wesley of packing and despatch know about anything anyway? 'Look, for quite a long time I worked in the office of a legal firm. Nothing special, but I got to see stuff about cases just like this. Okay? I can tell it's not been done right. A friend of mine is a lawyer there. I'd just like him to have a chat with you.'

'You know what lawyers charge?' asked Averil.

'Yeah, I know, but it would be just a talk — no charge.'

'I've got a little saved.'

'No. My friend would just give an opinion. There's no promises. I'm not saying you'll be reinstated, just that things weren't done properly. Hadley is making an example of you, I reckon. They haven't been fair, and the law's clear on procedure concerning that.'

'Would I have to go to court?'

'I don't think so.'

'It's good of you to bother,' said Averil. 'I don't know anything about the law.'

'What do your family think?'

'My daughter lives in Dunedin.'

'She'd want you to put up a fight, wouldn't she?'

'She's angry. She knows I didn't do anything. Anyone could've done it. I touch a lot of packets every day I'm there. Sometimes the machine plays up.' As she talked, Averil tapped her fingers gently on the table. It was the only sign of any distress.

'Serge Foster. That's my friend's name. He'll give you a ring. He'll deal with Hadley on your behalf.'

Averil came to the door with him. 'People have been good coming round,' she said. 'Especially Bruce. Like you, he's not happy how things were done. Kind really.' She stood by the smiling gnome as Wesley walked to his car. A thin, nondescript woman in her late fifties: a faithful woman who couldn't understand why the world had turned on her.

Serge came to Wesley's flat eleven days later, his large Volvo saloon arousing some interest among the kids skateboarding along the block in the slanted sun of the summer evening. He'd seen Averil and made contact with Hadley Group. 'Wide open,' he said. 'They're wide open to challenge on half a dozen issues. I think they just wanted to make an example of someone. I don't think they bothered about getting much legal advice at all. Neither fair nor reasonable in process taken. A thin case for accusation in the first instance, and then no preliminary formal letter, no opportunity for Mrs Knowles to present rebuttal. Their mind had been made up from the start.'

'Who did you see?'

'A Dr Beardsley and a Keith McEwan. She's a head honcho, right?'

'Yes,' agreed Wesley. 'So what's happening?'

'Beardsley didn't concede anything at the meeting, but I think they've got the wind up now after taking my summary to their lawyers. Brian Saxton from Crombie and Neave rang me and was conciliatory. I think we'll get reinstatement at least, and I'll go for a few thousand for emotional suffering and harm to reputation. They don't want to go to court and that gives us the advantage.'

'Great. That's really good,' said Wesley. 'I couldn't put my head up officially. I appreciate this a lot.'

'No big deal. These outfits have to learn to play by the rules.' Serge sat relaxed in the small, warm room. He smiled at Wesley and let time go by before changing the subject. 'You okay?'

'Not too bad.'

'We don't see you enough. People would like to see you, you know. We're still your friends, whatever.'

'I'm just sulking,' said Wesley. He wasn't ready yet to go into the offices: meet people with a smile, both he and they aware he'd been cut down to size.

'Well, at least come round home more often. It'll save you cooking.'

'It's a real bugger letting people down,' said Wesley. 'I want to be with Debbie and Patrick, but when I go there's this bloody awful sense of how they must see me, well, Debbie anyway. I never know what Patrick's thinking — closed shop there.'

'He'll come around in time.'

'I've hurt them and they've withdrawn. No bloody wonder. I feel like an insurance agent, or a vacuum cleaner salesman, when I go now.'

'Things will get better,' said Serge, 'and anyway keep in touch. I'll let you know how I get on with Hadley. And we need to talk to people about you making an application to be readmitted to the bar. You should have only been suspended anyway. Crap decision.' He was a good friend to Wesley, yet even that friendship had altered because of what had happened, as if Wesley had suffered some disease and so made Serge more aware of his own social health.

It turned out much as Serge had predicted. Hadley Group management took legal advice and Averil was reinstated, given a formal apology and four thousand dollars. She wanted to give money to both Wesley and Serge, but neither would hear of it, so she baked a fruit cake for each of them and topped it with marzipan and a butter icing. On the day she returned to Hadley, her workmates clapped her in. Mrs Herangi and Ruben Best made sure they were there to show support.

Out of it all, of course, came knowledge of Wesley's background despite his having no formal part in the dispute. It wasn't rocket science. The Crombie and Neave lawyers ferreted out his connection with Serge Foster, and made Hadley aware of who he was, his initiative and also his disgrace, but having been once burnt, the management took no action. Their personal animosity wasn't a basis to move against him. Not immediately anyway.

Wesley decided to leave, however, and find another job where again he would have no more past than he wished to disclose. Maybe later he would apply to be reinstated as a lawyer, as Serge and others urged, but he rather fancied being a driver somewhere: a courier perhaps, or a rural mail delivery guy. At Hadley the drivers seemed cheerful and carefree, helping with the cartons at the loading bay and then driving off into the world while Wesley, Rhonda and Malohi had to go back to the artificial lighting of the factory and work of constant repetition. Maybe, even, he should show some entrepreneurial enterprise and buy a van, set up for himself. Patrick would like that, wouldn't he? Driving with his father after school, going to all sorts of places, the opportunity to talk and share.

Wesley wasn't sorry to have worked for the Hadley Group, though. The chance to see the place from the bottom up, rather than from the top down as had been his professional custom. The chance to be with Rhonda, Malohi, Bruce, Ruben Best, Mrs Herangi, Averil and all the others, to have no protection of status, no presumptive importance. The chance to do something for somebody else and feel good about it. A small enough redemption, but a beginning, and to get anywhere you have to have a beginning.

14.

Discovering Australia

It was always winter in Dunedin when I was a student there. Sure, I spent the vacations in the Maniototo working on my uncle's farm, but there must have been some summer weather in the city during term time. Any memory of it is crowded out by the recollection of the bone-chilling flats in North East Valley, my duffle coat spread over the heaped blankets of the bed, the slippery frost on my walk to the campus, scarf-wound fellow students with their chins down, puddle freeze stamped on to make spider web patterns. Maybe it's just that a micro ice age coincided with my time there.

The first flat was right under the hill. Jesus, it was cold. Neville had a kerosene heater in his room and Richie and I would often go there seeking warmth rather than companionship. We followed Neville to another flat the next year mainly because of that kerosene heater, and would have done so the next year again, but he hooked up with Alice, and the heater was lost to us. Actually, Neville was a humourless prick and it was only the heater that we missed. Alice was too good for him, but perhaps she feared the cold as well.

So it was Bevan with Richie and me in the third year. Bevan was a really okay guy, but my God that was a frigid little wooden place.

The cold air seemed to funnel down the valley right onto it and there was no insulation. Several times the pipes froze and the landlord got really snarky, as if it was our fault. There was a cramped open fire in the living room, but the heat just seemed to whoosh up the chimney, and we were always short of wood. All three of us tended to work in the varsity library during the day, whether we had lectures or not. It was warmer there. Richie reckoned the reason we didn't have many girls coming round was because of the cold, an explanation that disguised our personal deficiencies. I did hook up a bit with Joanne that year, though.

It was through the need for warmth that we got to know Mrs Ritter, who lived alone next door. Her house was one of the best in the street — two storeyed, brick and roughcast and with a roof of orange tiles. Even the garage was tiled, and there was a large concrete bird bath shaped like a seal balancing a bowl on its head. By the steps of the imposing and enclosed front door was a chestnut tree that had grown to block the sun and shed leaves profusely into the gutterings of nearby houses. As mere tenants we didn't care, but other neighbours had complained, and although she loved the tree, which had been planted by her dead husband's grandfather, Mrs Ritter said herself that it had outgrown the section and must come down.

One Tuesday Bevan noticed her talking by the tree with an arborist, his occupation clear from signage on the battered Commer truck. Bevan became excited about the possibility of cutting the tree down ourselves and keeping the wood. He called Richie and me to the kitchen window to watch them talking and gazing into the branches. I told him that even if Mrs Ritter agreed, green wood couldn't be used for ages, and Richie said that cutting down a big bugger like that in a suburban backyard was a job for experts. And how would we ever get rid of all the rubbish left? Bevan was set on it, though, and said you could hire all the equipment needed. 'I've done it,' he said, 'I've helped cut down trees. No problem for three fit guys like us.'

In the end we were persuaded, and the next day we went over and made a pitch to Mrs Ritter, whom we'd rarely seen that close up before. A tall, rather stately woman with grey, straight hair, dark brown stockings and a man's face. Bevan did most of the talking. We would fell the tree for $400 plus the wood from it, and we'd clear up afterwards. 'I've a quote from professional people,' she said, 'and taking down a big tree like this close to the house is quite a business. You can't just topple it, you know. You realise that? It could smash right onto the house.'

'You take it down from the top,' replied Bevan. 'Bit by bit, working down from the top. The trunk would be the very last part we touched.'

'You've done some of this sort of thing?' she asked.

'Yep,' said Bevan confidently, and as if in response to some unspoken further question he flexed his rugby shoulders and did a sort of soft shoe shuffle to demonstrate agility. Mrs Ritter grinned. Not many elderly and stately women do that, but Bevan was a bit of a specimen.

'What are you all studying?' she asked, in a complete change of subject. We told her. History, me, maths, Richie, and geology, Bevan. 'I have a degree in German,' she said, 'from the University of Bristol, not here. Do any of you speak German?' None of us scored with that. 'Pity. Never mind,' she said.

'Anyway,' said Richie, 'what do you reckon about us felling the tree?'

'Murder, that's what it is,' said Mrs Ritter. 'Murder, and I have the responsibility for it. I have to accept that. It's murder so that I can have sunshine at the front of my house. Murder as an indulgence.'

'But these chestnuts aren't even edible, are they — not that variety,' Bevan pointed out.

'Depends how hungry you are,' she said, 'and it's the life of the tree I'm talking about, not eating anything.' I could tell she was beginning to enjoy talking to us. She put a thin, dark-veined hand on the door frame, and smiled again. We never saw many people come to the house and maybe she was a lonely woman. For whatever reason, maybe pity, Mrs Ritter gave us the go-ahead to cut down the tree with just one change to Bevan's proposal — a trailer-load of firewood was to go to the Salvation Army.

Bevan was the boss of it all and Richie and I just hoped he knew what the hell he was doing. He hired a chainsaw, loppers and what he called tether ropes, which were used to direct the fall of main branches and also secure us when up the tree. He hired a trailer too, and asked Mrs Ritter if we could use her Honda with the towbar. We didn't admit it, but the whole event became a welcome diversion from study. I got the lowest grades of my uni career that year, and Richie flunked stage three calculus. Bevan of course got straight A's. He was an annoying bugger in the way that things came more easily for him than the rest of us.

The day we started was a big day and a hairy one at times. We wore gardening gloves, but didn't have helmets like tree people I've seen more recently. Things were less regulated then and we had little idea of what was required anyway. We secured a ladder that gave access to the body of the chestnut and Bevan was the first one up to show us how things should be done. He had the small chainsaw on a heavy sash so he could climb with his hands free. He went way up, way up until the branches were too slight to take his weight. I don't know how much experience he really had, but he always possessed an air of casual confidence that was reassuring.

It was as he said: a process of taking the tree down from the top. The outer spread cut to fall and be gathered below, the larger limbs roped, chainsawed in sections that had a dramatic fall through lower branches, wild noise and the flurry of debris. Mrs Ritter sat at the living room window and watched. Mid-morning and mid-afternoon she brought us coffee and Gingernuts. Five days it was before there was just a great stump higher than our heads and great rounds lying on the lawn with growth rings like ripples on the surface of a pond. Five days because we were amateurs and also had lectures and sports obligations, and it rained most of the third day and we couldn't work then. But that wasn't the end of it. There was the rubbishy stuff to cart away behind Mrs Ritter's red Honda, and all the big pieces to be sawn and split into firewood lengths.

Mrs Ritter would talk to us as we had coffee on the front steps, or in the large kitchen if it was especially cold outside. She was interested in our lives and talked quite freely about her own. You tend to forget, don't you, that old people who never seem to do anything, may once have had lives of some significance and venture. Mrs Ritter was born in the Shetland Islands, but said her family way back came from Norway. It was her husband who was a Ritter and a Kiwi. De Ritter was the name earlier, she said. There were quite a few Jewish de Ritters, and another possible derivation was the German name Von Richter. She liked the second possibility because of her familiarity with the country and its language.

Mrs Ritter must have been a bright kid to go from a bakery in the Shetland Islands to Bristol University, the BBC and media work in Berlin. And quite late in life marry a New Zealand entrepreneur, end up a childless widow in Dunedin with three provincial and impoverished students living next door and little other company. I liked talking to her and would stay doing so when Richie and Bevan had wandered off. She had a clear, confident voice, a large-featured face with heavy eyebrows that would become expressive when she was interested, and she would sweep her straight, grey hair back with thin-skinned, long-fingered hands. She enjoyed talking about her past, and the future for the three of us. She had tutored in the language department when she first came out and had begun a doctorate in German, but let it lapse when she became an essential part of her husband's electronic import business.

The last of the chestnut tree was the most valuable and the most difficult to deal with — the great lower trunk. No chainsaw would have been big enough to slice through the base in one go and we had to saw out chunks piece by piece. It made great firewood, though. It was a round cut from a main bough, however, that intrigued us. Bevan and I were carrying it over to be split with iron wedges when I noticed that it had a map of Australia on its cut surface, clear as anything. A growth ring, darker than the others and forming an outline as if drawn in purple ink. The western seaboard wasn't entirely true, but the eastern one was strikingly accurate. The bulge of New South Wales and Queensland, the York Peninsula and the Gulf of Carpentaria. We left it unsplit to show Mrs Ritter, and also two of Bevan's rugby mates who came around to collect him for a run. The father of one of them worked at the *Otago Daily Times* and appeared the next day with a camera. Once he'd convinced himself that we hadn't doctored it at all, he took a photo of the outline, and another of the three of us and Mrs Ritter standing behind the slab.

These days it would be all over Facebook, with umpteen thousand likes, but we were happy with the brief fame of appearing in the local paper. Some tree guy wrote in and said that the outline was so distinct from the other growth rings because that year would have been one of extreme weather, or because of one-off soil additives.

We kept that one circular section. All the rest became firewood, some of which we sold, but the map of Australia was hoisted onto the front verandah, rolled into the corner by our bikes to be away from rain. Interest in it persisted for a while: the proprietor of a coffee bar in St Andrew Street said he'd buy it and have a veneer taken off for a tabletop, but that came to nothing. And as it weathered and dried the outline became less definite and a fissure developed across

Queensland. Eventually it just sat there, in full view, but with no more attention paid to it than to the rusted downpipe, or the broken deck chair close by. I imagine some later tenants chopped it up and burnt it to stay alive.

My friendship with Mrs Ritter continued, however. Although her academic background was in languages, she'd lived through a lot of history and was interesting to talk to, about post-war Germany in particular. Also her house was well insulated and heated, which was another reason I quite liked the visits. Several times we sat in the front room with the chestnut tree no longer blocking the sun and had coffee brewed on the stove, a novelty for me. She told me about the black market in looted paintings as ex-Nazis tried to shed their links with the past, and the mass rape of German women by the advancing Russian army at the end of the war. She asked about the papers I was doing in colonial and political history. Mrs Ritter always wore those brown stockings and had multiple rings on her hands, with large coloured jewels rather than diamonds. She said she'd left most of her friends behind when she came from Europe and had found New Zealand a bland country. 'I wish my husband had lived longer,' she said. 'He was cruelly taken and I miss him a great deal. I'll show you his photograph some time.' She never did, though.

Joanne and I had stopped seeing much of each other by exam time. She'd got really involved in the drama society and I couldn't get excited about that. They all seemed to be very aware of themselves and a bit posey. I saw her several times with Maurice Tishop in tow, who was a wanker of the first order and even wore cravats to parties. So at the year's end Mrs Ritter was my most consistent female company, and that not often. A rather sad commentary on my social life. I did win a badminton title, however, and passed my units. Just the low grades.

I was head down at the end of the year, but not long after exams I went next door with the papers. I thought Mrs Ritter might be interested in them and my choices. She didn't answer the bell, yet the red Honda was in the garage. I noticed that its left back door was open, and when I was closer I saw Mrs Ritter lying on the old brown carpet that lined the garage floor, and with scattered groceries around her: lots of stuff including milk, broccoli and bananas, a shiny tin of golden syrup that had rolled to the entrance and was glistening in the drizzle there.

You don't register something like that all at once, and I seem to stand looking for too long before going in to her. I knew nothing about first aid, but I knelt down to check if she was breathing, and she wasn't. Her teeth were showing in a way that made her face unfamiliar and her legs with the dark stockings were drawn up somewhat as if in skipping. I knew Richie was home and I ran back to the house and shouted for him to ring the ambulance. It seemed a long time coming, but it wasn't. We didn't want to leave Mrs Ritter lying there alone and so we waited at the garage entrance with the tin of golden syrup and in the drifting rain. I said maybe we should put something over her, but Richie said she could still be alive.

The St John paramedics briefly tried resuscitation and then got her away in a hurry, but we knew she was dead. She might well have been there for hours. It was still quite early in the afternoon and later a policeman came to get a statement from me. A tall, older guy with a weary expression, and still just a constable despite his age. We stood in the doorway of Mrs Ritter's garage out of the drifting rain and he jotted down a couple of things as we talked. He wanted to know about her relatives, but I couldn't help there. He gathered up the groceries with due care, even getting down to look under the car, and then checked that both doors to the house were locked and the windows secure. He asked if I'd seen Mrs Ritter's car keys and said if they were still with her he would come back and lock the vehicle. 'Don't let it all upset you,' he said. 'She was an old lady after all.'

If the constable came back I didn't see him, and nobody else came about anything at all to do with Mrs Ritter. No relatives of her husband seeking more information, though we did see people on the premises at times afterwards. Nothing in the paper about it that I saw, not even a death notice, or something about the funeral. Only a few days later I left for the Maniototo to help my uncle for a bit before going home for Christmas. I was surprised how suddenly it had all ended — an acquaintance established over the chestnut tree and maintained by our occasional talks of history. All just cut off with no chance of a farewell, and things went on just the same. I hadn't lived long enough to know anything about death, but every time now I see a map of Australia, or a really big chestnut tree, I think of the three of us in that cold flat and old Mrs Ritter in the big house next door.

15.

Double
Bubble

He hadn't paid much attention to the news of the virus on the other side of the world. Wuhan might as well have been on Mars. Catastrophes in places like Guatemala, Uzbekistan and Somalia had never in the past had any effect on Colly's life in Tekapo. Even things that happened in cities just over Burkes Pass were a long way off for him. Not that he was a recluse, or a moron, just that his life had become comfortably localised. He had television, a laptop and a cell phone. He could pay his bills online without too much swearing at the perversity of information technology. All of that, though, was peripheral to how he lived his life and what was important in it.

So Colly was caught on the hop rather when Covid-19 swept in and lockdown at level four was announced. It had the unreality of a Hollywood dystopian movie. Despite the high-pitched clamour in the media, he still looked out from his small home to the narrow shingle beach and calm, blue water of the lake; the high arcing sky, the ducks and gulls, the far line of pine trees to his right. Colly's house was small, wooden, aged and well kept, with a sizable section around it that was also well kept. He was well kept himself, disliking anything slovenly, whether physical or intellectual. Most of his working life had been spent in specialised libraries such as the Hocken and the Alexander Turnbull, and he had a degree in history, which had inculcated in him a love of accuracy and verification, and also, it must be admitted, a certain reluctance to endorse change.

Librarians don't make a fortune, but Colly's property, originally purchased by his father as a bach when Tekapo was little more than a petrol stop, had a prime position and had become worth a good deal of money. Developers and real-estate agents contacted him often, and his two sons and their wives took pleasure in pacing out the boundaries and estimating their gain when the time of his sad passing came. I'm not suggesting in any way that because he was seventy-nine his susceptibility to the Covid virus was for them anything but a real concern.

Colly was a bubble of one. Several people in the township offered to shop for him and give any other help he needed, but he was used to being alone and not at all afraid of going to the supermarket. He was reasonably fit, liked to walk and that was allowed. No, the problem that Colly faced was that two days into lockdown he discovered an overseas backpacker in his shed. It was a large shed by the silver birch and close to the lakeside road. The Mazda was there and a stock of drying wood, but there was still room for a work bench, relegated household odds and ends, and apple boxes of tools that Colly rarely used because of his mechanical ineptitude.

Also there on that morning was a dark-haired man sitting in a sleeping bag with a pack beside him. Colly was starting on his early lake-front walk and the guy looked up at him, smiled apologetically, and in good English despite a noticeable accent, explained his presence. His name was Giulio Moretti and he was hitching and hiking his way around the country. He'd ended up in the half dark in Tekapo the night before with no one willing to take him further because of the lockdown, and not enough money for accommodation even if it had been available, so he'd walked into Colly's open shed and slept there. He was a young man and young Italian men are always presumed to be good looking. Giulio was an endorsement of the stereotype, despite Colly knowing from his own travels long ago that there were many young Italian men who would find no role in a Hollywood Mafioso saga.

Colly's first reaction was annoyance. The temerity of someone just coming onto his property and settling down for the night, but Giulio said that he hadn't wished to startle anyone in the house as darkness fell and had meant to be away again before being noticed. 'I will travel now,' he said. 'I'm sorry and thank you. How lovely is the view of the lake and mountains. I saw the small stone church too.' As he praised the surroundings, perhaps to mollify Colly, he rolled up his sleeping bag and put on his boots, having slept fully clothed.

'You probably won't get a ride today,' said Colly. 'Where are you heading?'

'Christchurch.'

'Hardly a soul will be on the road and they won't want to pick you up anyway. It's the personal distance thing and especially as you've come from overseas. You're not supposed to travel.'

'I've been here over seven weeks,' said Giulio. 'I've done my quarantine on the road before there was a quarantine.'

'Well, anyway it's too early to head off yet. You might as well come inside and have a coffee.' Colly's natural helpfulness returned as his surprise faded.

Giulio had more than coffee, of course. Young men are always hungry, and he had three pieces of toast and Marmite, commenting on the unusual taste, and two cold sausages left over from Colly's dinner the day before. Colly was interested to find out where he was from, where he'd been and how come his English was so good. 'My home is Gubbio,' Giulio told him. Colly had been to Italy, but the name Gubbio meant nothing to him. 'I went to the University of Perugia and studied French and English,' said Giulio. 'I had a municipal scholarship.'

'I've been to Perugia,' said Colly, pleased to make the connection. 'I went to Assisi from there: to the cathedral.'

'All tourists go to Assisi,' said Giulio, and yes, Colly remembered how crowded it was, overrun almost. How open in its pursuit of money from visitors. 'Come to Gubbio next time, or Lake Trasimeno. More natural and true.'

'I liked Perugia a lot,' said Colly. Perugia was big enough to swallow tourists and retain its own identity. He remembered the ancient high walls and narrow paved streets, and the lovely soft, green-leather coat his wife passed longingly several times, and that he bought for her the day before they left.

'An Etruscan city and now famous for higher learning. It's my home now,' Giulio told him.

'You've finished studying?'

'Yes, finished now.'

'So what will you do?'

'I hope to get work in the Ministry of Foreign Affairs, or Culture and Heritage.'

'Languages are valued, are they?' Colly asked.

'More and more,' said Giulio. 'But now there is this virus, so who knows.'

It was difficult, however, to feel the threat of Covid-19 as they sat together and looked out to the sunlight flexing on the blue lake and talked of who they were and where they came from and, in Giulio's case, where he wished to go. Together by chance, and at very different points of their lives. 'You haven't got much money, have you?' Colly said.

'Very little money.'

'How will you manage even if you get to Christchurch?'

'Something will work out. Maybe I will get in touch with the Italian embassy. Is there an embassy there?' He didn't seem worried. He sat relaxed in a kitchen chair as if he and Colly were old friends. He was young and had no fear of the world. He was young and all experience was welcome. His jeans were tight and accentuated the bulk of his suede walking boots. On a fine silver chain around his neck was hung a small medallion. Colly couldn't make out an image, or inscription, but thought it was probably of religious significance.

'I don't think there's an embassy there,' said Colly. 'Maybe, though.'

'There will be other travellers like me there. I can talk to my parents for money if things don't work out. Lots of people visiting must have gotten caught out by what's happened.'

'Did you have an American English tutor at the university?' asked Colly.

'A woman from Nebraska. Dr Rona Kinks. How did you know that?'

'No one says gotten here,' said Colly.

So they began to talk of language rather than illness, or Giulio's cheek in sleeping uninvited in the shed, and then they moved on to his experiences on the road, the encounters, the high points and the difficult times. Giulio did most of the talking. He didn't seem much interested in Colly's life, but then most of that was a long time ago and there wasn't much happening in the present: not on the surface anyway. Colly was interested in a view of his own country from a different perspective;

things observed and admired, or criticised, by someone who came from a foreign country. A young, active, intelligent person who sifted experience and made judgements with assurance, sometimes excessive assurance, but challenging and insightful nevertheless.

They were still talking when the sun was high, and they'd had coffee and biscuits, and Giulio had spent time on his phone. 'Why don't you stay here during level four?' Colly said. 'There'd just be the two of us. You'd have no hassles with authority then. It wouldn't cost you anything and in return you could give me a hand in painting the house. I've been meaning to do it. I've got the paint and everything. What do you reckon?'

'How very kind,' said Giulio, the words formal, but his manner relaxed.

'There's no urgency for you to go home?'

'Where could I be more safe than here?'

'Okay then,' said Colly. 'We'll give it a go and either of us can call it off if it's not working out.'

'Okay then,' Giulio repeated.

'A bubble of two.'

'Thank you.'

Colly made no special effort for lunch. His guest would see what sort of midday meal would be before them during the weeks of lockdown — tomatoes and lettuce from Colly's garden, cold sliced meat, bread and butter. No wine at lunch, but Giulio was to find that made a welcome appearance at the evening meal. Colly pointed out the spare bedroom, even laid a flannel and towel on the plain, clean bed he made up, as he had seen his wife do so often. 'It takes a while for the hot water to come through in the shower,' he said, 'but it does eventually.'

After lunch they walked around the outside of the weatherboard house and Colly talked about the work needed; not just the painting, but the stripping back and the replacement of a bargeboard under a drainage pipe. 'It's no good just slapping paint over everything,' he said. 'Half the job's in the preparation.' Giulio professed an enthusiasm that was not to last and said he'd do the ladder work so Colly wouldn't have to take any risk.

'Fair enough,' said Colly. 'Thankfully it's a single-storeyed place and there shouldn't be hassles. Everything seems to involve scaffolding these days, and that's a hell of an expense.'

Colly said they would start on the house the next day, and they walked together through the Tekapo township, swerving to pass occasional people, and being swerved themselves by a few others. It was strange to see the place so quiet, the main road almost deserted despite it being still the tourist season. They walked along the lakefront on their way home, collecting some chunks of driftwood to add to the pine and blue gum in the shed, and Colly told his bubble companion about the Scottish Highlander and sheep stealer whose name had been given to the Mackenzie Country.

When they returned, Giulio asked if he could use the washing machine, and he put all the clothes he had, except the shorts and singlet he wore, in one easy load, and sat on a kitchen chair and talked as Colly made the evening meal. Potatoes, kumara, broccoli and schnitzel. Colly ate a good deal of schnitzel because it was quick and easy to cook in the fry pan and had no bones. And they drank a Bannockburn riesling. There was no dessert, but Colly put out bought biscuits to have with their coffee. Giulio's appreciation was expressed only in the alacrity with which he consumed all he was offered and could otherwise reach without offence.

It was different having someone else in the house. They watched television together — pandemic news, naturally, but also a programme on the restoration of French châteaux. Giulio told entertaining stories concerning his family's history. The Morettis had been preeminent in Gubbio once, he said: had led forces for the Pope in long-ago wars. There were statues of his ancestors.

Colly went to bed after ten and found it odd to be lying there with lights still on in other rooms and someone else present, but it was comforting too, and he was able to see himself as a benefactor in a small way. He thought of his family, especially the grandchildren, and hoped it wouldn't be too long before he could see them, and because of his talk with Giulio he thought, too, of the European trip he and his wife had taken many years before — the one-armed, retired vicar on the Scandinavian bus tour, Delphi, a bad bout of diarrhoea in the Dordogne, the green-leather coat from Perugia that was the only one of his wife's garments still in the wardrobe.

They began the preparation for painting in the morning. The house wasn't markedly shabby, many people would have been content to leave it as it was for a few more years, but Colly was conscious of minor bubbling, disfigurement and discolouration, especially on the southern side close to the poplar trees, and the wooden sills had suffered in the hot sun. He told Giulio he wanted to pick them out in a bright blue, and the doors too. Colly scraped and sanded from the ground and Giulio used the ladder for the higher parts. He was a bit slapdash, but then it wasn't his place and he would be far away before any negligence was revealed. He was, however, quick, agile and strong, and Colly realised the job would be completed so much more rapidly with two of them. Before the afternoon coffee, Colly said that would do for the day, and they washed up. Colly's hands had abrasions from the sanding blocks, for his old skin lacked elasticity and tore like paper at any knock.

'We'll have a walk and also go to the supermarket,' he said, 'but you'll have to wait outside. It's one person per household.' He knew that with Giulio's appetite to consider he needed more supplies.

'It's an empty lake,' Giulio said as they walked its rough shore, and Colly could understand why he should think that, especially during lockdown, but Colly saw space rather than emptiness, and there are more things to observe in a scene than people, boats and buildings. There were the mountains to the west, the peaks of which caught drifts of cloud, there were seagulls without the sea, a straggle of clean and natural debris at the final reach of the small, lapping waves, a pair of Canada geese, male and female in different colours, as were the beach stones themselves in subtle ways. Giulio picked up stones, but not to peruse them, feel the smoothness, or notice variations in composition. He took them to throw into the lake as far as he could, or to skim them as young guys like to do. And Colly joined in, reclaiming briefly that boyish satisfaction.

Paige Merrill arrived at the shop entrance at almost the same time and was obviously surprised to see Colly had a companion. The Merrills were Colly's neighbours, and Paige, back from university, was serving out her lockdown there. Colly introduced her to Giulio and the three stood rather self-consciously and unnaturally apart to talk. Paige was studying law, not languages, but found Giulio interesting because he was unexpected in a predictable and diminished domain, because he was foreign and because he was a good-looking guy and she was a young woman. She herself was too thin for conventional beauty, but her skin and hair had the gloss of youth and she had a manner of friendly inquisitiveness.

The two remained talking for a while when Colly went inside and later he raised a hand to her as she stood by the milk, yoghurts and cheese. He could remember her as a skinny child calling to him from the fence top as he worked in his section. Balls, hoops and even clothes would appear on his lawn, and he would throw them back over the fence good-humouredly. Occasionally she had just climbed over and stood as he worked to tell him that she was soon to have a birthday party, or that her cousins were coming to visit. All of that was years ago and Paige now understood the adult protocols of private territory.

Giulio carried the groceries on the way back. He said the high rate of Covid-19 infection in Italy was because of the traditional lifestyle there and also because of economic hardship for many. 'Most people don't trust the authorities,' he said. 'It's always been the same. Official positions are seen firstly as a means for personal enrichment, and for protection from those who would impose consequences for that. It was the way in Caesar's time. Still is.'

'Are your family okay?' asked Colly.

'I think they are. My father has a bad leg, but apart from that his health is good. I don't check as often as I could because I haven't much left on my phone.'

'I could give you a few dollars.'

'How would we get it on?' said Giulio. 'How would we get it on with things as they are?'

'I don't know, but there must be ways.' But the Italian's thoughts had drifted elsewhere.

'This Paige we met, so she lives next door?' He pronounced the vowel in her name as in 'large'.

'Paige,' said Colly, with the correct pronunciation. 'Yes. The section behind. That family's been here a long time, like mine.'

'I like her,' said Giulio with natural openness.

They finished the preparation of the woodwork by lunchtime the next day and started painting in the afternoon. It was the more enjoyable task for Colly: easier on his hands and he had the satisfaction of seeing the new coat grow over the weatherboards of the house. Giulio did the ladder work, as he'd promised, wearing some of Colly's fishing clothes. Despite that detraction from his appearance, he was quickly down from the ladder and over to the fence when he saw Paige next door. They talked there for a long time and Colly had caught up on the lower painting by knock-off time, which was well before five. Colly said concentration and good workmanship couldn't be maintained by non-professionals over long periods. 'It's easy to become slapdash,' he told Giulio as an indirect admonition. And he also told him of the advantages of modern water-based paint when it came to getting the stuff off your skin. His bubble partner was more interested in the time he'd had with Paige, and in what Colly had planned for the evening meal.

'She is going to be lawyer,' Giulio said. 'Lawyers have money in their face. You don't see a poorly dressed lawyer.'

'I try to keep away from lawyers,' said Colly. 'I've got nothing against Paige, though. I read that there's more women at law school now than men, and that's probably a good thing. Rapacious, though, lawyers, which is tough for the rest of us. What's Italian for lawyer?'

'Avvocato,' said Giulio.

There was a strong nor'wester the next day and they didn't continue painting, because wind-blown stuff would stick to the side of the house. Even walking was unpleasant, and they stayed inside. Colly cleaned the shower, the kitchen, sent emails to his sons with news of his bubble companion and began reading a book on the history of the Otago settlement. Giulio watched television and in the afternoon rang Paige on the landline and talked openly and with considerable familiarity in Colly's presence.

'We should walk together by the lake tomorrow if the wind departs,' he said to her. 'In the morning I will get in touch.' Colly thought he should perhaps remind him of the lockdown rules, but decided against officiousness. What harm could there be in such a limited extension of contact in such a community, and what was his company in comparison with that of Paige?

Colly found himself rather less tolerant when it became apparent that Giulio's growing interest in his neighbour was accompanied by an inversely proportional enthusiasm for house painting. 'I don't wish to paint today,' he told Colly at breakfast the next morning. He was not at all hesitant in the statement. 'I hope that Paige will walk with me sometime and I don't want paint over me. There is a lot of time to come for painting.' The nor'wester was over and Giulio and Paige had their walk in the afternoon. Colly didn't expect an invitation to join them, and didn't receive one. Giulio had slicked down his thick, dark hair with water, and his olive skin and solidity were a contrast to Paige's slim paleness. Colly waved them off and then continued to work on the house. They were adults, he told himself, and would do as they wished.

In the bathroom that night he noticed that his electric razor case was not as he'd left it and there were a few dark hair cuttings in the razor head. Colly disliked the sort of intimacy represented by that, and also Giulio's failure to ask permission. 'The batteries have run out in mine,' said Giulio without contrition when Colly reprimanded him. 'I was going to ask you and forgot.'

'You need to get some tomorrow,' said Colly. 'Don't forget. It's not good using other people's bathroom stuff.'

'Yeah, yeah, okay.'

Perhaps to regain Colly's good opinion, Giulio was promptly onto the painting next morning, barely half an hour behind his host, and as they worked he talked entertainingly about casual jobs he'd had in his own country and since coming to New Zealand. He said he'd worked in a chocolate factory in Perugia and eaten so much of the product that he'd gone right off it: the city was famous for its chocolate, he claimed. Vineyards in Umbria too, including Cantine Giorgio Lungarotti, where he had learnt to hand pick grapes and play the card game briscola. He said once he went into the mountains and saw wolves there. Mid-afternoon he washed and changed his clothes, told Colly he'd arranged a walk with Paige.

'Get some batteries,' Colly told him.

'No money,' he said cheerfully, and so Colly got his wallet and gave him fifty dollars. He was helping on the house after all.

'Maybe tomorrow we will finish the white, I think,' Giulio said. 'Then there will be just the blue for the doors and windows.'

'And the bargeboards,' said Colly.

The walk with Paige must have gone well, because that night when in bed Colly heard her being let into the house by Giulio, and afterwards their soft voices from the spare room. Colly wondered if he should do something about it: not burst in on them and demand her expulsion, but talk to Giulio in the morning, check with Gerald and Wendy Merrill, have a word with Paige herself perhaps, but he decided that surely there was no victim and no crime, just human nature playing out. People made their choices and would live with the consequences. There were no unruly sounds of lovemaking, or doors slammed, and Colly drifted into sleep.

Neither he nor Giulio said anything of the visit the next morning. Giulio seemed no more in love with life than before — less in fact. He was slow to go to the ladder and complained that the paint was drying the skin of his hands unnaturally. Hardly anyone was dying in this country, he said, not compared with his own and others, and he was sick of level-four lockdown. 'Why should these things apply to me,' he said, 'when I am not a citizen of the country?'

'When in Rome do as—'

'Very clever,' cut in Giulio.

'We're lucky here and I'm not moaning,' said Colly.

'I would like to be in your Christchurch,' said Giulio.

'The rules are the same.'

Paige and Giulio didn't walk together that afternoon, and if she came to his room in the night, Colly heard nothing. Giulio had become less inclined to talk, shared fewer of his experiences and expectations. There were no more stories of popes and war and wolves. Colly supposed he'd become bored: what young guy wouldn't, cooped up by accident with an old codger who'd spent almost all of his career buried in specialist libraries. Giulio's view of life was one focused on the future, Colly's was largely concerned with the past, and so they tended to look in different directions.

The next morning was very still and blue, just as Colly liked his world, and he decided on an early walk before continuing with work on the house. Giulio preferred not to go, giving no particular reason. He came from the kitchen, though, with his coffee mug in hand, and watched Colly making his way to the lake, lifted a hand in salutation when Colly looked back before disappearing from view. The lake was calm, with just a soft susurration from the water's edge. Without Giulio as example, he didn't throw, or skim, any stones, but he did keep an eye out for firewood, as was his habit. Coming back, he met the Merrills and stood the required two metres away to talk with them a while. Giulio was the main topic, for although they'd never met him, they knew of him from Paige. Colly mentioned his help with the house painting, his random arrival, the considerable appetite, but said nothing of Paige's visit in the night, for he thought they would be unaware of that.

'It's very kind of you,' said Wendy. 'What's happening must be doubly worrying for someone away from family and in a foreign country.'

'He's earning his keep,' said Colly, 'and he's company too.'

'It's kind of you all the same,' she said.

Giulio wasn't about when Colly got back. Colly thought he might have been with Paige, but when he went into the living room he saw his wallet open on the low, polished table and a note beside it. 'Thank you for everything. I have taken a loan and left something in return. In bocca al lupo.' Colly assumed the Italian phrase was an expression of goodwill: he was more sure of what had been taken and what gifted. Over three hundred dollars gone, all he had in notes, but his visa card remained, and beside the worn, leather wallet was the silver chain with the ornament that Giulio had worn around his neck. Nothing else of his remained in the house, but much later in the day Colly found he had also taken a sultana loaf and a tin of baked beans, maybe more. He'd be on the road to Burkes Pass, Colly thought, flagging down some essential services vehicle and spinning a line about how he came to be there. He'd be looking for places to doss down, as he had in Colly's shed: nobody to please but himself, nobody he need return to, nothing for which he need account.

It wasn't how Colly had expected them to part, although he knew what comradeship they'd had was wearing thin. The monetary loss didn't worry him over much, but he regretted the manner of it. There was the necklace, however, and what else had Giulio to offer? He could just have shot through without leaving even that. Colly looked closely at the small medallion on the chain: the image it bore was worn, but looked like a porpoise, or a dolphin. Maybe it was a cheap, mass-produced thing, maybe it had value and a story to tell of Giulio. Maybe.

As he painted in the still, warm morning, Colly found he missed the young Italian, even though no intense bond had been forged, and differences had been increasingly apparent. He missed that casual courage in the face of life the young possess, the risk and high endeavour that he could only dimly recall in himself. He wished Giulio no harm — good fortune even.

When Colly was about to knock off for lunch, he heard Paige calling from the fence, and he walked through his garden to where she waited. Her long blonde hair looked freshly brushed: it formed a frame for her narrow, small-featured face.

'I just wondered if Giulio was about,' she said, and smiled.

'He's gone,' said Colly.

'Gone for good?'

'Yes.'

'Well, he never said anything to me, and he shouldn't be heading off during level four, should he?'

'Not really,' said Colly, 'but he was getting restless, I think.'

'What an odd thing, though, to just go off like that.'

'Maybe he was worried about his folks and wanted to try to get back home.'

'He didn't have any folks, no mum or dad anyway.'

'He told me he did and said he was in touch.'

'He told me they were dead,' Paige said. 'Told me he had nobody close to him over there. I don't know what to believe now.'

She didn't look especially stricken: puzzled, disappointed perhaps. Colly made a quick decision. 'He left something for you,' he said. 'Wait here a minute and I'll get it.' He went back to the house and took the silver chain, returned to the fence where she waited. 'It's for you,' he told her. She held it heaped in the palm of her hand for a moment, the medallion uppermost, and then strung it out from end to end in front of her and studied it.

'What a strange guy,' she said, as if it was Giulio himself held up before her. 'I liked him, but he thought we should get it all on after just a few days and that's not me.'

'Well, he liked you. He didn't have much else except the chain, I guess, and he wanted you to have it.' Maybe he did, thought Colly, perhaps he knew that it would be passed to Paige, for what use did Colly have for a silver chain to wear around his neck? 'It'll be a reminder of him.' He said nothing of the note that had no mention of her, didn't tell her that he'd had no warning of Giulio's leaving, no face-to-face farewell.

'But he's just shot through. Rude really, and those lies about his family. Maybe he's got problems despite his confidence.'

'You'll have his cell phone number, though,' said Colly.

'No, we never used it,' she said, 'but if he gets in touch with you, tell him from me he's a rude bugger, but thanks for the necklace.'

'Okay.'

Colly never heard from Giulio and didn't expect he would. He hadn't got to know him well and wondered how much of what he'd been told was untrue. A young guy on the road in a foreign country pretty much makes up his life from day to day, and enjoys the freedom as a consequence of that. All sorts of lives are possible when you are young and about the world, and Colly, even Paige, would soon for Giulio be merely ancillary figures in his own history.

16.

Other People

Only time grants a full compass of understanding, for the old know what it is to be young, but the young have no experience of age. And are in no hurry to acquire it, Alistair was tempted to add to what he'd written, but that didn't fit with the serious intent of his paper, 'Trends Towards Pessimism in the Later Fiction of Jean-Paul Sartre and Simone de Beauvoir', so he just paused in his composition and gazed beyond the screen of his computer to the view of a faculty carpark, a grassy mound with two cherry trees and the rear end of the music and art history block. The late afternoon sun was lengthening the shadows of the campus and the passing students moved languidly in the heat. A tall girl in pale shorts carried a yellow balloon on a string, and nobody took any notice of her. No sooner had she disappeared than another girl, slim and Asian, came over the cherry tree mound with a white balloon, and nobody took notice of her either.

Enough of pessimism for the day. His mood was contrary to the topic. He could go to the staffroom and have tea, or coffee, but it was a drab place. He could cover the greater distance to the staff club and have beer, or wine, but he'd been there for a lengthy lunch and didn't want to appear as one of those blowsy academics with no place more enlightening to spend an afternoon, no studious preoccupation that guaranteed advancement. And there wasn't time. Michelle Cole was coming at five for a preliminary discussion concerning her thesis on Robin Hyde. Michelle was a pleasant and able student, but Alistair was ambivalent concerning his appointment as supervisor because of his limited knowledge of her subject. He had read of Hyde's life, had a cursory acquaintance with the novels and poetry, but was ignorant concerning the bulk of her journalism. The supervision of the thesis had been foisted on him by Professor Cedric Ransumeen, head of English and media studies.

He would visit his fellow lecturer in office B223, Alistair decided. Michael was both friend and rival, and the first relationship was strong enough to permit relaxed acceptance of the second. Before leaving his room, Alistair wrote on the small whiteboard fixed on the corridor wall next to his office door. Its purpose was to relay messages, but every few days he also put a quotation on it, hoping to arouse student interest. 'In heaven, all the interesting people are missing,' he wrote. He never included an attribution, hoping to encourage students to find the source for themselves and so have their intellectual curiosity aroused. A pity Google made it so easy.

On his way to B223, Alistair debated again with himself concerning the best home for his essay. He had reduced the choice after much deliberation to three — the *New England Journal of Literature*, the *Literary Review Quarterly* and *Hathaway Magazine*. Simultaneous submissions were not permitted, and the choice for Alistair came down to what he gave greater weight to: the likelihood of acceptance, or the prestige if successful. He'd had a 5200-word piece on grammatical shifts in Australasian fiction in *Hathaway Magazine* the year before, and a friendly exchange with the editor, but both the other periodicals had a larger circulation and greater mana in the academic world. Michael had appeared in the *Review*, and Ransumeen had featured there and also the *New England Journal*. Of course Ransumeen was ubiquitous in terms of publishing, found in everything — except *Hathaway*, of which he seemed unaware.

Dr Michael Seedon, B223. Alistair gave three staccato knocks, paused, then one more. It was the secret code between them, for there were occasions when they wanted to seem absent to all but themselves.

'Yes,' came from within. Michael was sitting by the window with his shoes and socks off. He was cutting his toenails with large, orange-handled paper scissors. Well, attempting the task. 'How are you feeling?' he said. He gestured with the scissors without waiting for reply. 'Useless,' he said of them. 'The podiatrist told me that fingernails grow three times faster than toenails. Did you know that?'

'No.'

'An evolutionary thing. Australopithecus's toenails would have grown equally with his fingernails, I expect. I've got this fungal infection on one big toe. It's no big deal, but not easy to get rid of. The chemist showed me an elfin-sized bottle that cost $72, and I told her what to do with it. I'm trying the natural antiseptic property of sunlight.'

'Probably isn't effective through a window.'

'Really?'

'Well, I know that the part of the ultra-violet spectrum that's needed to absorb vitamin D is blocked by glass, so maybe other benefits are too.'

'Bugger,' said Michael, without being much concerned.

Alistair sat in the other chair. The room was the same size as his own, but seemed more confined because Michael had an extra bookcase stuffed with volumes: some jammed on their sides above others upright, some teetering on the top shelf. The view was more attractive, though. A walk path, a plot of rampant blue-flowered agapanthus, the broad steps to the terrace of the main library. 'I'm taking a break from existentialism,' said Alistair.

'How's it going? Nearly finished?'

'No. Nowhere near. I've got bogged down.' It wasn't entirely true. The essay was well through, but he didn't wish to arouse his friend's competitive instinct.

Michael flipped the scissors back into the drawer impatiently and began to put his socks on. 'I wrote a poem,' he said. 'Just before you came I wrote a poem. It took me four and a half minutes, which must be the fastest poem I've done.'

'About what?'

'Balloons. A woman came past the library with a yellow balloon on a string, and the poem came just as easily and just as unexpected. I saw a guy as well later with a balloon.'

'I saw someone too,' said Alistair. 'Maybe there was something on at the Students' Association. Balloons remind me of birthday parties. Is that what you wrote about?'

'No. My poem's about the imprisonment of breath.'

'Oh, okay.' Alistair didn't write poetry because too many people did, and also it paid so poorly. Nevertheless he was a little jealous of Michael's collection, *Paces Towards the Light*. Any publication added lustre to one's CV.

They sat for a time without further talk, lulled by the full and angled summer sun and at ease with each other, then Michael did up his shoelaces and stood up. 'I have to go down to the assignment box,' he said. 'Lunchtime today was the deadline for the level three people to hand in their pieces on post-modernism. So it's a marking weekend for me. Mind you, a bunch of them asked for extensions. I must be getting soft. I need to crack down. Most of them have no good reason: they're just bloody slack.'

'Tell me about it.'

They went down together, taking the stairs, as was their habit. The lift was irritatingly slow and imprisoned occupants from time to time quite randomly. A visiting professor from Alabama had been stuck between floors for hours and forced to pee into his satchel. On his return to the States he published a nebulously located poem in the *Montgomery Gazette* entitled 'Southern Purgatory'.

Alistair didn't accompany Michael all the way. On level one they saw Professor Ransumeen entering his office. 'I think I'll talk to him,' said Alistair. 'Have another go at getting out of supervising Michelle Cole's thesis.'

'Good luck with that,' was his colleague's response. 'Catch you later maybe.'

There was, of course, no good luck with that. Ransumeen was happy enough to give Alistair some time, but not disposed to relieve him of any responsibility. 'Someone has to do it,' he said. 'We've all got a full quiver.' Alistair suggested that a woman staff member was perhaps more appropriate, but was rebuked for reverse sexism. The professor then lunged across his desk, and Alistair put his hands up instinctively as protection, but Ransumeen's target was a blowfly on the side window. He squashed it on the pane with the flat of his hand and rejoiced in his victory. 'Yes!' he exclaimed. 'I just cannot abide blowflies. It's impossible to work with the buzzing of them and they're filthy creatures. Just the pitch of their noise is anathema. I could scream.' He wiped his hand casually on a tissue, but left the corpse of the fly on the window adhered by its own yellow guts. 'Where were we?' he said.

'The Robin Hyde thesis.'

'Miss Cole's a scholar. There'll be nothing for you to do except make a few structural suggestions. No awkwardness in regard to its academic acceptability. None at all.'

'It's more my own suitability,' said Alistair. 'There's a heap of journalism involved. I haven't the time to get on top of it.'

'That's her job. Yours is to direct, encourage and evaluate. Besides, she's happy with you. When I suggested you she was okay with it.'

It was no use persisting: to do so would only convince Ransumeen that he was a slacker. The HOD had peculiarities enough, but wasn't a lazy man. Yes, he wore the same clothes for many days on end, swam naked in the winter ocean at night, stalked blowflies and championed the poetry of D'Arcy Cresswell. But isn't eccentricity often the mark of the original mind? Ransumeen also lectured often and well, ran an efficient department and was objective in his treatment of staff. Even the shapely Dr Lucy Millrose was given her share of semester courses, and chided on occasion for her tardiness in returning assignments. Most nights the professor's office window was lit when its fellows were darkly opaque, and no one could recall a sick day.

After a pause that marked his victory, Ransumeen changed the subject. 'In love, one and one are one,' he said with significant emphasis. 'How is literary pessimism coming along?' Alistair recognised the Sartre quotation, but didn't think it one of his best.

'Slow progress, I'm afraid. It's getting the time, isn't it.'

'Quite. One thing I've noticed over the last few years is an increasing editorial sensitivity to length. Anything much over 5000 words has become difficult to place. It's a bit dispiriting. If the academic journals don't provide space for in-depth scholarship then we're on the slippery slope.'

'I have been wondering where best to submit it,' said Alistair.

'I often send a note of intent to several editors,' said the professor. 'From the response I can gauge interest, which helps. Sometimes I've had invitations to submit, even pieces commissioned. There's an element of luck: the editorial shaping of an issue, a recent symposium, a notable death.'

'I have thought of the *New England Journal*,' Alistair said, but Ransumeen was distracted, baring his teeth at a blowfly bumbling close to his open door, and taking up a folder of maintenance returns in readiness for a swipe.

'Thought which, what?' he said after the fly had swerved away.

'The *New England Journal*. I thought maybe that.'

'I've had work there from time to time,' said Ransumeen complacently. 'The present editor has a discerning judgement.' Ransumeen still had the folder in his hand and he'd forgotten why. 'Trivia, trivia,' he said. 'I must get these returns done', and he began to scrutinise the top one.

'Well, thank you. I'll be off to talk with Ms Cole about her thesis.'

'Mmm?' said Ransumeen. Already his focus was turning to administration, but he raised his head to smile absently. His round face was pale and his glasses caught the light. It was an amiable enough countenance, despite the mismatched socks visible beneath the desk. Alistair tried to imagine him standing naked in the night surf, as Michael claimed to have witnessed.

'I'm off then.'

'Thank you, Alistair.' The professor gave considerable emphasis to the Christian name, as if pleased to be able to bring it to mind.

Michelle Cole was punctual, naturally, and despite never having done Alistair's level two course, she recognised the whiteboard quote. She was that sort of attractive, attentive, talented young woman that Alistair had found such dispiriting competition when a student himself. Straight A women students with a non-assertive serenity that cloaked steely resolve. She thanked him for agreeing to be her supervisor and gave him a five-page provisional 'structure' that she planned to follow.

'Tell me first why you chose Robin Hyde,' Alistair said. When he had her motivation he would have the key. He thought Hyde a rather sad person and hoped Michelle could prove her otherwise. He hoped that not too much of his time would be taken up over the coming months with a dead Kiwi writer who didn't appeal to him, despite her talent. Michelle was a pleasant intermediary, though. He admitted that. He liked her fitting, pink top and her loose, dark hair. He liked best her intelligence and contained enthusiasm. He could well learn from her, but said nothing of that. As she talked, Alistair visualised the interior of his refrigerator and wondered what was there that would make a meal. He was still unaccustomed to his domestic responsibilities, having been separated from his wife for less than four months. And not just separated, but abandoned by a partner whom he'd thought as content with him as he'd been with her. Enough of that. 'The poetry doesn't do much for me. I find the prose much stronger,' he said. 'What about you?'

'The more you know about her life, the more the poetry comes to mean. Each unlocks the other I find, although only the fiction is much read now.'

'A sad life, don't you think? Not an easy time to be a woman writer here. If she'd been born thirty years later maybe things would have been easier.'

'Probably,' said Michelle, 'but her personality would be the same. An impulsive, unsettled woman in many ways.' Alistair was impressed by the objectivity Michelle displayed, despite her admiration for the writer. Surely the thesis would be fine, the sessions straightforward and not demanding much more of him other than encouragement. Sausages: he knew he had sausages. He liked sausages, not the cheap, homogenised, supermarket crap, but butcher's sausages that showed proof of real meat by exuding fat when cooked. Snarlers, he and his flatmates used to call them. How many hundreds of them they must have eaten over the student years together, and he'd never tired of them. Catherine had preferred superior meats, but since her departure he'd come back to sausages. If you did a few at a time, those left over could be used in a sandwich the next day. He had potatoes too, beneath the sink, and a few carrots sweating in the fridge tray despite the chill. A clean-up was overdue in there.

'How important do you find the Chinese experience?' he asked. 'She said she wished she could be reincarnated as a Chinese woman, didn't she?' The sun was low in the west and lit his office with a heavy glow. He reminded himself to update his essay onto a memory stick to take home, so that he could continue working on it in the evening. He needed to get more done; to apply himself, work harder. Michael had his poetry collection published, but still had placed more academic pieces during the year. Ransumeen noticed such things. At staff meetings he made sure to mention any scholarly success from within the department. Our flags of achievement, our individual and collective laurels, he called them. Alistair needed more such distinctions, and the supervision of theses didn't provide them. Yes, sausages and a potato and carrot mash would set him up for a night with the pessimistic existentialists. He smiled at Michelle. Everything she said had the stamp of a perceptive intelligence, and soon they would finish talking of Robin Hyde, and Michelle would go. He wished the writer's life hadn't been so sad.

'Frederick de Mulford Hyde, the fighter pilot. Such a Monty Python name it's hard to believe he really existed. And he proved all Mr Hyde and no Dr Jekyll, didn't he. If he hadn't met her and got her pregnant, he'd be just another in oblivion.'

'Now he'll always exist as a tag in her story,' said Michelle.

'Those people are fascinating. Saved from the general oblivion just because they had a random walk-on part in the life of someone who mattered.'

'Like the workman Charles Langridge, who helped break into Sylvia Plath's apartment after her suicide,' Michelle said. 'There are interesting parallels, I think, between Hyde and Plath.' And Alistair encouraged her to explore them, went with her to the door, said he was looking forward to the next meeting, and that he had confidence in the general direction she was taking.

'Do you know if there was anything special on today?' he asked. 'I saw people with balloons earlier.'

'It's Te Reo Awareness Day. They had it in the theatre.'

'Of course. I'd forgotten. I should've gone over.'

'Quite a lot of staff were there,' said Michelle without accusation. 'The balloons had Māori words.'

'That explains it.' He watched her go blithely down the corridor. He should have remembered Te Reo Day. He was a supporter in principle and, more significantly, Ransumeen would have been there and noted who was present from the department. How was it possible a real person called Frederick de Mulford Hyde had existed? And a fighter pilot, for Christ's sake!

Pessimism didn't go well for Alistair over subsequent days. Not for a lack of instances in the writing of either Beauvoir, or Sartre, but because he couldn't decide on his unifying theme. Whether to seek the origins within the philosophic parameters of existentialism itself, or the more specific issues of the nature of the writers' personalities, relationship and the passage of time.

And fellow senior lecturer Amanda Forsyte received an award for best teacher in the department. The selection was by the students, but Ransumeen had heartily endorsed it at the staff meeting and foreseen a bright academic career for her. Alistair had no reason to expect the award himself, but nevertheless was privately aggrieved. Amanda was younger, relatively new to the university and had the advantage of lecturing in media studies, which the students favoured because of a reduced reading requirement. Michael and Alistair congratulated their colleague in public, but privately agreed she lacked a certain academic rigour.

'Anxiety is the dizziness of freedom.' Alistair wrote on his office whiteboard before leaving for a Tuesday brunch at the Ransumeens. Cedric and Elaine hosted such a meal for the department twice a year at their villa in an inner suburb. A large, rambling, wooden house containing many original gouache and oil paintings that indicated considerable artistic discernment in at least one of the marriage partners. Section maintenance, however, was of little importance to either. Each time Alistair came to the place he found the roughly mown lawn significantly reduced because of the encroachment of rampant verdancy that had once been garden, but overrun by gangster convolvulus, twitch and tree suckers. In time the lawn might be engulfed completely and nature rule it all. Maybe in time the house itself would be assaulted.

For the brunch, trestle tables had been set up on the verandah and the hosts carried out trays of food for their guests. Alistair knew from past experience that almost all of it would be vegetarian, and cold to boot. Carrot and celery sticks, corn balls, diced cucumber with guacamole, tofu skewers, cauliflower with lemon and garlic sauce, stuffed mushrooms, rustic Tuscan bruschetta, pygmy tomatoes. Perhaps the Ransumeens considered their guests to be goats that, after clearing the trestle tables, would move on to reducing the neglected profusion of the section. Even as Elaine offered him a tomato and cheese wafer, Alistair felt a Palaeolithic urge to knock the platter from her hands and demand a well-fried steak, battered cod, at least a thick slice of ham from the bone. But instead he took one for politeness' sake and carried it with him to the steps where Reg and Michael sat talking by themselves in the sun. Alistair and Michael liked Reg, whose qualifications for teaching media studies were practical rather than academic. He'd been a script editor, director of short films and most recently employed by the Film Commission. Before any of those occupations he'd been a primary school teacher in rural Poverty Bay. Reg was the oldest member of the department and his completely bald cranium and trim, white beard made him appear even more venerable. 'How are you feeling?' Reg enquired.

Alistair was pleased to find that the intent of their earnest conversation was to decide the best Western film of all time. They had before his arrival agreed, after fierce debate, on two final contenders — *High Noon* and *Shane*. 'What do you think?' Reg asked him.

'Yes to your finalists,' said Alistair. 'And I'd have to go for the Gary Cooper, although it's a close thing. It's the doubt and fear behind the courage that's the subtlety so often lacking in Westerns.' He showed his own resolve by flicking the tomato and cheese wafer at the lawn — unsuccessfully, for it fell with a wet slap onto the step below his own.

'John Wayne complained he wasn't a proper hero,' said Reg.

'None of Wayne's own roles were as nuanced. Just gung-ho stereotypes.' Alistair remembered the last time he'd seen the film. A crummy flat in Sydenham and a gale outside that made the TV aerial rattle so much he could hardly hear Cooper's laconic delivery. Wet hail striking the window in the dark and sliding down the glass. Whenever he thought of the film later, that's the weather the actors had — wind and driving hail they had to speak against rather than their arid environment on film.

Michael was talking of the church scene when Elaine appeared, a meatless platter in each hand. Reg was the only one to take advantage of her offer. 'You're not talking shop, I hope,' she said. 'I can never get Cedric to talk about anything except his work, or bugs.' Nor could anyone else, of course.

'Films,' said Michael. 'We were talking Hollywood.' But Mrs Ransumeen had spotted the cast-off wafer.

'I see there's been a little accident.'

'Sorry about that,' said Alistair humbly. Heroism is fine in dusty Hadleyville's high noon, but in modern life, circumspection rather than defiance is sometimes called for, yet he was aware of Michael's slight, derisive smile.

'Anyway,' said Elaine, 'do come and help yourself to anything. The punch is a new recipe that Amanda has given me. It's become popular again in England,' she said, 'and among the young set too.' Only Elaine would talk of the young set, or any set. Alistair couldn't remember anyone else ever using it in conversation. Surely it belonged in an Oscar Wilde play.

What was he doing there at all? Apart from ingratiating himself with the professor, he saw little advantage, or pleasure, in it. He could be restoring order in his own section rather than observing the victory of riotous regeneration in the Ransumeens'. He could be reading Proust, even marking essays on the rise of a new West in American literature. He could be completing his piece on existentialist pessimism for the *New England Journal* or *Review Quarterly*. He could be eating sweet and sour pork at the Golden Dragon restaurant instead of enduring the baleful regard of raw vegetables.

And being at the professor's home reminded him of Catherine, who had been a special favourite with Elaine Ransumeen. Both of them had an enthusiasm for Kiwi art in general and Rita Angus in particular. Elaine wasn't so insensitive as to ask after his wife, but Alistair knew she and Catherine kept in touch, and sometimes he saw in her expression as she regarded him a mixture of pity and knowing accusation. He recognised it again as she turned with platters in hand, paused, glanced at him before moving back towards a group centred on her husband and Amanda Forsyte. Reg began to extol the element of vulnerability in the screen character presentation of both Alan Ladd and Gary Cooper, but Alistair had become preoccupied with his own life and moved after Elaine Ransumeen to make apology for an early departure. He left the entire gathering browsing contentedly on the vegetarian smorgasbord, and as he made his way to his car he decided on the new quote for his whiteboard. 'To be happy, we must not be too concerned with others.'

'How're you feeling?' asked his neighbour when Alistair had reached home and was coming from his garage. Vincent owned a plumbing business and regularly beat Alistair in their squash games without displaying any triumphalism. His wife was also a good sort.

'Fine,' said Alistair, but didn't stop to talk.

'Six-thirty tomorrow as usual?'

'Fine,' said Alistair. He could feel the raw resistance of Elaine Ransumeen's vegetables in his gut. He recalled reading that an elephant has to eat over 250 kilograms of vegetation every day and forage almost non-stop because of the low nutritional value of its diet.

It was odd the things he noticed now that he was living alone, but unaccustomed to it. One of his observations was that his home no longer altered in his absence. The unmade bed retained an exact topography, the *Listener* magazine remained open and face down on the kitchen island, and the half-eaten piece of morning toast that he'd left and forgotten on the hall table on his way to the lavatory had taken permanent residence there. Nothing had changed in anticipation of his return and as any welcome to him. Even a large bluebottle blowfly that he had noticed in the morning was still traipsing the window above the sink in bewildered frustration, but safe at least from Professor Ransumeen's implacable butchery.

Alistair decided he would have a beer and then go to his study and work on his article. With no commitment to a partner, or to children, he was free to concentrate on his academic career. It would blossom surely. He saw himself addressing the plenary sessions of London and Berlin symposia, and receiving offers of professorships at United States universities of considerable standing and abundant endowment. He saw himself in the relaxed company of female colleagues who were equally committed to academic excellence, but casually generous with sexual favours in the manner portrayed on American television programmes.

In his study he sat watching the neighbours' cat that was licking its bum by the letterbox, quite without any consideration for onlookers. Alistair had his essay up on the screen, but found concentration difficult. During the day he always worked better in his university room. He supposed that cats had no existentialist dilemma: that for them 'Life is not a problem to be solved, but a reality to be experienced'. That could be next for the whiteboard he decided. And he must remember to ring Elaine Ransumeen and thank her for the day's hospitality. Catherine was very good about such things and he didn't want to seem a boor in comparison. He would choose a platter for fulsome praise that had at least the pretence of animal protein in its make-up. A candidate didn't come to mind.

On Tuesday morning Michelle came again to his office to discuss her thesis. Alistair was both impressed and depressed as a consequence. Impressed by the progress she'd made, depressed by the comparison with the snail's pace of his own essay. But then she had no marking, no lecturing, to distract her. Michelle had made contact with members of Hyde's family and been well received. There was the likelihood of some personal letters hitherto unavailable. He was pleased for her and said so, but when she left, enthusiasm went with her, and he remained with glumness gathering about him. Did Michelle have a boyfriend? Certainly not one in evidence, or that she spoke about. Alistair knew several attractive women who appeared to have no need of sex, and unencumbered by such urge achieved all the more. It wasn't a level playing field really.

Amanda was like that too, he decided, when at the staff meeting in the afternoon. Lots of male friends and colleagues with whom she fraternised with friendly off-handedness, but never permitted to distract her from academic ambition. She was a slight woman. Red hair, pale skin and an oval face of porcelain calm, the features reduced, almost as if painted on: a face essentially feminine. She was explaining the online tutorial program that she'd initiated while at the University of Canberra and Professor Ransumeen was impressed. Alistair found it difficult to concentrate because it was hot and crowded in the small common room. He'd been the last to arrive and so had to take one of the uncomfortable low chairs close to the bench, his head level with the gaggle of assorted and stained mugs. And Dr Hugh Neilsen beside him, who always breathed noisily through his mouth, and when sitting slipped off his left shoe to lessen the discomfort of an ingrown toenail. Foot problems were rampant within the faculty. Hugh had the physique of a truck driver and was a world authority on the ethereal poetry of Christina Rossetti.

'Let's by all means embrace the advantages of information tech-nology,' said Ransumeen warmly. 'Perhaps, Amanda, you might find time to organise a seminar for us on the program you're familiar with.' Serve her right, thought Alistair, but she seemed not at all loath. No doubt the initiative would advance her further in the professor's good opinion. Discussion moved on to the next agenda point — the expenditure on A4 paper purchased for the photocopy room. Absolutely unsustainable, said Ransumeen. He was forced to the unpleasant conclusion that staff were taking considerable amounts for their personal use. Alistair was one of those, but felt no guilt. Instead he thought of his squash games with Vincent. Until recently he had been able to win occasionally, but Vincent had won four sessions on the trot. Somehow he seemed able to dominate the T. Alistair regarded the gaping, stained mugs and wondered if he should go more often to the club and practise. Maybe Vincent was already doing so. 'I hope not to have to introduce a sign-out policy and restrict stocks to the main office,' the professor was saying. His socks matched and that wasn't always the case. Alistair registered the check pattern so he could keep track of how many days elapsed before they were changed. The round lenses of Ransumeen's glasses caught the sun from the window and the greater circle of his pale face was also lit, almost in a celestial manner.

Hugh rested a caring hand on Alistair's arm, leant confidingly, breathing like a shunting engine. 'How are you feeling these days?' he asked. The whirling galaxy seemed to unwind during staff meetings, speech and movement slowing until the danger that all there would be caught for ever in characteristic poses of assumed interest, or undisguised lassitude. Alistair began to ponder a new quotation for his whiteboard. It came to him as Dr Mellors was stressing the need to make their courses more relevant to the sort of career opportunities presently available to the department's graduates. 'Society cares for the individual only so far as he is profitable.' Yes, that would do nicely. He and Catherine had once gone on a skiing weekend with Mellors and his wife. It hadn't been a great success and wasn't repeated. The women had a disagreement about the heating in the motel and stopped speaking to each other.

Over the next few weeks Alistair made a big push on the essay — at the expense of his squash. Vincent vanquished him with increasing ease. There was considerable satisfaction though in completing the piece, for he found himself tiring of Sartre and Beauvoir. Michael said that anyway he should be concentrating on writers closer in both time and space. Antipodeans who hadn't been dug over by a procession of academics. 'We need to promote our own,' he said. 'There are Kiwi and Aussie people who deserve it. And we should be teaching them too, instead of some of the fusty crap lingering on that the students have absolutely no interest in.'

'Trends Towards Pessimism in the Later Fiction of Jean-Paul Sartre and Simone de Beauvoir.' Alistair was pleased with it. Probably the most insightful piece he'd done in several years. He sent it to the *New England Journal of Literature*, with a covering letter that was all restraint, modesty and scrupulous grammar. Its completion left another gap in his life, though smaller and less enduring. His squash improved, however, as did the appearance of his section. Also he gave more time to Michelle Cole and Robin Hyde, updated his lectures on the contemporary American novel and curried favour with Professor Ransumeen by volunteering to assist with the fledgling creative writing programme.

He heard nothing from the *New England Journal* for seven weeks. Not a good sign. Eventually a letter that wasn't an outright rejection, but offered only to hold his essay for consideration in regard to a possible issue the next year on existentialist writers. An offer couched in decidedly lukewarm terms. It wasn't at all as Alistair had hoped. Maybe he would submit his work to the *Literary Review Quarterly*, even, perhaps, lower his sights to *Hathaway Magazine*.

Ransumeen asked about it after he and Alistair had a discussion in the professor's office concerning the initial semester course for creative writing. 'What about the Sartre paper?' he said.

'The *New England Journal*'s offered to hold it over until a themed issue proposed for next year, but I think I'll send it off elsewhere.'

'I see. It's a lottery, really, isn't it. A coincidence, though, that you mention the journal. Amanda told me just yesterday they have accepted her piece on suffragette poets.'

Ransumeen leant back in his chair so far that his face disappeared from sight and Alistair expected him to fall, thought he might be experiencing a spasm, but he was merely tracking a blowfly on the window behind him. He then righted himself and took up a plastic ruler in readiness for assault. 'Humans have subjugated every creature larger than themselves,' he said, 'but there are still insects, bacteria and viruses.' He paused and began to edge his chair around so that he could use the ruler. 'A fly is a malignant thing, Alistair,' he said. 'The Israelites knew the truth. Satan as Beelzebub, Lord of the Flies. We must all carry on the fight against evil.' He turned slowly until he faced the window, lifted the ruler behind him so as not to give warning to the fly then took aim with such concentration that his tongue began to protrude from his gaping mouth.

The professor was normally a clumsy, even ungainly man, but when engaged in his persistent and deadly war with flies he seemed endowed with a preternatural agility. The blowfly lifted noisily from the window as Ransumeen made his swoop, but the professor adjusted without hesitation and the ruler connected with a smack, the blowfly

Return to Harikoa Bay

hurtled to the bookcase where it lay inert, upside down, on the cover of a collection of essays by Charles Lamb.

'Actually,' said Ransumeen, after a pause to allow transition of personality, 'I've had some correspondence with the journal myself concerning that same issue. They're keen for me to contribute a piece with an overview of the major French authors concerned. I think it's only fair to tell you that if I find the time to get round to doing so, I would be including both Sartre and Beauvoir. No survey would be possible without them. Of course, the broad scope of my essay shouldn't negate the value of your more focused study. I hope we will be fellow contributors.' The professor took off his glasses and smiled at Alistair as if bestowing a gift rather than almost certainly scuttling his chances.

After leaving Ransumeen's office, Alistair met Amanda on the stairs. Despite her intelligence, her skull was small and her short, ginger hair framed the porcelain features. 'How are things, Alistair?' she said. He said things were fine and congratulated her on the journal acceptance of her suffragette poetry essay. 'Thanks. I got the impression they were short on contributions. Probably would have accepted almost anything.' She meant it as self-deprecation, and laughed, unaware of the implication for him. He held the rigour of a smile as he trudged on up the stairs and along the corridor to his room. At the door he paused before the whiteboard, cleared it of the existing quote, and wrote, 'Hell is other people.'

17.

Pīwakawaka

Margaret, my mother-in-law, was a practical woman and of a resolute frame of mind, with all the common sense of a farmer's wife. I got on well with her and experienced few of the exasperations popular in conventional humour concerning mothers-in-law. I came to realise, however, that like all of us, she had her own powerful and individual superstitions. Especially she feared pīwakawaka — the fantail. She'd grown up in rural Northland with Māori families among her neighbours, so maybe that's when she learnt that this little bird, despite its nimble beauty, is considered to be of ill omen. My own experiences of the fantail are benign and come mainly from tramping in the bush. The fantail is quite common there and seems to wish to join you on the push through the ferns and trees. I'm told it's not just a pert compatibility, but that pīwakawaka takes advantage of the insects stirred up.

My father-in-law was a convivial man, yet by the nature of his occupation had to spend most of his time working alone with stock, or driving a tractor, so in the limited leisure time he had, he liked to be with others. The saleyards, the gun club, bowls, euchre evenings, rugby matches, the racetrack and the Victorian Hotel. Margaret was also at ease with people, but preferred to spend her free time in the garden, which had gradually expanded around the wooden, red-roofed farmhouse, protected from the appetites of sheep and cattle by a wire fence. She was also an excellent cook, a skill my wife inherited. Once, when I complimented Margaret on a meal, she said matter of factly that she was a good plain cook, and my wife, Carol, explained that meant she didn't go in for anything fancy. Carol also told me that women make a distinction between cooking and baking, which I'd never realised before.

Roses were what Margaret loved best. Like her they were hardy and could withstand the commonplace droughts of the place. She had all sorts and a name for each. Surely the rose, of all flowers, has the most individual varieties and all with their own names, many romantic, some even grandiose. 'Blushing Lucy' and 'Rose d'Amour', 'Archiduc Joseph' and 'Princesse de Lamballe'. Roses exact a price for their beauty, and although Margaret wore gardening gloves, her forearms were often marked with small bruises and scabs from the thorns. She was a tall, strong woman who shirked nothing in the house, or about the farm, but I recall her best in her country garden, among her roses and dahlias with a straw hat she also wore to bowls.

I was at her house quite often before Carol and I married: less afterwards, but that was because of where we lived, not any disinclination. Thinking back, though, I can recall very few conversations just between the two of us in which any personal and meaningful connection was made. Perhaps she thought to do so would be a trespass on her daughter's territory. Almost always it was the comings and goings of family, Christmases and Easters, greetings and farewells, kitchen chat and focus on the kids. Maybe that's the usual way with in-laws, after all they and you are brought together not by the desire of either, but through an intermediary. Margaret was a much-loved nana and the children strengthened our friendship, but again with an indirectness that deflected personal focus.

The farmhouse is no longer there, and the property has become part of a large dairy unit with rearing irrigation machines to stalk the land. The hay shed remains, and around an impressive water trough are a few straggling roses: yellow mainly, although I don't know their botanical name. When I went back and witnessed the change, I was pleased that Margaret never saw what had happened to the place: the neat, wooden farmhouse demolished and so little left of the extensive garden that had enhanced it.

While returning from that visit I picked up a German backpacker not far from the bridge. So typically Teutonic with his blond sturdiness that I had to smile, but made no comment. He was going down to the lakes, he said, and I told him about the rail trail and the old gold mining towns. He was pleased that I'd visited his own country and found beauty there too. We talked about the wine country along the Rhine and the splendid windows in Cologne Cathedral, both places that he knew. The backpacker has no particular relevance to my mother-in-law, but then this is not a story, and need conform to no rules of unity, or genre: it's just a recollection from the motley of unscripted life that drifts past.

The incident of the fantail is part of that: the pīwakawaka, with which I began. I glimpsed then something about Margaret that was of the inner person, usually kept to herself. She and my father-in-law had been holidaying with us in a bach at Tekapo and after the second day she found they had forgotten to pack enough of his blood pressure and prostate medication. It wasn't a good year for Norman's health and things didn't improve afterwards. I was happy to drive her back to the farm, and so we had over an hour together in the car. It was a big, blue summer day, I remember, and we had the air conditioning on. Even the harrier hawk seemed to be drowsy in the sky. The sort of day that sometimes brought later a fierce nor'wester to buffet everything about.

I suppose we talked about the family, the kids especially, Norman's health problems maybe, her forgetfulness, the impending decision regarding the sale of the farm, the holiday we were enjoying. And when we didn't talk there was no uneasiness. I do remember she said our daughter, Alice, who was six, reminded her of Carol at the same age: the same determination not to be left out of anything, the same unwillingness to wear the clothes chosen for her. Alice then had a powerful aversion to some clothes, a trait thankfully completely lacking in the other two. She would hide the garments she hated behind the water cylinder, or discard them in the neighbour's bin, or slash them with the garden snippers, irrespective of value. The few times I smacked her all involved her clothes. In time she grew out of the habit just as she grew out of those clothes that received her approval.

The garden was looking good when Margaret and I reached the farm, especially the peonies and roses. Roses must have a long flowering season, or maybe it's that different varieties are out at different times. I was going to stay in the car, but it seemed more supportive to go into the house with her rather than stay and so suggest impatience. The key was hidden under a pot plant by the front step — probably the first place an intruder would look, but burglars were uncommon then in the country. Margaret went through to their bedroom and I stood in the straight, wide hallway with a view of the kitchen table at the end of it, bearing bands of sunlight from the window above the sink.

Margaret's cry from the bedroom wasn't loud, more a sort of involuntary high-pitched gasp, and quite out of character, and accompanied by a flapping, scratching sort of noise. She came out with her hands to her face. 'Oh, a fantail, a fantail's got in,' she said. I was relieved that was all, and surprised at her agitation. She retreated down the hallway and I went into the bedroom and shut the door. The fantail was small and dark and frightened. I opened the window and tried to guide it out, but of course it fluttered and butted in the high corners and I was afraid of hurting it. Finally I caught it in my cupped hands and released it through the window. In its desperation it shat over my fingers and I went to the bathroom to clean up.

'Has it gone?' Margaret asked quietly when I joined her in the kitchen. She was sitting in the same patch of sun that lay on the large, wooden farm table.

'I got it out the window.'

'I'll get Norman's stuff,' she said. When she came back she said she needed a cup of tea before going back to the lake. 'A fantail's really bad luck, especially inside,' she said. 'Somebody's going to die. That's what it means. And there's no way it could have got in. Everything was shut up.'

'The bathroom window had been left open though,' I told her.

'It still means someone's going to die,' she said. She stayed sitting and so in role reversal I made the tea — black for both of us because there was no milk.

'Don't worry about it,' I said. 'Birds get in when things are quiet and people are away. Probably it was catching insects around the window frame.'

'A fantail came before my father died,' Margaret said, 'and he hadn't even been sick. Hardly sick a day in his life. It came twice and fluttered at the kitchen window when it was getting dark. The second time Mrs Wetere was there talking to my mother about the women's auxiliary, and she just got up and left without saying anything: couldn't wait to get away. Dad was killed two days later when the props on the logging truck collapsed. At the funeral Mrs Wetere gave me a hug and said she wished she hadn't got the warning. She meant the fantail for sure.'

'Who knows about these things for certain,' I said. 'There's odd coincidences that just happen. Don't worry about it. It just gave you a fright to go in and find it there. If we hadn't come back the poor thing would probably have died in the bedroom.' I didn't want to be dismissive, and I didn't want her worrying either. She didn't say much more about it then and made an effort to move on. She washed the cups, checked the windows and then we left.

She didn't say anything more about her father and the fantail until we were almost back at Tekapo, and we talked about other things: Norman's enthusiasm to be closer to people when they moved into town, and whether she would have room for her roses there. Then, as we drove down from the pass, with the spent lupins lining the road, she asked me not to say anything about what happened to anybody else. 'I'm all right. I'm over it,' she said. 'I don't want the others to know about it.' I was okay with that and said I was sorry about her father, that I hadn't known before how he'd died. 'He was away a long time at the war and wasn't allowed all that many years back with us,' Margaret told me. 'Mum said she lost him twice. She was very bitter about it. Promise you won't say anything to the others. I've never told the family about Dad and the fantail, and I don't want anyone else anxious about what happened today at the house.'

Margaret never mentioned it again and nor did I. I imagine she worried a lot over the following days, but she didn't show it, and nobody died, well, not anyone close to our family anyway and not soon after. So although Margaret was a private woman, and my mother-in-law, not a blood relation, we shared the secret of the pīwakawaka at her father's window and in her bedroom. A secret that even her husband and Carol knew nothing about. And sharing it added something to how we were with each other, although we never talked of it afterwards. One thing, just one personal thing, that was between us alone. As far as I know the fantail made no visit, gave no warning, before her own death, but then Margaret's quiet and painless passing years later was clearly presaged by practical medical indications. I miss her more than I expected, and always when I think of her I think, too, of the fantail, pīwakawaka.

18.

Frost Flowers

Wally Tamihana was captain of the first fifteen when I was in the fourth form, and famously told the headmaster to get off the fucken field. Beth Attwood was thrown from a steer at the Geraldine rodeo, broke her neck, but came right with time and ended up the chief of Work and Income. Amelia Muirton went on a Rotary exchange to America and was killed by a lightning strike in Lincoln, Nebraska, after a high-school prom. Bernard Eldermere was bald at twenty-nine, but became a multi-millionaire because of mānuka honey, while his more likeable brother, Albie, was jailed for corporate fraud, and Belinda Burge, who failed all her units at varsity, is now a worldwide celebrity as a creator of fashion hats and fascinators.

All of these people have a story, but I'm going to talk about Mrs Poole and Greg, who lived pretty quietly and hardly went anywhere when I knew them. We lived next door for quite a few years and got on well as neighbours. Mrs Poole was a widow, but her husband left her well provided for, as he'd been the main shareholder in a Lower Hutt factory making plastic guttering. She was small and thin when I first knew her, and both attributes became accentuated as the years passed. Her movements were staccato, as if clockwork provided her propulsion. A smart little woman, always well dressed and never without make-up. I got to know all of her children: Erin, who's married to a biology lecturer at Massey University, Sue, a parliamentary journalist, and Greg, who lived with his mother.

I'm not sure what the matter was with Greg, but he couldn't walk, had awkward arm movements and his speech was difficult to understand. I've always assumed it was some problem at his birth. He could laugh, though, and I liked to hear that. We could hear his laugh even from next door: explosive, deep and unrestrained. Less frequently we heard him crying, and that, too, was loud, and equally affecting in a quite different way.

When I was still at primary school Mrs Poole often invited me over to have a game of draughts with him. I took it as a compliment, and never thought that maybe he had no better, or more willing, company than a kid some ten years younger than himself. I still think it was more than that, though.

They both made me welcome. I remember winter weekend afternoons spent sitting with them in the warmth of the nearby woodburner. Milo and Afghan biscuits, TV movies sometimes. Greg was good at draughts, although he tended to scatter the pieces. I think he let me win more times than I deserved.

In later years I took him for walks, well, I walked and pushed Greg in his wheelchair. He never did have an electric one and I don't know the reason for that: certainly it can't have been financial. In the year before I went to varsity I remember quite a few walks. I'd like to say they were always the result of spontaneous consideration on my part, but my mother often made the suggestion. It wasn't a drag, though, and I was happy to do it. Greg must have been nearly thirty then, but because of his dependence and limited experience of the world, he seemed much younger, despite his encroaching baldness and hairy arms. His thin legs were always aligned the same way in the chair, rigidly together and slanted to the right. He would grip the arm rests when we crossed a gutter, lean back to look at me and chortle if I did anything at speed. The park was his favourite destination, especially the playground where he could watch the little kids' antics, and the pond where the black swans presided over a scrabble of lesser birds. There was a bench by the silver birches that caught the sun nicely and I'd sit there with Greg's chair pulled up alongside. We'd talk a bit, which wasn't always easy because of his garbled words, but we weren't uncomfortable with silence.

One of the first times we went was a Sunday soon after an Anzac Day. I remember because Greg still had two fabric poppies pinned to his green jersey and when I asked him why two and why still, he said they were for lost great-uncles. It was a blue, windless afternoon and people had been drawn to the park, families at the pond's edge feeding the ducks and swans, young people with Frisbees, or soccer balls, strolling couples. One pair came slowly past from the direction of the old band rotunda. The guy was self-consciously casual, endeavouring to disguise his pride at accompanying such a good-looking girl. She really was a stunner: Hollywood legs in red shorts. There seemed a slight vibration in the air around her. When they'd gone on, Greg turned his head towards me in his ungainly way and said slowly, 'Wow, now she was something. Jesus.'

Yes, Jesus, she was something, but it seemed strange coming from Greg, and I realised that I had made the stupid assumption that because of his disability he didn't have the same responses and feelings as the rest of us. Why shouldn't he see a beautiful woman and think of taking her in his arms? Why shouldn't he see a white mountain slope and imagine himself skiing there, regard the quivering sea and visualise the plunge into it, or watch a craftsman create something of balanced perfection and wish to share that satisfaction? Why must he accept the full imposition of such a savagely limited life before he had done anything at all to deserve it? You don't get any guarantee of a fair deal, do you?

Greg went on set days to a sheltered workshop, had for years, even played wheelchair basketball for a while, but his condition deteriorated steadily. The last few times I spent with him everything about him seemed to end on a slant, no matter which way I propped him up, and he talked less, perhaps because he'd become more difficult to understand.

He died during exam time in my second year in Auckland and I didn't get down for the funeral, but when I came home for vacation work at the woolstore I went over to see his mother. A blustery, warm Friday with shrubs convulsing and shadows dancing. 'He liked you,' Mrs Poole said as I followed her into the sitting room. The photos of her husband and of Sue, Erin and Greg, were still on the sideboard by the woodburner, but there was a new reminder of her son. His wheelchair by the window and propped on its seat a large, framed image of him, smiling his slanted smile. It was to become a sort of memorial, the wheelchair and photograph, always there.

'He used to ask about you,' she said. 'He knew all the subjects you were taking and how you got on. He would have loved the opportunity to go to university himself. He started a polytech course offering preparation for academic study, but became too debilitated to continue.' Mrs Poole got up as she said this, went to the wheelchair and adjusted the photo frame in her clockwork way, just as she habitually used to help Greg change position there a little for greater ease. 'You liked to hear him, didn't you?' she said, going back to her green armchair.

'Hear him?'

'You told me once you and your mother liked to hear him laugh.'

'Right, yes, we did, even from next door. It *was* pretty loud, wasn't it.'

'One of the workshop supervisors mentioned his laugh at the funeral.'

'*The Simpsons*,' I said. 'He really loved that programme. We watched it sometimes together.'

'He understood the social and political satire behind it. He knew it wasn't just cartoons. He knew a lot more than he could be bothered saying.'

'I remember us playing draughts too.'

'So do I,' she said.

'It can't have been easy.'

'Looking after him?'

'Yeah. Everything that had to be done, especially when he grew up.'

'Everyone said I should put him in care, even Erin and Sue, though they loved him. Everyone said it was too much for me and not the best choice for him either, but I couldn't do it, and he didn't want to go.' Mrs Poole lent forward from her armchair and lowered her voice, an unconscious emphasis of significance to come, rather than to ensure privacy, because we were quite alone. 'He knew we wouldn't have that long together. I won't make old bones, he used to say. He knew all right and so did I.'

Mrs Poole was of a different generation to me, and a different gender, and I was a bit surprised by her openness, the honesty with which she spoke of Greg, the equality she assumed I felt. I suppose it was because he and I had known each other for a long time and now he was gone, and there weren't many people she could talk to who remembered him. And she was a well-educated woman and unconventional in her own way. She wasn't swayed by others.

Even after I left home permanently, I used to go over to see Mrs Poole if I was back visiting my parents. The wheelchair was always there, and Greg in his frame. I knew she loved all her children, but for her son there was a sense of fulfilment lacking, for which she held herself unaccountably responsible.

On my last visit, before she moved to Palmerston North to live with Erin, she told me as much. We were on her deck, out of sight of the wheelchair and Greg's image, with a view of her large, well-kept garden that she took much interest in, but didn't need to maintain herself. My mother was envious. Lot and lots of peonies with their large, roundly compact heads, already tinctured with a range of colours, ready to burst into flower. Mrs Poole made a point of congratulating me on my marriage — her generous gift had been a small, inlaid Italian table — and she was interested in my work at the ministry, but we came around, of course, to talk of Greg, for that was the bond we shared.

'Towards the end,' she said, after we had been talking for some time, 'he had this thing about frost flowers. Did I ever tell you about that?'

'I don't think so.'

'He watched this nature programme that featured them — fragile petals and stems of pure ice that form and grow when certain plants become frozen. Very strange and very beautiful, and very rare. He really wanted to see them and we began to plan a trip overseas, although we both knew it wouldn't happen. We made up a full itinerary and he had pictures of frost flowers on his wall. He could have been a scientist if he'd had the chance. He never blamed me, but you can't help thinking what might have been, what you might have done differently.'

It was odd, and rather sad, that last conversation with Mrs Poole: sitting in the sun with a view of the profusion of peonies and talking of frost flowers, and what life might have been for Greg if he'd been given a chance. It made me realise that the love of a mother for her child is incalculable in its intensity, unassailable in its loyalty, unbearable in any perceived betrayal.

Return to Harikoa Bay

19.

Running Bear

hile at a Civil Defence seminar in Hamilton in July I met a guy I recalled vaguely from high school. I introduced myself and, yes, he'd been in the same form. 'You bullied me,' he said almost immediately, as a statement rather than accusation. I hate bullying: I believe I've never bullied anyone in my life. I said he must be confusing me with someone else. 'No, it was you,' he said calmly. His face was as round as that of a mantelpiece clock, and it came back to me that he'd been especially good at maths and not much at anything else. 'You probably don't remember, because it wasn't you being picked on, but you were a bully. Once you made me throw away a pie, and it was my lunch,' he told me.

That's what you find sometimes, that there are people who believe your failings to be just those impulses you most despise in others, and it gives a jolt to the comfortable assumptions you have about yourself. That guy at the seminar was called Nick and we were in the same workshop group at least once during the three days, but we never talked about our time at school again, and it wouldn't have done any good. He will always have me cast as a bully, and I still think his memory is false. It got me thinking though, about bullies, about school, about the stereotypes we accept even when we've grown up.

Everyone comes across a bully from time to time: not just someone who punches you in the face for nothing, but people who belittle others, or use some small authority for their own advantage. The insecure person who persecutes another as an outsider to emphasise their own allegiance to a community, or the one who salves his own despair by inflicting pain elsewhere. Such behaviour is inexcusable even though explicable, but the worst bullies seem to have no reason for cruelty except the pleasure they take in it. Razzer was one of those.

You didn't want to attract Razzer's attention. He was a year ahead of us at school and the oppression of the vulnerable, or those possessed of oddity, was his entertainment. If you had a tight group of friends, it was usually sufficient protection; you'd just get a sneering put down, or threats of what might happen after school, but he picked out the isolated, the apprehensive, to torture, as the wolf finds the straggler from the herd. He had several regular victims whom he used as punching bags if he could catch them in some empty corridor, or a corner of the buildings not open to view.

Tommy Datt, who was my year, was one he picked on. Tommy had ginger hair, a pimply face and no sporting ability whatsoever. Razzer, on the other hand, although not especially big, was strong, agile and aggressive. Why didn't we tell some teacher about him, for God's sake? The head went on enough at assembly about respect for our fellows. Why didn't we gang up on the prick when we saw him close in on some kid, his elbow working as he gave quick, savage punches? I suppose because we knew that after formal authority, or our vigilante group, had meted out punishment, then he would come looking for us as individuals. Would come looking for me.

I might as well say now that there was one time in particular when I could have done something and didn't, that the guilty shame is with me still. It was after the school cross-country, and Razzer had finished in the first half-dozen, of course. Most guys had already changed and gone home. Andrew and I were ready to do the same and were walking back behind the gym to get our bikes when we saw that Razzer had Tommy penned up close to the wall. Razzer stared brazenly as we passed, and Tommy made no plea for help, just remained hunched and with his face turned from us. 'It's just a bit of fun,' said Razzer in an offhand way, but also as a challenge. 'He's a useless prick.' And Andrew and I didn't say anything, didn't do anything: we looked away and went away and talked of something else. Andrew went down in my opinion after that, but not as low as I ranked myself. There are quite a few things in the past I'd like to change, but there's no other recollection that brings quite the disappointment in myself as that of walking away from Razzer and Tommy Datt despite knowing what would continue there.

There was another occasion when I saw Razzer enjoying himself. It was in the baths enclosure and he had some junior kid cowering naked, half under the wooden seating, and was flicking him with a towel. The kid was crying and on his pale skin were red marks where the towel end had snapped back. There were more of us that day, though, including some seniors who finally yelled at him to bugger off and leave the kid alone, and I joined in the chorus. Oh, what bravery!

In my last school summer, though, I learnt something else about Razzer. It was a Sunday and some of us were down at the bay courts playing tennis, less concerned with improving our game than with trying to hook up with girls there. Razzer came walking by, alone as he almost always was. He'd got a job at the ANZ Bank that year, I heard. You don't imagine a bully working in a bank, do you. He sat down on a green bench by the netting and shouted cheerfully at us, although we weren't friends: something about us being useless wankers. Maybe he wanted to remind us that he'd been to the same school, that we should remember him. He seemed just the same, except that his hair was much longer and he wore winkle-picker shoes. He had a transistor radio, which he put beside him on the seat, then turned it up to listen to pop songs. We didn't acknowledge him, although Andrew and I were having a spell, sitting on the warm asphalt not far away.

After a bit, a couple of older guys came along, both wearing black jeans, and the taller of the two had sunglasses. They stood watching the tennis in a casual way, clapped with sarcastic intent when someone double faulted, called advice to the girls concerning their lack of ball skills. After a bit they moved and sat beside Razzer. The one with the sunglasses put the transistor on the ground to give himself more room. 'And turn that fucker down, mate,' he said. 'Nobody wants to hear that crap.'

The transistor was playing the song about Running Bear and Little

White Dove that Johnny Preston had made a number one some years before. The one with the ugga-ugga chant in the background. And that's when I learnt something about human nature. Razzer picked up his transistor and without a word put it back beside him, close to the guys, and he turned up the volume so that Running Bear was loud over the courts and the playground close by.

I'm not sure who gave the first hit, but all of a sudden it was full on, two on one and Razzer not backing down, and the rest of us startled and just watching, even those on the courts. There was a savagery and malice to it that were both enthralling and repugnant, and as they fought, Johnny Preston kept singing loudly about Running Bear and Little White Dove, and the doomed love between them.

The bully is always a coward, right? That's what the films and books show us, but life doesn't make assessment that easy. For a short time Razzer even seemed to be winning, and although bleeding from the nose himself, he had the tall guy bloodied at the mouth and the other one backed off. It was two on one, though, and both of the others seemed competent bullies themselves. They got Razzer pinned to the bench and gave him a kicking, and one of them booted the transistor as well, which put an end to Running Bear. Razzer backed into the netting fence, kept his fists up, and after flinging the damaged transistor over the netting the guys went off, having won, but also having got more than they bargained for. The whole thing must have been over in less than two minutes. Razzer stood and watched them go. 'Fuck,' he said vehemently and snorted blood onto the ground. He didn't look at any of us. He didn't retrieve the transistor. He just walked off in a different direction and said 'Fuck' again as he went, his voice muffled because he was clenching his nose and leaning forward.

He got what he deserved all right, and Andrew and I were happy with that, but that's not why I remember the whole thing. I remember it for the lesson that someone can be a cruel bastard, a bully, and yet be valiant. Life's strange like that. People don't always fit the mould we find most reassuring to assign them.

20.

Return to Harikoa Bay

Yes, that flickering presence of the past behind the substance of the present, as always when you come back to a special place after many years. Ivan opened the road gate and they drove down the steep unsealed track towards the bay. There was that feeling again of being perched on the spur, with native bush swelling in the gullies, the five higgledy-piggledy baches close to the pale beach and the blue sea run of the sound spread beyond.

'Here we are then,' said Ivan unnecessarily, but as a greeting to the place.

'Yes, here we are,' agreed Nicky. 'The track's a lot better now, though.' She remembered how hot it always seemed to be travelling here with the boys. How her clothes stuck to her and the car seat; how good it had been to arrive and unload, to be in the open, but also in the shade. This day was just as hot, but there were only the two of them and the Audi was bigger, had air conditioning. So she had travelled better, yet as they wound down to the bay she missed the excitement with which the boys had always greeted their arrival. Now there were just the two of them in contained agreement that here they were then: at Harikoa Bay. Hugh was in Italy, or maybe Turkey by now, doing the big OE thing, and Danny had only the month before left home to go to a university hall in Christchurch. A fifth time, at least, coming back to the bay, but now Ivan and Nicky were coming alone and for different reasons.

Only the five buildings still — well, the two rickety boatsheds closer to the water as well, but no more residences. The Palmer bach had been tidied and repainted, even had solar panels on its tin roof, but the other places looked much the same. A little more settled among the long, brown grasses and straggly native shrubs. Each building at sufficient remove from the others to give a measure of privacy, although some in clear sight of a neighbour. In all of the holidays at the bay with the boys, they'd stayed in the McDermott bach, but Ivan hadn't been able to get that this time, instead taking the place owned by the Blenheim Pipe Band. Who knows how a pipe band ends up with a place by the sea?

Both of them were a bit disappointed not to be staying in the place they knew, but Nicky's nostalgia was soon outweighed by the better kitchen facilities that bagpipe players enjoyed, and the chemical toilet that was quite modern. On their first visits years ago the McDermott bach had only a long drop.

There were two small bedrooms with a couple of narrow beds in each, and Nicky chose for them the room that had a blind on the window. Their larger cases they placed on the other beds to save space in their own room. The place hadn't been aired, was very stuffy, and the golden air moved, languid and liquid around them. There was a smell of fish from old parkas by the door and the inoffensive smell of an insect population seldom disturbed.

Before fully unpacking they made coffee, put on their soft fabric sunhats and sat on the bleached wooden form outside by the door. A view over the beach to the sea where the sunlight flashed on the small waves like flying fish, and on the other side of the sound, far off, they could see the dark, forested hills.

'Not much changes,' said Ivan.

'You're right there,' Nicky said, although they both knew it wasn't so.

'I still would've liked to have had the old place.'

'Better facilities here.'

'They've probably upgraded at the McDermott place too, after all this time.'

'That's true,' Nicky said. 'I'd like to look inside, but I suppose we won't be able to do that.' Actually she didn't especially want to do that:

not if changes had been made. She wanted it to be as it had been when they came as a family. There was change enough happening now.

'Do you want to wander down to the beach?' he asked.

'I'll finish getting organised. You go on, though. Maybe I'll come later.' They had been together in the car for hours without disharmony, but now she preferred to be by herself, to draw the familiar setting around her without any necessity to explain her feelings. When Hugh and Danny were part of the family there had been more opportunity for natural emotional disengagement between husband and wife; now the continual focus was their own relationship.

He stood up and handed her the large, stained coffee mug with faded words on the side extolling idleness. For a moment they held the mug between them as connection, and then Ivan smiled, released it, walked towards the beach and the false flying fish, with a hand held up for a moment as signal of both goodwill and farewell. How familiar he was, yet strangely unknowable too. The loping walk he had and the forward jut of his head. The thinning and greying limp hair, but no baldness, which she knew was beneath his sunhat. His shoulders folded forward slightly as if he were still at his desk in the offices of Doar and Jarvis. He would be looking forward to being alone on the beach, mooching along the shore and happy to see what the ocean had cast up for him. He would bring back some shells, or smooth stones that glittered enticingly when wet, but proved unexceptional once dry. And such debris would build up in the bach and she would have to throw it out before they left. He was like a kid in some ways. Perhaps all men are.

Beachcombing never lost its appeal for him. At any coast he liked to go out in the mornings and walk the high-tide mark, especially after a rough sea. Once he'd found a bikini top, another time a pink fishing float, even a dead albatross, and a small homemade paddle with a pāua shell oval set in the handle. That first afternoon back, there was nothing unusual on the deserted shore, but he enjoyed the driftwood pieces, grey and worn smooth, although still sometimes contorted, and the strips of seaweed laid out as if by hand for inspection. The beach was not of sand, but fine, worn gravel, some of it quartz with a rusty colour. There were shells, mainly broken and with no splendid sheen, and the occasional crab case, light and fragile in the hand. Ivan wondered what their sons were doing: Hugh on the other side of the world and Danny at university. They were men now, and had turned out well, but in a strange way he still thought of their boyish selves as retaining an independent existence, would have been unsurprised to see them come running down ahead of Nicky to join him on the beach.

He and Nicky hadn't talked a lot about the days to be spent at Harikoa Bay, but he knew there would be some pretty serious stuff laid out; a reckoning, although neither had used the phrase. With Danny gone, the two of them could put their individual views of how life should play out with the welfare of their sons no longer paramount. It seemed better to both of them somehow to make decisions away from their home, in a neutral place, but one in which they'd been happy. Like representatives of the powers convening at Geneva, or Brussels. Ivan smiled at the thought and lobbed stones into the small waves that flooded up the beach and then sucked back again, rustling the fine gravel. He knew Nicky would be resolved, sure in what she wanted, while he was caught in a curious apathy and had no cherished plan for the future. He would see how it turned out. He hoped there wouldn't be tears. He hated it when she cried, and she seldom did, probably because she knew how that disarmed him. She wasn't into emotional blackmail. When he reached the end of the beach, where the headland rose up, he decided he would walk past the baches on his way back: see how many were being used.

The pipe band secretary had told him there was someone more or less permanently in the top hut: an old guy who'd been a teacher. The top hut was always called that, just because it was closest to the headland. As he walked past, Ivan could see there was a reasonably fresh wood stack, and a Toyota Camry parked close to the door. No sign of anyone about the Palmer, or Allymont places, and the Allymont dinghy had been dragged almost up to the house, which was a sign no one was staying there. Also bricks had been placed at the base of the door to stop stuff blowing inside when the wind was up. On their second visit to the bay they'd gone often to that bach — when Rob and Esther Allymont had been staying there while their Nelson home was being built. Pleasant, hospitable people with whom they got on famously, and had never seen since.

He knew of course that the McDermott bach was occupied and there were signs enough, including clothing and two coloured beach towels on the line strung between the woodshed and the overhang of the door. He'd told Nicky the place had probably been improved since they were last there, but there was little external suggestion of that. As he went past, though, he saw someone standing by the raised back of an SUV. A youngish woman in yellow shorts and white T-shirt. A woman with pale skin and dark hair, but too far away for him to gauge her expression. Ivan raised a hand and she gave a wave in return. Instead of going on immediately to join Nicky at their own place, he turned up the gully and into the bush, followed the creek into the abrupt shadows and crowding trees, was aware of the sudden coolness and the sound of the small surf abruptly muted. The shadowed intensity of New Zealand bush had been borne home to him as a characteristic only after he'd experienced the woodlands of Europe. Ivan liked the cover of his own country: the entering into anonymity, the stepping from sunlit focus to invisibility.

The bay sloped steeply back, the creek had cut deeply into the ground, ferns trailed on the sides and the reduced summer flow was clean, but with just the faint brown tinge that bush streams have. Ivan scrambled up far enough to reach a concave bank beneath a tōtara tree where he had brought the boys at night to see glow worms. The reward had been in sharing the small star-spangled heaven beneath the bank, rather than his own appreciation. There was nothing to be seen, of course, and crouched there for a moment he had a sense of his own absurdity — a forty-eight-year-old accountant seeking glow worms in the afternoon, instead of returning to his wife and providing companionship.

Nicky could see him approaching. The skinny legs in his second-best jeans propelling him in a slightly ungainly walk, the minor shoulder hunch, pale arms, his expression subtly changing with the realisation that he might now be under observation. He looked what he was — a city and office dweller on a country excursion. She didn't dislike him; she just didn't love him any more. She could find a statutory reason for that if necessary — the three occasions he'd screwed Mrs Flowerday on the quality carpet of his office at Doar and Jarvis, lying close behind the desk so as to be invisible from the window. It had all come out through Irene Flowerday's sense of guilt, and it was agreed her business be handled by another partner in the firm henceforth. It wasn't because of that, though, Nicky thought as she watched him, as he came and sat down to join her on the form outside the door, began to talk about seeing someone at the McDermott bach. She had ceased to love him long before Mrs Flowerday lay down with him, but could assign no dramatic cause and no specific time. It had been accomplished gradually and with no intention on either side. She thought maybe it was a natural biological thing — that once a pairing had produced offspring the drive for intensity in the bond was no longer necessary and so waned. She saw it so often in the marriages of others, some of whom had parted, some settling into placid companionship, some continuing together with ill-disguised impatience. Nicky found it difficult to remember quite why she had chosen Ivan rather than any other of the men wishing to be with her.

'I saw a woman at the McDermott place as I came past,' he said.

'Did you talk?'

'No, too far away. Quite a young woman and she was unloading stuff from her car, I think.' He put a finger in his mouth and scraped briefly at a side tooth. Nicky thought maybe she'd taken to him initially because he could dance so well. What she liked to do with men was talk and dance, and people didn't dance as much now, except at weddings and perhaps school reunions. It was all cabaret dining, string quartets and concerts. She liked to dance with agile, well-dressed men, close to them back and forth, but with clean, quality fabric between her flesh and theirs. Strangely, perhaps, Ivan was an accomplished dancer. It was a contradiction to his ambling locomotion when not responding to music. His mother had taught him, sweeping him around the dark, polished floor of the Athena Academy where she had students three evenings a week. He'd become accomplished almost despite himself. It was how Nicky and he met, the dancing. And he had mastered the tango as well as the waltz and quickstep. It had interested her, more than that, intrigued her, this awkward, studious man who transformed on the dance floor to a gliding maestro who took the lead with deft, courteous command. They didn't dance much now. More a lack of opportunity than inclination? Maybe not.

'I saw a fairly new Toyota at the top hut and there was a good stack of wood. It'll be the old guy we were told about. Must be pretty lonely for him here in winter.'

'You could ask him about the fishing,' Nicky said.

'Yeah, I might.'

'I thought we'd just have soup tonight and the buns while they're fresh. Okay?'

'That's fine.' Habitually she sought his approval in this way, but always she had already made up her mind.

'It's not soup weather, I know, but it'll give us more room in the fridge. That's one downer here: a small fridge.'

'Good we brought plenty of tinned stuff then,' he said.

All the baches were close to the water, and although the waves were small they could hear the sea breathing and it was a lulling sound, and the slanting sun was still strong and high-up gulls passed with a steady beat, or swerved against the wind with fixed wings. There was no hurry for the soup: they weren't going anywhere. 'I went up the stream a bit to where we used to see the glow worms in the bush,' he said, and she smiled and nodded.

'The sea smells, doesn't it,' she said. 'I'd almost forgotten that. Not so much of salt either, though people say that. I've been sitting here and trying to make it out. It seems a smell half of something living and half of something dead.'

'Does it smell the same always and everywhere, do you reckon? Did it smell just like this when we were in Florida, or Corsica? There should be regional smells, shouldn't there?' Neither of them could remember. 'Can I do anything?' he said after a time.

'No, I'll go in soon. We could even eat out here.'

—◊◊◊◊◊—

They did that, staying on the bench until dusk gave everything a soft indistinctness that seemed to gather about them and to amplify the sound of the sea. When they had done the final sorting of their things in the small rooms, they sat in the largest of them, which was both kitchen and living room, Nicky with an Annie Proulx novel and Ivan with his laptop. Neither preoccupation was a bar to occasional conversations that came and went in a way quite customary to them, sometimes ending with small accord and rapport, sometimes lapsing because interest, or agreement, was lacking, even perhaps some minor hurt inflicted.

'Have you thought more about the sections?' Nicky asked.

'They're appreciating all the time, so why do anything? It's a hell of a lot better than money in the bank these days,' Ivan said. They had bought the city sections as an investment seven years ago. There were rates to pay, and maintenance costs, but they were appreciating assets. He'd had approaches, some good offers, but the land was important in his diversified investment plan. He liked to drive there sometimes, walk the boundaries — once he found a neighbour had been throwing rubbish over the wooden fence and had it out with him in what became a testy exchange. Ivan knew why Nicky brought it up as they sat there in the bach, why she wanted the sections sold. It was part of her increasing wish for division, a separation not just of property, but of themselves. A separation of their lives. 'So you still want out?' he said. 'Your mind's made up?'

'It's best, I think.'

'Best for you?'

'Yes.'

'But maybe not me and the boys.'

'I think we can leave the boys out of it now, Ivan,' she said. She had drawn him into serious talk and she put down her book to concentrate on it before the opportunity passed. 'I'm not going to just plod on,' she said, 'and neither should you, but that's your business.' In three months she would be forty-five years old. Not old, not nearly old, but at an age at which she needed to make a move if she was to take a significant, new path in life. She knew people would assume that when she did so it would be because of a man, a romance with violins and attraction impossible to resist.

There was a man — the head of her department who had bad teeth, despite his professorial salary, and a habit of picking his lip during meetings. They shared respect, even academic admiration, but not even a kiss. He was a scholar of some distinction who had wide contacts and influence: who had mentioned to her that there was an attractive position at the University of West Virginia that could almost certainly be hers. He'd held a visiting professorship there, said the faculty were congenial and the landscape pleasing, that he'd mentioned her in recent emails and the people who mattered were very receptive.

Nicky hadn't been to West Virginia, but she and Ivan had spent some days in adjacent states. What she wanted wasn't a new partner, but a new opportunity. 'I don't feel fulfilled here,' she said. 'I want new challenges and new places while I still can. You don't have to come — why should you? I'm happy either way. I'm not going because I want to get away from you.'

'A brave new world, eh,' he said, conscious of a tinge of bitterness, or perhaps cynicism, in his voice that he didn't entirely intend. So she didn't feel fulfilled? It was the language of magazines and he was surprised she used it. Who felt fulfilled, for Christ's sake. He didn't want to live in another country, accommodate the views and habits of people with whom he had no history. Sure, he'd enjoyed all the times they'd been overseas, but returned always knowing it was here he belonged. And although Nicky said wanting separation wasn't a part of her decision, it would almost certainly be a consequence, and what did that reveal of their marriage? She was prepared to go alone: he was reluctant to go with her. Ah yes, the bonds of matrimony and new priorities that stretch them.

'I might not get appointed. I might not like it if I do. Maybe I have time there and come back again. I don't know. I'm going to take a chance, though, and see how it works out, and I don't want to feel guilty about that. Each of us should do what's best for us as individuals now, and support each other too. It's the twenty-first century, for God's sake.' He had assumed a small, rueful smile, his flag that he had no faith in her logic, but saw no point in voicing his disagreement.

'We don't need to make a proclamation if it,' she said. 'No big deal, surely. It happens.'

'What happens?' he said.

'People taking on some project, or whatever. Going off to save orphans, or guard white rhinos, or, I dunno — you know what I mean. Not a divorce, unless that's what you want. Nothing that needs a lawyer at all. I know what you think of them.'

'I'd rather we keep away from lawyers, for sure.'

'There you are: nothing need be formal at all. No business of anyone except ourselves.' He gave his smile again. 'I don't see any great failure in it,' she said. 'What you need — I mean I don't want you to feel it's some sort of punishment, or that I regret us being together. It's a new stage, isn't it? The boys away now and everything. And as I say, you're welcome to come if it happens. There's a choice for you as well as me.'

'But for me it's a choice I'd rather not have. I'd rather not go to West Virginia, and I'd rather not stay here alone.'

'I can't alter that,' she said, 'but it's good we're talking like this. It's why we came, isn't it?'

'Well, I don't feel much like talking about it any more tonight,' Ivan said.

'Okay.'

'It's just I'm a bit pooped, though I've done nothing.'

'It's okay.'

'You're sure?'

'I won't be long myself,' she said. Well, it was a start. He could go off and mull it over and they had days together at the bay to come. She didn't want him to feel she was always at him. When you pushed him he became more resistant in a quiet, mulish way.

—◈◈◈—

Ivan didn't want to mull it over. Rather he wanted to put it out of his mind, because he knew it would come up enough in the days to follow. He knew what the end would be, but also that they must work through all the stages to satisfy her desire for a considered, bipartite agreement. She would feel better then. He knew her intention was not to hurt him, but to advantage herself, and who could argue with that? He and almost everybody else shared that motivation. He took the coins from his jeans pocket and put them as a small tower on the stunted wooden chair by his side of the bed. His side was always the same, no matter where in the world they were, and required no negotiation. As he put his pyjamas on, he decided he would think about the glow worm underhang, and about taking the dinghy out if tomorrow was calm. He should have checked the boatshed in his walk along the beach. Surely the pipe band would have a decent dinghy. There used to be a place well out from the headland, and in line with the track, where blue cod were abundant. Maybe it was so still. Ivan lay in the small, sagging bed, the closeted, insect-scented air still a novelty. The smell of this place was the same as he recalled of the McDermott bach. All of the baches would be the same, no matter who lived there, except maybe the top hut, which now had a permanent resident. The blind on the single window was ill-fitting and although the light bulb wasn't bright, he could hear the soft, fluttery thuds of moths on the glass. He would think of fishing and glow worms: of moths, and times when there had been four of them together at the bay.

— ·»} {«· —

After breakfast the next morning he was preparing to go down to check out the boatshed when the couple from the McDermott bach came over to introduce themselves. The pale and dark woman who was called Heather, and her partner, Bowden, who called out hello several times as they approached, as if he thought the new arrivals might be involved in some intimacy and he didn't wish to surprise them. He tapped on the door when reaching it, plainly seen through the window. A big, blond man with a heavy chest and so his belly was less noticeable. Four people in the living room cum kitchen of the bach seemed to make a congregation. The visitors were offered the soft chairs; Nicky and Ivan sat on kitchen ones. Bowden said they didn't want to bust in, just come to welcome them as neighbours. 'How long you folks here for?' he asked.

'Only till Friday,' said Nicky. 'We used to come here years ago. It's a special place for us.'

'You honeymoon here or something?' said Bowden cheerfully.

'No. We used to come with our boys, when they were young,' she said.

'We used to stay in the place you're in. The McDermott bach,' added Ivan. He didn't say that they'd hoped to do so on this visit too.

'It's all new to us,' Bowden said. 'I'm sort of between jobs.'

'We both are,' Heather said. She had been making an appraisal of the room while her partner spoke.

They talked a while, and it seemed Bowden and Heather were in no hurry to leave, having had no company but themselves for days. Nothing that was said was either especially interesting, or significant, and after allowing sufficient time not to seem dismissive, Ivan remarked that he'd been about to check out the boatshed. Bowden said he was happy to walk down with him, which wasn't the response Ivan had hoped for.

Bowden was one of those people who assume physical proximity is sufficient to justify personal revelation, even between strangers. As soon as they were out of earshot of the women he began to confide in Ivan, opening up with little reservation. He said Heather and he had been together only a few months, that she had escaped an abusive relationship and he'd found her virtually destitute in Picton, in a camping ground. 'She's had a hellish rough patch,' said Bowden. 'We've hit it off pretty good actually. She's a dynamo in the sack.' He gave a laugh that suggested he was accustomed to arousing such response in women.

'Right,' said Ivan in a neutral tone.

'Never a bad thing in a woman, is it.' Bowden talked on, keen to prolong the topic of Heather's willingness to fuck, but Ivan didn't reply. It was something she wouldn't have told him herself and he had no wish to hear of it any other way. He wanted to be alone to enjoy the stillness and warmth of the summer morning, the colours of the bay, the familiar discordance of the gulls and the regular susurration of the sea. 'We were in the Picton camping ground for a while,' Bowden told him, 'but even a hut there costs a fair bit. It's okay here until we get ourselves sorted. I can turn my hand to most things mechanical. It's just I never got the qualifications.'

The boatshed had no lock. Just a spoon pushed through the catch to keep the door closed. That was the way of things at Harikoa Bay. Inside was an old, clinker-built dinghy, striped with sunlight from the gaps in the warped plank walls, and a pair of oars on the floor, one spare rowlock lying alongside, a plastic jug to bale with, an old sou'wester on a nail, stiff as a seal skin. The anchor rope was white and furry from so much time in both the sun and the sea.

'I could help you push her out,' volunteered Bowden. A generous enough offer, but Ivan didn't want him there; didn't want to share the boat, or the bay, with him, or be told more about Heather's habit of initiating sex when she woke in the mornings, rubbing against her partner like a lioness on heat. Not only was it a betrayal of intimacy and a male boast, but also the evocation of something lacking in his own life. He said he wasn't going to do anything with the boat right away, that he had work emails to attend to before he could think of taking the dinghy out. He said how much he enjoyed fishing by himself as a change from the constant presence of clients and colleagues at his work. He said it artlessly, casually, yet with a message that even Bowden couldn't misconstrue.

—◈》《◈—

With the men gone, Nicky had shifted to the vacated soft chair, and she and Heather began to talk with more intent, both knowing that they were making an assessment that would determine how far they let each other in. There was no easy match of age, profession or background, but Nicky soon decided she liked this woman for her intelligence and wry fortitude. Heather didn't heap disclosure at first acquaintance as Bowden did, but was open nevertheless. She talked with glancing humour of her own life and was interested to hear of Nicky's. There is a sub-text to the conversation of women that is often lacking in that of men: flags flown that have meaning additional to what is said, sometimes contrary even. Bowden had been good to her at a difficult time, Heather explained. 'He's rough enough round the edges, but he knows what it's like to have a crappy break-up. He's been married. Kids too, and that's sad, isn't it?'

'He must be a good deal older.'

'Oh yeah, much. He's been good to me, though, when I needed it. I don't kid myself that it'll last, but we're okay for each other for now. Neither of us have made any promises: we're just taking things as they come. You never know with guys, do you. I like it here at the bay. Not to live always, but for a while. You must too?'

'I do. We didn't come all that regularly, but it seems more often than it was. Some holidays are like that, aren't they, longer and brighter than other times.'

'As kids we had holidays in camping grounds. Rotorua, Taupō, places like that. Nothing special. It must be different now your boys have grown up.'

'We're thinking of going to the States,' Nicky said. 'I'm applying for a university position there.'

'Wow,' said Heather. 'You must be a real brain box.'

'I had a lot of support. A lot of advantages. Ivan's not keen to leave his work here, but I hope he'll come. I think both of us would benefit from a change. You can get too set in your ways, and it's a small country.'

'I'd like to go overseas. If I had the money I'd be off. Maybe I could do a working holiday, meet a super rich Italian guy.' She got up and went to the kitchen part of the room. 'Things are better here than ours,' she said. 'The oven and microwave look pretty new. The kitchen in our place is crappy.' How old would she be, Nicky wondered. Thirty maybe, no more. Below average height, but with a good figure, and she wore small ear studs with blue stones that were attractive, even if somewhat out of place with shorts and a T-shirt. She had a demeanour of resilience and adaptability, as if accustomed to taking life on despite the contest seldom going her way. With difficulty she opened one of the deep, wooden drawers beneath the sink and looked in. 'Yeah, this stuff though's just like ours. Things that have been here for ever and never a bloody tin-opener that works. All nana stuff.'

'I guess old bits and pieces get exiled to the bach,' said Nicky. 'The bedding here's mainly army surplus by the look of it.'

'Same with us. Anyway, I've held you up long enough. Bowden's probably back by now. You should come over sometime and see the place again.'

'I'd like that, and perhaps you can both come over for a meal before we go.' They went to the door and after saying goodbye, Nicky stayed in the sun, sitting down on the form and watching Heather walk through the straggly brown grass, the dark broom clumps and briar, the trios of small, violet butterflies that skirmished at head height. Nicky wasn't keen to go to the McDermott bach, she had all she needed of it as a memory, but maybe she would, just to have Heather to talk to again. And she would have a lunch for them all. Now that the boys were gone she realised that Ivan's company wasn't enough. Fine in itself, but not enough on its own.

Ivan was on the shore, standing looking out to sea. Nicky could see no sign of Bowden, which was no surprise. Those two wouldn't hit it off. She wondered what sort of a life people had in Morgantown, West Virginia. From what she knew of American universities she assumed staff were more collegial there, more social, welcoming to a woman whether she had a partner or not. She would be invited to thanksgiving dinners and star-spangled banner parades. The number and variety of academics working within her own speciality would be so much greater than in New Zealand. The relevant periodicals would be more numerous, and their editors more well disposed towards her submissions if she lived there. Ivan had begun to walk along the beach. She could watch him quite dispassionately: a decent, unexceptional man who was a good father and dependable partner, despite his lapse with Irene Flowerday. Probably he'd choose not to go with her to the States, but Nicky wanted the decision to be his. She was a little amused, and disappointed, by the degree to which he fulfilled the stereotype of an accountant — the industrious dependability, aversion to risk, a certain inwardness and social reserve. There was the dancing, however, and the sex. Men always wanted more sex than their wives, didn't they, at least until the blood cooled.

Nicky had found lovemaking overrated — even with men more attractive and talented than Ivan. The localised physical pleasure never outweighed the sense of intrusion, of being overwhelmed, almost of being used. Always she experienced a sense of detachment, and although attractive herself, she wasn't captivated by the human form. Naked people are not beautiful. Not even young women, when viewed free from the haze of lust. Humans need the addition of colours, coverings, fragrances, coiffuring and adornment to approach beauty. They are too close to apish ancestors to be attractive to an impartial observer, and bipedal walking hasn't yet attained the natural grace of four-footed creatures perfected by a far longer evolution.

She remembered on their trip to Singapore a visit to the zoo, and the tigers there, close and at ease, one swimming in the moat. Now there was beauty. All sinuous and glowing hide, great liquid eyes and whiskers like pale quills. All cats were lovely, but the beauty of tigers was accentuated by the element of threat, the awareness of a terminal savagery at their disposal.

Nicky didn't dislike men. She enjoyed the company and conversation of intelligent guys and the balance they brought as colleagues. She even admired their characteristic of ignoring, or not noticing, the trivialities of relationships that so many women got hung up on, but she didn't much want them lying on her, handling her, getting inside her. She understood that a woman's body was a valuable currency in dealings with men, but unlike Heather she wasn't dependent on it.

Yes, definitely an application for West Virginia. She would complete it after lunch when Ivan would be fishing, but she wouldn't make a secret of it. She could no longer see Ivan, and assumed he was on the track, walking back to her. She wished him happiness, but not at the expense of her own.

—◦⟫ ⟪◦—

'How did you get on with Heather?' he asked her as they ate.

'Quite liked her, actually. We're going to meet up again. What about you and Bowden?'

'He's okay, I suppose. We haven't much in common, though, and I didn't take to him. I don't think there's a hell of a lot to him, yet he talks all the time.'

'Is he going fishing with you?'

'No, so if you don't mind I'll need your help to push the dinghy out. The tide's up so it shouldn't be too bad. You don't want to come fishing?'

'No. I'll come down with you and then have a walk along the beach, maybe a swim. I need to get onto my application, though.'

'Right.' Ivan recognised the prompt for a reopening of their conversation about the future, but didn't want to go there. 'You could read your draft to me tonight and we can talk about it then,' he said, assuming a falsely positive tone.

'That's fine.'

'They seem to me a bit of an odd couple. He must be a lot older than her. He went on about how she'd had a bad time with some guy in Hamilton and run off, ended up in Picton on the bones of her arse. I can't see it lasting.'

'She said he's been kind to her. She needs someone right now, even if it's not permanent. They seem happy enough.'

'Well, that's something,' said Ivan. Everything seemed to have some relevance to the unease within their own relationship, even the single white cloud shaped like a cartoon bone drifting overhead, and a bumble bee walking clumsily in the grass by the bench seat. Even the way they concentrated on those things rather than looking at each other. Especially the McDermott bach not far away, where they had come with the boys and been like a family in a happy television shot.

When they'd washed and dried the few dishes, they walked together down to the boatshed, and with Ivan pushing and Nicky pulling, they dragged the boat the short distance to the water, where he hopped in and she waited for a time, and waved, as he rowed out. Occupied with the oars, he couldn't wave back, but smiled and nodded as he diminished, facing her, not the direction in which he was headed.

Nicky walked on then along the granular shore, glancing sometimes to see Ivan becoming smaller, pulling steadily to the place where there was the best chance of cod. She walked right around to the rocks of the headland and then turned and began to walk back, but farther from the beach, along the wandering track that led past the baches. Yes, as Ivan had said, there was a car by the top hut where the old guy lived, and as she came closer she saw him sitting in a driftwood chair, watching her. None of the baches had fences, or gates: their individual boundaries indeterminate.

'Hello,' Nicky said and stopped.

'Good afternoon and welcome,' he replied, and clumsily, but courteously, stood up . Yes, an old man all right, but not unkempt and quite able to initiate and maintain a conversation. He introduced himself as Wiri Purdue and said he'd been watching Ivan rowing out to fish. 'I think he knows where to go,' he said with a smile, and Nicky told him about their past visits to the bay, about their boys and the McDermott bach. She could see he was part Māori and asked about his iwi. 'Too many affiliations to burden you with,' he said, 'and half Irish as well. Now that's some sort of a double whammy, isn't it.'

Wiri had been a high school teacher, mainly in the Bay of Plenty and Marlborough, and was an interesting man to talk to. His wife was dead, but he had a married daughter in Nelson. 'Close enough to keep in touch, but far enough away not to be a bother to them,' he said. 'I've always lived close to the sea.'

'Bit lonely in the winter though?'

'I go over to them for quite long spells sometimes, but I'm used to being on my own.' He had one of those aquiline Māori faces that Nicky saw in paintings more than real life. She could imagine him with a moko. Wiri was interested in her work at the university, although his qualification was in history and hers in drama. Nicky was keen to tap his local knowledge. She knew nothing of the bay's history, little of the wider area's. 'Harikoa means joy, happiness,' he told her, and when she mentioned her sons' fascination with the glow worms years ago, he said the Māori name was titiwai. Wiri talked, too, of present ownership and occupation, and the ban on major alteration to the existing baches, or the building of new ones. 'All here is under sufferance,' he said. 'These old places were built without any land titles whatsoever.'

They talked for some time, standing in the hot sun together, and before Nicky left he wished her well, and she said maybe he'd like to come to their place for a drink: sometime during the next couple of days when it suited him and when Ivan would be there. She was going to have a swim, she told him, and Wiri smiled and nodded. He wore a white, formal shirt, blue shorts and sandals and was clean shaven. 'Enjoy your stay,' he said with a cheerful smile, bestowing benevolence, as if suzerain of the bay.

In the bach she changed into her swimming costume, and with a multi-coloured beach towel around her shoulders walked down to the shore, discarded the towel and sandals with hardly a pause and waded into the water with a brief intake of breath. Unlike Ivan, she wasn't a good swimmer, clumsy in the sea although graceful on firm ground. Yet another way in which the two of them differed. When in the water he regained the assurance and mastery he displayed when dancing. She could see the dinghy at the fishing spot, but it was too far away for her to make any signal. She was beyond the small breaking waves, but still had the reassuring touch of the clean sea floor when she stood up, just her head above the water. How strong the taste of sea water, and not merely of salt. She let just a little into her mouth to reacquaint herself with its complexity, and of course it triggered recollection of the earlier visits, of Hugh and Danny and a happy Ivan, although there was no one else swimming and no one on the beach. She would, however, write her application that afternoon: already she was turning over phrases that were true but glossed, as was customary, to present herself in a favourable light. The beach was a lipstick swathe around the bay, the five baches weathered and low in profile amid long grass and shrubs, the bush gullies frog-green despite the summer. Nicky had read somewhere that sea water had medicinal value, and she took a couple of sips as she thought of West Virginia and what life might be like there. Challenge was what one needed in life, otherwise all was mere repetition.

—◦≫ ≪◦—

Two cod and a trevally. Ivan was pleased with his catch when he returned late in the afternoon. He brought them inside, already gutted and cleansed at the water's edge, and made no reference to the laptop on the table before her. She'd said what she was going to do, but he wasn't ready to talk about that. The evening would bring engagement soon enough. 'Well done,' she said. 'I'll do some now. I'm glad I brought those lemons. Which do you want?'

'Cod,' he said. 'What's better than fresh blue cod?' He was sunburnt despite the floppy hat, and he smelled a little of fish and sweat. It was a novelty for him to spend so much time outdoors and to come back as a provider.

'You need a shower,' she said.

They ate later at the small wooden table with the laptop pushed to one side: no cloth, mismatched plates and cutlery, salt the only condiment, wine in plastic mugs. A good wine, though, a Marlborough riesling they had bought when in Blenheim the day before. Nicky talked about meeting Wiri Purdue at the top hut, about expecting some sort of hermit and finding an articulate, educated man with family in Nelson and other links with the world. They talked some more, too, about Bowden and Heather, the way life sometimes brings people together in what seems quite random ways. Nicky did most of the talking. He could have described how his fishing line had angled in refraction in the clear water of the sea, how the dinghy had jostled as he'd rowed into the swell, how the tails of the hooked fish had twisted in futile opposition as he hauled them in, how much he missed his sons, and how much he would miss her now that she was determined to go away, but he said nothing of those things.

After the meal they tidied up and then went for a walk on the beach. It was still hot and they walked slowly, turning often to the slight sea breeze. There was always that smell of the sea: strong, unmistakable, yet mysterious in its elements. 'I wonder what the old chap Purdue does all day,' said Ivan.

'Well, he's onto the fishing spots. Knew where you were heading. He knows a lot of history stuff about the area too.' She told Ivan of the glow worm name — titiwai. And the meaning of Harikoa.

'You could end up in a lot worse places than this,' Ivan said.

He stooped and took up a stick, as white and smooth as a bone, and used it to fossick as they went. His face and legs were angry with sunburn. 'You've got to remember here to put lotion on at least a couple of times a day,' she said. Habitual concern and consideration for a partner often survive the passing of passion.

'I know. I should keep some in the boat maybe. The reflection off the water makes it worse, I reckon.'

He enjoyed walking on the beach with her, being the recipient of her attention, knowing, however, that later they would disagree again, hurt each other with reluctance, but hurt each other all the same.

— ⁂ —

That time came with the late dusk, as they sat in the main room, occupying the two easy chairs, Nicky with the laptop on her knee. 'I'll read it now, shall I?' she said.

'Okay.'

'It's good to get an objective view.' What view could be less objective than his, as they both knew, but she read it because she didn't want it kept from him: she read it to show that he was still important to her. She read it so that it was plain to them both what the future was most likely to hold.

It was an impressive application, as he knew it would be. Afterwards there was a silence for a time, then he said, 'You don't go into your family circumstances at all.'

'Well, that's something that would be discussed if and when I got offered the position. And also I don't know yet if you'd be coming. You haven't said. You won't say.'

'Maybe you won't get it,' he said, not unkindly.

'I think I will. I say that only to you, but I think I will. There's been some unofficial encouragement as is often the way in academic appointments. Nothing's certain, of course.'

'Maybe I could decide when it is.'

'Okay,' she said. 'I just don't want you to pretend anything's a surprise when it happens. Everything in the open, right?' She put the laptop on the floor beside her and leant forward in the poor light of the single bulb. 'I'll go whether you come or not, and you need to know that.' She said it in a soft, deliberate voice, almost as if explaining to a child, and he gave in reply his customary, small exasperated sigh. 'We'd just be moving on,' she said. 'If you don't come, we'll still keep in touch and I trust you about any division of money, or property, if it comes to that. That stuff's not something I worry about. We're not like those people who want to punish each other.' She knew that in any separation the financial decisions would be important to him, not at all because he wished to advantage himself, but because by nature and profession he feared the financial loss that so often ensued when marriage ended.

'It's not that. We could manage that. It's more that splitting up diminishes everything that's happened before. What's the point of all that we've done together if then we just bugger off on our own.'

'It wouldn't be easy, not at first, but there are gains as well, aren't there. Freedom things, you know? I mean things difficult for — difficult if we're still together.'

'Such as?'

'Well, you could find some accommodating woman to fuck, and feel okay about that.'

'First blood to you,' he said.

'What?'

'I knew that would come up.'

'I'm just saying. I know that's important to you.'

They were getting to the nub of things now, talking of matters they normally avoided because the edges were too sharp. Awkward things and dangerous to handle. Ivan had brought the driftwood stick inside with him, as was his habit, and he picked it up from the uncarpeted floor, held it between his flat palms and made the tip rotate on the floor, as if it were a fire stick. But he did it slowly without generation of heat at its tip, or within himself. 'And what about you?' he said. 'What special emancipation have you got in mind?' Was there sarcasm there? He intended none.

'Not being a housewife, for a start. That's pretty important. I'll be concentrating on a couple of research projects I've had in mind for years. The boys don't need me now the same, and I don't think you do either. It's a cliché, I know, but people change and want different things. For nineteen years I've put myself fourth — not first, second or third, but fourth, at the end of the line. I don't regret it. I'd do it again, but I don't have to now and I don't feel guilty. There were things important to my work that I had to put aside. I feel entitled to selfishness now.'

'We were happy, though, weren't we?' Ivan asked.

'Mostly we were, but I've got catching up to do now. It's exciting for me.'

'I can understand that.'

'I'm in credit now, aren't I? In your own accounting terms, I'm in credit.'

'Yes, I grant you that all right. I can see how it's quite exciting now for you, but does going overseas have to be part of it?'

'It's where this opportunity is. A new country, new people. I think I'd like that. Wouldn't you?'

'I don't think I would, actually — not long term,' he said. It came to him that Nicky was more optimistic, more trusting of the future, while his inclination was to hold fast to what he had in the present — and perhaps in the past too. You could put too much at risk and come a cropper.

'So you wouldn't come with me?' she said.

'I don't think I would. I'm not sure, though. When it comes to the crunch, who knows.'

'Fair enough. I think we should make selfish decisions. Best in the end, I think.'

'Selfish decisions?'

'I do what I want and you do what you want. Anything else will just fester, I think. We've had a good run really, with the boys and everything. There's no shame in taking individual directions now. No shame, no blame. We'd be friends and keep in touch. People change.'

'You've said that,' said Ivan.

'I know.'

'Can't people change and stay together?'

'I don't think they can always. Every situation's different. Why not face up to what we've got, which is that you think staying here is more important than being together, and I think going's more important than being together. I mean, that's it, isn't it?'

'So much honesty. It's like talking with no clothes on.'

'The naked truth,' Nicky said and touched his arm lightly as rapprochement. She remained leaning towards him a little for emphasis, and he continued to turn the driftwood stick, but with his eyes to hers.

'It isn't what we thought would happen,' said Ivan.

'What did you expect to happen?'

'Have the boys come back as often as they wished. Have money enough for any trips that took our fancy. Build a new home on one of our sections perhaps.'

'As long as we don't bullshit ourselves, I think we'll be okay. I really do. We do this knowing what it is, and see how it works out. It's not about either of us winning.'

'What do we say to the boys?'

'We tell them exactly what it is. You think they haven't been with us long enough to know how things are? They'll still have two people to visit who love them, just living in different places.'

'I guess so. They're bright enough.' There wasn't anything of significance in what Nicky said that he could take issue with, and he knew the resentment he still felt was at the way things had turned out between them, not at her. Disappointment, really, rather than resentment, and he was no doubt largely responsible for it. It made him feel sad. It changed the way he felt about where they were. 'How do you feel about going home tomorrow?' he asked. 'We've thrashed this thing out enough for now, haven't we, and we're hardly in holiday mood.'

'You've pre-paid, remember.'

'I don't care about that.'

'I did mention a catch-up to Heather, but I suppose we could just pop in before we leave and say goodbye.' There was Wiri Purdue too, but she knew Ivan wanted to get home, that the bay had altered around them, or rather that they weren't the same people. She knew, too, that he didn't want to talk about the marriage any more and that it seemed to him the future was being shaped more by her than him. 'We can work through it as long as we're honest with each other,' she said. 'Change this big isn't easy, I know, but we'll come out the other side better by facing it now.'

'We're giving up on each other. That's it, isn't it, when you strip it down.'

'In a way, yeah, but in another way we're just making a new

agreement about how we are, and that doesn't mean all we've had and done together is less important. Not to me.'

'Time will tell,' Ivan said. 'My guess is we'll just drift further and further apart.'

'Well, we work at it then.'

'I'd rather work at what we've got.'

'But it's not enough, what we've got, is it? It's not going anywhere.'

'Do we have to be always going somewhere?'

'Now you're just fucking with words so you don't have to engage,' Nicky said. She didn't want to get angry. She didn't want him to get angry. Success depended on them being able to keep talking through the whole thing: keep talking even if they ended up on opposite sides of the world, as looked to be the likely outcome. Pull back now, she told herself, leave communication open. 'Anyway,' she said, 'you've heard the application. Maybe, as you say, I won't get it anyway, so there's time. There's — I'm making sure you're in the loop, though, aren't I?'

'Yeah.'

'Well, that's important, isn't it?'

'Fair enough,' he said, but with that same small smile that was dispute to every word.

'Anyway, let's leave it there for now and have a coffee. Okay? Just remember all of this isn't a criticism of you.'

'I just never thought it would be us.'

'It's like I said. People change and circumstances change too. What fits now doesn't necessarily fit the future, or the past.' Nicky got up and went to make their drinks. 'I thought we might've heard from Hugh,' she said. 'He was going to let us know when he got to Istanbul.'

'But he's not flying. All manner of hold-ups when you're going by train or bus over there.'

—⟫⟪—

They talked about trains and planes and buses, about over there, as they had their coffee, as proof that they could debate crucial things, disagree, parade emotionally naked, as Ivan said, and re-emerge fully clothed to behave conventionally once more. They were educated, sensible people of substance and experience who would work things through. Nicky knew that, and Ivan hoped it was true.

'I think I'll have a walk before it's properly dark,' he said later. 'Go up maybe to see if the glow worms are there, but I won't be long.'

'Okay,' Nicky said.

It was very still outside: the hiatus between the sea breeze and the land breeze, with the temperatures of both ocean and earth at brief equilibrium. The moon gave a pearl lustre to the thin cloud that obscured it, and the breathing of the sea was lulling in the gloom. Ivan needed the torch as soon as he entered the bush and in its bouncing light the trees and ferns pranced grotesquely around him. It always seemed to take longer at night to reach the glow worm bank, as if the bush extended its domain once the sun was gone. He switched off the torch just before reaching the underhang and crouched, breathing heavily from the scramble, the jeans he'd put on making the sunburn sting. Even when his breathing had subsided and he'd been still and quiet for several minutes, there were no stars on the moist bank, no miniature cosmos that Hugh and Danny had found so fascinating. Hugh had been interested, too, in the science of it: how an organic body came to bioluminescence. He'd done 'research', he said, and told his brother with delight that it was the glow worms' arses that were shining. Boys enjoy such humour.

But there were no shining arse stars for Ivan. Just the dark creekbed in the bush, and memories and a regret already formed in regard to the future. Maybe it wasn't the right time in the life cycle of glow worms; maybe they knew he was there and didn't trust him. He went back down and stood for a moment outside the bach, part of the general stillness. In dimness all about him, the only light, apart from that of their own place, was from the McDermott bach where Bowden and Heather were staying — a big, unqualified blond man and a small, feisty, hard-done-by pale and dark woman, both beleaguered, but trying to make a life together despite the odds.

Nicky was still in her chair in the main room, with a book and a mug. 'I've just made myself another drink,' she said. 'Do you want one?'

'I'll get it.'

'Did you see the glow worms?' she asked.

'No,' he said. 'I don't think they're there any more.'

21.

The Dreamer

Children open their hearts to anyone they trust, but we learn as adults to keep secret the things most dear to us. An emotional armour is necessary against both the malicious and unintended treacheries of life. There are just a few people, however, who never acquire such protection and walk with a dismaying vulnerability among their fellows. Matt is one of those, despite his solid, reassuring sort of name.

I was flatting with Ewan, a long-term uni mate, and writing a thesis on the degradation of our alpine vegetation. Money was tight and we had three rooms and a shared kitchen and bathroom in a rambling wooden house close to the river, from which the mist rolled like smoke in the winter. There were other tenants — Briar and Karen in the front rooms with a bathroom of their own, and Matt with just a bedroom. The women had been there a year, but Matt was new, like us. The kitchen was our common space. Sometimes in the evening all five of us would be there employing the stove and microwave, manoeuvring around each other, the women making fun of the rest of us because of our eating habits. Matt existed on tinned soup and baked beans, or reheated takeaways, and we weren't much better, although Ewan had a distinguished family recipe for fish pie. Karen laid down ground rules regarding washing up and putting the rubbish out. I found out in time she had ground rules in personal relationships as well. Both she and Briar were attractive, but she had greater awareness of it and more craft in its deployment.

Matt was on the council's park staff. Gardens, not cars. No family or friends came to visit him. He belonged to no groups, received no personal mail that I noticed in the box, walked, or biked, by himself with an aura of fierce intensity. He had hog-bristle black hair, a roll of flesh at the back of his neck, heavy lips with the downward pout of a blue cod.

'Can I come in and talk?' he asked when I'd been just two days in the flat. It was evening and the slanting summer light flooded through the green glass of the front door and made an aquarium of the large, old-fashioned hall. He stood at our door, his lips lifting slightly in what I would come to recognise as his smile. He had a direct, persistent gaze that made evasion difficult.

'I've got a bit of stuff to get through,' I said, 'but sure, come in for a bit.' Ewan was there and Matt seemed glad of a larger audience.

'How you guys settling in?' he asked, as if he wasn't himself a newcomer.

In reality he wasn't much interested in us except as recipients of his own visions and ambitions. 'You're graduates, right?' he said. 'You know about poetry and books.'

'I'm doing law,' said Ewan. He had written Matt off within five minutes of meeting him. Ewan was a noted athlete and had no time for also rans.

'Geography,' I said.

'But you've done English,' Matt insisted. He took one of the four creaky cane chairs that came with the room, jettisoned from some suburban gazebo and forlornly out of place in the dingy sitting room. 'I'm writing this book about my life,' he said. 'Almost a hundred and forty thousand words and I'm just about finished. But I'm not using "I", or "me". I'm writing it as if it's someone else, see.'

'Third person,' I said.

'Someone else,' he said. 'It's really searching stuff and I've put a lot into it. I thought maybe you'd like to read it. It would be good to get feedback as I go.'

Ewan stood up and said he had work to do. Our desks were in the bedrooms. Matt kept his eyes fixed on mine and his lower lip drooped wetly. I said I wasn't much at literary criticism. 'But you can be the average reader, can't you?' Matt said. 'They say it's good to pitch to the average reader and I can explain the difficult parts. Some of it's quite deep, actually. Life's deep, though, isn't it.'

'Maybe a professional appraisal and editing service would be better,' I said. 'People who know what publishers are looking for.'

'I tried one,' he said. 'It cost bloody heaps and they didn't seem to get it at all. Went on about apostrophes and paragraphs when I'm dealing with life-changing stuff. I don't think the woman could cope with the intensity of it. Anyway, I'll just get it. I won't be a jiffy.' And before I could think of any way to prevent it, he was off to his room and almost immediately back with a much-scuffed laptop that he put on one of the cane chairs drawn close.

'Just choose a typical section,' I said firmly. 'Representative of your style and intentions. I've actually got something I have to get onto quite soon.'

'There's this part about getting fired from Toomeys' for nothing, well, just a small accident in packing that wasn't really my fault, and Melissa saying I was bothering her. I really nailed it: wrote six thousand words over a weekend, I was so pissed off with how I was treated. There's therapy in writing, isn't there.' Matt found the place and hitched his chair closer to mine. As I read, he kept switching his gaze from the screen to my face and back, smilingly intent, waiting for some expression of amazed admiration that I would be unable to contain.

I don't claim to be a critic, but the writing wasn't that bad, it just wasn't special. It was the sort of earnest self-revelation that you could find in any number of letters and diaries written by ordinary people, but how could I say that to Matt, whom I hardly knew and who had created a hundred and forty thousand words of the stuff instead of getting a life.

'So, what do you think, eh?' Matt said for a third or fourth time. There was a lot of swearing in it and I noticed that because he didn't swear much when he talked. That was about all I could come up with.

'Seems to be a lot of swearing,' I said.

'I want it to be real life,' replied Matt. 'Nothing held back at all.'

'Yeah, but you don't swear a lot, do you.'

'It's impact, though. The appraisal I got said that language has to be heightened for fiction. She said I hadn't achieved lift-off. What's lift-off?'

'I'm not sure.'

'I could show you the appraisal?'

'No, that's okay,' I said. 'Actually I'd better get on with some work of my own, but thanks for the chance to see some of your stuff. A hundred and forty thousand words is pretty impressive, I have to say.' At least I could praise his work ethic.

'What do you think I should do?' A few days in the same house and he was asking my advice as to what direction his life should take. His face had become blue cod again and I could tell from his tone he was disappointed by my response.

'Why not send it off to a publisher? That way you'd get another professional opinion. Maybe the assessment woman missed the point. Finish it and send it off so you find out one way or another. That's my advice.'

Matt was keen for me to read some more of what he termed 'crucial passages', and even when I said I didn't have time, he wasn't in any hurry to leave, kept talking about the reluctance of publishers to accept work that broke new ground. 'I'm breaking new ground, you see,' he said.

'Good on you. A last revision, perhaps cut down on the swearing and sex, and then send it on its way with fingers crossed, I reckon.' Sex and obscenity can be winners in fiction, but the former in particular seemed remarkably foreign to Matt's experience, and it showed.

'Maybe I will — send it off soon, I mean,' he said as I manoeuvred him to the door. 'I wouldn't mind you having another look over more of it before then.'

'No, strike while the iron is hot.' I was all enthusiasm, but for my own benefit.

That's what he decided. He came to see me as a confidant and button-holed me regularly to talk of his masterpiece. Less than three weeks after showing me his writing, he came to me in the kitchen when I was checking on Ewan's fish pie. 'I've sent it off to Penguin,' he said in a tone of suitable solemnity. 'In the accompanying letter I said—', but his voice died away as his attention was taken by Ewan and Karen passing in the passage, each unconsciously drawing to full height and with foreshortened pace as they exchanged hellos with distant courtesy, yet with a lost intimacy still a fragrance about them. 'He's screwed her, hasn't he?' Matt said softly after they were gone.

'I think he has,' I said. The qualified admission made it less a betrayal of confidence.

'Jesus.' His gaze lingered on the green lit hallway, part wistfulness, part incomprehension, as a chimpanzee gazes at the full moon. I had no sympathy for him, and envied Ewan, although he'd been denied a permanent bed in paradise. Ewan was an alpha male and would move on. 'Anyway,' said Matt as the moment passed, 'I told Penguin I needed a response within a fortnight.'

'Perhaps not a good idea to put too much pressure on.'

'The work will speak for itself.'

'Good luck with that then.'

'I sent it to the top person,' Matt said, 'so there's no reason for it to get stuck on a desk lower down.'

Well, he was right about that at least. The typescript came within nine days, with a formal note, which Matt brought to my bedroom quite late at night. He wanted to be sure we'd be alone, he said. His expression was one of suppressed suffering as he proffered the editor's note. It lay on the flat of his hand rather than being held in his fingers, and I remember the oddity of that. As you might hold a dead butterfly, or a marshmallow.

'Unfortunately, not at all suitable for our list,' the letter said, and not much more.

'What list?' said Matt morosely. He'd been weeping almost certainly.

'It means the sort of books they go in for, I think.'

'A hundred and forty-seven thousand words about the world as it really is and there's no room on some list?'

'You could try other places. Some great books were turned down time after time at first.'

'It's a conspiracy,' said Matt. 'Everything's written and chosen by women these days. There's a feminine aversion to forthright masculinity.' He must have read that somewhere, surely.

I did feel sorry for him. Not just because all that beavering away in his room had come to nothing, but because I was evidently the closest thing to a friend he had for consolation. I wasn't his friend, but he didn't understand that, and it wasn't the moment to disillusion him, so I put aside my notes on the effect of climate change on *Ranunculus grahamii* and listened to him go on about hopes he'd had for recognition, how his fellow workers in the parks division gave him a hard time, and his failure to hook up with any girls, including Karen and Briar. 'I took my room mainly because they lived here,' he said. 'You'd think you'd have a good chance, wouldn't you, when you're actually living with girls, but they're not interested in anything about me. Briar avoids me and I heard Karen tell her I'm creepy.'

She told me he was creepy too. A retarded, creepy guy, she said. She chatted often enough with me, but said she wasn't interested in a relationship. A very direct person, Karen. Always she would sway slightly in a womanly way as she talked to you, though, just so you were aware of what was possible. Her father had quite an important job at the council and she said she could have lived at home if she wished. She was out of my league, but I had some hopes regarding Briar, whose legs weren't as good, but who had more empathy and a more natural manner. She was at training college and sometimes asked my advice about her essays.

When I came back from a field trip in the upper Rakaia, I expected a disconsolate Matt to be soon at my door, but he seemed quite up when I met him in the kitchen heating some fried rice and chicken. I asked him about his book. 'Oh, I've moved on,' he said blithely. 'I've found my real path in art. Text is ultimately unable to encompass life. I've realised I've got this natural gift for oils and it's all coming together. Colour, shape and composition are the best means to express yourself.'

'I didn't know you were into art as well,' I said.

'I went to a talk in the gallery on modern non-representational trends and I took out books from the library. I don't suppose you know much about art?'

'It's not really my thing,' I said.

'I'll show you what I'm doing. Come, come,' he said, both impatient and condescending, and with one hand on my shoulder and the other carrying his meal, he ushered me down the hall. I knew his room well enough. The smallest in the large house. A sagging wire-strung bed with a wooden headboard and a tartan cover, a kitset table with his laptop among the jumble, a solitary cane chair, brother to others elsewhere in the house — it must have been an extensive gazebo the landlord had raided. There were things new, however: an easel which held the painting he was working on, and an intangible addition, the fragrance of oil paint that dispossessed the accustomed smell of Matt's neglected body. 'Look at this,' he said with affection surpassing that of a new parent, indicating the painting.

I was relieved at his pleasure, at his recovery of purpose and belief. I'd expected him to be still cast down by the rejection of his hundred and forty-seven thousand words. I wasn't Matt's friend, despite his assumption of it, but he had no one else I was aware of and I didn't want him to be sad. He sought me out more when he was forlorn. That was my main consideration as I looked at his painting, standing before it and with Matt close, avid for response, his eyes flicking from my face to the work and back, just as when he'd presented his writing. The painting was in brutal stripes of black and red, and over them the bold lettering in yellow — 'TELL IT NOT IN GATH.'

'It's from the Old Testament,' Matt said, sensing my bewilderment.
'Right.'
'Biblical significance.'
'Right, but you said text wasn't able to encompass art?'
'It's integrated, though,' said Matt. 'Integrated with the visual elements to achieve emotional unity and intellectual gravitas. There's this book I could lend you.'
'Right,' I said. It didn't look much to me, but then what do I know about art. Mainly I just wanted Matt to be happily engrossed in something and not always coming goblin-like to my door late at night to open his sorry heart. Extended commiseration can be a chore, especially when you're young.
'How do you know when you've finished it?' I asked.
'It just about is, I reckon, but there's some left of the red and I might as well use that up. It'll add texture. There's red over because the black bands grow bigger from top to bottom. Did you notice that?'
'Yeah, I did actually.'
'To give a sense of darkness burgeoning,' said Matt.
'I can see that.'
'The burgeoning is symbolism. Colour symbolism is pretty much what I'm into with this.'

'I do like the red,' I said, 'and yeah, I can see symbolism there. I mean blood, fire, danger, stuff like that. It's visceral even, red is.' I was quite pleased with visceral, and Matt seemed impressed.

'You're bang on there,' he said, and went on to tell me he was planning a triptych: a green and white, and a blue and pink, to accompany his black and red.

The rice had become cold during our talk and Matt came back with me to the kitchen to give it yet another burst. 'Come in any night and see me working on them,' Matt said. 'I don't think it would be a distraction at all and you could learn a lot. Painting's different to writing. I find I can even listen to music when I'm painting.'

'Might be better if I come in to be surprised when you're all done. There must be a lot of concentration needed for painting.' Did I wish to spend my nights watching Matt slap on his coloured stripes?

'I really feel it's natural for me, though,' he said. 'It's what I'm meant to do, I'm sure of that.'

The new priority in Matt's life kept him buoyed up for weeks. Whenever he saw me he offered a fulsome rundown on how his triptych was progressing. He would have done the same for the others, but they brushed him off. I couldn't quite bring myself to tell him I wasn't interested in his pursuits, not interested in him. Ewan said he was a total bore and a loser, Karen said he was a creepy weirdo and even Briar said he was just a dreamer. Maybe I was a little less secure in my sense of superiority.

You knew, though, that Matt's euphoria wouldn't last. The bluebird of happiness was migratory in his world. On one of the coldest nights of August, when I was about to go to bed, he came tapping on my door, jauntiness lost once more. He took a cane chair to the side of the oil heater and positioned himself to absorb most of the limited comfort it provided.

'People don't value my talent,' he said despairingly. 'No one seems to understand.' It would never occur to Matt to open a conversation by enquiring as to anyone else's wellbeing. 'I took the red and black Gath to the city gallery and couldn't even get to see the director. No bugger was interested. I offered it for the coming exhibition of emerging local artists, but a curator there said they'd already made the selections. She suggested I take it to the stall day at the arts centre where there's lots of amateur art.'

'I've seen some quite interesting pastels and watercolours there,' I said.

'They're just weekend painters. All scenes of lakes, mountains and sheep runs. They may as well be photographs, but not as good.'

'Ordinary people maybe feel more comfortable with representational stuff. They don't have to read a critique to know what it is.'

'You know how much time I spent on the triptych?'

'I know you've been seriously into it. Nobody could fault your commitment. It's just that abstract art's more demanding.'

Matt spread himself a little more by the heater and absently started eating the chocolate chippie biscuits from the packet on my desk as a consolation. 'Well,' he said, 'I went to the arts stall, didn't I. I took the entire triptych by taxi and sat by the entrance. Not one of the panels sold. No offers even. One jerk said they reminded him of old rugby jerseys.'

'Give it more time maybe for people to catch on.'

'It's expensive too, painting. A lot more than writing. I don't know how much longer I can keep it up. You've no idea the cost of oil paints.'

'Don't give up, though,' I said. The longer Matt was both absorbed and inspired in his bedroom by the muse, the better for the rest of us, especially me.

'It's not easy having an original talent. Most people operate on herd instinct.'

'Always a price to pay,' I said, and mine was to spend the next two hours bolstering his spirits while Ewan, Karen and Briar slept — maybe together.

Matt persisted with painting for several more weeks, but with a failing conviction that meant he hung around the kitchen and hall more often, came tapping on my door to enlighten me with the latest knockback, or frustration. Eventually, however, he discovered yet again his true calling and genius. Music was this time his inspiration. I should have seen it coming. If I were making this story up it would be bagpipes, or drums, of course, the cacophony of which we bore for the benefit of having Matt as euphoric recluse in his room rather than roaming in Lear-like despair. In fact it was the clarinet he decided on. He took some private lessons from an honours student at the university, and carried the black leather case with him almost everywhere as a mark of sophistication. A second-hand, but quality instrument, he told me, and I wondered how many hours on his knees within the council tulip and lily plots it represented.

As with his other cultural endeavours, he showed just that degree of hobby talent sufficient to delude himself that greatness beckoned. In those last weeks of the year, I was working on the final section of my thesis, and even now I can never revisit it without hearing again, muffled somewhat by the green hallway of that once grand house, the sound of the clarinet, repeating catches over and again. The largo from *Xerxes* by Handel, or 'Ode to Joy', which Matt told me was Beethoven, or maybe he said Bartok. A conflation of the plight of indigenous alpine vegetation and clarinet solos from traditional European composers. Life can be like that. My mother was something of a musician and I'd learnt enough to be able to encourage Matt in this latest dream of greatness. Music was better than art and writing, he told me. Top musicians travelled the world from one great venue and opera house to the next. Music was the one true universal language, he said. 'When I'm working in the gardens,' he said, 'I can feel a sort of music from the flowers and trees, especially in a breeze, and it's as if I'm in tune with universal things. Music lets you travel in an emotional world. It's transporting, I find.'

But maybe not far enough. The others complained that his playing drove them mad, but then they never had him plaintive and distraught, tapping at their doors when a dream had failed. I was willing to have the sound of a clarinet rather than the black hole of Matt's presence, but agreed with Ewan, Karen and Briar that if he intended to remain in the house next year we wouldn't come back.

When the time came, I told him that I was leaving because my thesis was finished and I wasn't sure of future plans. It failed to arouse in him any significant expression of interest in my own life. 'Whatever you do, don't go without giving me your contacts,' he said. 'I'm so close to the big breakthrough and I'll be able to keep you in touch with my path. I really feel I'm on the brink of destiny.'

I was pleased for him. I wished him no harm, but I was certain that another crash was what awaited him, despite the present animation, the temporary uplift of his codfish lips in a revelatory smile. I went away without leaving any means for him to contact me. I left him there, alone against the pitiless derision of the world.

22.

Koru
Lounge

Loneliness is a form of pain, but not of the variety that prevents observation and comprehension, that narrows everything to fretful self-absorption. At least that's what he thought as he sat in the Koru Lounge and waited for his boarding call. He was Wallace Lowry. An unremarkable name, but he had been a judge in courts that entitled him to be addressed as Justice Lowry, which added gravitas. A slight, elderly man with flat, white hair and a somewhat imperious nose. A calm man, sitting relaxed and still in the busy Koru Lounge, but yes, a lonely man nevertheless and he knew that of himself.

He had been working on his laptop and there was more to do, but he was allowing himself a break. The lounge and the people within it were familiar to him, the groups always the same even though the individuals changed. There were those like himself who sought only comfort and the opportunity to work, those who were determined to eat and drink as much as possible to justify their membership, and those whose main pleasure was the sense of privilege, of being elevated and apart from the restless, basic throng of waiting passengers.

Wallace Lowry had always felt different from other people and perhaps that sense had encouraged a propensity to be a student of human nature: an inclination reinforced by his occupation. People were placed consciously before him and he had to judge them, to see behind their appearances and their stories to an essential self. One's profession becomes customary and its requisite skills habitual. Even at a Christmas party the doctor notices the pallor of a fellow guest, the real estate agent makes assessment of the property without intention.

When he was about to return his attention to his screen, Wallace noticed a young woman coming towards him, smiling, her eyes seeking his. He knew he should remember her, but the name didn't come, nor did a context to their acquainceship, but he wasn't disconcerted. He was an elderly and somewhat important man. The young woman would remind him of all he needed to know, just as he'd been able to ask for clarification in his rooms, or in court.

'Justice Lowry?' she said. He smiled and stood up. His mother had taught him that more than fifty years before. 'I'm Rebecca Allison. We met several times at my father's place in Oriental Bay.'

'Of course,' he said, and remembered. Rebecca was the daughter of a colleague and already a senior lecturer at the University of Sydney. Art history, he recalled.

'My father often talks of you,' she said.

'And I of him,' the judge replied, not altogether truthfully. 'Are you on your way back to Sydney?'

'Via Auckland, and I should be in the air right now. My flights always seem to be delayed.'

'I know the feeling.'

'What about you?'

'I had a meeting and I'm on my way home,' he said. 'My plane doesn't leave for almost an hour, but this is as a convenient a place as any to work.'

'I don't want to disturb you.' They had remained standing.

'Not at all,' he said. 'Sit with me and tell me how things are with you and your family.'

It's no hardship to listen to an intelligent and attractive woman. He liked many women although he had never slept with one. He'd never done that, but he could still admire them for their appearance as well as their talents. He knew Rebecca was married and had a family, and he guessed her to be about thirty-five, maybe more. She was slim and fair and neat, and she looked very fresh and clean, despite the delay to her travel. She had a warmth to her manner that added to her appeal. Wallace knew that despite his many natural advantages he lacked warmth, but then the great majority of people did, and he possessed courtesy, acumen, innate consideration and a lack of malice as compensation.

When Rebecca had talked of her parents, her family and asked after his own life, listened with interest and made empathetic response, she told Wallace she was to go to Greece the next month: to a symposium on religious art.

'Actually Crete,' she said. 'Heraklion. I've never been.' Crete, Heraklion, the words were like exotic birds released among the drab verbal commoners that swarmed about them. He'd been to Crete as part of his long-anticipated OE after he was admitted to the bar, and his time there was still clear, while many other places more prominent in the brochures had faded. Yes, Heraklion, of course, and the ancient site of Knossos, the splendid Minoan artefacts of the archaeological museum, but it was the city of Chania, farther along the coast, in which he'd stayed much longer, that had greater significance for him. He had met Nikos there on a very hot day. Hot days were common, but the meeting with Nikos was special to him, even now after so many years and the loss of contact.

'I went to Crete when I was a young man,' he said. 'Such a rich history. So many overlays of culture.'

'My main interest is Christian religious art of the medieval period,' said Rebecca. 'I've been to Greece several times, but never visited Crete.'

'If you get the chance, you should go on to Chania. I'd say an hour and a half's drive. There's the wonderful Venetian harbour and a history to match Knossos.'

'There may not be a lot of time for sightseeing unfortunately. It looks a tight programme and I have to be back at the university almost immediately.'

'Go to Chania if you can, though,' he said. He remembered the old sea wall and small enclosed harbour, the promenade and the bow sweep of many cafés and tavernas, the small, colourful boats nodding and jostling in the hot sun. He had come from Heraklion on a bus that had deviated and stopped many times on the way, so he was hot and exasperated after walking to the sea after arrival, especially as he had a sizable backpack to carry. There were many places to eat and drink in the old part of the city, but on that first day he wasn't selective, entering one of the first on the harbour curve, to escape the sun. He put his pack on a chair beside him and tugged his shirt free from the sweat of his back. 'Any sort of beer,' he told the waiter, who seemed to understand, and later confirmed that by taking his order for breads, tomato and olive salad and more beer. After that he was no longer exasperated, not during all his time in Chania.

The waiter was busy, but still friendly, lacking the air of slight disdain that Wallace had noticed in the staff of restaurants and bars in Paris, Florence and other cities. Short in stature, as many Greeks are, and seeming then to be old because Wallace himself was young. It was the waiter who understood that Wallace didn't have the money, or inclination, for a hotel, and suggested he go to the house of Mrs Volanakis in the street Agiou Markou. When he did he found it an apartment rather than a house, part of an old building that accommodated other families and also a shop where lace was made and sold.

'I spent nearly two months in Chania,' he told Rebecca. 'People in Crete liked Kiwis. I was there a long time ago and older folk still remembered the war and Kiwi soldiers, some of whom joined the partisans to fight when they missed evacuation. It may well be different now.'

'I've always got on with Greek people. It's a pity that economically things aren't so good.'

'What places do you know best?' he asked, and she was enthusiastic in her response, talking especially of churches, monasteries and convents of which he knew nothing. There were places, though, that they had both visited and enjoyed.

'Sifnos? You've been to Sifnos?' Rebecca exclaimed. 'I love it. My favourite island. Definitely.'

'Only a few days, but yes, well worth it and not crowded when I was there.'

'I love it, love it,' she said and leant forward, then back in her enthusiasm. Wallace remembered the small villages like squared white icing on the rugged and parched beauty of the landscape, but he'd met no one who mattered to him there.

Chania was different. He remembered walking in the heat to Agiou Markou Street and finding Mrs Volanakis and her rooms with some difficulty. A Victorian novelist would have called her stout and her face was heavily lined, yet she moved gracefully and had a pleasant voice. Like most of the local women she wore black. Yes, she had a room, and he could afford the price. Her English was limited, but equal to the basic requirements of their exchange. 'New Zealand like is Australia,' she said.

'Almost, yes,' he said. It was easier and more polite to agree. He had a wash and lay down for a time, then went out in the afternoon heat, but free of his pack. He wandered the harbour, visited the maritime museum, then had more beer at the same café. The helpful waiter was still there and Wallace thanked him and said that he was set up at Mrs Volanakis's place.

'She has no husband now and one empty room to help her live,' the waiter said. When he turned to go, Wallace noticed the bald spot on the top of his head, like a tonsure and with a gleam as if regularly polished.

Mrs Volanakis was talking to a neighbour when Wallace returned, a woman much like herself, in appearance at least. He had become accustomed to the Mediterranean habit of having the evening meal quite late, and although it was nearly seven, he went to his room and wrote in his journal. The room was small, the bed was narrow, the one high window looked out to a second-storey string of washing, but there was a bare cleanliness to it all. As he wrote, the shadows of the clothes did a slow dance on the pale wall before him, as if in welcome.

Mrs Volanakis had said nothing about her family, not even if one existed, and he knew there was no longer a husband only from the waiter's comment, but when he went from his room to the kitchen, Nikos, her son, was there.

Rebecca was telling Wallace about visiting the Convent of Faneromeni and the relics and icons there when they were interrupted by Bruce Porter, who came purposefully towards them, a drink in one hand, a plate of small cakes in the other. Wallace took no pleasure in his approach, was disappointed talk of Greece was interrupted, but introduced him to Rebecca, causing Porter to balance his drink precariously on the plate so as to free a hand.

'This man is a bastion of the judiciary,' said Porter enthusiastically. A silly comment, and Wallace remained formal. Porter was an influential businessman who had appeared before him some years ago charged with tax evasion by the use of overseas subsidiaries. Wallace had found him not guilty and Porter saw in that a personal endorsement, whereas in fact the judge disliked him, but applied the law. Morality is an individual creation, the law is imperfect, but must have common application and be upheld despite its failings. It wasn't the only time Wallace had been scrupulous in carrying out his duty despite his own inclination.

There was no empty seat close to Wallace and Rebecca, and after Porter had talked disparagingly about the government for a time and invited Wallace again to make use of his holiday home in the Coromandel, he somewhat reluctantly returned towards the buffet. Wallace admitted to himself he was a good-looking man who dressed well. He had dark eyes, and the whites of them were clearly visible also. Whenever Wallace looked in a mirror, he noticed how little of his own eyes was visible, how the heavy eyelid folds pressed in as if to shut out the world.

'Tell me more about your visits to Greece,' he asked Rebecca. 'I never went to many religious institutions when I was there.'

'I shouldn't say it, but sometimes I'd rather have been on the beach,' she said and laughed.

'I went to Corinth on my last visit and was disappointed. The city streets were very dirty and most buildings shabby. It put me off.'

'Ordinary people are pretty much up against it,' she said. 'The national debt's sky-rocketed too, and there's this whole huge problem of illegal immigration. A surge of desperate people who don't care about border rules, who just want to be somewhere else.'

'There've become too many of us in the world.'

'It's such an enormous challenge for the Greeks, those refugees.'

'Even a history such as theirs isn't enough,' Wallace said.

—◦≫ ≪◦—

Yes, he'd been to Greece several times since that first trip, but never back to Crete, never back to Chania. There would in all his life be only one time for him in that place. A time spent mostly with Nikos

Volanakis. It's not only some fortunate women who have warmth, though it is less often found in men. Nikos had warmth, apparent at their first meeting. He was sitting on a wooden kitchen chair talking with his mother when Wallace came in. No doubt Mrs Volanakis had told him of the New Zealand backpacker in the spare room, and Nikos stood up unsurprised to greet him. His English was much better than his mother's and he showed a friendly interest in their lodger.

'You will like it here,' he said. 'It's a fine place. An old place where lots of things have gone on, and a new place too where lots still goes on. People like to come here.'

Nikos wasn't especially good looking, yet better than most: chunky, but without fat, active but not restless. He had the clear, attractive skin of young Mediterranean people, and the dark, abundant hair. He was happy, optimistic and young. Mrs Volanakis didn't join them at the table but bustled about to ensure Wallace was well looked after. The meal was mainly mutton with spices and bread.

No doubt it had a special name, but Wallace didn't ask. Just enjoyed it. During that first meal together he and Nikos talked about things other than food. They talked of their own countries, Nikos imagining New Zealand fully as exotic as Wallace found Greece to be. They talked of their lives and aspirations. Nikos had an academy diploma in economics and business management, and for two years had worked for the airport. It was shortly to offer international flights, he said, and he was involved with the planning.

'I will take you out to see everything there,' he said generously, and so he did two days later, but Wallace had only a subdued recollection of that. Nikos even organised casual work for him at the airport, handling luggage, and that time, too, had almost completely faded, except for a single incident in which he'd caught a finger in a hatch door.

What remained vivid for him were the hot, long evenings spent strolling on the waterfront with Nikos, or in the cafés and restaurants with outdoor seating spreading unchecked onto the promenade. Sometimes friends of Nikos would be with them, both men and women, laughter, extravagant talk and drinking, but the names were gone, and usually it was just Nikos and himself. Nikos knew all the interesting places and was proud of his city and its history over many hundreds of years. One weekend they took the small bus inland to the high villages of Lakkoi and Omalos, places of lemons and oranges. Places that looked as if they had fully accomplished evolution and would change no more.

The recollection of those places still spun out like dreams for him, redolent with weighted sun, rural fragrances, the soft sounds of the grasses as they walked together. At such times he had a strange awareness of the scene, as if he were outside himself and looking down upon them both, knowing the experience was special, knowing, too, that it was passing even as they lived it.

There were nights also when they sat in the family kitchen making plans, talking of places already visited and people met there, sometimes playing draughts while Mrs Volanakis ironed pieces of lace for the little workshop in the building, or cleaned the patterned copper and brass salvers she hung on the walls.

—◊》《◦—

'Some of the religious sites need to be better looked after,' said Rebecca. 'It's not that people don't care — they do. But resources are scarce and curatorial practices aren't always understood. Often I have a testing ambivalence, wanting to have things taken into better care elsewhere, yet at the same time knowing they're best appreciated in their original setting.'

She told him of the theft of scrolls from the monastery of Karakalou. Wallace was pleased by her earnestness and animation. He liked to find people dedicated to something worthwhile, rather than the crass, or depraved, men and women often put before him.

'Life is a scrabble for so many these days,' he said. 'Those going under in the present don't give a damn about the past, or the future, and that's understandable. And is religion still important in Greece, or on the wane as in so many so-called Christian countries?'

'More superficial now, I feel,' she said, 'but that's not an opinion I can substantiate.'

'Well, that's certainly true here. I sometimes think science is our new faith and perhaps no less a consolation than any other. We believe in pills and space travel rather than gods.'

Their discussion was interrupted by the boarding call for Rebecca's flight, and Wallace stood up again to wish her a pleasant trip and a worthwhile conference in Heraklion. 'Do see more of Crete if you get the chance,' he said, and watched her go off towards the door with a turn and wave. He was sorry to see her go, although he had work to do. He was sorry because she was an interesting and worthwhile person, because she was the daughter of a valued colleague, because she was young and had warmth.

She left a gift, however, which was the memory of Chania and Nikos activated by her talk of Crete and Heraklion. Wallace put his hand luggage on the chair where she'd been, to discourage the return of Bruce Porter with his specious summaries of life, although there was no sign of him among those in easy view. He didn't immediately take up his laptop again, but returned to his youth.

Wallace had a brother and a sister, but felt closer to Nikos in just weeks than he did to his siblings in all the time he was growing up. Maybe the intensity was because Nikos and he knew a parting could not be far away: maybe it was because they sensed love, though there was no kissing, no late bedroom visits in the Agiou Markou Street apartment. Wallace didn't know if Nikos was gay, didn't then fully understand his own inclination. He knew it was not unusual for guys there to walk arm in arm, to wrestle, to dance together and laugh at it all.

On the evening before the day Wallace was to take the bus to Heraklion and the ferry, the two of them went again to the harbour and chose the café with the old waiter who knew Nikos and his mother, and they drank there with another young man Nikos knew and who had noticeably small hands. Wallace drank raki with them, although he disliked the taste, but it was the last night and to make the same choice emphasised togetherness. Late evening was often the very best time in Chania because it was still warm and with natural light, but not blazingly hot. The waiter took a photograph of the three in which Wallace's sharp nose was evident above his smile, and in the background a tall man stood with his head averted, looking out from the café to the people passing.

The friend had difficulty in remembering where he'd left his scooter and went off in search of it after a brief farewell. Wallace and Nikos walked along the old stone sea wall to the Venetian lighthouse as they had often done before, and they sat there and looked back over the blue harbour water to the bobbing coloured boats and the sweep of the small shops, cafés and restaurants behind. A pleasant and steady breeze that had come a long way across the Aegean Sea bore only clean, natural scents. Nikos had one arm casually on Wallace's shoulder for a time, the slight pressure felt through the thin cotton of the white, collarless shirt, and as his friend spoke of things they had done together, and his ambition to work in Athens, Wallace had heightened awareness of the pressure, light and passing though it was. They talked of the airport and people there, but more of the places they had visited together like Omalos, and the ruins of the Ottoman fort in the olive trees close to Rethymna.

'Why should you go home at all?' Nikos exclaimed. 'Every city needs lawyers. There's money here.'

'Money's the same everywhere, but the law is different from country to country, and the customs around it. Anyway, you can come to New Zealand and I'll show you round. Maybe we'll get motorbikes. Have a road trip.'

'I will come. Of course I will.' He said it enthusiastically, but he never did come. 'I like motorbikes,' he said with equal vehemence. 'Italian bikes are much the best, yes? When I have money I will come and see you. But now you should stay here.'

Nikos said goodbye the next morning at breakfast. On work days he left quite early for the airport. 'I will come, yes, you will see. When I have more money I will come and we will have motorbikes to ride. And you must come back here. Come back any time. Come back soon.'

'Of course I'll come,' said Wallace, but he never did.

When Nikos had left, Wallace didn't want to stay in the house any longer. He had nothing against Mrs Volanakis, but it was an empty place without her son. He gave her a gift of money from his airport earnings because he knew that was useful for her, then took his backpack and walked in a leisurely way the considerable distance to the bus terminal and waited there out of the sun. Yes, he was sorry to leave Chania and Nikos, but he was young and looked forward to other places and other people before he went back to his own country.

—·>> <<·—

Now, however, he was old and realised that although he had travelled much farther in the world, and in ways that were not all physical, he had never forgotten Nikos and Chania, and sometimes he wondered about his choices there. And choices made since, which were also judgements in a way. He had never slept with a man, even after 1986 when the law was changed. He had been wary of the effect any committed emotional attachment could have on his ordered, purposeful existence, and casual carnality was repugnant to him and dangerous in a life always under scrutiny. He had devoted himself to his own advancement, but also to service in support of the law, and found the two not mutually exclusive.

Given the opportunity, he would probably make the same decisions again, but nevertheless the passing years had brought a greater awareness of the isolation that was the price. The boarding announcement came for his flight, and he gathered his things in an unhurried way and made his way to the door. A slight man, almost dapper, with a composed face, prominent nose and white hair combed forward in the Roman way. He passed a seated couple, and the man looked at him keenly, but Wallace didn't notice and the man said nothing until the judge had gone by.

He then turned to his wife and said, 'That's Justice Lowry. I'm sure of it. He's heading the royal commission on waterways. I've had some dealings with him. Such a dispassionate man, but scrupulously fair. Sharp as a tack, the old bugger, and you don't put one over him easily. He sleeps with law books, they say, and that would be right. Total commitment.'

'Sweet dreams there,' she said. 'I'm going to leave my bag here and go to the toilet. Look after it.'

'That's Justice Lowry for sure,' said the man aloud again, even though his wife had moved beyond earshot. 'I should've said something.'

But the judge was already walking down the corridor to the plane and preparing to think of legal matters that he would consider during his flight, yet buoyed somewhat by the unexpected meeting with his young self, and with Nikos. Almost he could smell the lemons of Omalos and fragrances borne on the sweet wind across the Aegean Sea.

23.

The Light Fandango

Real fucken villains don't always have a leer and a scar on their face. Corruption is usually on the inside. Mr Prick Pryor's one of those, for sure. What he's prior to is just about every setback I've had in this rat-arse flat he owns, and I've got the full story. Tenants have rights now: you can't just kick somebody out for being behind a few weeks. I've got Pryor pinned, though, pinned as a butterfly in my lyrics for 'The Intestinal Magician'. Vortex of the moon, man. Yeah, I'll tell you all about Prick Pryor. This place wasn't ever meant to be lived in. It was an office block and where we are three floors up was a murder house with resident dentists. Pryor did a tight-arse Mickey Mouse conversion and our front door now comes off the fire escape. There's better flats alongside and below and a laundromat at street level that seems to go twenty-four seven. It's like living in a long-haul freight spacecraft. Sometimes I find myself humming along. From the fire escape entrance you look down at the arse end of Bruck Burgers and Corinthian Patio Furnishings, and down the alley there's a glimpse of the heavy traffic in Whitney Street, shimmering through the carbon monoxide. Police and ambulance sirens, impatient crowds at the lights. Yeah, let it be. Trash people come sometimes and set up in the alley, sleeping in cartons and under car covers, shouting at each other, shooting up and pissing up, climbing the fire escape and pushing their loser faces to the small window. Summer usually. In winter they go off to a warmer place, like the European nobility.

There were three of us, but Shaun's gone now. A pity, really, because his parents have money and used to bring round meat, cakes and stuff. But he was an uptight sort of guy and intent on passing exams. What can you do with a fucken BA these days, I ask you? Bugger All behind your name. I'd say kindergarten teaching needs a BA now. These days you can buy degrees from hick universities in Arkansas and Idaho. And he used to listen to Barry Manilow, so enough said. It's just me and Ryan now. At least we don't have to share a room any more, but effectively our rent's gone up and that's a bugger. Pryor doesn't see the logic.

I've just about given up on lectures. I mean either you've got it, or you haven't. You've got soul, or nothing. It's all tangential, right? I reckon pushing on with my own stuff's more important than sitting listening to some pedantic turd rabbiting on about existentialism, or the prefiguration of capitalism in the American novel. I'm published and didn't have to pay for it. Check out *Sport* magazine. Every Thursday I read at the open mic session at the Cannery and I'm regular on several sites. Okay, they don't pay, but you're out there, aren't you. You got to do your time with poetry, and I'll look back on all the shitty stuff and smile — and riff on it.

I don't bother with tutorials much now either. Not since Dr Royden didn't agree to another extension on the Pynchon essay. The old fart said he'd decided to adopt a three strikes policy like the justice system. Thought it was funny, sat with his stupid, round glasses and fat guts as though he mattered at all. I could've told him why the essay's late: that I had Natasha Feldelei in bed with me for nearly two weeks and barely time to eat, let alone a dissertation on Thomas bloody Pynchon. Royden wouldn't have known what to do with Natasha, just lain there with his Billy Bunter glasses misted up. That Natasha, man, I tell you. You could die happy after Natasha. But she emptied me out altogether. Even had to sell the Suzuki 125, and the morning she left she went through the cupboards and took the tins of baked beans and spaghetti. And the almost new, yellow cap I found by a dumpster behind the Cannery. Farts like Royden wouldn't have a clue about life's real possibilities. They live in an academic mausoleum, never see a live naked woman.

That's another thing about Prick Pryor. He says we're tearing the place to pieces, says it's a P lab and he'll have the police in. As if. Ryan and I keep well away from the hard stuff, just keep stoked on first-rate West Coast shit. Pryor wouldn't know the difference. What you want is to let the imagination range free, but not shut capability down. Astral perfumes, man. I'm tapping into the subconscious as a deliberate ploy in my writing lately. I've been reading a lot about dreams and the freely connected imagery you experience there. I set the alarm to wake me at random times and that way I usually catch the dreams before they dissolve. You dream every night, lots of dreams, but hardly any of it sticks, and it's such great, hallucinatory stuff.

Just the other night, Tuesday at 2.14 a.m., I caught the tail of a sequence in which I was riding a camel, part of a caravan strung along the Silk Road. I sat not in a saddle, but on a Persian rug of rich yellow and royal blue and the camel's head a nodding metronome before me, outlined against the shimmering dunes. Soft, pale tassels swaying on the bridle. It had two humps, and even in the dream I thought that peculiar, but I looked it up afterwards and yeah, there's a two-humped camel — the Bactrian camel. The unconscious mind stores this stuff. That dream was the inspiration for a quatrain sequence I'm real fucken pleased with. First one:

> *Back to Bactrian camels swivel*
> *moonlit valleys in atomic sand.*
> *Carry silks, spices and heresies*
> *bribes to some preposterous land.*

Yeah, in the dream it was daytime, I know, but the sweltering desert thing's too clichéd. Anyway, I bet they travelled at night when it was cooler. No matter what time it is when the alarm goes, I write down what dream I'm having in a notebook on the floor. Dreamus Interruptus. It pissed Natasha off actually. You make sacrifices for the muse, I guess.

I'd be able to get more done if I had some money, but much of my time has to be spent doing cruddy jobs that pay fuck all. Mum and Dad don't want to know any more, and when I offered to take a first-year tutorial, Dr Royden wouldn't recommend me. He holds a grudge a long time, does Royden. I even applied to supervise swimming classes at the municipal pool, but you need a life-saving certificate, or something. I can swim, can't I? What more do they want? Kids float naturally anyway. So what I do now is unload crates of vegetables behind the supermarket early mornings. Not even under cover and often as cold as a disused urinal. Barely the minimum rate, but at least I can usually get a cabbage, or a cauli. I leave my helmet close by and sneak one in. Now that the Suzuki's history, it's good the helmet's still some use. Not that green stuff is my favourite. Good for you, no doubt, but who wants to end up looking like a fucken rabbit? I don't tell Ryan the stuff's nicked, otherwise he'd be on about me paying more of the food bill. All winds across the desert, man.

Ryan isn't keen on cooking. He's a great one for stuff from Bruck Burgers, even though the backside of Bruck's that we look out on is a stinking offal pit. The only good thing about Bruck's is Miranda. She comes outside sometimes if it's sunny, in her breaks, and sits on a crate to have a smoke. Sometimes she pulls up her smock to get the sun on her legs. She has damn good legs, has Miranda. Ryan and I can lean on the fire escape rail and have a rather public conversation with her below. She has a good sense of humour too. We've invited her up, but she says the breaks she gets are too short for visiting. That whole back alley seems a different place when she's there, but I suppose that's partly because she only comes out with the sun.

I don't go home much. Dad's not one for the arts and keeps telling me how well my brother's doing with two courier vans and a third on order. I told him that in twenty years nobody owning courier vans will be remembered, but songwriters and poets will still be renowned. 'Is that a fact,' he said, 'and you'll still be listening to the buggers for sure.' His greatest talent is in growing supertoms, despite working as a carpet layer all his life. I think of him when the tomatoes come in to me at the supermarket, but without any surge of affection. Supertoms can take you only so far as a human being. My mother I've got nothing against: Mahjong's her thing, not supertoms. I don't know the rules, but she's got an authentic set, real ivory inlay, and the pieces I've always thought quite beautiful, and they've cropped up in dreams. In one recently I had the box and used the pieces one by one at toll gates on a Chinese path that wound ahead past cliffs and strangely contorted trees. If I wasn't so busy I'd look into the history of Mahjong. The Chinese possess an authentic artistic culture.

Prick Pryor nabbed me as I was coming back from work yesterday. He says he's getting the lawyers and Tenancy Tribunal onto me. I've told you about how he hounds us, no toleration at all, how he tried to change the lock and holds back the mail. Even that scuffle over the push bike that I found by the laundromat and he reckons I stole. He's strong for an old bugger is Pryor. I told you about his wife too.

What I'm after is lift-off in my writing. 'The Emperor of Ice-Cream' was transformative in its day, and Dylan does his best, but a new kicker is needed. Dreams, good shit, mic highs all give a boost and I've been experimenting with trauma and coital energy too. With my left hand I use a needle on my calf muscle and as the pain increases I write down the words that occur to me. Involuntary response and some great juxtapositions that I've put on my blog. Similar with my sexual climax associations, although recording the words becomes more difficult with someone else so closely involved. Emotional power though, man oh man. Some words I didn't even know I had in my vocab, some not even in the language. This is the key in art of any sort: direct transfer of the most essential and powerful emotions with the minimum loss through acquired and conventional channels. Roll the coloured fluffy dice, man.

It's not rocket science, is it. I'm not saying even that I'm the first to see it, but do you think I can get any substantial support. I sent a grant application to Creative NZ for my Notional Neanderthals chapbook. Just about needed a doctorate for the application alone, which took a week to complete, but not a bloody thing, and no joy with any of those residencies that the clique of smug, published wankers rotate among themselves. I even sent letters to some fellow Kiwis on the rich list suggesting the time had come for a return to significant individual patronage in the arts. Only Sir Whitby Frottager replied. He told me to get a job, but when I said I was happy to accept one, I didn't hear back. Typical.

There's an unspoken literary censorship these days, too, that discriminates against men. Oh yeah. It's a feminist thing about their freedom and assertiveness. Women can talk about fucking any way they like. It's a claim to equality and liberation, but when a guy does the same it's the imposition of male intention and objectification. At an open mic session last month in the Students' Association building I got shouted down by women when explaining my coital energy process — hadn't even read the poems, for Christ's sake. No wonder I do get depressed at times: there's a certain drudgery even in creative work when you're misunderstood. Sometimes I wake in the night almost overcome with a sort of desperation to have my work seen for what it is.

I walk a lot late at night too. The inner city never sleeps, just hosts an alternative population. In lit offices the cleaners erase the sweat of day, the trash trucks visit the overflowing bins, final party groups howl together, taxis have unimpeded sway, the homeless take possession of alcoves, recessed doorways and underpasses, hedgehogs come from the small parks and stare into the drains, wolverines sneer from the band rotunda. Sometimes I stand on the plinth of Seddon's statue and declaim a poem or two for my own benefit. I feel better afterwards, and also because I have somewhere to go home to. It's salutary to remind yourself of people worse off than yourself. Self-belief is the motif of the true artist. You have to disregard any majority opinion because most people are fucken stupid. That never changes.

The group at the Cannery on a Thursday night is different. They know me there, mostly guys and they cheer when I get up. They're pissed, of course, but that relaxation makes them more open to innovation in poetry, less inhibited by outmoded definitions of what constitutes artistic expression. One night last year they chanted my name to get me back behind the mic. It hasn't happened lately, but my new stuff will rock them. I'm putting in mime interludes and strut sessions and stronger satire about deficiencies in education and welfare policies. Pub poetry can give you a real high when it goes well. You can't understand until you've experienced it. I sweat like a pig when performing: more than running on a hot day. It just pours off me. I feel it on my chest and behind my ears. It's being locked into the moment and giving your all. Everything is focus and the world right way up with the colours vibrating. Just not long enough, or often enough, and there's been rumours there might be a change in format, with less open mic and slam, more name poets invited to have readings. Tell me about it. Nature poets waxing lyrical over ruffled tussocks and sunsets, academics smirking at their self-referential cryptic crap, loose-haired women chirping on about sex and family grief. Yawn bloody yawn.

I told you about Pryor and the lawyer's letter and the big bastard he sent around to claim the bicycle, and Ryan saying he's about ready to move on. If it came to it, I could go home, but they'd want board anyway, and no way could I ever have a woman there. Girls like Natasha Feldelei wouldn't be understood by my parents, wouldn't even exist, according to them. Then again Natasha doesn't talk to me now. I guess she's not into dropout guys without a motorbike, without much of a job and facing eviction from a cruddy fucken flat. To be at the forefront of one's art is to be crassly and grossly misunderstood by the mass behind.

However, language continues to inspire and sustain me. Roger Simpson at the supermarket is my immediate boss — everyone there is my boss one way or another. He told me last week that he's been designated inward goods supervisor and could hardly keep the enormity of it from his voice. It's even on a plastic badge he wears. You have to bloody laugh, don't you, though he didn't appreciate that. A sort of nomenclature inflation goes on. The coffee maker becomes a bloody barista and the rubbish guy a garbologist, the rabbiter's a pest eradicator and the secretary a personal assistant. It's a proletarian expression of the same urge that compels the royal dukes to cover themselves with sashes, insignia and medals when on the balcony. Fancy dress vaudeville dudes.

Anyway, I told you about Prick Pryor's last attempt to take possession of the place: the false fire alarm and so on. I make sure Ryan's in the flat when I'm at work and I don't go out much apart from that, except late at night. I may have to barricade myself in if Ryan leaves for good. If Pryor brings in the police I'll ring the press and TV and make a last stand. The publicity could even be advantageous: give me a platform, a profile, and persuade publishers to look anew at my work. All I need is that sort of boost to get recognition. I see myself standing on the fire escape with a crowd and TV crew below, and giving some of my best stuff to the world. You only need that one break. Just the one big fucken break. All the colours of the rainbow are just behind the cloud, man.

24.

Thunderflash Days

I've never marched in an Anzac parade, never been under enemy fire, or suffered severe privation, as they say, never even sailed away on a troopship with a band playing on the shore and a girlfriend tearful there. But I have been awarded a military medal. It's the colour of a penny and much the same size. The ribbon is striped in subdued hues of blue, red and green, and there's even a rather impressive black presentation case with a crest on the lid. All at the taxpayers' expense.

The sacrifice I made to earn such an award was completely involuntary, even reluctant. I was a birthday marble national serviceman of the 1960s. I knew nothing of this rather bizarre form of conscription until, as a twenty-year-old university student, I received a letter informing me that I was obliged to undergo fourteen weeks of basic military training at Waiouru and afterwards serve part time in the territorial force for some years.

None of my friends was selected in this lottery and I seemed a solitary victim of fate. My fellow students thought it a great joke, and because it was so removed from the life I led, and not to take effect for some months, I joined in the mockery. Eventually, however, reporting time arrived, and instead of taking a well-paid vacation job on the wharves, or in a woolstore, I faced a longer, poorly paid sojourn in the army.

I remember standing on the railway station platform of my home town waiting to leave and seeing several other guys of a similar age and disposition who were probably heading north for the same reason. One I even recognised — a school acquaintance whom I'd partnered in the tennis team in my last year. We travelled up together: the train to Picton, then the ferry over and finally the charter bus from Wellington to Waiouru. I was glad of the company, but I never saw him again after we were allocated to our corps. I've no idea how many of us there were in that total intake. You trained with others of your own platoon and became part of larger units only occasionally on full parades, or field exercises.

Almost the first thing we did on arrival at camp was hand in our civvy gear and get the army issue. As you walked along past stacks of clothing, stores blokes made a cursory assessment of your size by sight and dumped a garment in your arms. The only item selected with any care were boots: boots and feet are important in the infantry. Black boots, they were, and they laced up high on your shins. We undressed in the issue store to put on our uniforms because our civvy clothes were bundled up there and stored until our training finished. Lines of us undressing awkwardly as strangers and feeling even more discomforted in the unaccustomed gear. I was embarrassed to find when I took off my jacket that a biro in the pocket had leaked onto the lining, blotched my shirt, even left a stain on my chest that took several days to go, but nobody laughed, or drew attention to it. The stores regulars just wanted to get rid of us as soon as possible; my fellow rookies were preoccupied with the unsought introduction to military life.

There was no welcome as such on arrival, or later, just the impersonal processing that takes place to turn a civilian into a recruit. We were each given a number and soon learnt that it was as important to the army as our name, often more so. You don't forget your number when you've been in the army. It goes on almost everything you own and it's how you're identified in a regimented society. A lot of stuff about national service escapes me now, but I can still rattle off my ID number.

Another important number is that of your rifle, though I no longer remember that. We were issued with our rifles on the second day. They were FN SLRs — self-loading rifles that I rather liked, though they've long been replaced by subsequent issues. You cleaned your rifle at the end of every day, and afterwards they were inspected and placed on a rack in the centre of the barrack room. A chain was drawn through all the trigger guards and padlocked. To lose your rifle was the greatest crime and fear.

It was while we were being instructed on weapon cleaning during that second day that I met Chris. We were sitting on ground sheets on one of the grassed areas, and Corporal Delmar was going through cleaning and assembly. He'd done it so often that even as he spoke and named the parts his glance and real attention were on two armoured vehicles being loaded onto transporters beyond the field. I could tell that Chris was familiar with firearms, but he went through the cleaning rigmarole with the rest of us. 'Would be good for deer, eh,' he said quietly, sighting along the barrel.

He was the first friend I made in the army, and became the closest, though he had more mates than I did. An easy-going guy who was good at almost everything without much seeming to try. His parents had a farm in the King Country and he was doing an agri course at Lincoln. Almost everything to do with the land interested him. We'd be pushing up some damn tussock ridge with full packs and he would say how much such poor soils responded to aerial topdressing, or urge me to stick my hand beneath the heavy growth to feel the difference there. 'Micro-climate,' he told me. 'Cooler in summer and warmer in winter.' As if I cared. I was doing law.

I also got to like Nikora, who had the bed two over from me. He was mostly Māori, but didn't look much like it — tall, thin, not very brown and with a narrow nose. There seemed to be a lot of Māori in the army, in the training intake and as instructors and regulars. Our best instructors were all Māori. They would tell you what to do and how to do it without ridicule, or hectoring, just evincing sometimes a resigned awareness of our ineptitude. Nikora worked for the Auckland City Council, part of a team responsible for recreational funding. I was impressed, but he said he hadn't been there long and was doing a tech course as well.

The three of us tended to hang out together, although there were other buddies as well. Often in free evenings we played poker, the cards spread on a bed. On Sunday afternoons we usually chose the same sport to play. The choice you didn't have was not to play a sport. I'm sure the army saw it as physical fitness training under the guise of recreation. It was okay, though. Usually we chose cricket, not because of any special ability, but because when your side was batting there was ample time to do nothing except sit around and talk.

Most of the guys I trained with had full-time jobs: some had been out working for years and had a fully adult view of the world. All sorts of young men were thrown together and had to learn to get along, or at least stay clear of one another. A few couldn't cope and were released on compassionate grounds ranging from ingrown toenails to panic attacks, but most of us put up with it and sought amusement and comradeship where we could. In all my time there I never saw a serious fight, despite what I'd read, and seen in films, about savage confrontations in such places. We just wanted to get through the fourteen weeks and back to our lives again, and were quick to learn the tricks to make things easier — like washing our clothes underfoot in the showers, putting cardboard stiffeners in our bedrolls before inspection and spitting on the nugget when polishing our number one boots. Few of these skills were ever useful afterwards, and even the friendships tended to fade away unless we ended up in the same units after training. At the time, though, such things had importance — especially friends.

Chris was the best with firearms of the three of us, and the fittest too; Nikora was the best on drill parade; and I surpassed them at map reading, which we spent less time on, of course. I had a knack for visualising landforms from contour lines when we were on field exercise. It came to me quite naturally. Nikora was a bit of a satirist in his own way and took a wry pleasure in the oddities of army life, like the nose-to-nose and eye-to-eye posture when a dressing down was given, or the distinction between a grunt stick and a swagger stick. I guess he knew that laughing at things can be a way of diminishing their threat. He often imitated Corporal Delmar's 6 a.m. strident wake-up chant as he came through the barrack room. Hand off cock, feet in sock.

There's a lot of repetition in army life — the same things done in the same way at the same time with the same people — and so I don't seem to have enough memories to spread over all those weeks. Maybe, too, in that sort of environment you shut down some emotional receptors and let a lot just go by. It's the guys who were a bit different whom you remember — Rick, who had the fame of a national swimming title, Evan, who jerked off in the showers, Ash, who got occasional bloody awful migraines that made him puke, but carried on just the same. I admired him for that. And two guys whose names escape me, but not their personal idiosyncrasies. One sang the sad, drifting songs of the Big O, seemingly in his sleep, and the other had a photo on his locker of a really sexy chick that he said was his girlfriend, but was revealed to be a Hollywood starlet. We gave him heaps over that.

There are some incidents that do stand out from the impersonal routine, and the essential boredom at the heart of enforced activity. Falls on the swaying logs of the confidence course, someone spraying dangerously off target with a Bren gun, the unexpected army benevolence of a trip one Sunday for a mass swim in a small, cold lake. Our transport was always those green Bedford trucks with canvas canopies that sucked in dust to combine with sweat as a greasy coating on your face.

Our thunderflash fiasco was memorable in its own way. We were on a three-day exercise not long before the end of our training, far up on the tussocky hills. Chris was hoping to see wild horses, but there were only birds and soldiers, and not many of either. Nikora, Chris and I quite liked getting away from Waiouru, but the first night out some regulars, acting as the enemy, came whooping in among our tents, firing blanks, kicking out pegs and throwing thunderflashes to imitate grenades and shells. Thunderflashes are just big-daddy fire crackers, but you wouldn't want to be too close when one went off. We had to turn out in the dark, take position in the rifle pits and share sentry duty for the rest of the night, so there wasn't much sleep.

There was a lot of steep walking the next day on the slopes of the mountain: advancing in open order, camouflage training, skirmishes with the regulars and so on. And rifle cleaning of course at the end of it. All that playing at soldiers, which has a serious and necessary purpose, but also an element of absurdity. I actually got a compliment from Sergeant Matene on my map reading.

Chris reckoned we should show some initiative and get back at the regulars somehow. Just the three of us cook up something and follow through. 'I know Matene's got thunderflashes with him,' he told us.

'We'll lift one or two and catch these smart buggers by surprise tonight. They won't be far away, and expecting nothing.'

The idea of slogging around in the dark to find the 'enemy' and give them a hurry up didn't appeal all that much to me, and pinching any of the sergeant's thunderflashes was surely dicey — not so much any difficulty in achieving the theft, but his reaction to it. Maybe he'd commend our initiative as Chris said, more likely he'd be highly pissed off. Nikora, though, was just as keen as Chris, and so I went along with it, not wanting to admit to a lack of adventuresome spirit.

We all had individual crawl-in tents with little room inside. Matene's and Delmar's tents were side by side and between them lay their packs, which would be taken in last thing. At dusk when the instructors were doing a round to set sentry points, Nikora and I kept a lookout as Chris nipped in and nabbed a couple of thunderflashes. They were like yellow relay batons, and he hid them inside his own tent tucked in the groundsheet.

We sat together with most of the other guys to cook up from our ration packs and muck about, but afterwards the three of us stood a while by ourselves and made a plan of sorts. None of us had a duty that night, and we reckoned Colin McIntyre, who had a sentry stint after 2200 hours, would let us head off without question. A pleasant Wellingtonian, he was most notable for receiving more mail than anybody else in the platoon. There were guys who didn't get a letter in the whole time.

Nothing of our preparation was any use. Darkness had come when Sergeant Matene turned up at Chris's tent with a torch. I heard him stop at a tent close by and ask which was Chris Bland's. I thought, Jesus, he knows about the thunderflashes already, so I crawled out and went over to take my share of the blame, but the sergeant said nothing about that at first, although they must have been unmissable in the torchlight. 'We've had a radio message,' he said. 'You've got a sister called Janice, right?'

'Yeah,' said Chris, half sitting up, pushing the thunderflashes stealthily behind his back.

'There's been a car accident and your sister's involved.'

'How bad an accident? She's not really bad, is she?' Chris asked.

'All I've been told is that she's in hospital and you're to go down at first light and meet a Land Rover to take you back to Waiouru.'

'Okay. Jesus.' Chris blinked in the torchlight and then looked away.

Sergeant Matene shone the torch where the thunderflashes had been. 'And what've you got to tell me about what's behind your back, eh?'

'We were going to give the regulars a bit of their own medicine,' said Chris.

'Give them here. We don't need your bullshit plans. There's enough going on.' He took the batons and then turned the torch on me and Nikora. 'And I could've guessed you two would be in on it. When we're back I'll have enough cookhouse fatigues for you to keep your mind off playing silly buggers.' He adjusted the green towel tucked around his neck, stood for a moment looking over the darkened scatter of small tents among the tussocks, and sighed, as if it were obvious that all of them were occupied with guys as useless as the three of us. Then he turned again to Chris. 'Anyway, make sure you're all set to go at daybreak. Corporal Delmar will walk you out. I hope your sister's going to be okay. You know she's in the right place anyway.'

'She's got a baby only three months old,' said Chris.

'Daybreak you'll be on your way,' said the sergeant. He stood with the torch in one hand and the thunderflashes in the other, then turned and went into the dark.

Nikora and I gave awkward expressions of support, but Chris didn't want to talk much, and after a bit we went back to our own tents. I guess emotionally he'd shifted to a close, personal part of his life that had nothing to do with us, nothing to do with the army and with being on a dark hillside with a chill breeze nosing the tussock and the moon flitting behind the clouds.

I don't suppose he slept much, and I was woken by Corporal Delmar's voice nearby in the first grey light of morning. Chris was already waiting with his pack and set to go. 'Let me know how things turn out,' I said, and we shook hands. 'Look after yourself.'

'Yeah, I will. You too. See you, mate,' he said, and they moved off downhill, both with loose, accustomed strides. It wasn't the way I expected our parting to be, and we've never met up since. If I'd known that, maybe I would have managed a farewell that better expressed the value I gave his friendship.

I did get in touch when back in camp. Sergeant Matene got a phone number from the adjutant's office and Nikora and I rang. Chris's mother answered and went off to find him. It took a while and he said he'd had the chainsaw out cutting firewood. His sister was in hospital with a punctured lung and spinal injuries, but she wasn't critical. 'They say she'll pull through,' Chris said, 'and should come fully right in time. It's a bugger, though, especially with the baby and everything.' It was different talking to him on the phone, not being able to see his face, knowing he was no longer in the same world as ourselves. 'Yeah, yeah, we'll keep in touch for sure,' he said, before I handed over to Nikora. We didn't, though, just took our separate ways.

Training finished not long after Chris went home: he didn't come back, Nikora headed for Auckland and I returned south. I did my years of part-time service with 2 Battalion and there were some good guys there, but once I'd finished, the whole army thing receded, became increasingly like a story told by someone else, because now it has so little connection with my life. There's the medal and a cap badge in a drawer with my swimming certificates, graduation photograph and a piece of uncut opal from my Aussie outback visit. And I guess I could still handle the map reading if I ever had to take to the hills for sanctuary.

25.

Three Women, One Morning

Elizabeth is one of six deputy chief executives at the ministry. She's responsible for organisational culture and capability. Sometimes we call her Elizabeth Regina, but you can't deny her relentless efficiency. I'd say she's mid-fifties, but looks after herself: a bit of a power dresser, but not great with shoes. Low heels and often open toes in summer. I've wondered if she has a problem of some sort with her feet.

We didn't have a lot to do with each other usually, because she's top echelon and I'm twenty-six and a member of the chief information officer's team. My degree's as good as hers, though, and I've got time. She knew who I was and was always pleasant — if slightly distant. We'd talk in the lift, or in passing at a staff gathering. She would raise a hand in the supermarket perhaps, but not pause to chat. So-oo much to do, of course. But that sounds bitchy and really, she was fine. I didn't dislike her.

Last month she needed to attend a conference day at Massey University — addresses by overseas people, mainly — and she wanted someone from the information team to accompany her, and later write it up, which she was too busy to do. A couple of us were available and Elizabeth chose me because she wouldn't be back till evening and the other woman had young children. Elizabeth is considerate of such circumstances when there's a choice, although her own children left home years ago, and her husband not long after, I gather.

That Wednesday morning the weather wasn't great. The Cook Strait southerly towed in low cloud, and although the wind lessened as we drove north in the congestion of early traffic, the drizzle continued and the outside world was cold and hunched. I did the driving, so Elizabeth was free to use her mobile to answer queries that arose even before we'd left the city. There was time also for talk, and it was unforced, and the silences, too, were comfortable enough. Unequal in age and institutional position, okay, but with common ground in our employment, and aware of boundaries. We discussed the seemingly endless restructuring within the ministry, the workloads, agreed on the ugliness and personal intrusion of the new open-plan office that was home for the information and relations teams. Nothing that might make it awkward when I met her in the lift again, perhaps, or when I submitted my report on the Massey conference to her for sign-off.

We were well past Ōtaki, and Elizabeth busy on her screen, when the engine died and there was just enough momentum for me to guide the car into a farm gateway with straggling kōwhai trees behind the flanking wooden planks darkened by the rain.

'Bugger,' I said.

'What's happened?'

'No idea. It just gave up all of a sudden. A red light was showing, but it's been on ever since we started, I think.' We sat for a moment in silence. The vehicle wasn't going to recover a sense of duty and start itself, though. I gave the key a twist, but there was just a click from the starter motor. 'Scotty says it's almost always something electrical when cars won't go, but it started fine this morning,' I told Elizabeth. She didn't seem all that interested in that opinion.

'I know nothing about cars,' she said.

'Me neither.'

At least we were out of the way of the traffic continuing to pass. We sat and looked out at the grey sky, the drizzle tapping lightly on the puddles of the farm drive, magpies in the branches of the kōwhai. It wasn't an inviting scene, but it was up to me as the junior to show willing. 'I'll have a look under the bonnet,' I said, with greater purpose than I felt, and Elizabeth nodded. After a hunt I found the release catch beneath the dash and then the latch beneath the bonnet lip, but there were no prizes for that. One engine looks pretty much like another to me — lots of leads and pipes and hoses and containers for radiator water and windscreen fluid. Nothing was dribbling, nothing seemed broken. I didn't poke around at all. The last thing I wanted was to be sitting in the Massey venue with crap all over my Country Road jacket and grease on my hands. 'I can't see anything,' I told her when back in the driver's seat.

'Two choices, I think,' Elizabeth said. As an executive she'd been considering the options. 'Either we flag down someone and get a lift to Ōtaki, or Levin, whichever is closer, or we get onto the AA service. All ministry cars have that.'

'Yeah, but I don't think AA would have people in Ōtaki or Levin, would they? Better a garage person there than waiting for someone from Palmy, or Wellington.'

'You're probably right.'

For that, one of us would have to stand out by the road and flag down a passing car, and was it quicker to go on to Levin, or back to Ōtaki? Elizabeth came up with an okay plan: use Google to check the distances and then contact a garage and have someone come out. At this point a white ute came down the farm track, and as we were blocking the gate, it had no choice but to stop. A tallish man got out and came casually towards the car. He wore a crumpled parka brown with age, and he was smiling, as if he'd quite expected to find us there. Everything about him, smile included, was oddly pixelated by the fine raindrops on the windscreen glass. When I lowered the window his image came together, the smile accentuated. He lightly rested one hand on the door frame; the cuff of his parka was completely worn away. 'Can I help?' he said.

When everything was explained to him, he gave only a cursory glance at the engine, and one turn of the key. 'I'd say it's the alternator for sure,' he said.

'But it started okay this morning,' I said.

'If the alternator fails then the battery gets drained even if you're driving,' he said. 'Especially with the heater and stuff on.'

'My husband says it's always electrical,' I said. Second-hand knowledge.

'Yeah, usually,' he agreed.

'We're blocking your way,' said Elizabeth. He made no reply to that and instead introduced himself as Donald Munro, enquired as to our circumstances and took charge of the situation without assertiveness. No use waiting for ages in the car and the cold. We were best to come with him to the house and he'd get onto a garage he dealt with in Ōtaki, and see whether something could be done about still getting to Massey. If I'd been alone I don't think I would have gone up to the house with him, despite his manner, but there were two of us and Elizabeth had no hesitation at all.

'I did an agri commerce degree at Massey,' Donald said as we drove in the ute, shoulders touching, past pine trees and towards a wooden, two-storeyed farmhouse with verandahs top and bottom. An old house, but well kept, with high hedges and established magnolia trees as a frontage. Even though the cloud was low and sullen, the fine rain drifting in, there was beauty too. The moisture made grey beards of the spider webs on the hedge we passed and the large magnolia flowers on the bare branches were like fluted clams, white, cream, pink or purple, some tinged with all.

'How lovely,' Elizabeth said.

'My mother planted them over sixty years ago when she came to the farm.'

The front door was protected from the wet and flanked by coloured-glass panels; a well-worn, patterned carpet led down the hall behind it. 'Mum,' called Donald when inside, 'we've got visitors.' He led us into a large living room. The lights were on and an open fire burning. It was a room of heavy, old-fashioned furniture, including two large display cabinets, the silver and china inside flickering and glinting in reflection of the flames. Mrs Munro was already coming from her chair to meet us. Tallish, like her son, but thinner and with a face so heavily lined it seemed folded in on itself, yet still able to smile. She was a bit like those very old English actors who play duchesses, but more simply dressed. Neat clothes, however, and not inexpensive — a pale blue, fine wool jumper over a white blouse and a tweed skirt. Her shins were thin and seemed solid bone.

'I'm Rose,' she said, and we introduced ourselves in turn. 'Come by the fire, both of you, and you, Donald, go straight away and get rid of that disgusting coat.'

'Well, I was working, wasn't I,' but he went off cheerfully.

'We're sorry to be a nuisance,' said Elizabeth. 'As soon as we can get someone for the car we'll be on our way.'

Donald returned coatless, but now showing a worn collar to his work shirt and white paint stains on his jersey. Elizabeth had been remarking on a blue and white cup, plate and saucer that she said brought memories of visits to her grandmother many years ago.

'Spode,' Mrs Munro said. 'Nobody can be bothered with it all now. Women haven't the time to be pampering china, or cleaning silver and brass. Neither of my daughters wants any of it, and I've got rather tired of polishing and cleaning it myself, and I never use any of it now, whereas years ago good china was put out, silver cake trays, cut crystal, cheese knives. All a lot of nonsense, really, and my daughters are quite right. There're more important things.'

'It's so lovely, though,' I said. 'And it's the provenance that makes things special. Things handed down, things gifted, all with a part in the family story.' Not that there was much of that in my case. No gentility in the Walters clan.

'Exactly,' the old lady said approvingly. 'That's what gets lost of course.'

Donald, of a more practical nature, brought talk back to the present situation. 'Well, anyway, we need to decide what's next. I've rung the garage and they're sending someone out as soon as they can source an alternator. Seems to me the first thing is, do you still want to get to Palmerston North, or are you going to flag that?'

'If at all possible,' said Elizabeth. 'The first talk starts at ten. I'd just like us to get there as soon as we can, so the whole day isn't a waste.'

'How about this then. Mum takes you in our car to Palmy and back again afterwards. Hopefully by then your car will be okay to go.'

The offer surprised us, especially his mother being named as driver. Mrs Munro seemed very old to me, and probably past it.

'That's very kind, but we don't want to put you to such a lot of trouble,' Elizabeth told them.

'Mum's a great driver. She drives a lot, no trouble. My sister lives in Palmy. I'd take you myself, but the agent's coming out to look at stock I've shedded up.'

'A pity to miss your meeting having got this far,' said Mrs Munro, and she stood up and placed a heavy screen in front of the fire, as if the decision was made. Generosity breaks down reserve. Donald and his mother didn't feel like strangers. I told them how kind it was and that the ministry would reimburse them for petrol and anything else.

'Forget it. Mum will enjoy an outing,' Donald said. 'I'll go down and get your car out of the way and I'll bring ours round.'

Mrs Munro asked if we'd like tea or coffee, but getting on the road promptly was the priority. She excused herself to get tidy, and Elizabeth and I were briefly left alone. Dark leather sofa and armchairs, glass ornaments on the mantelpiece and a large aerial photograph of the farm above. I don't think Mrs Munro changed, and had no need to, but she had pinned on a large lapis lazuli brooch and carried a dark padded jacket. I was aware of perfume too, something floral and classic like Chanel No. 5. 'Off we go then,' she said cheerfully, and we went and stood sheltered outside the front door with the flanking panels of richly tinted glass — yellow, purple, green, royal blue. How on a sunlit day they would cast colours into the hall.

I'm accustomed to garages as part of the house, but the red-roofed car shed forty metres away from where we stood revived memories of my uncle's farm in Canterbury. Better Donald than us, reunited with his parka, to trudge down to get the car. I expected a small vehicle for his mother, but of course it was the family car: a big Ford, not an elderly woman's town runabout. It drew up by the wet and defiantly gleaming magnolia flowers. When we were inside, Donald told his mother that he'd phoned his sister, but she wasn't going to be home. 'It doesn't matter,' she said. 'I can go shopping. I can fall asleep in the mall.'

'I hope it all goes well,' he said. 'We'll try to have your car right when you come back. Give me a cell phone number and I'll keep in touch.'

I wondered why he wasn't married, if he'd ever been. Maybe having his mother so well established in the family home had been a disadvantage and he was getting on now. Close to sixty, I'd say. A bit older than Elizabeth, maybe, but an outdoors life had stopped him running too much to seed. He had thick, dark hair and scaly tops to his ears because of exposure to the sun. His teeth were good. He talked quietly and used no more words than were necessary for his message. He was what Scotty would call a decent bloke.

Elizabeth took the front passenger seat as of right. I was in the back with both of our satchels, and couldn't see the speedometer, but

Mrs Munro didn't hang back. She was a confident, almost flamboyant driver and passed quite a few others. I guess she knew the road well. 'Tell me about the work you do. Both of you,' she said. We kept it to a precis: the ministry's activities and responsibilities are worthy, but not exhilarating for outsiders. There's protocols for everything, and outspokenness is dangerous. There was nothing in what Elizabeth said that indicated her position, or its superiority to my own. I liked that about her. The more time we spent together, the more she came fully into view; the more there was to respect.

'So many working mothers now,' Mrs Munro said as she passed a milk tanker on a sweeping bend. 'It's good, I know. Women have more options than in my day. Yes, it's good, but you feel sorry for the children sometimes, bundled off to care and supervision rather than being with Mum.'

'But there's better qualified care nowadays and too many mothers felt trapped with their children at home. Not all women were cut out for it. It's a balance maybe. Not that it's perfect now, I agree.' Elizabeth's tone wasn't a challenge.

'Little ones, though. I always think those first few years are so special. Little ones with their mothers.'

'But for many couples now a double income's almost essential, especially in cities,' I chipped in. We planned kids and Scotty's job doesn't pay a fortune.

'I see some families — well, everything's different now,' said Mrs Munro. She seemed to find the exchange invigorating. 'I'm eighty-three and remember my father coming home from the war. It's better for women now, but I still like to see families together. Of course, people don't have so many children now, do they: that's something else that's happened. When I was little the Willocks next door had nine children and that wasn't unusual. Not unusual at all.'

'Poor woman,' said Elizabeth.

'The older ones looked after the little ones. That was the way then. Six in our own family.'

Mrs Munro talked about such things as we drove on. And credit cards, computers, foreign people ringing her up trying to get her banking details, all the passwords that she found difficult to keep track of. Not chattering, but interested in us and interested in her own life too. I think Elizabeth would have appreciated the chance to use her mobile to keep up with things at work, but was too mindful of the help being given to do so, and Mrs Munro was amusingly forthright in her opinions. She complained about the increase of dairying in the district at the expense of sheep. 'Cows stink, don't you find?' she said. I don't imagine Elizabeth had ever been close enough to one to notice. 'Even driving, you smell them. There're just too many of them. Cows stink whereas sheep have a pleasant smell. It's the fleece. People say sheep are stupid, but I've never found that, unless you panic them.' She talked about wind farms too. She knew more about them than either of us. She said Donald was keen on wind farms and they were the responsible way to go for power now. 'I like the lazy movement of them on the skyline — like giant people signalling,' she said.

The rain got heavier as we reached Palmerston North, but Mrs Munro continued confidently. She knew where the university was, she said. Not far past the square, when we were halted at lights, a bogan shouted at us from what Scotty calls a skite car: a big red thing low to the road, flash wheel trims and with exhausts altered to make a hell of a noise. It drew up alongside and a pale-faced guy, wearing a white T-shirt despite the weather, gave us the finger and made chimpanzee lips. 'Get a fucking move on,' he yelled. 'Move that useless fucking tank.'

'Charming,' said Mrs Munro, but not addressing him, or looking his way.

'He just wants to be noticed,' said Elizabeth, 'and, lacking any talent, this is his only way.'

'At Woodford House I was taught not to swear, but sometimes I think it,' said Mrs Munro. 'It gives the release without disclosing vulgarity.' We watched the skite car turn off and accelerate away, the guy's bare arm and finger held high in the rain.

Mrs Munro said it was a pity it was so wet because the university grounds have lots of trees and walkways. 'What's that special name for the grounds of a university?'

'Campus,' Elizabeth provided.

'Campus, that's right, campus.' She repeated it with emphasis, as an aid to memory. 'I think I'll go along the bottom road and drop you there.' I asked her what she'd do for the rest of the day, and she said she'd go into the shops, also that she had a friend in a retirement home who still had her wits about her.

'You're welcome to come in with us. It's all open session. It's just that you could be bored silly, with hours about pharmaceutical products and research trials.' I'm sure Elizabeth had no expectation that Mrs Munro would accept, but she did. After all, she said, she could always leave between speakers if the going became too heavy. I think it was the company she wanted. Maybe it got lonely in that big, wooden house on the farm, even with a son as loyal as Donald.

As it turned out, she never heard even one of the speakers, and neither did we. She parked on the lower road okay, and we walked up steps to the campus. Once there, she unfurled a large, red umbrella and, beneath it, rather uncomfortably crowded together, we went in search of the venue. The conference was well under way and there were no other people about to direct us. The noise of the rain striking the umbrella was loud, and although close together, we could hardly hear one another. We hadn't gone far when Mrs Munro stopped abruptly, caught her breath loudly, began to walk again and then fell to the ground, almost taking Elizabeth with her as the umbrella caught around her shoulder. I thought Mrs Munro had tripped, but Elizabeth, with typical competency, knew at once something serious had happened.

She knelt down and pushed the umbrella aside, settled Mrs Munro on her back on the wet asphalt, leant to her face to check her breathing and then began vigorous resuscitation. The university bookshop wasn't far away and a couple of women students must have seen us. They came running out. 'Ring an ambulance,' I called, and they turned back immediately.

'You ring too, just in case,' said Elizabeth urgently, her shoulders jerking as she worked.

'By the bookshop,' was all I could tell the operator when asked where in the university we were. I hadn't been to Massey before.

'It's just confirmation,' he said. 'It won't be long.'

Yet we seemed to be there in the rain a long time — Mrs Munro lying in the puddles, Elizabeth kneeling by her and me holding the big, red umbrella over them, phone still in the other hand. A few people gathered, but no one willing, or medically competent enough, to take over. Elizabeth kept trying until the paramedics came, but I think she knew it was hopeless. The ambulance was able to get close and Mrs Munro was placed inside, where activity continued. As she was stretchered in I saw how wet she was, thin hair plastered to her scalp, and how grey her long face: grey as sand, and with the deep creases of her cheeks like striations in the sand. Only the large lapis lazuli brooch seemed embellished, so rich and glistening in the rain.

One of the St John guys rushed over to get information from us. We couldn't even give a specific address, or Donald's number, though I said surely Mrs Munro had a phone in her bag. Before he went, the paramedic said, 'You don't know much about her, do you?' but in a tone of surprise, not accusation.

When he'd gone, we sat together in the bookshop's warm office, out of the rain and conscious of the sympathetic glances from the staff. The partly furled umbrella on the floor formed a small, but expanding pool. 'You okay?' Elizabeth said. 'My God, what a morning it's been. I can hardly believe it's happened. The poor woman. We'll get a taxi and go on up to the hospital, though I know what we'll be told. What a hell of a shock it'll be for her son. What else could go wrong today, eh? I can hardly believe it. Poor old soul.' She put her hand on mine. 'Sure you're okay?' she said again. She wasn't Elizabeth Regina to me any more, rather a friend forged quickly and truly by a shared and intense experience.

I couldn't get my head around it. Mrs Munro had seemed so with it. Hard to believe she could go so suddenly. What could we say to Donald? If it wasn't for us maybe she'd still be okay. I said so to Elizabeth.

'He'll get a full report. There'll be a heart history for sure, or maybe stroke, and it's just a coincidence it happened when she was with us. Sad, sad thing.'

The paramedic was right, Elizabeth and I didn't know much about Mrs Munro, didn't know she existed until a few hours before, and then she was dead. We don't know much more now, even though we went to her funeral. We know she disliked cows and approved of wind farms, that she could swear without saying anything and was an accomplished driver. That she had cabinets of delicate china and family silver. We know that she was old, curious and kind, and that's how we remember her — especially that she was kind.

26.

Mr Prince

I spent the holidays at the end of my sixth form year working on a North Canterbury farm west of Cheviot. It was dry country and sheep were what mattered. It was a bigger property than most and run by Ross and Glenn Astell, whose family had been there for generations. Glenn was married and lived in the main house, which was two storeyed, wooden, quite old, but still well maintained. It had a set of back stairs, which Mrs Astell told me was for the servants years ago so they could come and go largely out of sight. 'Now I have to do everything myself,' she said, and laughed.

Ross lived in the smaller, more modern place by the entrance windbreak, and there were shearer's quarters, too, by the yards. They were a bit run down, but not too bad. That's where I stayed with Piripi Ngata and Paul Prince. I was just an odd job boy, really: rousie in the shearing shed, helper with fencing and a hanger-on during musters. I even helped Mrs Astell in the garden sometimes. Piripi was there permanently. Early twenties, I'd say, and able to do almost anything well: shearing, fencing, tailing, mustering — only machinery he wasn't that interested in. I liked working with him; he showed me how to do a lot of stuff without being bossy. We did a fair bit of fencing together at the back of the property, loading up a trailer early behind a four-wheel farm bike and being away for long, hot days. He had dogs of his own and was good with them. He liked to laugh and his laugh had a sort of hiccup in it. He's the first Māori guy I got to know well. There were hardly any Māori boys at my school.

Paul Prince was the other one in the quarters with us, and he arrived a week or so after me. He must have been at least in his forties and I began by calling him Mr Prince, but everybody called him Paul, even the Astell twin girls who were only at primary school. He wasn't permanent either, but was building a new hay shed: huge, but with only two shielded sides, which faced south and west to the worst weather. I gave a fair bit of help with that, too, but only as a gofer. He worked five days of the week and then went back to Christchurch for the weekends, usually with a trailer behind his crimson Commodore. Paul was proud of that car and particular about it. Part of his arrangement with the Astells was that it would always have garaging. I found him okay, but he could get tetchy if things didn't go right. It wasn't like working with Piripi.

The three of us in the shearers' quarters got our own breakfasts and lunches, but everyone went up to the big house for the main meal. Eight of us if the twins were at the table. Mrs Astell was a good cook and there's always plenty of meat on a farm. You go a long way to get better than a leg of hogget well roasted with pumpkin and potatoes. I ate more than at home, but never put weight on over those weeks. There was television in the quarters, but the reception was pretty hopeless and we were usually outside working until near dark on those long, summer days. The three of us did play cards a bit, and Piripi listened to the radio, but most nights we just had a couple of beers and a yarn before turning in. Nothing was ever said about my age and drinking. It was just a natural thing and no one overdid it.

I was there for nearly six weeks and would've stayed longer if I didn't have to go back to school. The Astells paid me pretty well, considering my lack of skills, and Mrs Astell gave me a hefty fruitcake to take back home. Looking back, I realise how little use I must have been, but the Astells made me feel welcome. Probably the flower garden work was the most useful stuff I did; Piripi wasn't keen on that.

It worked out well about getting back to Christchurch to catch the bus south because Paul was happy to take me on the Friday, even if it meant leaving a bit earlier than usual. Everyone came down to the quarters to see me off in the Commodore, even the twins. Paul said another couple of weeks and he'd be heading home for good himself. Years later I read in the paper about a Monica Astell who was appointed to some marketing board and I wondered if that was one of the twins. I'm pretty sure one was called Monica.

Anyway, I went to Christchurch with Paul Prince, and he invited me to have tea at his place before I caught the bus. He was married and had an eight-year-old son with a scab on his chin from a fall on the jungle gym at school. An odd kid who kept jiggling his head and smirking. I felt awkward about being there, partly because Paul hadn't bothered ringing from the farm to let his wife know I was coming with him, but more because of the way he spoke to her. I didn't have a lot of experience then about how married people were with each other. I went to the homes of my friends, of course, but when you're young the way your own mother and father are is what you expect in other people. My parents were happy enough together and the odd disagreement never came to much. I don't remember any shouting at each other, or us, come to that. If my mother was angry, or disappointed, she just seemed to withdraw into herself and there was an indefinable sense of tension in the family, but that didn't happen often and warmth would return. I do recall my father sitting my brother and me down when we were still at primary school and saying that you never hit a girl: under no circumstances.

I'm not saying that Paul Prince ever hit his wife, but he showed her no kindness, or respect. He belittled her in a casual, but deliberate way as if to show off how completely in control he was. She'd made macaroni cheese and he scoffed when she brought it to the table. 'Jesus, woman, call this a meal for working men. I don't know why I bother to come home. They have a decent spread on the farm, don't they, Hughie. What do you do all bloody day? Powder your nose?' And he laughed and looked at his son and me in turn. I just wished I were somewhere else, and couldn't think of any way to disassociate myself from what he said. I was just seventeen years old, in someone else's home and didn't know how to deal with it. Maybe for Paul Prince, putting his wife down was the easiest way of building himself up.

It caught me by surprise too, because it was so different to the way he spoke to Mrs Astell, the only other woman I saw him with. I guess he knew no one there would let him get away with slagging a woman off. I can't remember his wife's name. He didn't introduce me to her, but must have used it sometime, though if so I've forgotten. Everything about her was pale. Pale hair, pale eyes, pale skin, pale life, as if she were gradually wishing herself away. Even her dress was pale, and hung limply from her thin shoulders as if from a coat hanger. Paul ignored her most of the time, unless he wanted to criticise her. 'I thought at least you'd have a decent pudding and have smartened yourself up for visitors,' he said, even though she had no idea I'd be coming.

I wasn't there long, because I had to get to the bus station, and I couldn't wait to leave. I didn't want to have to witness the on-going humiliation, he on at her like a rogue dog worrying a ewe, and her taking it with a wretched smile to pretend it was a joke. And the boy. Jesus, what sort of an environment was that, but he didn't seem to notice. He knew nothing else, I suppose.

'Maybe we should get going, if that's all right,' I said. 'I need to check in and everything, and I'm not even sure if I've got the right departure time.' I thanked Mrs Prince for the meal and she smiled and nodded.

'She's a crap cook and not much of a screw either,' said Paul, and she smiled again. The same shamed smile as always when he ridiculed her.

'Oh, Paul,' she said quietly, without looking at either of us. 'You're embarrassing him.' And she was right. She must have taken years of it. I can't understand why she didn't just get out. Why would a woman put up with being treated like that? She stood in the doorway when we left and lifted her hand low at her side in a small, awkward goodbye.

While we drove to the bus station, Paul talked about the farm and how he'd be sorry when the hay shed was finished. He didn't say anything more about his wife. 'I like getting away from the city and meeting new people,' he said. 'I've always been good with people.' He pulled up by the bus station and kept the engine running as I got out to get my case from the boot, but then he decided he needed to have a pee, switched off and headed off inside. I took a coin from my pocket and made as good a scratch as I could along the left side rear door where he wasn't likely to see it for a while and where a bicycle pedal, or whatever, could well have done it. I know, I know, but I didn't have the courage, or the words, to say anything to him. Now it would be different, but it wasn't now.

I was sitting on the depot seats outside when he finished, and he just gave a wave as he walked past. If it hadn't been for that last day, I would've thought him an okay guy, but he was a prince without principles was Paul, and I got to see that whether I wanted to or not. What can you do except walk away and forget, which, as you see, I haven't been able to accomplish.

27.

Refuge in the Present

When I started teaching there were still a good many Second World War men in the profession, some taking the lead, some happy just to relax and resume a normal life. There were a few at the boys' secondary school I went to after training college. Their background didn't come up much at all, certainly not from them, but as time went by you gleaned bits and pieces casually referred to in conversation, and realised that the deputy head had trained as a pilot in Canada, but the war had ended before he got to fly in combat, and that the HOD social studies had been on torpedo boats in the Pacific. And Neil Pike, who taught maths, bore a visible history in the puckered machine-gun scars on his left arm.

Ray Sillitoe had been in Europe too, but like Neil didn't talk about it. Maybe they did when they were together, but I doubt it. I never saw any particular huddle of ex-war guys: some of them didn't even get on all that well. Ray was the metalwork teacher and a very heavy smoker. Often when I went past the workshop he'd be sitting on the concrete step, puffing away. A small, thin man with the darkened complexion that some heavy smokers have. He rolled his own because it was cheaper that way. While the class fooled around noisily inside, riveting the sides of their fourth-form tool box project, or whatever, Ray would draw on his ciggie, rub his bony elbows and look into the far distance across the playing field.

At several staff meetings the head had emphasised that under no circumstances were classes to be left unsupervised in labs and workshops, but Ray took no notice. Maybe he thought the doorstep was close enough to pass as a place of control. Probably he knew he wouldn't be that easy to replace anyway. Staffing was always an issue and Ray was quite popular with the boys. He treated them with distant casualness but nevertheless almost as equals. He would get them started, wander off and reappear at the end of the period to make sure they tidied up. Unless it was raining, most of his time was spent smoking on the step and in a far scrutiny. Around the pale doorway steps were the stained, squashed butts of his fags, like bird droppings.

The school inspectors' report specifically commended the woodwork programmes, but mentioned that elsewhere in the manual department the projects were outmoded and the students not sufficiently challenged. I liked Ray, most people did, but he was lazy all right, no denying that. It was easy to feel a bit superior to him because of his laziness and lack of professionalism. Condescending even, though he was older than most of us. Ray had been married, I know that. Whether his wife had died, or they'd split up, I'm not sure. He had a daughter and grandchildren in Perth and went over there a couple of times, I remember.

Despite the difference in our ages and in the length of time we'd been at the school, I got to know Ray reasonably well because we were paired up to look after the bus boys. I think Ray was even made dean of the bus boys. Dean was a title new to secondary schools then, introduced to give spurious dignity to additional tasks that paid little, or nothing. Ray made an unreliable list of the boys and routes at the start of each year, and I did all the work after that, including any hassles with the boys' behaviour, or changes to the pick-up points. Ray was strong on delegation and comradely in its application. At any formal gathering of the bus boys, he would yarn to one or two seniors about farming, while I coped with what was required with the throng.

Anzac Day wasn't such a big deal then as it's since become, perhaps because there were still many who knew first hand the reality of war. There was a dawn service in the town if you wanted to go and usually an invited speaker at the morning school assembly. Poppies, of course, but if you hadn't got round to buying one, nobody much cared. On one Anzac morning I happened to be talking with Ray by the staff lockers when he opened his and rummaged in the top shelf until he found a crumpled fabric poppy. 'Ah, knew it was somewhere,' he said casually. 'Had it for years, but I never seem to find the pin. You haven't got a spare, have you?'

The head had a variety of ways to encourage the involvement of staff in school activities, from flattery to vague promises of promotion, from veiled threats to appeals to professionalism. Putting people on the spot publicly was another. I've been caught by that myself. It's difficult, when you're not expecting it, to refuse a request to perform an obviously worthy task. Ray wasn't taken in, however. He had greater experience in deflection, I suppose.

It was at one of the head's impromptu staff addresses on a rather dour July day when the southerly flurried the puddle surfaces of the main quad outside, and groups of students stood listlessly beneath the building doorways and overhangs. The head only came into the staffroom at morning tea time when he had special reason. He didn't wear his gown day to day, but tended to hold the lapels of his suit when speaking formally, as if in academic dress. A few late comers padded quietly to the sink bench to make themselves tea, or coffee, offering a smile of obeisance as they passed him.

'There's gratification in selfless endeavour,' said the headmaster grandiloquently in conclusion. 'A reward in itself.' He was exhorting us to volunteer for greater involvement with sporting teams. Masters competed for the coaching of the top rugby and cricket teams, but the head's enthusiasm for broadening the scope to badminton, hockey, soccer and volleyball wasn't shared by many at that time in traditional schools. There was no spontaneous upwelling of offers after the head's appeal. 'Let Mr Collins know if you can help the school in this significant way,' he said. Norm Collins was the sports master, coach of the first fifteen, and considered any boys who dodged rugby as slack twerps, but he smiled grimly to show willing. He once told me he disliked sponge cake for being all bloody fluff and air like a bouffant hairdo and that a man needed solid fruitcake in the belly.

The head had turned back on his way to the door, apparently

struck by an after-thought. 'Travel, that's right. That was the other thing,' he said emphatically. 'Travel for the inter-school fixtures is quite a time-consuming task, and I'm sure we'd all like Mr Collins to be relieved of that at least. You came to mind, Mr Sillitoe, with your existing rapport with the bus companies.' The head stood still, eyebrows slightly raised in an interrogatory way, and looked directly at Ray.

'I have sufficient on my plate, thank you,' said Ray, quietly, yet without embarrassment, as if he were refusing the offer of another sausage roll. I remember that he was smoking. Strange now to recall how natural it seemed then to have people smoking in the staffroom. Several teachers smoked pipes. You just don't see pipe smokers these days, do you.

Ray became sick, but said nothing about it — not to me anyway. I only found out because I heard him retching in the staff toilets. I'd come in during a free period just as he disappeared into one of the cubicles and closed the door. He sounded pretty bad and it went on for some time. I didn't know whether it was better to wait for him to come out, or just go so he'd never know he'd been overheard. In the end I stayed. It was a bit awkward for both of us, but I wanted to make sure he was okay. I offered to go over and supervise his class, but he said it wasn't necessary. 'I've had this crook gut quite a bit recently,' he said. 'I'm having a few tests to check things out. I can manage all right, but it's not getting any better.'

It got worse, not better. An advanced cancer, oddly enough not of the lungs despite a lifetime of smoking, but further down. 'Spleen,' Neil Pike told me, who had known him for a long time. 'Not good in the spleen.' Ray didn't talk about it, but we could all see that he was slipping quite quickly, and he left teaching and the school at the end of that second term, went into hospital and soon after was transferred to the hospice by the public gardens. I visited him a couple of times. He looked smaller each time, though quite calm lying there. There was a television in his room, but he said he didn't watch it. He never asked me anything about the school, but talked about his daughter, who had come over from Australia to be with him. She and her husband had evidently done well and, on both my visits, Ray told me the same story of their flash home in Perth, the matching BMWs, the business trips her husband took to advise on distribution hubs.

Return to Harikoa Bay

'At least I never held her back at all,' he said. 'At least I can say that.'

He didn't talk much, though, and I didn't stay long. Most of the time we just sat there and he seemed to forget about me unless I started up a conversation. The sun was setting during my second visit, and I remember looking over the gardens and duck pond to the hills 'where the dying sun made sullen embers of the western cloud'. That's what seventh-former Peter Craddock wrote in a story that won the Guthrie Huddlestone English Prize that year. I judged it. He was inclined to romantic excess as the young are, but a talented boy nevertheless.

A good many of the staff went to the funeral, and we missed Ray although he'd been a quiet man and less than dedicated as a teacher. It was strange to walk past the metalwork room and see a new, animated teacher inside with an attentive class, instead of Ray smoking on the step and the boys within mucking around and talking.

Sometime afterwards his daughter donated his medals to the school, and among them was the Distinguished Conduct Medal for gallantry. The head was delighted and tracked down the citation and Ray's service record. He decided to make the library foyer a memorial alcove and display Ray's medals there with other war material the school had gathered. It was almost as if he found Ray more interesting and worthy dead than alive. At a staff meeting the head told us Ray had been a sergeant and distinguished himself particularly in Crete. The head rattled everything off as if he'd known about it all along. As if they'd been staunch comrades and confidants.

Afterwards I talked with Neil, who knew Ray best of all of us. 'He had an absolute shit of a time in Crete,' Neil told me. 'He was captured and escaped, led a small group who hid out in the hills, but was caught again and badly beaten. He got away a second time and did some desperate hit and run stuff with the partisans. He was a wreck at the end of the war, I gather. Never really came right. Everything afterwards was pretty much just a shelter, I think, from what he'd been through.'

So that had been part of Ray's life too. An idle man and a poor teacher, who had risen to an extreme, exacting challenge in the past and sought only refuge in the present.

28.

Leaving Emptiness

The Indo-European origin of the word widow means 'be empty'. It's great, isn't it, what you can learn now just by using Google. Noeline made a sexual joke of it when I told her, but then she's got a lot to be cheerful about — and so have I, really. Noeline's divorced, but has a successful career as a real estate agent, and a pleasant partner who's not dependent on her. I like Lloyd, who has sufficient authority in his role at the IRD not to need an assertive manner, or a self-referential conversational bias.

It seems to me a widow generally gets greater sympathy than a divorcee, the assumption in the first case being that a union made in heaven has been sadly disrupted by the call for one partner to return there, whereas divorce is a personal failure.

To be honest, my marriage wasn't great, and I accept my share of responsibility for that. Our mutual and contained disappointment was assuaged by the presence of a daughter, and reciprocal love with her formed a tripartite bond. No matter what divergence grew in other matters, we always had Sonia in common. Mark was at his best as a father and our happiest times together were as parents, not lovers, not even partners. I know from the people around me that's not uncommon, but sad I think and not what was hoped for, or expected.

But Mark's dead and Sonia's left home. I'm sorry he's dead and it wasn't fair that pancreatic cancer struck when he was only forty-two. We had some long final talks in the hospice, but they were healing only for our feelings towards each other. Had he lived, I think we would have separated when Sonia went to varsity, and we would have accomplished that in a resigned, business-like manner, but with a sense of failure and underlying resentment just the same. Amicable — am I the only one so cynical as to smile when the term is used in reference to separation? He was strong at the end, as men consider they need to be, but he felt somewhat cheated in life, I think, and not just by death. I do grieve for him, but not for us.

Sonia comes home often. She seemed to skip that difficult, rebellious time of adolescence that Hollywood makes much of, and we get on really well. I love her company and we talk of anything and everything. She's keen for me to 'meet someone'. The someone being a man, of course. She tells me I won't find a man in the garden. I do love the garden, but I'm not using it as refuge. I've always been a keen gardener, perhaps because my working day is full of contact with people I haven't chosen. That's what it's like being a dentist. A lot of people meet up through their work, but I don't think it happens much with dentists. It's not like running a riding school, planning house renovations, or advising on family trusts, not even like giving violin lessons, or lecturing in microbiology.

People aren't at their best in the dentist's chair. There's that sense of recumbent vulnerability, someone looking inside you, pain and expense to come — and it's not great for me either. I've never fancied a guy because of the state of his choppers, but have been put off often enough by bad breath and close-ups of nasal hair. Quality conversation is difficult also.

It's not that my experience of marriage dissuades me from having a relationship, even marrying again. There are lots of men I like, and I prefer mixed society to always being in the company of women. My best friends are women, but there's a casualness, almost an indifference, among men socially that's a relaxing counter to the intense scrutiny and determined involvement that mark female friendships. So much stuff seems to just pass guys by. Whatever, they say, whatever. Mark never remembered the birthdays of his friends, never felt slighted if he wasn't invited to join some group going to a game, or show, was happy to pick up with someone from years before and just as happy to let him drift away. A hen party can be fun, but you don't want to live in one. And the admiration of a man has connotations distinct from that of a woman — not better, but different. Two sexes are surely better than one.

I'm just so busy, really, that's the thing. I do draw sustenance from time in the garden, being out of the house and the surgery, but it's quite a tie. Mark always said I should plant lots of shrubs and ground cover for easy maintenance, but I love the perennials, delight to see the froth of peonies and phlox after winter. I enjoy working among all the scents of the garden, how they vary as I move from one place within it to another, from one season to the next. I love fostering the delicate gentians, restricting the aggressive climbing roses, remorselessly hunting down the convolvulus. But I won't find a man in the garden, Sonia likes to remind me. Unless it's dark and he's looking through the bedroom window, she added once. She likes a laugh.

Gardening's not all I do. I still ski. The garden's largely passive in winter, and the mountains have always been a draw for me. Cold weather makes some people close down, but I feel more energetic when it's chilly. There's a pureness about the mountains in winter. I'm vain enough to say that I've won slalom trophies and display them still in my workroom. Mark wasn't a skier — it wasn't something anyone in his family could afford. He always felt that I had an easy passage in life. There's the share club too, the bridge, the hospice committee and the pro bono work at the community clinic.

I actually met a pleasant guy through bridge. A maths teacher at Sonia's school, who was better at bidding than playing the cards, but very sound overall. He asked me to be his partner at a tournament and we had lunch with others and drinks alone afterwards. We were fourth out of twenty-two tables and he asked me if I'd be his partner for a twelve-week session. I was pleased with fourth, but I could tell he was keen to unite for more than cards and I didn't want to lead him on. His teeth were sound, he was slim and he wore a jacket well, but he had a donkey bray laugh and kept putting a finger in his ear. Such habits are very hard to break. And Noeline told me he paid maintenance for a family in Palmerston North. Oddly enough, whenever I play against him at the club now, he and his partner seem to win. He doesn't comment on that, but it's almost as if he's out to show me what could have been.

I've been out with a few guys, but not via computer dating. All of that online stuff seems creepy to me and too calculating. You must become like one item of many on a shelf, open to perusal and appraisal. Noeline said I'd make an ideal cougar, but I don't like the word, or the concept. It's not the sort of feminism that appeals to me.

Your friends try to set you up sometimes when you're single: discreetly, usually, and with the best intentions. I met Kieran at one of Patsy's dinner parties. He was a Londoner, but had been here for years working as a journalist. He was well travelled, well read, and not bad looking, but full of himself and rather surprised I think when I didn't encourage him. And he wore a red jersey with a purple shirt when even a man should know better.

At Eleanor's I was introduced to John Huang, who's a Fonterra scientist. I like him. His Otago family has been in New Zealand longer than most European Kiwis, and he talked in an interesting way about his trips back to Hunan province in China to discover something of his ancestry. He's had his DNA profile done too. I think I might do that myself. As you get older, you grow more curious about your family history. My grandfather always said there was an admiral way back in the family.

I saw John a few times, once at Eleanor's birthday party, and he invited me to go with him to hear the symphony orchestra. It was an enjoyable night. We went to other musical events too. He's a really nice man, but the more I got to know him the more I realised that he was still, in a subtle way, mourning the death of his wife. He hardly talked of her. A lot about his three children, but she was behind that family happiness of the past. I didn't want to buy into that. We still see each other occasionally, with other people, but understand without ever talking about it that we have no future together. He's off to China again soon, able to combine work with more family investigation. He found out he'd lost relatives in Mao's Great Leap Forward and also the Cultural Revolution. I have to say his teeth aren't great. He should have had work done when he was young.

Then there's Todd. He was so persistent, kept texting and ringing, but it was never going to be on. He coughed and spat a lot and I just can't stand that. Not at all romantic. And Alec? Alec is probably the best-looking guy I've been out with, a sort of late-model Brad Pitt, but I went right off him after a visit to his place. He had a dog that kept barking while we were having a drink. When he went out to stop it, I took the wine glasses into his kitchen and happened to see him at the kennel. He hauled this small, brown dog out by the chain and kicked it hard twice. Anyone who could kick a pet like that could kick a person just as easily. So bye bye, Alec, and he never knew why. Since then I've never thought of Brad Pitt in quite the same way.

Maybe it sounds as if I've had lots of guys interested, but I'm talking of three years since Mark's death. There's been months on end when I never went out with a man. It wasn't always me shying away either. I know what it's like to be rebuffed, even if it was with gentleness and no intention. Sonia said she was sure Terry was the one. Strange how persistent the myth that there is a single, predestined and perfect partner for each of us, whereas there are a great many people in the world with whom you could make a successful couple, provided there's compromise and agreement. Look at all the arranged marriages that work. And I see no psychological reason why you can't love two men at the same time, but that's denied, of course, because of the personal and social difficulties it creates.

Terry was in the city on secondment from the head office of Contact Energy in Auckland. The one guy that I met by accident, just like a rom com. Noeline and I were at the main art gallery, not to view an exhibition, but to have a hot drink after giving up on shopping because of the rain and wind. Neither of us can have been looking our best. There was a sparrow in the café: not distressed at all, but flitting and hopping among the tables to get crumbs where it could. It came cheekily to our table, and in waving it into flight again I struck the small, yellow teapot in front of me and it fell onto the floor without breaking, but splashing hot Earl Grey onto the trouser legs of Terry, who was sitting alone at the next table. The three of us were soon talking, and not just about how tea stains are best removed from light material. Turned out Terry was a bit of an art freak and had been looking at the Rita Angus exhibition I'd seen days before. Turned out she was a favourite for all of us, and so we went back to the gallery together.

Noeline invited him to dinner because he was new to the city, and that's how it began. He may not be as good looking as Alec, but in all other respects he's pretty impressive: bright without trying to be smart, perceptive without being probing, caring without being clingy and with a sense of humour that appealed to me. Not a bad résumé. Both of us had busy lives, but we managed to meet often. He's the only man I've been to bed with since Mark died, and I felt it brought us closer. Quite enjoyable most times, too, although I'm not mad about the doggy style stuff. He made no promises, but I hoped there might be a future for us as a couple. When his secondment came to an end, however, there was no talk of that. Two nights before he left, we had dinner at Restaurant Pompeii. He said my friendship had made all the difference to his stay and that I should get in touch if I came north. There was no awkwardness on his part, and I realised I'd allowed myself to assume his feelings matched my own, though he'd never said so. I missed him a good deal, but made no effort to hold on, and after a few emails and phone calls at increasing intervals there's been not much contact. I still think of him sometimes: I still like him. I hope he still likes me. Not everything works out.

Anyway, that's not the end of the story. There's Jole now. Yes, an unusual name, and spelling. He said it's one of those family ones that get handed down and not to do so would be thought disrespectful to all the dead Joles gone before. I met him in Methven in July when I was skiing at Mount Hutt. A man has to have the right build to look good in alpine gear; it's so easy to look overweight. Jole has the right build: tall, rangy so that the heavy clothes don't bulk at the waist. His face is lined, but the lines go straight down his cheeks in an outdoor sort of way. Men seem to have an aversion to moisturiser: no, more likely just can't be bothered. Men can't be bothered about all sorts of things.

Jole's dark haired — the romantic heroes always have black hair, right? I bet Mr Darcy was dark. I've read the book, but can't remember if his colouring is ever mentioned. Jane didn't go in for a lot of physical detail, more emphasis on deportment, and attitudes revealed through behaviour and conversation. I hadn't met him before, but we have friends in common and were introduced in a scruffy Methven diner with off-putting food and offhand staff. I've had a special affection for the place ever since. 'You're the dentist, right?' he said, leaning forward because of the chatter. He talks quietly, which is another thing that recommends him. 'I've heard about you,' he said. He'd probably heard that I'd been disappointed over a chap from Auckland, but what he mentioned was my skiing. 'I'll have to watch out for you on the slope seeing you're such a whizz,' he said. Actually he proved pretty competent himself.

Jole's an interesting cross between an inside and outside sort of guy. He's a scientist specialising in stock improvement through genetics, but spends a good deal of time visiting properties and advising cockies on their programmes and equipment. I like going with him when I get the time. He's a natural with both people and animals, despite being a typical boffin when he needs to be. Empathy, that's what he's got. Sonia, the little witch, says he'll have to do now that Terry's no longer on the scene. I feel safe when I'm with Jole. I guess that's something that only a woman, or perhaps a child, feels when in a man's company. In a dingy street, among strangers or unsettling activities that could pose a threat, I'm not apprehensive when with Jole. Not that he's especially formidable — he just has that male ease, and the feeling of security is contagious.

After a couple of farm visits with him, he said it was time for me to show him my surgery. 'In situ,' he said, 'I need to imagine you in your professional role, and I'm counting on treatment at mate's rates.' I think he's looked after his teeth well enough, but it's hard to tell. Some people naturally show a lot of teeth, just in talking and the way they hold their mouth, but Jole's not like that. He smiles with his lips together, but it's a nice smile and comes often.

I took him in with me on a cold Sunday morning. A southerly was punishing the foliage of the lilac tree outside the window and everything in the room was cold to the touch. He was interested in the equipment, especially the new KaVo x-ray machine and imaging equipment, but what amused him was the Simpsons cartoon I have on the ceiling to distract children. 'You're onto it,' he said. 'What a great idea.' He lay back on the chair and gazed up at Homer and Bart. 'Have you ever made love in this chair?' he asked.

'No,' I said. 'I keep my duties and my pleasures separate.'

'Fair enough,' he said, still looking up at the Simpsons. I think, however, he was disappointed, his question more intended as a suggestion. Most guys seem keen to have sex at the drop of a hat. It never bothers them about when they last had a shower, or occurs to them maybe it's the time of the month.

Jole and Sonia get on well. Several times when she's been home

Return to Harikoa Bay

we've gone out together at his suggestion, and I don't think it's just to please me. 'Looking like Brad Pitt isn't everything,' she said, 'and his car's better than yours.' It's a Volvo SUV, whatever those initials stand for. He has a nice place in Cashmere too, with a view over the city. It's well kept. He even has pot plants inside and they're well cared for. His partner died in a bus accident when they were holidaying in Malaysia. They weren't married. Jole's still close to her son. I like it that he's kept contact. He'll talk about it all with me, but doesn't dwell on it. He's a very open sort of guy when you get to know him, and honest in his responses. If I ask his opinion about my clothes, he takes it seriously and isn't afraid to make a criticism. Generally he seems to think the less women wear the better.

Last Sunday we went way up the Rakaia to a run owned by the Standish family, who are successful merino stud breeders. Jole was taking them his analysis of the computer data they'd collected from the flock. He's at his best in that sort of environment, loving the landscape, the people and the stock, and obviously keen for me to feel the same. It is grand country, especially when the wind is down and the blue dome of the sky sets off the mountains. Ron Standish had just had a small operation on an ingrown toenail and wasn't getting about much. 'It's damn embarrassing,' he said. 'It's such a ludicrous complaint. Who can take it seriously? I usually tell folk that I've sprained my ankle.'

Because of his toe he didn't come down to the yards after lunch to see the rams that were penned up there, but his wife, Kate, walked down with us, talking knowledgeably about the dangers of overstocking on drought-prone country. I liked her, and thought she must have come from a high-country family herself, but she said she was a GP's daughter, and had been a radiologist before her marriage.

The rams were big, confident creatures, but used to being handled. They had three tags in their ears, each a different colour, and Jole said that way their individual genetic and developmental profile could be tracked. 'It's shape up or ship out these days,' he said. 'We know everything about them in this business.' As he talked his hand strayed naturally to the head of one of the rams and his fingers played in the wool. The merino seemed happy enough with the fondling. I like the way Jole is with animals.

I liked Ron and Kate too, and we stayed on for afternoon tea, date scones as broad as a bread slice and meringues with whipped cream.

Stayed on even later, had dinner, and when we went they invited us to come back soon. It was evening when we left, but the summer sun persisted, the arch of the sky still clear and blue. Jole drove down the long, unsealed track, stopped by the delivery box to get out and close the gate. He didn't drive immediately on his return to the car, but sat looking at me. 'I'm serious,' he said. 'I want you to know that,' and then he started driving again, started talking about the Standish family and how Ron's great-grandfather had drowned in the river while crossing on horseback. I knew it was important though, what he'd said about being serious.

The next morning he came to my rooms and left a parcel for me with Adrienne. I didn't see him because I was busy with a young woman who had an impacted wisdom tooth and consequent second molar decay. Evolution hasn't been kind to the human jaw, but has benefited the practice of dentistry. It was lunchtime before I got a chance to open Jole's rather unwieldy parcel. No coloured ribbon in a bow, the joins were clumsily done with Sellotape: most guys have little sense of presentation. Inside, though, was a fabulous Mons Royale merino ski jacket and note that said, 'I hope this will soon have a permanent home in a wardrobe at my place.'

Well, I haven't moved in yet, but it's on the cards. It's a happy time and I intend to do my best for both of us. Sonia's supportive, Noeline, Eleanor, Patsy and my other friends say I should go for it. What's not to like?

I surprise myself with the pleasure I feel now that I'm with someone, and it's Jole. I think I'll be a better partner this time round because I'm more realistic, and I know what it's like to be alone.

29.

Third in the Back Row

In my final BSc year at university I became a tutor for a small organisation offering subject help to secondary school students. I can't remember how I heard about the job: probably there was a notice on the common room board. Anyway, it wasn't through someone I knew who was already employed there. Even at the time I was surprised how little care was taken to establish my suitability and qualifications. That I'd passed units in maths and the sciences seemed distinction enough. I'm even unable to recall the name of the man who interviewed me. He wore a suit, was short and brisk in both manner and appearance, and asked me within a few minutes when could I start.

It was one on one, not group instruction, and that made a good deal of difference. Discipline didn't really come into it. The sessions were held in a couple of second-storey rooms close to Bealey Avenue that belonged to a ballet and dance academy. It used the spaces most of the day and from 7.30 at night. Acme Tutorials put out some desks and chairs in the time between, and that was our workplace. I had three students for an hour each once a week: two of them on Thursdays. Generally, there were several other tutors at work scattered about the rooms.

I had two girls and a boy, all from different schools, but all for maths. Maths seems scary to a lot of people, but I had no trouble with it. Teaching it is a different matter and I wisely chose not to make that a career. Angela Muscroft is the only one whose name I can recall, and for reasons other than the time we spent together. The boy always seemed as if he were there on sufferance, shuffled his feet about a lot, kept looking at other people and sniggered easily. The other girl was very shy and made little improvement because of that. Angela was a fifth former at Papanui High School. She passed all her subjects in School Certificate that year, including sixty-one per cent in maths. I don't claim any credit.

Her father brought her to the first session. It was bucketing down. They put their raincoats on the backs of the tubular chairs and drops fell to the polished dance floor. Adults were permitted to stay during the tutorials if they wished, though hardly any did. I guess Mr Muscroft wanted to check out the place and who would be teaching his daughter. Apparently he was satisfied, as he just dropped her off after the first time, and Angela's sister usually came to collect her. It's the sister, Diane, who makes all of this something important to me, something still clear in the mind, something of reproach.

Certain women have an aura that forms a charge in the air around them: not a colour so much as the unconscious extension of charm in the magical sense. A spell. She was sexy enough, but more than that was an integration of appearance and personality. A sense of completeness. She came up to the rooms during the second session and sat waiting on a form by the wall bars. She wore faded jeans, shiny red boots and held a light jacket on her lap. She smiled at her sister, but didn't interrupt, sat composedly, glanced at those of us at the spaced desks. She wasn't close enough to hear what Angela and I were saying, but awareness of her presence made me self-conscious, and Angela sensed that, I think.

When the hour was over, Diane introduced herself, and I found myself praising her sister's application and ability in order to continue the conversation, and then following them downstairs and onto the street. I barely restrained myself from climbing into the back seat of their car and was halfway through a nonsensical comment about the fragrance of the twilight when they drove away. The air was cooler once Diane was gone, and the immediate world diminished. Mundane noises of the city resumed a jarring tone.

At the flat I described her to Warwick and Iosefa, who were eating cold sausages as they played table tennis on the kitchen table. 'Sounds well out of your league,' said Warwick casually.

'Yeah, man,' said Iosefa, 'You wouldn't be up to it.' I decided that if I ever did get to know Diane, I'd never bring her to the flat. Not because it was squalid, though it certainly was, but because Iosefa was six foot two and possessed exotic allure for women.

I spruced myself up the next time I went to tutor Angela. The new pair of burgundy corduroy trousers and the black jersey with the polo neck. I cleaned my teeth thoroughly too, though I knew the possibility of kissing Diane on such slight acquaintance wasn't great.

'Did your dad drop you off?' I asked when Angela arrived.

'Yes.'

'Diane will pick you up maybe?'

'Maybe,' she said.

'She's a good sister to you.'

'Mrs Grainger said I should practise the use of prime numbers, common factors and multiples.'

'Okay.'

'And powers, including square roots,' Angela said, and that's what we did.

It's not easy when you're talking about such things to work the discussion around to what Diane's job was and whether she had boyfriends. 'Lots of boyfriends,' said Angela patiently when we were having a short break. But no academic qualifications, it turned out. She worked at the local radio station, mainly arranging advertising, but aiming to get behind the microphone. You don't need any other qualifications, though, when you're young and beautiful. What's a PhD in microbiology compared with the legs that Diane had, the dark irises in her large eyes, the small bones of her wrist, the smooth muscle connecting neck and shoulder. I wanted to ask how old she was too — you don't want a girlfriend older than yourself — but I felt I'd shown enough curiosity.

Diane did come up shortly before the end of the session and sat by the wall bars again. She pulled her hair back and put in one of those elastic band things. Her hair was dark, she had a high, pale forehead and she watched the several tutors and students with a slight smile, or looked down at her hands.

When the hour was up I went down the stairs with them and along the street half a block to the car, which was a scruffy, blue Ford Cortina. I asked Diane if it was hers.

'All mine,' she said. 'I call it The Pimp because it takes most of my money.' I guess I laughed louder than the joke deserved.

'Do you think you'd mind dropping me off if it's on your way?' I said quickly, because she and her sister were already in the front seats. 'Just if it's on your way, of course.'

'Where do you live then?'

'Fitzgerald Ave,' I said, 'but anywhere close would do.' I'd biked in to the rooms, but needed to be with her for longer.

'The river end,' Diane said. 'I'm happy to drop you there. Okay?'

I had hoped for a chance to talk to her during the ride, but the Cortina was noisy, the river not that far away by car and she chatted with Angela most of the time about netball. 'Did you go to the same school?' I butted in to ask her.

'Yes,' she said.

'Did you like maths?' Why did I say something as stupid as that?

'Not really. No, actually I hated it, especially the algebra. All x's and y's that didn't add up to anything. What sort of a career can you get with x's and y's?'

'Right,' I said.

'Maybe I needed extra lessons like Angela,' she said.

'Right.'

'Are they helping you that much, though?' she asked her sister.

'They're okay. We haven't had exams yet to tell,' Angela said. Her voice held no special enthusiasm for my instruction. Obviously she would have preferred to keep talking netball.

'Well, let's hope so,' said Diane with emphasis. 'Dad told me they're costing plenty.'

'I don't get it all,' I said. 'Acme takes a fair whack.'

'I bet they do. I think I might talk to them about the advantages of radio advertising. Maybe you could tell me who the boss is and how to get in touch.'

'Sure. No probs,' I said.

And that was about it. I wanted to get around to asking Diane if she would like to meet for a coffee or something, but she pulled up just over the bridge. 'This do?' she said. I walked up the avenue until the Cortina was out of sight and then retraced my steps, began the considerable hike back to the dance rooms to get my bike. Things hadn't gone exactly as I'd planned. I wondered if perhaps the new corduroy trousers had been a mistake. Women notice clothes, don't they? But neither Diane nor Angela had remarked on them. I was worried, too, that Mr Muscroft might cancel the tutorials because of the cost and I'd never see Diane again.

I already knew the Muscrofts' phone number. It was on the sheet I'd been given with the details of my three students. I decided to ring Diane and ask her out, rather than having Angela overhear everything — perhaps witness my rejection. What possible authority could I retain in maths if that happened? The call would be too much out of the blue, though, until Diane and I knew each other just a little better. But her wish to secure Acme Tutorials as a client for Radio Heights was something that could achieve that, and when she next came to collect Angela I had the boss's name and contact. They were on the sheet as well. Director was what he called himself. Thinking about it more now, maybe it was one of those Scottish Mac something names, though he was definitely Kiwi. Odd, isn't it. I can see him so clearly, short, upright in stance to compensate, and with a dark suit and pale face, but I can't remember his name.

'I managed to get the info for you,' I said to Diane the next week when the tutorial was over. 'The director's name and contacts.'

'What's he like?' I hardly knew him, but I hinted that I did, even that I had some influence with him, and she said perhaps I could say something to him in support.

'Sure, happy to,' I said. 'If I see him. He's not around all that much but I'll certainly put a word in if I have a chance. I definitely agree they should be advertising on radio.' I thought everyone should be. Imagine the pleasure of sitting down with Diane Muscroft and talking about publicity for your business, or talking about anything at all, or just sitting down with Diane Muscroft.

At the car she actually asked me if I'd like to be dropped off again, but it looked like it might rain and I didn't fancy a long, wet walk back for the bike, so I said thanks, but I had stuff to do in the rooms. Also maybe it would improve my chances not to be too slavishly a supplicant. And they'd just go on about netball, wouldn't they? I knew it wouldn't rain as long as Diane was with me, but after I was left at the bridge the normal functions of nature could resume. From the driver's seat Diane reached out to close the door and there was just a glimpse down her blouse. It's just not fair when that happens. Atavistic Neanderthal genes come to the fore at such moments. 'Don't forget to look at my test,' said Angela.

'Right. I'll remember,' I said, and still had a hand on the car to steady myself when Diane drove off, spinning me around so that I almost fell. It rained on the way home.

I thought a lot about calling her. I practised in my room. I rang on Friday night when Warwick and Iosefa were at the movies with two girls they'd met while in the supermarket. Nobody had a cell phone in those days. Mr Muscroft answered and told me that Diane wasn't in. Of course she wasn't. Girls like Diane were never at home on Friday nights. I should have known that. They were at dances and cabarets, or driving with guys in V8s with stripes on the bonnet. I rang again on Sunday afternoon when my flatmates were watching television. Mr Muscroft answered, which was better than it being Angela, not as good as it being Diane.

Diane took a while coming to the phone. 'Hi Diane, it's Roland,' I said.

'Who?' Obviously I hadn't been on her mind all that much.

'Roland. From Acme Tutorials.'

'Oh, okay.'

'I just wondered how it went with the director. The radio stuff and everything.'

'I haven't been in touch yet.'

'Well, I hope it all goes hunky dory.' I don't know where that came from. I'd practised the bit about contacting the director, but the rest was just nerves.

'Hunky what?'

'Doesn't matter,' I said. 'Look, I was wondering if you'd like a drink sometime. I'm keen to hear more about your job, radio and so on. Sounds really interesting and maybe afterwards I'd be better prepared to sound out the director if you still haven't seen him. You know, just a wine, or coffee, at Orlando, or maybe The Lincoln?'

'I'm extra busy this week,' Diane said. 'Flat stick. You could ask whatever you want when I pick up Angela on Tuesday.'

'Sure, sure. Okay, see you then.'

It wasn't an outright rejection, I told myself later, just that she didn't understand that I was interested in more than merely the nature of a career in radio advertising. Maybe, however, Warwick was right and Diane was well out of my league. Maybe I needed to pay more attention to Simone in my metric, normed and Hilbert spaces class, who sometimes smiled and said hello, who once came and sat beside me when there were plenty of other seats. She was thin though, Simone, extra thin. I know there's a lot more to friendships with girls than just physical attributes. I understand that, but there's not much to actually see with very thin girls, is there. I mean even if the conversation is stimulating, you need something to rest your eyes on.

Diane didn't turn up until right at the end of the session on the following Tuesday. Angela was already packing her stuff. I'd given up on the burgundy corduroys and wore a pair of dark cotton trousers with narrow legs and a little fob pocket near the front. Quite big money, but the shop guy said they were the latest thing. Okay, I didn't have a car, or a motorbike, but I could look sharp, couldn't I? The shop guy had said that. 'Yeah, they look pretty sharp on you,' he'd said.

As we went down the stairs I asked questions about Diane's work at the radio station. She was a bit worried that her voice wasn't quite right for announcing. An opportunity was coming up and she wanted to give herself the best possible shot. The station head was encouraging but had said something about enunciation. 'What is that exactly?' she asked me. 'Pronunciation? Is that the same thing?'

'Enunciation's more about clarity, I think.'

'So I'm not clear?'

'I reckon you are,' I said. Diane said if she didn't get to be an announcer she'd probably quit. She was clearer than any of the other idiots there, she said. I could have told Diane that the thing against her on radio was that she couldn't be seen. That was the only thing. Television, that's where Diane belonged. Once you could see Diane, it didn't really matter what she said.

I accepted her offer to be dropped off at Fitzgerald Ave, partly because rain didn't look likely, and on the way endured Angela's complaints about the phys ed teacher who hadn't selected her for the top under sixteen netball team. Big deal, Angela. When I got out of the car at the bridge, Diane also got out and came round to the back of the Cortina so that she could talk without her sister hearing. 'Angela told me you were asking about my boyfriends. What's that all about?' she said.

'It was just in passing,' I said.

'But it's personal stuff.'

'I was just wondering, that's all. Maybe we could have a drink or something.'

'Stop wondering,' she said. 'Stop thinking with your cock, okay? Nothing doing, okay Roland?'

It sounds brutal and it was in a way, but Diane said it calmly, almost nonchalantly. I suppose she was used to dealing with queues of guys thinking with their cocks. What twenty-one-year-old guy isn't? 'Sure,' I said, 'I just wondered. No probs.' I tried to be casual, gave a laugh and a shrug before beginning to walk along the avenue, and then turning back to the studio rooms for my bike when Diane had driven away. There seemed to be dogs barking derisively at me from gate after gate, and trees reared back in the dusk and sneered as I passed. Reality's not always the story you wish for.

Diane still came to pick up her sister after the tutorials, but there was no meaningful conversation between us. Sometimes she waited in the car. During the last session Angela mentioned that Diane had told their parents about my absurd infatuation, and that Mr Muscroft had said he'd thought me a pleasant enough lad, but destined to be always someone third from the right in the back row. Angela also thanked me for the maths tuition, and I wished her well for her school exams and for netball too. Nothing that had happened was her fault. In fact nothing had happened, and that was my disappointment and failure.

Perhaps Diane made it in radio. I didn't listen to it a lot, but I never heard her voice. Maybe her enunciation hadn't been up to it and she went on to something else. Married a very rich and important guy, or became a super successful real estate agent. And if we were to ever meet up there would be no embarrassment because she'd have no recollection of me — just one of the guys in the back row who'd been lucky enough to see her go by.

30.

The Undertaker's Story

How wonderful it would be to be born old and have the joy of growing young. I'm thinking of that as I sit in my car at the domain and watch small boys playing rugby. As always with kids at that age they find it irresistible to pursue the ball instead of maintaining position, and so they cluster and swarm despite the shouted instructions of the coaches. A mist drifts over the field and the soft spring foliage of the silver birches droops with a heavy dew. A fox terrier runs among the players, but they take no notice and continue pursuing the ball and one another. From the carpark comes high-pitched laughter and, indistinct within the mist, seagulls sheer overhead. I, too, used to play footy here when I was a boy and often on days like this, biking through the fog with my boots tied to the handlebars. It's a pleasant reminiscence, but I can't stay long as there's a long drive ahead and Leonard Withnaill's body is close behind me in the Mazda SUV, covered with a tartan picnic rug of my dear mother's. You need fear no grotesqueness, however, for he's in a mid-range Bunzl body bag: out of sight and with just the faintest scent of formaldehyde.

Leonard and I weren't friends, although we knew each other and had affiliations in common. We weren't enemies either. Acquaintances, you could say. We both had homes in Vogel Street, just two apart, beside the course of the Felton Golf Club to which we both belonged. He was on a twelve handicap, two better than me, but then he practised more: golf is a game that rewards persistence. We were in the same Rotary Club too. He was a rather successful solicitor and enjoyed making jokes about my profession, which is that of undertaker. People seem led to levity by mention of my occupation, perhaps as a form of protection from deeper reflection. I've become accustomed to the comments. You don't start off in life with an ambition to be an undertaker, do you. Train driver, astronaut, rock star when you're young, accountant, lawyer, diplomat maybe when you're older. To have dead people as your clients doesn't appeal. To many people death seems contagious, whereas I've found that working alongside it has given me a greater appreciation of the wonder and privilege of life. I can watch a butterfly, a cloud, twilight on the retreating tide, for many minutes at a time.

Anyway, as I say, Leonard and I knew each other, though almost always we met in the presence of other people — Rotary, Business Association and as members of the golf club. Otherwise it was just a wave, or phatic greeting as we passed in Vogel Street. I was never invited to his house, although he was a convivial man. If I'd been married it may have been different of course. Leonard was married. Ngaire was her name. A large, ginger-haired woman with considerable physical presence, but a quiet and gentle personality, as I found from occasional conversation at functions. She's the reason I have her husband's body behind me in the Mazda now.

No, there's no story here of unbridled sexual passion and infidelity, but there's cruelty to be found, and death, of course. At the back of my section, close to the Cleopatra magnolia, which flowers wondrously on bare branches, is a small wooden gate that gives access to the golf course, not far from the twelfth hole, which is one of the longest on the course. There's a water hazard too, in the form of a long pond with blue gums at the north end. As the trees have grown it's become increasingly difficult to par the twelfth unless your drive is spot on. A couple of times, before any golfers have been on the course, I've seen a scrawny kid fishing for balls with a whitebait net. That's showing some initiative. Early in the morning and also in the evening, I often walk to the pond, past the McIvers' place next door, and the Withnaills' two along. Both winter and summer offer their contrasting attractions: a summer dusk is magical, with the colours fading and the fragrance of the freshly cut grass of the fairways, and winter also with a metallic frost and that frozen stillness. Even the rain I don't mind, for this is a dry region. A wind is unpleasant, though, no matter what the season. I don't like walking in the wind. Leisurely reflections don't seem to come in the wind.

I like it that there are lots of trees on the golf course. They're there for strategic purposes, but have aesthetic value as well. Trees have individual fragrance: the resinous pines, the lemon, petrol smell of the peeling eucalyptus, the smoky blue gum. Macrocarpa is most evocative for me. When I walk among them I'm a boy again, sitting by the great, evergreen wall that surrounded the red-roofed wooden farmhouse, and hearing from the yards my father's voice of command and the barking of the dogs in response.

It was almost dark on the evening I witnessed Leonard strike his wife. I was strolling past the low paling fence that marked the boundary of his property with the course, when he and Ngaire came to the french doors leading to their patio. They were clearly outlined by lights behind them, while I was unable to be seen. Without conscious decision, I stopped to watch and listen: nosy, I know, but there's something atavistically satisfying in watching others, unbeknown to them. A man within the bounds of his own property feels free to liberate his true personality, and what I observed was ugly and unexpected. Leonard and Ngaire were arguing and when she turned away he roughly pulled her back and punched her on the side of the face. 'Silly bitch,' he said. 'You're a useless, silly bitch.' Her body gave a sort of quake, but she didn't fall, only put her hands to her face and turned away again. She made no resistance, just gave a bursting sob and stumbled back inside. What a species we are.

What do you do in a situation like that? If it had been a movie I would've strode through the Withnaills' landscaped section and clouted him, comforted Ngaire, turned a grim face to the camera, but it wasn't a movie and I knew I was a sort of peeping Tom at the edge of their privacy. So after waiting just long enough to see the blow wasn't repeated, I walked on in the darkness of the golf course and the shadow of cruelty.

Naturally I saw them both differently after that — his affable suaveness revealed as preening arrogance and her pleasant compliance as the symptom of oppression, but marriages are private arrangements by those concerned and I said nothing of what I knew. You don't forget something like that, though, and when I sat with him during meetings of the golf club management committee, or on Rotary occasions, I remembered not just the words, but the tone. The blow too. When he announced that he was donating a defibrillator to the hospice, I felt no gratitude. When he offered pro bono work to the Salvation Army, I was unmoved. What I had seen from the sweet dusk of the golf course was the real Leonard Withnaill.

Less than a month later, Ngaire died from a fall on the stairs of the old Augusta theatre in Maple Street: steep stairs, marble and uncarpeted. She and Leonard had been part of a small group visiting to make a recommendation for a Historic Places listing. They left early, while others of the group had remained behind to inspect some original tasselling, and barely heard Ngaire's cry as she fell and Leonard's shouts soon afterwards. A terrible thing to happen.

Leonard didn't ask me to handle the funeral. He went to Stengler and Kayes, the largest firm of undertakers in the city. They did a professional job as always, but their main room, spacious though it is, has a rather dispiriting outlook onto the firm's carpark and the workshop of Beta Refrigeration Services. People want a pastoral scene when they contemplate the end of life. My own chapel looks out on rhododendrons and lemon trees through which Monty's Tyre Shop is barely visible. Ngaire's sister gave the best eulogy and there were affecting clips of Leonard and Ngaire, some when their children were small.

I know Murray Stengler well, and like him. He doesn't play golf, but he's pleasant company and very professional in his work. His father founded the firm and Murray has advanced it. We talked briefly of Ngaire's death when we met at a recital of the Burns String Trio. 'No one saw it happen,' he told me. 'Leonard said she just slipped on the smooth marble and went down with a hell of a wallop. It must have been too, because when she was on the table there were all these terrible bruises on her head as if she'd banged over and over. She must have bounced down several steps. It wasn't easy to prepare her for family viewing.' Murray had no suspicions and I aroused none.

Nigel Robbins plays at Felton. He's what we call a bogey golfer because he's on an eighteen handicap. An inveterate slicer of the ball and a great swearer because of it, but then he's too old to improve now. He's a senior sergeant and I deliberately got into casual conversation with him when I saw him practising alone on the putting green. I brought the conversation round to Ngaire's death and said there was something I'd appreciate his view on. 'It's awkward actually,' I told him, 'but I once saw Leonard hit Ngaire and wondered if I should mention it. After what happened to her, I mean.'

'Where did you see that?' Nigel picked up his ball and came closer.

I told him I was walking past their place on the course, in the evening as I often did.

'And he didn't see you?'

'No.'

'Was it a punch, or just a shove?'

'A punch.'

'Just one?

'Just one.'

'And what did she do?'

'Just took it.'

'I wouldn't say anything,' said Nigel. 'Not after all this time. You'd only be opening up trouble for yourself. Stuff happens in marriage and they always seemed an okay couple.' He put the golf ball on the smooth grassed surface again and took his stance. 'It's all water under the bridge now anyway,' he said. I could tell he didn't understand what I was getting at, but I just left it at that.

Leonard didn't come into money as a result of his wife's death, he didn't quickly pair up with an attractive younger woman with a marked libido, he didn't buy a Mercedes convertible, change his dress code, or travel to Machu Picchu. He displayed due contained sorrow for a time. His life went on as usual as far as I could tell. I was unable to accept that, despite knowing that Nigel Robbins' advice was sound. I felt an unwelcome burden even though Ngaire had played no significant part in my life. If the agencies of justice in a society see no reason to take action, there's still individual responsibility, isn't there? On the night Leonard hit his wife I'd evaded that, but couldn't any longer. For a clear conscience, one must act on what one knows.

There was no particular hurry. I've always been an organised, systematic person. It's an advantage when you run a business, even a necessity, especially if you lack a compelling personality. I know my own failings: that I lack charisma and that easy engagement with my fellows that draws people in. I overheard once, in the locker room at the club, Gordon Hight saying to someone that I dealt with stiffs all day and I was pretty much a stiff myself. Gordon's useless as a golfer. No consistency in his swing at all, despite the flash Cleveland clubs.

No particular hurry, but I got things sorted in my mind. Each month the Felton committee meets at the clubhouse and Leonard often stayed on alone afterwards to catch up on work as treasurer. I took what I needed to my locker, but Leonard didn't stay on so I just waited a month. He did stay on the next month, perhaps because the AGM was coming up when his report would be due. I said goodnight with the others and walked towards my house through the darkened course, but I didn't go home, just waited a while by the quiet pond at the twelfth hole. In summer the sprinklers were often on, but that night was cold and still and the blue gums were outlined against moonlit sky. The smell of trees is not so strong in the cold.

When I walked back to the clubhouse there were no cars, and through the committee room window I could see Leonard working, so I went briefly to my locker, then to the shallow bunker of the eighteenth, then back to talk to Leonard. He looked up, not especially surprised, since he knew I was a bit of a course prowler.

'Hi,' he said, 'what's up?'

'You'll want to see what's in the bunker out there,' I said.

He got up in his unhurried way and we walked down the corridor, passing the bar and locker room, and out into the night.

'What've you got there?' he said as we went.

'A body bag,' I said. 'It was dropped off for me here.'

'You've got some job, haven't you. Jesus,' and he laughed. He seemed pleased to find further evidence of the demeaning peculiarity of my profession. I didn't mind telling him about the bag, but made no mention of the iron bar I held beneath it.

In the fine sand of the bunker, which was an almost luminous white-grey in the moonlight, was the stub of a putter with a blue ribbon tied to the face. 'Now there's an oddity,' I told him, and when he knelt down to have a look, I hit him hard just above the right ear, before giving him a massive injection of formaldehyde. There was very little blood and just a few convulsions after the injection. I sat with him for a few minutes until it was over, then I left him there in the body bag and went back to the clubhouse to get Guy Hanley's electric golf cart. A body bag fits on a golf cart almost as well as a golf bag, and off we went over the course towards the twelfth and my place. I came back later, of course, to return the cart, clear a handful of clotted sand from the bunker and lock up the clubhouse. I remember the sharp shadows cast by the moon as I walked home and the black, scurrying orb of a hedgehog by the fourteenth tee. Most hedgehogs you see are dead and you don't realise they can move quite fast. The golf course is a different place at night — the soaring trees, the manicured, delineated surfaces, the spacious silence.

I'm not anxious with bodies. Leonard was safe in his bag in the cold garage. Most people panic with a body, and that's when things go wrong. They want shot of it at any price and so make mistakes. I left him there the next day, and in the evening took him to my work when my staff had all gone home. In the embalming room I gave him due respect — no indignities inflicted despite his crime. I'd taken his life after all and that was quite enough. I felt no personal gratification, just a sense of duty and justice done. As I said before, we all have a responsibility to look out for one another, to uphold fair play, decency, social and personal rights.

In my job I often encounter curiosity, even fear, concerning the process of embalmment. Visions of gaping Egyptian mummies and sarcophagi perhaps, when modern science has made it quite straightforward. The body is washed in a disinfectant solution, limbs massaged to relieve stiffening, a shave if necessary, the eyes closed with plastic caps and the lower jaw secured by wires, or sewing. The blood is removed through the veins and replaced with formaldehyde-based chemicals through the arteries. Then through a lower abdomen incision the organs are punctured and drained and more formaldehyde injected. The rest is really just cosmetic, to prepare the body for viewing in the casket. In Leonard's case that was unnecessary, of course. The whole process was over in about three hours. I don't mind doing embalming: there's no need for aimless conversation and no objection to the professional decisions I make. When people question my sense of humour, I say I may not be able to make people laugh, but I can always make them smile.

I could have retained Leonard's company at home for some length of time without any problems, or indication of his presence, but he needed to be put to rest. Do you know the Catlins in Southland? There's some lovely, unspoiled country — native bush untroubled for rolling miles, long beaches with a sucking surf and stiff sea winds. I'll find a place for the body there. A quiet, respectful spot, and have time to dig a proper grave and lay him in it. There'll be no cross, or stone, but the beauty of the place will be a marker and one better than he deserves. I love the smell of the wet bush and the calls of the birds in it.

I'm on my way to the Catlins for the long weekend now. I just turned in here to the domain on impulse because I saw the kids playing rugby and it reminded me of being here, right here, at the same age and for the same reason. I can't remember what I wanted to be in those days, but I did read lots of books about soldiers and sailors and sticking to your guns. And now I'm an undertaker. I could have done a lot worse. I'm fine with it, actually. In a way we all have to be undertakers.

31.

What
Eddy Sees

ALL RIGHT, EDDY, LET'S START WITH WHAT YOU HEARD FROM YOUR PLACE BEFORE YOU WENT OVER TO THE WEYMOUTHS.

Well, I've just been watching *Terminator* on Netflix, see, and I'm heading off to the sack when I hear this shouting next door. Nothing unusual in that, but this time there's a different voice as well, isn't there. Another loud guy that's not Todd Weymouth, so there's three of them having a go.

THE WEYMOUTHS AND SOMEONE YOU HADN'T HEARD BEFORE?

Right, as I say. So anyway I go to the window to have a look. You see into their main room from my place. The hedge just cuts a bit off. Todd and Irene nose to nose and this tall joker in a green jersey right in there as well. There's a grown-up son I've never seen, but this guy's too old for that. And he's not backward in having his say. But then Todd backhands this guy and it's all on with Irene screaming and everything. It's pretty lively for two older guys and I decide I better go over there.

WHY DIDN'T YOU CONTACT US?

They row all the time, the Weymouths. I've been over before, and they wouldn't thank me for bringing in you guys. No way. So anyway, I put my jersey back on and go over there pronto. I know the front door will be locked so I go straight round the back, through the kitchen and there they are. Todd started it, from what I saw, but the other guy is getting the best of it by the time I come, has him pinned down by the telly and smacking him about, so I grab him and haul him off and Irene's yelling at me just to fuck off and that Todd had it coming. And Todd just crouches there and snorts blood and keeps swearing.

DID THE GUY HAVE A WEAPON OF SOME SORT? A STICK, OR ANYTHING, OR WAS HE JUST PUNCHING?

I didn't see anything. There's things on the floor, ornaments and stuff, a broken chair, but the guy's not holding anything. I think he might start on me, but he goes off the boil once they're separated and I just keep between him and Todd. I ask him who the hell he is, and he says he's Irene's boss. He's come round to see her, finds her crying and sticks up for her. Irene works in the office of McGlashan Motors, so I guess he's the manager or something. A biggish guy, not someone you'd choose to pick on.

YOU'D NEVER SEEN HIM BEFORE, RIGHT?

No idea who he is. Still don't know his name.

HIS NAME'S BILL CULLIN.

Never heard of him. Never seen him before.

MRS WEYMOUTH'S NEVER MENTIONED HIM?

No, why would she?

PEOPLE SAY YOU AND MRS WEYMOUTH ARE GOOD
FRIENDS, GOOD NEIGHBOURS.

I've lived next door for years, so I know them both. Irene doesn't have
it easy with him, mainly because he's a drinker. It's got worse since
he lost the hearing in his right ear, and the other one's not much cop.

DO THEY FIGHT A LOT? HAVE YOU SEEN HIM HIT HER,
OR ANY SIGN THAT'S HAPPENED?

What does she say?

COME ON, EDDY.

I think he slaps her sometimes, but she probably won't say that, so I'm
not. I keep out of it. Stuff goes on in a marriage, doesn't it.

SO WHAT HAPPENED AFTER YOU SEPARATED THE GUYS?

This Bill, as you call him, says Irene should go somewhere to stay the
night. Her sister's or somewhere, until Todd sobers up. He offers to
take her, but Irene says why should she have to leave her own home.
Turf the bastard out, she says. The guy's keen to get you people
involved, but Irene says she's been there before and it only made
Todd even more shitty towards her in the end. He's not an easy man,
our Todd.

HE CLAIMS YOU, OR BILL CULLIN, SMACKED HIM ABOUT
AFTERWARDS. IN THE DARK AFTER HE'D GONE OUTSIDE
TO MAKE SURE MR CULLIN HAD LEFT.

Could be anyone in the neighbourhood, couldn't it. That's how folk
around here see him. Todd just wants to pin it on someone — anyone.
Probably falls down on the concrete without needing any help, he's so
pissed. Pissed and angry.

YOU DON'T GET HIS SORT OF INJURIES JUST FALLING DOWN ON THE CONCRETE. HE'S IN HOSPITAL NOW AND NOT GOOD AT ALL.

What's the matter with him?

QUITE SERIOUS HEAD INJURIES AND HE'S BEEN KICKED IN THE SCROTUM AND BACK. HE'S NOT IN GOOD SHAPE AT ALL AND HE BLAMES YOU.

Or this Bill Cullin, right?

MORE YOU, EDDY. HE RECKONS IT WAS YOU. HOW ABOUT YOU TELL ME WHAT HAPPENED WHEN MR CULLIN LEFT.

So what does Cullin say? You asked him too, right?

HE SAID HE RANG 111 FROM HIS CAR AND THEN DROVE HOME. NEVER SAW TODD WEYMOUTH AFTER LEAVING THE HOUSE, NEVER ASSAULTED HIM AFTER INTERVENING TO PROTECT MRS WEYMOUTH IN THE HOUSE. SO YOU TELL ME WHAT HAPPENED AFTER THAT.

Irene says she won't go anywhere — shouldn't have to leave her own home, doesn't want the police. She wants him locked out of the house, or taken away, and Cullin says he's not doing that, and I tell her the same. Who knows what he'd get up to in the state he's in. Cullin's getting the wind up, I think, and just wants to get away out of it. He says if she won't be helped there's nothing he can do, and he goes off. Todd goes after him almost at once. They must have had this second set-to out there in the dark.

YOU DIDN'T TRY TO STOP HIM?

Stop who?

TODD, GOING AFTER MR CULLIN.

Well, it gets him out of the house, doesn't it, and that's what she wants. I just want to get out and go home, don't I. The whole thing's a mess and the Cullin guy goes off and leaves me with Irene damn near hysterical and Todd nasty drunk.

YOU DIDN'T GO OUT AFTER THE OTHER TWO, EDDY? YOU DIDN'T CATCH UP WITH TODD WEYMOUTH OUT THERE IN THE DARK AND HAVE ANOTHER GO?

Hey, I didn't have a first go, remember. I'm the guy who broke it up, remember. I'm the neighbour doing the right thing.

SO WHAT HAPPENED NEXT?

Irene races and locks Todd out, doesn't she. Says why should she leave the house when she pays most of the rent, that she never wants to see the bastard again. I've heard that before. I tell her I need to go home, but she says to stay in case he smashes a window and climbs in. You never know with him, she says.

CONSTABLE ANDERSON SAYS THAT WHEN HE ARRIVED MR WEYMOUTH WAS LYING ON THE PATH BARELY CONSCIOUS. YOU'D JUST LEFT HIM THERE?

All I knew was that he was outside, where Irene wanted him. I only go out when the ambulance comes and the cops come to the door.

THE THING IS, EDDY, THAT MR CULLIN HAS A RATHER DIFFERENT STORY. HE SAYS THAT HE DIDN'T HIT TODD, BUT JUST GOT BETWEEN HIM AND MRS WEYMOUTH TO PROTECT HER. HE SAID YOU ARRIVED ALL STEAMED UP AND SAILED INTO TODD.

Well, he would, wouldn't he, but what does Irene say, eh? That's the clincher, isn't it. She knows the whole story. I bet she backs me up on this.

MRS WEYMOUTH IS STILL UPSET AND FINDING IT

HARD TO RECALL EVERYTHING. AND MAYBE ALSO
SHE DOESN'T WANT TO POINT A FINGER AT YOU, OR
MR CULLIN. UNDERSTANDABLE IN THE CIRCUMSTANCES.
I HEAR THAT YOU AND MRS WEYMOUTH ARE PRETTY
CLOSE AND HER HUSBAND DOESN'T LIKE THAT ONE BIT.
THAT RIGHT, EDDY?

You hear, you hear — what stuff do you hear? There's too many gossipy pricks around here. I'm a neighbour to her, aren't I, and I just try to keep an eye out as a neighbour should. Isn't that what you people are always on about? Eh? Be a good neighbour, right?

I'M JUST TRYING TO GET TO THE TRUTH, EDDY. IT WAS
PRETTY NASTY STUFF LAST NIGHT, AND WE NEED TO
SORT OUT WHAT HAPPENED — AND FIND OUT WHO'S
RESPONSIBLE FOR MR WEYMOUTH'S INJURIES.

And what about what he did to Irene? What about that? Family violence, isn't it, so what about that?

THAT TOO.

Just don't go making out Todd's some victim here. Anyone around here knows him: a moody bugger who turns nasty pretty quickly. Irene's had a hell of a time, and that's what you should be looking at here, not bloody Todd.

WE'LL HAVE TO TALK TO YOU AGAIN, EDDY. AFTER
MR WEYMOUTH IMPROVES AND WE HAVE A FULL
STATEMENT FROM HIM AND MR CULLIN ABOUT IT ALL.
MRS WEYMOUTH TOO. BUT THIS WILL DO FOR NOW. JUST
MAKE SURE YOU'RE AVAILABLE OVER THE NEXT FEW
DAYS. THANKS AND WE'LL BE IN TOUCH. OKAY, EDDY?

I'm just the neighbour, aren't I? Just trying to be what a neighbour should and I get dragged into all this shit. I should have just pulled the bloody curtains and let them get on with it. You try to help, don't you, and you get shit in return. So I don't want to talk again.

32.

Behind the Scenes

He became an old man at seventy-six. It happened abruptly. They cut out a length of his bowel because of cancer, and for some days and nights he wandered the hospital corridors with a colostomy bag. Only months later he couldn't pee, so they inserted a miniature meat grinder through his penis and minced most of his prostate. He noticed his balance failing too. Sometimes when he rose from a chair he had to take a step to stabilise himself. He had a simple, clumsy fall from a stepladder only a few feet high and fractured his left kneecap.

His body had been a longtime friend and partner, but he can no longer trust it. His hearing is going, yet always clear is the cicada chorus of tinnitus: his eyesight too — part of each day is spent searching for his glasses. Even his sense of taste has relinquished its subtlety. Most food seems just the same and only titbits of crass sweetness claim distinction. How he'd once enjoyed the singular piquancy of wild blackberries, the succulence of pork crackling. Often now he feels he could just as well be eating cardboard. He finds himself giving a grunt of exertion when he bends slowly to tie his shoelaces, and he can no longer swivel his head sufficiently to back the car with his earlier casual ease. He tends to bite his tongue when eating, as even instinctive and habitual responses become unreliable. At rest his fingers have a slight, mouse-like tremble, as if expressing inner anxiety. Frequently he is left behind in the rush of conversation, even within his own family, and his opinions are accorded less attention, his intellectual jurisdiction diminished.

'Richard,' his wife Fiona says with equanimity, 'you must accept you're an old man now. You're not an athlete any more, are you.'

'Dad,' say his son and daughter, 'you've got to learn to take it easy, look after yourself and not take on as much. We worry about you.'

'It's all downhill after your mid-seventies,' his mate Aidan complains. An odd expression, Richard thinks, because going downhill should be easier and more satisfying than trudging uphill.

'Old age never comes alone,' George, his neighbour, informs him. 'We'll all be folding our tents soon.' George is fond of such banal adages.

Both Aidan and George belong to a cycling group that moves forlornly in single file about the suburbs each Wednesday. They encourage Richard to join, but he refuses. It's too obviously a regime of submission, and most of them have e-bikes anyway, which is cheating.

'There's nothing to look forward to, is there,' says Aidan mournfully.

Richard refuses to give in, however. Okay, maybe there's nothing to look forward to, but he has much to look back on, and he finds refuge and pleasure in that. The past is welcoming and he still has citizenship there as someone gloriously young, or in his prime. As long as he retains his marbles there's a place for him in the theatre of former times. He's lived in the same city most of his life and there are settings within it that evoke memories, some that dismay and accuse him, others that flatter and sustain.

He chooses such places on his walks and drives, steps into the reveries they hold. The gardens by the museum, say, or the alley behind Sussman and Walker Ltd where he used to park his MGB: the site of the long-gone Anchorage Hotel, or the greywacke stone wall by the old reservoir.

—⋅≫ ≪⋅—

Richard's way to the shopping centre passes his old secondary school and he can see the prefab classroom in which he was taught biology in his final year by 'Burglar' Steelman. The prefab is used to store art equipment now. Richard has walked in and glimpsed through the stained windows the jumble of trestles, easels, boxes, crates, even a wooden spinning wheel. Burglar had been new to the school, maybe only five or six years older than Richard. He still had the professional idealism of a young teacher and went the extra mile. Richard enjoyed biology that year, mainly because of Burglar's enthusiasm. One day towards the end of the final term he asked Richard to stay behind after class, encouraged him to take biology at university. 'You've got a knack for it,' he said. 'You could do really well, and there's plenty of career opportunities in the sciences. Science is more and more the thing.'

Richard remembers his genuineness, his helpfulness, the way he used to crack his knuckles while standing by the window in the lab. 'Get stuck in at uni,' he'd said. 'Don't get sucked in too much by the pub crowd. I'll be interested to see how you go.' At a school reunion nearly fifteen years later, Richard learnt that Burglar had committed suicide by throwing himself under a railcar. Pancreatic cancer, and he'd known too much biology to wait around. He was still in his thirties. A tall, thin man and when he wrote on the board the naked expanse of his wrist extended a long way from his shirt cuff and the ginger hairs glinted in the sunlight. His Adam's apple was pronounced and drew attention by going up and down his throat like an elevator when he swallowed. 'I'll be interested to see how you go,' he had said, but Richard had never gone back to talk to him, to thank him, and he regretted that.

The kindergarten is still there, the catch on the road gate too high for childish hands to reach. Richard's work had prevented him from taking and collecting Melanie, or Nat, as a regular routine. It was his wife's chore and his occasional pleasure. He has ample time to pause there now, watch the children ride the narrow red slide over and over, see them astride bright plastic-wheeled ducks and horses, their small legs in vigorous propulsion. See also the child alone beneath the wintersweet, crouched in absorption over a bottle top, or a dead dragonfly. He remembers the disparate inclinations of his own children. It was Melanie whom he would see whooping in the playground, and Nat he would find inside the rooms even on the brightest days, moulding playdough by himself, or silently assembling a wooden jigsaw puzzle. How early the features of character are formed and how enduring they prove. In Melanie's time at kindy the senior teacher was a Māori woman called Mrs Pomare who encouraged the children to sing and dance together and told Richard that his daughter was naturally musical and naturally disobedient. What he remembers most vividly when he pauses at the kindergarten gates is how Melanie, or Nat, would reach up quite naturally to take his hand when he came for them. The time when you walk hand in hand with your children is not long, yet special. As he watches the busy playground he can almost conjure the former selves of his own children: see them running towards him, stretching a hand to his, to be taken home.

—◦⟫ ⟪◦—

In all his life, Richard has had only one serious fight, and there was no victory. Whenever he waits at the Ashburn Street bus stop, he can see the walkway to the back of the Anglican church hall where the argument began. Many of the dances were held in church halls in those days. Maybe the parsons and vicars hoped that being on religious premises would convert the young, or at least temper their lust.

The fight was the culmination of a mutual dislike between Noel Collier and himself. They'd fallen out as potato pickers, targeted each other in rugby clashes between their schools, belittled each other on the rare occasions they found themselves in the same company. Peer group assertiveness comes naturally at eighteen.

At the dance Collier had tried to cut in when Richard was partnering a quiet girl from a private school. Although she wasn't the girl he'd hoped to take home, he wasn't going to have prick Collier displacing him at will. They embarrassed her by the brief hostility, and she left Richard promptly and with relief when the dance was over. A quickstep: he could remember that, though not her name. He'd never been much of a dancer. Her dress was green and tight at the waist.

Collier came up again when it was over and people were drifting away to the carpark — self-absorbed couples, companionable single-sex groups, isolated guys mooching off. It had been raining, and the few outside lights gave a slick gleam where water still lay.

'Who the fuck do you think you are?' Collier said. He stood in front of Richard and Grant, who were walking to the cars. 'You think you're a smart bastard, don't you, and you're just a useless shit.'

'Knock it off,' said Grant in an offhand way.

'No, I've just about had a gutsful of Mr Smart Arse here,' Collier said. He stepped closer so that Richard would've had to move away to pass him. 'Let's settle it here. Let's see what you've got apart from a bloody big mouth.'

Collier wasn't an especially big guy and Richard wasn't overawed. He can remember taking off his jacket and giving it to Grant, but still wearing his bright pink tie. Single-colour ties were fashionable then. It was a brief fight there in the poorly lit walkway, not like the protracted punch-ups in films. They'd only exchanged a few hits when Collier kicked Richard so hard on his leg that he lost balance, and his opponent was able to give him a hefty smack on the nose. That brought enough blood to end the fight and Richard was left sitting on the wet seal with his handkerchief to his face. 'That'll teach you,' said Collier excitedly, his hands still up and fisted. He went off with his two mates, still talking, laughing.

Richard once walked to the hall from the bus stop, paused about where it must have happened. So long ago, but he can still remember the cold wetness of the walkway on his bum, Collier's derision afterwards, Grant's attempted commiseration by saying he didn't think kicking was really fighting fair. Richard has no recollection of pain, but the humiliation remains clear.

— ·›› ‹‹· —

In the museum gardens close to the river there is a green bench donated by the family of Robert Stephen Ettrick. The seat is only a few years old, but from it Richard can see the cluster of azaleas where almost sixty years ago he and Becky McGruder lay down in the dusk to make love. A high summer evening with the ground still dry and warm, and the softly moving air merely a further caress. She still wore her tennis dress. 'Take it easy and spin it out,' she said, but he couldn't. It was explosive and afterwards he was surprised to find the azaleas still standing. 'You like to go for it, don't you,' Becky said, but she was smiling.

They never fucked again and he couldn't recall why. He would have embraced the opportunity. They remained friends, even won a mixed doubles title together. Becky became a physiotherapist and shifted to Hamilton. A decade or so ago, Richard met her by chance in the Wellington airport Koru Lounge. She had a granddaughter with her. They talked easily and for some time, but of course nothing was said of the azaleas close to the river in the museum gardens. That Becky walked only in the past. He remembered the way her dark pony-tail swung when she ran, the gold studs in her ears, the flex of her smooth thighs, the walk they'd had afterwards along the dim riverbank with the mallards slipping evasively into the water with low, apprehensive chatter as they approached.

Snyder and Weir doesn't exist any more. The premises are still there, however, in Port Street and still occupied by a legal firm. Richard had worked at Snyder and Weir for twenty-three years. Despite Burglar's advice, he'd not taken biology at university, but followed his grandfather's profession. It's a coincidence that he knows Tony Grandhomme at the new firm, despite the twenty years between them. Tony's first employment had been at PFA Legal Services when Richard was a partner there. Richard goes to see him sometimes, the surroundings as much a motive as the company, for Tony's office was once his own. The large, dark wooden desk is still there, surely too big to fit through the door and so an inheritance even when firms change. How did it get in there in the first instance? The west wall has a floor to ceiling bookcase, but now the top shelves are empty of closely aligned legal volumes. More modern means of reference are represented by the technical paraphernalia on Tony's desk, and there are abstract art reproductions on the walls where once Richard had prints of works by Rita Angus and Austen Deans. And a new carpet in uniform, commercial grade grey, rather than the flamboyant pattern of Richard's time. The view, though, from the large window behind the desk has changed little — the small, contested carpark, the busy street, the glimpse of the Cashmere Hills between the Kingland Apartments and the SGA tower block somewhat enlarged because the earthquake took down McNally's. He enjoys the visits, but doesn't prolong them. He's aware that the elderly can often forget how busy younger people are, and he doesn't wish to become a bore.

The office is redolent with memories that crowd in when Richard visits, so that sometimes as he and Tony talk, their positions are transposed and Richard feels it is he sitting again behind the dark solidity of the desk and listening to those who have come for his professional assistance. Most conversations then were commonplace, at least for him, but there were the oddities that occur with long service in the job. The runholder who had a heart attack while discussing the formation of a family trust, a sex worker who offered a variety of services in lieu of her legal fees for property acquisition, a subdued, elderly woman from Papanui who sought advice on commissioning a $35,000 memorial to her beloved fox terrier.

Most of all, the office reminds Richard of Mrs Priske, who used to come to Snyder and Weir selling her home cooking: chocolate chip biscuits, apricot muffins, custard squares, Afghans and peanut brownies. Her food was splendid, especially the custard squares, but it was her history that made her memorable. She'd been in the Treblinka concentration camp in Poland as a child and every other member of her family had been murdered there. She never spoke of it, yet somehow it was widely known. Such an everyday-looking woman, with heavy eyebrows and a pleasant voice. Richard had bought her baking, talked of trivialities with her, given free advice, and only once was there a possible reference to a fearsome past. 'I need to have food about me always,' she'd replied to his compliments. How was it possible to suffer such cruelty, grief and deprivation, yet appear so ordinary and content?

Regularly he drives with Fiona to the eastern crematorium where her parents have plaques on a boulder wall by a lacy maple tree. His own parents are buried in Napier, but as Fiona cleans the brass name plates and places fresh flowers, he thinks of her mother and father: their warm acceptance of him, which had grown into friendship.

Perhaps because they had only daughters there was a vacant spot within the family for him. His father-in-law had died quite young and Richard remembers coming with his wife and her mother to tend the memorial, just as he comes with Fiona now to visit both parents. If the day was fine, his mother-in-law would sit on the wall by her husband's name when she'd done with cleaning and with placing flowers, and talk of him. It was the sense of being close again, Richard supposed. She would sit in the sun and reminisce. 'He spoke about his time overseas,' she once told Richard. 'Not many returned men like to do that, I gather. Nothing about the fighting, never, no, but lots about Italy, the people and the places they went through. He was on the push to Padua and Trieste and then spent months at Lake Trasimeno where the division was demobilised. They couldn't get home all at once, he said. He loved the countryside and the rural people.' Richard remembers how his father-in-law used to swear cheerfully in Italian after a few drinks, but always refused to translate.

It's a pleasant image, his mother-in-law sitting in the sun and talking of her husband. Richard has decided he, too, will be cremated when the time comes, and maybe Fiona will visit in this same way and talk of him to their children. He prefers crematoriums to graveyards: there is more of nature and less emphasis on death. Instead of subsided concrete, rearing gravestones and rusted enclosures — rose gardens, lawns and modest name plates.

Richard and Fiona belong to U3A and with others go regularly to listen to the visiting speakers, mainly university people, who share their knowledge of climate change, Debussy's preludes and the Viking Age. Within the audience is the will to be informed, and a greater determination to keep senility at bay. On their way to the meetings they pass the Golden Dragon restaurant, in premises that once housed the Mighty Mouse Coffee Bar. Richard washed dishes there as a first-year university student. He has sat in the Golden Dragon, looked into a kitchen unrecognisable, yet still seen shades of his former gangly self serving time there. The coffee bar had ropes across the ceiling, dim lighting, little choice of food, local musicians who played in imitation of the Kingston Trio, and a clientele of pseudo sophisticates who smoked almost continuously.

The manager of the Mighty Mouse had smoked even more than his customers — Turkish sobranies coloured pink, black and green. He'd failed in a career as a classical singer and regarded himself and the world with bitter derision. Richard had come to see that even his wit and superficial courtesy were cloaks for despair. In brief periods of idleness, he would lean in the kitchen doorway and entertain Richard with soft, but scathing, comment on the people he observed. Ridicule was his defence against life. A large, gaunt man with thinning pale hair and spaces between his teeth, who found no recompense in the success of the Mighty Mouse Coffee Bar. 'Would you look at that little tart,' he would say, though Richard at the sink was unable to do so. 'Look at all these useless berks pretending to be Americans. Jesus save us.' When the doors were closed and he, Richard and the waiters were cleaning up, he would sometimes talk of Peter Pears and Yuri Mazurok, but no one replied because they knew he was really talking to himself.

Richard remembers the coffee cups and saucers best of all, having spent so much time in their company. Both cup and saucer were in the same bright colour, except for the cups' inside whiteness — rich blue, red, orange, black or green, much like the sobranies of their owner. Despite a year of washing and drying them, Richard still admired the bold intensity and wishes now he'd taken a set as a keepsake. He'd had worse jobs, and left only because he was offered more money to cart hay in the long vacation.

Wherever he goes in the city, there are signs of the earthquakes — strengthened buildings, ravaged buildings, spaces buildings once occupied. The violence interrupted an essential continuity and Christchurch is not the same now. Their house in Merivale suffered little damage, but the river suburbs where he lived as a student and young man he hardly recognises. The Arts Centre is still standing. Richard played a supporting role in its repair and refurbishment, goes occasionally now to enjoy the old stone quads and lecture halls, recall a self who was a student there, biking in from run-down flats he shared. He'd had a camel-coloured duffle coat for the long winter months, and dark suede brothel creepers.

Close to the main hall is an upstairs room where he used to go for tutorials with Dr Crespe. Six or seven students usually, taking turns with minor presentations and the defence of them. Dr Crespe was semi-retired and very relaxed in his approach, no longer having career aspirations. He told them once that he tutored only to provide funds for an annual visit to Bologna. The room is privately owned now, and Richard can't go in, but he remembers it well, not so much because of the tutor, whom he liked, but because of Judy McIvor, whom he loved. She said she loved him too, but after four and a half months she left him — and the country. At the end of a Dr Crespe tutorial, she told him to come with her into the museum across the road, where they found a quiet spot by the display of ancient Egyptian pottery.

'Mum's very bad again and nothing here's any help whatsoever, so we're going to Mexico. A special advanced clinic in Guadalajara that's developed a new drug. A miracle drug. She hasn't got anybody else. There's just her and me, so I'm taking her.'

'You never told me anything about your mother being so sick,' Richard said.

'I don't like to talk about it, but now we have to go away. It's a last chance — the only chance.'

He saw her just once after that: a quick and sad goodbye. He wrote to the clinic address she gave him, but there was no reply. He hadn't said so to her, but he suspected the place in Guadalajara was one of those scams that preys on the desperately sick.

Richard may well have married Judy if she hadn't ended it. He remembers being with her in his small room with the single bed and broken blind. How she would close her eyes when the climax came and press her lips together. And how dark her circled nipples were against the whiteness of her breasts. When he walks through the quad, he can look up at the second-storey window of what had been the tutorial room and think of her there. She'd seemed happy, but in all the time they'd been together her mother had been dying, and nothing had been said of that.

—⟫ ⟪—

Richard used to run competitively, and then in later years for fitness and to experience the release that's the reward for pushing yourself physically. He no longer runs, but he drives sometimes into the Cashmere Hills and walks part of the track on which he used to train. He's become one of those old farts with a staff and toothy smile who call a greeting as you pass them. There is a rock outcrop shaped like a steeple where once he came across a tall Māori guy sitting with a dead Labrador at his feet. At first Richard thought the dog was just resting, but it was on its side with head oddly tucked in. He asked what had happened.

'Bunker just dropped dead,' the man said. He was in no way distraught and leant to stroke Bunker's shoulder as he spoke.

'How old was he?'

'Twelve.'

'Wow, that's not long, is it,' Richard said.

'Labs have a life expectancy of only ten to twelve years. He was pretty much at the end of things. I knew that, but he enjoyed our track walks. He was here and he was with me, so that's not too bad a way to go, is it.'

Richard had asked if there was any way he could help, but was thanked and told things were okay. After a little more talk, Bunker's owner stood up and put the body gently over his shoulder in a quite natural way, said goodbye and headed back to the road. Richard learnt Bunker's name, but not his owner's. Whenever he passes the steeple rock he can picture the grey-haired Māori man sitting there with Bunker, and then carrying him home. It's not an unpleasant memory. He's sometimes wondered why dogs have such short lives, while tortoises seem to live forever.

—»《—

There's a concrete step on the grassed riverside close to the Bridge of Remembrance that has resonance for Richard. It makes him smile as he recalls the comic busker there. He especially enjoys reliving the experience if Fiona is with him, for she'd been central to what happened. They were walking into the city centre, to the restaurant where they were meeting family and friends for their fiftieth wedding anniversary. The busker was dressed as a clown, but lightly clad, for the evening was very warm. Half circles of blue above his eyes and lips enlarged by garish red. He was playing a violin and came from the seat towards them as they approached. He circled and captured them in a lively, exaggerated musical rendition, then after a final flourish, held out his hand.

'Give him something,' Fiona had said.

'I've only got a fifty-dollar note and small change in cash.'

'So. It's our fiftieth, isn't it, so give him the fifty,' she said.

Richard had, and the busker bowed, followed them closely down Cashel Street, skipping and creating quick, jinking music. It drew attention to their progress so that other people paused to watch, even clap. Cavorting and playing, the clown accompanied them until they reached the restaurant, and when they were inside, he stood a moment at the window with the violin bow raised in salute. In costume and with his face painted, the only indications of his youth were his alacrity and a thick sprout of dark hair from beneath the coloured cone of his hat.

There were speeches and gifts and fine food at that anniversary, but Richard remembers best the happy busker with the violin, and Fiona's pleasure in being serenaded as they walked the busy street. 'We need more musical clowns,' she told him when last they passed the concrete step by the river. 'What's happened to all the clowns?'

— ·≫ ≪· —

Where else should we accompany Richard? There are so many choices. The courthouse in which he was admitted to the bar, the first home he and Fiona owned and in which happy place their children were small and close, the nondescript suburban corner in Avonside where he saw a cycling schoolgirl struck by a car. He drives sometimes to New Brighton and parks close to the sweep of the beach. In winter even, when there is no one on the sand and nothing outwardly to see, yet he can sit with a smile and conjure a private viewing of the midnight swim there after his capping day. The calling and laughter of his friends in the dark sea, the great cheese of the moon bright above them all. The past is a sustenance for him now. Always there is something to see within it — part memory, part dream, part a reliving.

33.

Being Frank

ecause I knew I would be soon passing not all that far away, I looked up the town on Google. Romans-sur-Isère in the department of Drôme. The location map showed Valence, where I had left the train and picked up a rental car, and Grenoble in the mountains, where I stayed afterwards for two days and gave a talk to English-speaking students at the university. From the web I learnt that Romans was famous for the making of shoes, that the International Shoe Museum there was housed in a former convent with Italianate architecture. Other things considered noteworthy were the collegiate church of Saint-Bernard built in the twelfth century, and Pogne, a ring-shaped orange-flower bread that's a tradition of the town.

I was aware of none of these things when I visited the town years ago. I came and went within the light of one day. My French publisher said I might as well go there on my way to Grenoble. 'I've enrolled you at Romans,' she said. The book fair was held in a large hall that has lost its detail and normal function in my memory. I recall, however, a large fabric banner above the door that flexed and billowed languidly in the breeze, and bore in bold, blue lettering the town's name and the words 'Book Fair' in both English and French. I recall, too, the uncovered trestle tables that we sat behind along the wall and the hard wooden seats. I'd never been to such an event before and have never since. Forty or more writers with their wares displayed like market bric-a-brac before them, and people strolling by, lifting and putting down, sometimes even purchasing. The books became objects distinct from any intellectual content and were assessed as such — weighed in the hand, the covers flexed, the pages briefly caressed and the bindings tested. I would not have been surprised to see someone press a thumb on the cover, just as a French housewife tests the ripeness of a pear.

I had that sense of dissociation that comes at times during travel, a feeling that we are outside our own experience, merely observers of a rapidly changing scene. The sense arising also from my inability with the language, despite sitting there with my novel in translation. I existed in a bubble of almost total linguistic incomprehension. Most of the few people who lingered before my table to talk soon registered my deficiency and moved on with a smile, or shrug, though I think five copies of my book were purchased during my entire time there, mainly by women who wished to display their own command of English, or because of their innate sympathy for someone so displaced.

The writers came from many backgrounds and countries, and most, it seemed, were unknown to one another. Name cards on the tables mentioned Germany, Italy, Ireland, Norway, Mexico, Australia among others; no one except me from New Zealand, I think. There was little chance for us to become acquainted, apart from those close at hand, but there was that general sense of goodwill that exists among common practitioners. Yet, by late morning a hierarchy had become evident, with those authors regularly patronised inflating with complacent satisfaction and those in comparative neglect subdued, and affecting artistic indifference to commerce. I was in the latter category.

The star was a fantasy writer from Uruguay, who twice left his place and the hall to replenish his stock. He was rarely visible to me because of the people gathered before him. I was told he was accompanied by a publisher's rep, which in itself was evidence of fame.

I was impressed, however, by how many people came, and the number of books they bought. Romans is merely a mid-sized French provincial town, yet overall the fair was distinctly a success. I can't remember if it was a well-established annual event, or a one-off occasion with the advantage of that originality. It was coincidentally appropriate as a venue, because the French word for a novel is *roman*.

The writer to the left of me along the wall was a short, Greek man with a fringing grey beard and a stack of graphic novels with lurid covers. After we had shaken hands, established our nationalities and a lack of each other's language, he returned to an intense scrutiny of his iPad, from which even the occasional purchaser found it difficult to divert him. On my right was a poet, a woman from Tennessee. Maybe in her forties, but I'm bad at guessing the age of women. She was tall, dark and one feature away from being beautiful — heavy cheeks that were accentuated when she smiled. She sold more books than I did, but I'm not just being defensive by thinking that was as much to do with her attractiveness and open manner as the poetry. And there is something about the Southern accent that most people find engaging, different, yet with familiar echoes from the movies.

Her name was Madison and we talked a little as the morning wore on: just generalities. The noise of so many people in the cavernous hall made anything more than that difficult. Each time, however, that the fantasy man from Uruguay strutted back with more books, we exchanged complicit glances of wry amusement.

There was a window behind me, an advantage denied most other writers, and when I grew tired of watching the scene within the hall, I could turn and look out to the peacefulness of a courtyard that possessed a lawn, neglected gravel paths, better tended plots of fluted, yellow flowers, and a fountain with a weak flow from a bronze gryphon glitter green with verdigris. The sun shone indiscriminately on it all and the cool breeze that I knew moved outside was not apparent from within the hall. I must go out there before I leave, I told myself.

If there had been any official opening of the fair, it had occurred before I arrived, and there was little sign of organisation, yet things seemed to work in a rough and ready way. It wasn't all that complex, really, despite the crowd, the bee swarm of chatter inflating the hall, the temporary tourist posters on the walls. Just a seated writer, a desk, some books, repeated more than forty times, and an eddying flow of people with mild curiosity.

There was one incident, which at first I thought legitimate. A young man appeared on the otherwise empty stage at the hall's far end, came to the edge, and began to talk loudly and passionately in French. He was thick set and wore a caramel corduroy jacket that wouldn't have done up across his chest. His pale hair was dense and seemed heaped up on his head, and he swayed as he spoke. For a short while he gained a puzzled attention that changed to laughter and a few cheers when several men came and with difficulty and firm grips escorted him from the stage. I gathered later that he'd been protesting about recent local restrictions on the use of common land.

The fair had no formal suspension at midday, but the food stalls set at the entrance of the hall were especially busy then. I stood in line for café crème and frites and was moving back with both hands full and held close, when I saw Madison with a croissant and coffee equally protected.

'It's not all that warm even in the sun,' she said, 'but I feel like a break from the tables.' I told her of the courtyard, with walls to hinder the drift of mountain air. 'Well, lead the way then,' she said. As we walked I was aware of her height and easy stride.

We weren't the only ones there, but found a wooden bench in the sun and beside a knee-high buxus hedge. A handsome, elderly man sat close by, but out of earshot if we talked quietly. His dark trousers had an immaculate crease and were tucked into highly polished tan boots laced well up his shins. I think I would've noticed him before if he was one of the enrolled writers, but certainly he was at least a confirmed reader, for he held one book before him and had others by his side.

'How splendidly he carries it off,' said Madison, and I knew she meant the whole presentation he gave to the world.

'So how are you finding it?' I asked her. 'A book fair is quite something, isn't it, and the people seem pleasant enough.'

She sat for a time without answering, intent on watching the handsome man, and then turned to me with a direct and steady look.

'How about this. How about we agree to cut the customary crap that strangers talk in passing? Phatic conversation, isn't that what it's called? I've gotten sick of it while travelling round recently. Here we are for a brief while before going back inside to the babble, so maybe we just relax and say what we think for a change. Sound okay?'

'Fine by me.'

'I bet you'd never heard of me before today, and I've never heard of you.'

'True enough.'

'It's humbling, isn't it. You have your own small ambit of recognition and complacency and then you travel to some festival, or a place like this, and realise you don't figure much at all. That even among those who give a damn for books, you're just one voice in the full choir.'

'But you've sold quite a few books,' I said. 'More than me. And it's an experience, a place like this.'

'True, and most people will give an author any sort of praise rather than buy the damn book. There aren't many women writers here, though, so I reckon that gives me an edge.'

'The fantasy man's doing okay.'

'And loving it,' said Madison. 'There's always an appetite for escapism.'

'But you haven't read him, have you, so you don't know. He may be the real deal.'

'That's true. You got me there, but after seeing him swaggering about I won't take to his work, just from jealousy and instinctive hostility.'

'I believe he combines humour with surreal fantasy.'

'Writing of significant power is always sad,' she said with conscious finality. 'Anyway, what do you think of him?'

'A bumptious dickhead,' I said, with no justification whatsoever, and her laugh was loud enough for the reading man with the high-laced footwear to look up and smile at us.

'Those boots are really something, aren't they,' she said. 'And he looks a really cool guy who does his own thing. He's a local guru, I bet.'

'Maybe he's actually an undercover man watching out for terrorists. Deliberately conspicuous because no one would expect an undercover man to be that way.'

'I like it.'

'When we go back in, I'll get you to sign a book of your poems for me,' I said.

'Let's not buy each other's books. It's not a good idea: only a sense of obligation and we're bound to be disappointed. Better just to have a memory of us both briefly in the same place with all these writers and their stuff, and the undercover guy out here with his great boots, and that fountain piddling in the sun as it's been doing for hundreds of years by the look of it.'

It did look that way. The fountain walls were dark stone, patched with lighter rock in places and the verdigris of the gryphon was matched by the moss adhering to the lines of seepage. The buildings surrounding the courtyard were not as old, and I wondered what had originally encompassed the fountain. Maybe the grounds of a château when Romans-sur-Isère was much smaller. Maybe it had always been for common use. There was one tree, on the far side, and it was very old, balding and with the base of its trunk a swollen excrescence with gills.

'You could write a fountain poem,' I said.

'No thanks. I'm enjoying a creative lull. I'm having a few weeks just mooching around Europe before getting back to work.'

Turned out she made a living from teaching at Belmont University in Nashville. Seems just about all American writers have a university post of some sort to keep them going. It's the modern form of artistic patronage there, I suppose. I told her I could well do with one of those myself.

We shared some stories about the more eccentric faculty members we'd come across. Madison had no inhibitions and her experience was more interesting than mine, or maybe it was just the novelty for me of life recounted from a female point of view.

'We haven't talked of sex,' I said when our conversation had wandered almost everywhere else. I wanted to see how far her wish for candid exchange extended.

'But isn't talk of sex an ineffectual substitute for the thing itself?' she said, not at all ruffled. 'Friendship is explicable, but sex is all urge and nerve endings: everything in the act, poorly expressed by language. Men talk more about it, I imagine. Among themselves, I mean. Is that right?'

'Well, I don't know how much women talk about it for a comparison. Not a lot in mixed company anyway. For myself, I find the greatest aphrodisiac is a woman's response. Pleasure together rather than her just lying there and putting up with it.'

'I can understand that,' she said.

'Are you married?'

'Not married, no, but I have a partner who I've texted to pick me up at 2.30 this afternoon. I'll have had enough of sitting in the hall by then. We'll drive somewhere quiet for a coffee and maybe later sort out a hotel. You should come with us.'

'I'm going on to Grenoble after this,' I told her.

'Plenty of time before then. If you don't come you'll just have to sit and watch the fantasy man sign his books. And everything will seem stale by late afternoon anyway.'

I thanked her and said I'd see how I felt later. I liked the idea but didn't want to barge in on their time together.

She was right about the afternoon session of the fair. The novelty had worn off. A few of the writers hadn't bothered to return after lunch, the bulk remaining seemed diminished, more ordinary, the people circulating fewer and less enthusiastic, even the fantasy man had time for sage conversation with the woman from his publisher. And I found that one of my books had been stolen while I was outside — fourteen rather than fifteen in the pile before me. A small price to pay for lunch with Madison in the courtyard, the almost companionship of the undercover reader with the fine, high boots, and the ancient bronze gryphon still bravely spouting in a modern age.

Madison packed up her poetry books before it was 2.30. She came and stood by my table.

'Come on,' she urged. 'Come with us.'

'Are you sure?'

'Come on. Enough's enough,' and she stood, her bag slung over her shoulder, and beckoned. She was wearing a jacket that I hadn't seen before — soft, dark leather, finely creased. It was well worn, but retained the distinction conferred by quality. As if my preparation to go with her aroused some sense of opportunity soon to be lost, a young guy came quickly to buy a book.

My first sale for the afternoon.

'I've been to New Zealand,' he said as I signed it. I like to think he bought the novel because he'd enjoyed my country. 'I visited Mount Captain Cook.' Outside the hall it was still sunny, and still cool because of the breeze coming down from the mountains behind Grenoble. I walked to my rental, left my gear there and came back to wait with Madison for her partner. I hadn't expected a woman, but wasn't much surprised. She was driving a small Peugeot, and we clambered in hurriedly because there was no parking place and she'd halted briefly on the road, obstructing following cars. I was introduced only when we were moving legally in the traffic. 'This is Lisa,' said Madison from the front seat, and she turned back towards me. 'And this is Frank.'

'No, not Frank,' I said, 'I'm—'

'I'm calling you Frank because that's what we agreed in the courtyard. To be frank with each other. Remember?'

'Cool,' said Lisa and laughed. I couldn't see much of her from where I sat, but there was a lot of wavy blonde hair. Later I was to find that also she was tall, but thin and with a face so sharp it seemed always in profile. Later too, I was to find she was an orthodontist and originally from Canada.

'What do you write, Frank?' she asked.

'Contemporary realistic fiction,' I said. I gave up about my name. What did it matter what I was called for just one afternoon?

'Are you an international star, Frank?' she continued.

'Not even famous in my own country.'

'Even I sold more books than him,' said Madison.

'But yours are cheap, aren't they,' Lisa said. 'All slim Jim volumes. And you probably fluttered your eyelashes as well.'

I was impressed with Lisa's driving. There was considerable traffic, but she had plenty of confidence and skill. And she was used to driving on that side of the road. When I asked her where we were going, she said she'd lunched at a pleasant café by the river and she'd take us there. She'd booked a place to stay that night in the oldest hotel in Romans, which had once been the mayor's office, she told us. 'Has it got a courtyard?' asked Madison.

I never got to check that out with them, but I did see the café close to the river Isère, the old stone bridge with four arches and the massed trees on the far bank. The proprietor was cheerful when we arrived, and recognised Lisa from earlier in the day, but after bringing our coffee he began a dispute with a man in the kitchen. Both of them were out of sight, but clearly audible. At first it seemed merely a matter of one giving a sustained reprimand and the other rarely replying, but then it blew up into a full-scale shouting match, and a young guy with hair to his shoulders strode through the small dining room followed, almost pursued, by the owner. They stormed across the road and stood not far from the bridge, still shouting and raising their palms uppermost in apparent despair and anger. When nothing was resolved there, the young man, still in a green work smock, walked off down the street followed by the boss man, both still shouting. For a time we could hear them even when they were out of sight.

We were left sitting by the window and open door, and there were people at two other tables who listened for a brief time and then resumed their own conversations. 'I don't think there's anybody else here,' said Lisa, meaning staff. 'We can take the money and run.'

'I'd rather have the croissant tray,' Madison said.

The more realistic question was how we would pay when leaving, but the long-haired guy soon came back. He'd discarded his smock to reveal a white shirt and tight jeans. He had blood on his face and teeth and he walked quickly into the back of the shop without looking at anybody, then came out again almost at once with a carry bag and a leather jacket. He shouted as he went through the door. The only word I understood was 'merde'.

'He's murdered his boss,' said Lisa. 'Throttled him and thrown the body in the river. We'll all be hauled in as witnesses.'

'Ah, the Gallic temperament. I love it,' said Madison.

Their reaction surprised me. I had a view of lesbians as serious people, resolute in maintaining an alternative lifestyle despite the difficulties and slurs. And, quite apart from that, I thought both women might have been upset by the violence of the disagreement. But they weren't discomforted and enjoyed the glimpse of life undisguised.

The proprietor came back quietly, almost thoughtfully, the green smock balled unobtrusively in one hand. He showed no evidence of any conflict, gave no explanation of what had happened and stood at his counter seemingly occupied with his computer screen. The show was over, an aberration already difficult to place within the peacefulness of the present scene. After a short time, he came to the occupied tables one by one to check if any further service was needed. To us he spoke English, and quite impressively, although talking of 'most weathers' when describing the season. He had worked in Paris, he said, but found it too expensive to live there. When we left, there was nothing in his demeanour suggestive of embarrassment, or evasion, and neither he nor we made any comment concerning what had happened.

Although I'd known Madison for less than a day, and Lisa for barely a couple of hours, I was comfortable with them, sorry to have to go off by myself again, but I needed to begin the trip to Grenoble and find my accommodation for the night. As Lisa drove back to the hall, we joked about what had happened in the café. Madison said the young guy would've been a lover, Lisa said he would have been the son, I said maybe he was an illegal and exploited immigrant. Their choices were more intriguing than mine. We elaborated on all three and laughed together at the misfortune of other people, being secure in our own happiness. Again there were no parking spaces close to the hall and Lisa pulled over a driveway to let me out, so leave-taking was hurried. 'Goodbye, nice Frank,' she said.

'Buy some boots before you go,' said Madison as I leant down to the window of the little Peugeot, and she smiled, which pushed up her cheeks and detracted from the symmetry of her face, but not the warmth of her nature.

'I hope your hotel tonight has a fountain and a courtyard,' I said. As they drove away, one dark head, one fair, I was conscious of the banner for the book fair still billowing lazily above the doorway of the hall, though there were few people coming and going, and some of the food stall holders were packing up.

Sometimes as you experience life, you have a strange awareness that its true power will lie in retrospection. I had that sense as I watched the Peugeot lose its identity in the traffic, and the fantasy man and his publisher's rep come from the hall and stand together for a moment at the entrance.

That was my day in Romans-sur-Isère, and although some years later I travelled through Valence again to a destination further south, I decided not to go back to the town. I have none of Madison's poetry, but I remember her so well, and Lisa too, and the shouting match in the café by the river, and the elderly man with splendid boots by the fountain with the bronze gryphon. The years rustle by like fallen leaves, and you can't go back, you can't go back, for as Proust knew, what you seek is not a place, but a time past.

❖❯❯

Acknowledgements

The following stories have been published previously in the places listed below.

'The English Visitor' was included in *Katherine Mansfield and Russia*, edited by Galya Diment, Gerri Kimber and Todd Martin, Edinburgh University Press.

'Refuge in the Present', 'Giving the Finger' and 'The Undertaker's Story' have all appeared as ReadingRoom short stories, published by Steve Braunias in *Newsroom*.

'Discovering Australia' appeared in *Landmarks* by Grahame Sydney, Owen Marshall and Brian Turner, Penguin Random House.

'Frost Flowers' appeared in the literary periodical *Landfall*, Otago University Press.

The author appreciates the grant from Creative New Zealand that substantially assisted in providing the time for the writing of this book.